HEART OF THE WOLF

The Wild Hunt Legacy: 6

CHERISE SINCLAIR

VanScoy Publishing Group

Heart of the Wolf
Copyright © 2022 by Cherise Sinclair
ISBN: 978-1-947219-40-3
Published by VanScoy Publishing Group
Cover Art: The Killion Group
Edited by Red Quill Editing, LLC

This book is a work of fiction. Names, characters, places, and incidents are products of the author's imagination or used fictitiously and are not to be construed as real. Any resemblance to persons, living or dead, actual events, locales, business establishments, or organizations is entirely coincidental.

All rights reserved. This copy is intended for the original purchaser of this eBook only. No part of this work may be used, stored, reproduced, scanned, or distributed in any manner whatsoever without prior written permission from the author, except in the case of brief quotations embodied in critical articles and reviews as permitted by law.

This book is licensed for your personal enjoyment only. This book may not be re-sold or given away to other people. If you would like to share this book with another person, please purchase an additional copy for each recipient. If you're reading this book and did not purchase it, or it was not purchased for your use only, please purchase your own copy.

Thank you for respecting the hard work of this author.

ACKNOWLEDGMENTS

Growing up, I thought an author would write "The End" and *poof*, the book would be published. That's not...exactly...how it works.

Much like a child, a book needs a community to become all it should be (and I'm so very lucky to have a fabulous community).

From the very beginning, I have my amazing crit partners, Fiona Archer and Monette Michaels, who get the first crack at the manuscript, and then content editor Bianca Sommerland jumps in.

After that, there's a back and forth between me, my wonderful Red Quill editors (Ekatarina Sayanova, Rebecca Cartee, and Tracy Damron-Roelle) and my incredible beta readers (Barb Jack, Marian Shulman, Lisa White, and JJ Foster). They're the reason you're not tripping over typos and wondering why the hero's brown eyes somehow turned blue.

When, the baby...uh, book...is ready to leave the nest, it still needs support.

And there you all are, my awesome readers. You have my deepest appreciation for sending happy emails, for writing reviews, for giving shout-outs for the book. For your enthusiasm that keeps me returning to the keyboard.

Hugs and kisses go to my marvelous Facebook Shadowkittens who stay with me from book conception to after the release date—and the next book. From begging for stories for different characters (no, the Murphy brothers will not get a book) to answering polls and having the most intriguing book discussions. And keeping me laughing.

I love you all.

PROLOGUE

A terror-filled chittering came from the rocky creek below. Pulled out of her grieving, Heather rose from her tree-shaded niche and wiped her tear-dampened cheeks. As she worked her way down the steep bank to the edge of the water, silence fell.

"Where are you, sprite?" She looked around, not seeing any movement. "Let me help."

After a long pause, squeaks came from a few feet away.

A young pixie not even the size of Heather's hand was caught between two rocks at the water's edge. She'd probably fallen from the tree overhanging the creek. "There you are."

"Whatcha doing, sis?" Daniel called from farther up the creek. Her brother was a tall, hefty male, muscular from working his ranch in Rainier Territory. Shaggy brown hair hung over his ears because he was "too busy" to get it cut.

Or he doesn't give a damn, which is more likely.

"Sprite saving." Heather knelt.

"What a surprise." Shoving his long black hair out of his face, Tanner, her other littermate, shot her a quick grin. "Face it, sis, you'll rescue anything, from females to OtherFolk."

Daniel smirked at Tanner. "Or brothers, like the time you and Gretchen—"

"Shut it, gnome-brain." Tanner tackled Daniel, dumping them both into the water.

Brothers. Honestly. Heather snorted. Yet their playing lightened her heart. A little.

"Hang on, pixie." Carefully, she moved a rock to free the tiny OtherFolk's leg and then held her hand out.

To her surprise, the pixie accepted the invitation and climbed on.

Slowly, Heather lifted her hand to under the lowest branch.

The sprite leaped and disappeared into the foliage with a happy chitter.

Turning, Heather saw her brothers had abandoned their tussling in favor of trying to catch a fish. It was many miles from the North Cascade's Elder Village to where they'd left their vehicles at a turnout. Since they'd been traveling in their animal forms, they'd stopped at one of the territory's clothing caches near here to shift to human and take a break.

Undoubtedly her brothers were getting hungry, and bears adored fish.

She was a wolf, not a bear. And right now, her heart was too sore to join them.

Mama is gone.

It felt just so...wrong. There simply couldn't be a world without her mother in it.

Shoulders sagging, she sat on the creek bank and put her bare feet in the cold water. The August sun was hot on her shoulders. The air held the resinous tang of the forest and the slightly fishy scent of water flowing over sun-warmed rocks.

Daniel made a snatch for a trout, missed, and grumbled.

Two silvery undines flashed around his legs, then went to tease Tanner. Water elementals had a wicked sense of humor.

Heather smiled slightly. It was nice to be with her brothers again. Her cabin wasn't far from their place—they were all in Rainier Territory, after all—but she was busy with her company, and they stayed busy on the ranch that'd been in their family for generations.

Pulling up her legs, she rested her head on her knees. This summer had been so filled with heartbreak. In June, Scythe mercenaries had attacked their summer festival. Shifters had died, and she had killed a human for the first time.

Then yesterday, word had come from the Elder Village their mother was failing. It'd taken too long to get from Rainier Territory to the village since the place was deliberately inaccessible to vehicles.

Mama was gone before they'd arrived.

We didn't even get to say goodbye. To tell her how much we love her. Heather blinked hard. Mama had known how much she was loved.

She'd known.

Wiping her eyes, Heather glanced at her brothers.

Having abandoned their game, they were watching her with concern.

"She wouldn't want you sad about her death," Daniel said gently.

Tanner's crooked smile held his own grief. "Nope, she's liable to come back and knock you into the creek."

"Like when we were sixteen"—Daniel splashed toward her—"and Mama found out the Martel brothers were messing around with you."

"Those assholes," Tanner growled. He'd always been the most protective of her two brothers. "They were, what, mid-twenties?"

"Mmmhmm." Heather tried to smile. They'd been the first to teach her that males weren't always honest in their interest. "The Martels are still lying cockroaches."

"We wanted to teach them a lesson, but Mama beat us to it. She'd already shifted to bear." Tanner splashed water at the undines, making them swirl in glee. "She scared the scat right out of them. It was great."

Mama had been the sweetest person, yet she'd take on the entire world to keep her babies safe. Heather had always wanted to be just like her.

"Mama bears—the terrors of the animal world." Daniel smiled, then frowned at Heather. "You sure had abysmal taste in males back then."

"Guess so." And it seemed her taste hadn't improved. Bitterness made her press her lips together. She'd grown better at avoiding liars, but not at choosing males who wouldn't cut and run at the drop of a hat.

Nobody stayed. She pushed her forehead against her knees, choking back a sob.

"Hey, we're here for you, you know." Tanner dropped onto the bank beside her and patted her shoulder.

Being bears, her brothers fumbled their way through emotional moments. But it warmed her heart that they tried.

Soaking wet, Daniel sat down on her other side.

"Thanks, dudes." They cared; she knew they did. But their lives were tied up in their ranch, just like hers was invested in her software business.

She didn't want them to drop everything for her. She didn't.

But she felt so *alone*.

Mama's death wasn't a surprise, not really. Daonain lived a long time, but Mama hadn't been young when she'd birthed Heather and her littermates. Her time had come, and she'd faded rapidly, as older shifters were wont to do.

Why couldn't she have lived long enough to see her first grandchildren?

Heather set her hand on her belly. She was pregnant—at long last, after so many years.

She wasn't very far along, having conceived at the last Gathering. In fact, the healer in Cold Creek had barely picked it up. She frowned. The way Donal's brows had drawn together was concerning. Still, he hadn't said for her to worry.

As she scrubbed her hands over her face, exhaustion pulled at her bones. She hadn't been sleeping well in her empty bed. After she'd told her two new lovers she was pregnant, they moved out, leaving the territory entirely. They'd had no interest in raising cubs, whether theirs or someone else's.

Had they ever been interested in her, really? Or had they just wanted an easy ride through life with a female who had money?

No, be fair. In all reality, her pregnancy was simply one problem too many. After all, they'd hated Rainier Territory where her cabin was located.

She couldn't blame them. Born and raised in Ailill Ridge, she loved Rainier Territory with all her heart...but it had become unwelcoming.

In truth, the territory was a disgrace. The Laws of the Daonain were ignored, and the clansfolk were alienated from each other. Most of the problems were Pete's fault. Shifters who should have been reprimanded by the Cosantir were allowed to do whatever they wanted.

Rainier Territory was no longer a safe place to grow up.

She put her hands over her still-flat belly—over the little ones growing within. *Don't worry, my babies. I'll protect you. If I have to slap every mangy asshole in the territory, you'll be safe.*

Giving them a gentle pat, she smiled. She was going to have *cubs*.

She bumped Tanner with her shoulder. "I'm ready to get moving and get home. I have a business to run."

As she rose, a tiny cramp started in her belly. Then there was a bigger one.

No. No, no, no.

Pain rippled across her abdomen. She felt a trickle of warmth, of blood, between her legs.

"Noooo." Her knees buckled.

"Heather!" Daniel caught her and eased her down.

"No, please." Pressing her hands to her abdomen, she felt her hopes and dreams simply end.

CHAPTER ONE

Is everything making you irritable, girl?

The answer was yes. It'd been two weeks since losing her mom and her unborn cubs, and all the joy and light had left Heather's world.

Having stopped at the coffee shop for much-needed caffeine, Heather walked down the sidewalk toward her offices.

The mid-August sun was already hot, intensifying the petroleum fumes hanging in the air. Located outside of Rainier Territory and an hour's drive from her cabin near Ailill Ridge, Cle Elum was a small human town with far too many cars.

She watched a woman drive two blocks before parking again. Really, humans depended too much on their automobiles.

"Fucking thieves!" Across the street, a man chased a couple of boys. The youngsters dodged, sped up, and disappeared around the corner.

Heather frowned. Why wasn't someone looking after those lads? They couldn't be more than twelve or thirteen. She'd never have let her...

Closing her eyes, she pulled in a slow grief-stricken breath. After a moment, she shook her head.

Leaves in the stream; nothing is forever. Time to move on.

Across the street, the shopkeeper returned to his electronics store, still swearing a blue streak.

She pursed her lips. Thankfully, Ailill Ridge, with a mostly Daonain population, didn't have gangs or thieves, at least as far as she knew. Of course, a badly run shifter territory like Rainier had its own problems—the growing animosity between werecats and wolves, the disregard for the Laws, and the poor condition of clan properties.

The whole clan suffered from a general malaise.

It hurt. Her ancestors were some of the founders of the town. They'd built her little cabin in the forest. She loved it...but she was starting to wonder if she wanted to stay in Rainier Territory.

Should she pack up her cat and wander the country?

She snorted. Considering what a homebody she was, her journeys might not last long, but maybe she'd find a welcoming new territory. It could happen.

Then again, she had a business to run.

Forgot about that little detail, did you, girl? Adjusting the shoulder strap of her laptop case, she grinned and continued down the street. She'd have to settle for a short vacation. One of these days.

A block down, she walked into the software company she and a friend owned. It was time to redo the advertising for the winter season. And she had to find a new cleaning company. And...

With a smile, she walked past the receptionist who was on the phone. In the beehive-like main room, cubicles lined the perimeter. Employees were intent on their work—although a few looked up with smiles of greeting. The far end of the room held the private offices.

"Heather, finally." Shaquana stepped out of her office. She wore a screaming red suit. Her black hair was in a perfect bun, her makeup impeccable. Her dark eyebrows drew together. "Woman, your bags have bags. Didn't anyone tell you sleep is a good thing?"

Heather managed a smile for her human partner. "I stayed up way too late last night. Maybe I had too much coffee yesterday."

Not...exactly...a lie. Was one cup too much?

Honestly, she thought she'd done well to get cleaned up and into her usual business attire of khaki pants, white button-up shirt, and navy blazer. It was a shame business owners had to look respectable. Really, the only dressing up she'd ever enjoyed was getting sexy for Gatherings.

"Stay awake for a while. We need to talk—and then maybe you should take the rest of the day off like you never do."

"We'll see." Heather glanced at the discussion table in the center of the room. "Is this an everyone meeting or an owner meeting."

"Just us. About the offer we got."

"What about it?" Over the years, their accounting software for small businesses had acquired an excellent percentage of the market. But, as often happened with software companies, bigger corporations wanted to buy their company to get the rights to the app. With previous offers, they'd simply refused.

So what was there to talk about?

Inside her white office with its sleek lines and burnished metal, Shaquana settled into one of the three black chairs.

Joining her, Heather took a sip of her coffee and waited. Her friend never took long to get to the point.

Until today.

"Spit it out, Shaq. What's wrong?"

Shaquana took in a long, slow breath. "I want to accept the offer. To sell."

Heather choked, feeling as if an elk had kicked her in the chest. Carefully, she set her coffee on an end table. "Sell. Our company."

"I'm sorry, Heather." Shaquana swallowed. "But we've been doing this for fifteen years—and I'm in my forties. I'm ready for something else."

"Girl, you can't possibly want to retire and sit around."

"No. John wants to move to Florida. His parents are there, and they're getting old. I plan to take a few months and travel, then see what's next. Florida seems like it'd be a total vacation."

Heather shook her head. Sell their company? *No!*

But Shaquana was so excited...

"You, uh, could buy me out." Shaquana bit her lip.

"I might—" *Wait.* Had they really started the company fifteen years ago?

Oh cat-scat.

Daonain aged much slower than humans. Despite being years older than Shaquana, Heather still looked around thirty. Everyone believed they were the same age.

Cat-scat. A shifter in the human world had to be careful.

She rose and tried to even out the shakiness in her voice. Her company—she was going to lose this too. "All right. Let's look at the offer again."

With a whoop, Shaquana jumped up and hugged her.

Heather hugged her back and tried to think of what she'd do.

She recalled the fleeting thought of packing up Greystoke and heading out. *Okay then. I will.*

Much as she loved her Rainier Territory, it was time to see the country and find a new home.

CHAPTER TWO

"Hey, Madoc, your brother just came in. And his is the last order for the night." The skinny human waiter clipped the order onto the order wheel in the restaurant kitchen. He grinned at Madoc. "You sure don't look like brothers."

"We had different fathers." Plus, Niall was a cahir. The God endowed his warriors with extra height and muscle, so Niall was a good six-four. But the waiter probably meant Niall's white-blonde hair, fair skin, and green eyes—so not like Madoc.

Madoc had hazel eyes and light brown skin, and... Well, any shifter looking at him would know his animal was a bear. He was big-boned and burly, with shoulder-length brown hair and a short beard.

Giving the order a glance, Madoc realized Niall must be ordering for André too. Good, they'd have a meal together. "I'll take the food out."

He slapped more burgers onto the grill. The lack of variety here made for a boring job, but small shifter towns didn't tend to have big restaurants. A cook went where he could work.

A few minutes later, he headed out with three platters of burgers and fries.

This late at night, the dining area had thinned down to only a few couples and his brother.

As Madoc approached, Niall looked up. "André just got off duty. Should be here in—" The restaurant door opened, and their brother walked in. Niall grinned. "—about now."

Although visibly tired, André still moved like a werecat, silent and graceful, something Madoc would never achieve.

"Yo, bro. Over here," Madoc called.

André started across the room.

Seeing him, a toddler in a highchair squealed, waved a spoon at him, and dropped it.

Chuckling, André caught it, handed it to the mother, then greeted the father and an older child at the table. Smiling, he listened as the girl chattered away.

After a couple of minutes, he bumped fists with the girl, then ruffled the toddler's hair, getting another happy squeal.

Niall chuckled. "Our own Pied Piper, eh?"

"Yep." Madoc liked people and got along with just about everybody. However, children *adored* André, and he always found time for them.

Madoc pushed a chair out for him.

André clapped a hand on his shoulder and took the seat. "My brothers. Thank you for arranging the food."

"No problem." Niall frowned. "Are you all right?"

André was an even six feet tall. Streamlined muscles and chiseled features made him popular with the females. Not in uniform, he'd left his dark collar-length hair loose. His skin looked grayer than the usual dark tan, and his brown eyes were haunted.

Haunted. André's job as an sergeant in the Royal Canadian Mounted Police could be gut-wrenching at times.

Madoc narrowed his eyes. "What happened?"

André rubbed the back of his neck as if it ached. "A logging truck hit a passenger car on a mountain road. The car went through the guard rail. The man and woman...didn't survive."

By the Gods.

Madoc set a hand on André's shoulder. "I'm guessing the accident was too close to how our parents died?"

André felt the warmth of his brother's touch, and it was a comfort. "It was." He drew in a breath.

A decade ago, the police had notified him of how their parents' car and trailer had slid off an ice-covered road. Their wooden travel trailer had smashed to bits like kindling. "You know, I'd always hoped they'd mellow with age, and we could have a normal relationship. But they died, instead."

Niall shook his head. "Brawd, they didn't want cubs. Their feelings were never going to change, even though we'd reached adulthood."

"I know." André sighed. Their two sires and mother had never abused them—just emotionally neglected them. He and his brothers were fed and clothed but always knew they were inconvenient. In the way. Annoyances.

If nothing else, the lack of parental love had strengthened the bonds between the brothers to unbreakable.

"I hear you, brawd. Me too." Madoc patted his shoulder. "I thought once we were out from under their paws, we might manage a friendly relationship, at least."

Niall's jaw tightened. "Can't be friendly with human-hating technophobes."

"If we'd chosen other careers, it might have happened," André said mildly.

"Maybe." Madoc's brown eyes were sad. "It hurts that Mama's rant about my working in a human-owned restaurant was the last thing she said to me."

"I had the same." André's heart ached. "How Daonain shouldn't be in a human police force."

Niall snorted. "Being called by the God to be a cahir gave me a few extra points...until they saw my laptop."

It'd been nearly fifteen years ago when the three of them visited their parents, hoping to reconnect. Shifters needed family. Instead, the reunion had ended badly. A few years later, their parents were gone.

André managed to smile at his brothers. "The seasons have turned; it's in the past." He took a long drink of his beer, the cold, smooth lager grounding him in the present. "Anything interesting with you two?"

Madoc ran a finger along his short, boxed beard. "My life is boring." He picked up a fry and made a circle indicating the restaurant. "I hope our next town has a restaurant with a more varied menu."

André flinched. "Sorry, brawd."

"Not your fault."

But it was. André's job with the Royal Canadian Mounted Police made for frequent moves—something they all enjoyed. But he tried to be stationed in remote, human-shifter towns, which meant small restaurants.

"I'm not bored." Niall smirked at Madoc.

André grinned. Unlike most shifters, the cahir loved human technology, especially computers. To look at him, a person would think *Viking marauder*, but a few minutes of talk dumped him into the nerd category.

"As it happens, I wouldn't mind a little excitement here and there," Niall added.

"A cahir wants an interesting life?" Madoc huffed. "Let's hope the God isn't listening, or we're doomed."

André agreed. As a warrior of the Daonain, a cahir's idea of *interesting* would qualify as a horror movie to anyone else.

"Aside from the accident, how's work going for you?" Madoc pointed a french fry at André.

"I thought it was fine, but…" André frowned. "You know I have a law enforcement conference in Vancouver next week?"

"Right. I'd forgotten." Niall made a choking sound. "You'll be stuck in a city."

"The location isn't the problem." André took a bite and chewed thoughtfully. "Moving from town to town keeps other constables from noticing how long I've been a Mountie."

Madoc looked up from doctoring his burger with ketchup. "I've lost track of time. How long's it been since the academy?"

"Would you believe a couple of decades?" The knot of worry in André's gut tightened. "The conference will have people who were in the same troop at the Depot with me, and some I worked with years ago. They'll look their age."

"Exactly." Like all Daonain, André wouldn't appear to age much until he'd passed a hundred or so.

"Fuck. You still look like you're in your thirties." Niall rubbed his chin. "I guess you can't do like me and switch companies every seven or eight years."

"There's only one RCMP." André shook his head. "For now, I'll apply some makeup and add some gray to my hair. But it's time to rethink my career."

The statement tasted like grief, and André turned his gaze away.

André had the same protective instinct as Niall, but it went a step further. He didn't want to just step between people and danger, he wanted to…help…as well. Working as a Mountie had mostly satisfied that need.

Now it would be gone.

Maybe he'd see about the Sûreté du Québec. It'd be nice to return to Québec where he'd spent his fostering years after First Shift.

"When are you leaving?" Niall asked.

"Friday morning."

"I have to head back to Calgary tomorrow to babysit the new

hires"—Niall rubbed his cheek—"but I'll see you two at the full moon on Thursday."

Madoc made a grumbling sound under his breath. He didn't like associating with shifter females, and full moons were a trial for him.

André bumped his shoulder. "Since Gatherings are getting a bit boring, why don't we see if any female would want a more... energetic...mating. We haven't shared a female in a while."

"And littermates share." Madoc brightened.

Niall nodded in agreement. "That would make the night more interesting, eh? There should be at least one female who'd enjoy being the center of our attention."

"It's a plan." André returned to his neglected food and realized he, too, was looking forward to the full moon. He'd missed being with his brothers.

CHAPTER THREE

"Almost packed." In her small cabin's bedroom, Heather grabbed a pair of fuzzy socks to tuck into the suitcase. "We just have... Oh *honestly*."

The corner of the suitcase held a plump, gray cat.

When Greystoke gave her a smug look, she could only laugh. "You're not being helpful, you little wretch."

Five years before, she'd rescued the starving juvenile from the streets of Cle Elum, then had been terrified at how he'd react to living with a shifter.

It turned out Lord Greystoke was a very flexible fellow. As long as he was supplied with adoration, petting, and food, he'd ignore her little idiosyncrasies—like changing into a wolf. Unfortunately, he had no hesitation in telling her exactly what he thought of canines.

She glanced at the window. Through the surrounding forest, the light of the sun was slanting toward evening. She needed to leave for the Gathering in Ailill Ridge soon.

She wrinkled her nose. Normally, the time before a full moon would set up an anticipatory tingle in her body, preparing her for being fertile and in heat and in a place filled with eager males.

This time? *Nothing.* Her body probably needed more time to recover from miscarrying. "I'm sure not in any mood to mate with anyone. And the males better not push me."

Greystoke rubbed his head against her fingers in sympathy.

Well, in the mood or not, she still had to go to the Gathering. Attendance was required of every fertile Daonain.

"I guess I'll finish packing tomorrow."

The sale of her company and office building was proceeding at breakneck speed since neither Heather nor Shaquana wanted to drag matters out.

"Soon we'll be exploring unknown territories." She picked her kitty up, and her snuggle set him to purring. "I love you, Lord Greystoke, my mini-Tarzan. And I'd be so, so lonely without you."

Oh look, I think I'm turning into a crazy cat lady.

Giving a half-laugh, Heather eyed her closet. "Now, what can I wear tonight that says, *leave me alone, or I'll bust your face?*"

Hours later, in the Gathering house in Ailill Ridge, Heather pointed toward the side exit. "Moya, I need to get out of here." The babble of too many people was abrading her skin—and her temper.

And the *smell*.

Testosterone wasn't supposed to have a scent, but she called bullshit. On Gathering nights, the scent of males wanting to mate thickened the air.

Not that she was interested. She hadn't mated with anyone this evening. The idea of sex simply didn't appeal.

She escaped out the side door and heaved a groan of relief at the silence and fresh air. "So much better."

Moya, her short, curvier friend, had followed her out. "Maybe you're not into sex yet, but you're looking better. Can we start our mini pack runs again?"

Heather nodded. Yes, it was time to get back to normal. "Next month. If I'm here." She was leaving her options open as far as how long she'd be traveling.

"Good. I'll tell Talitha." Moya leaned against the railing, then scowled at the paint flakes stuck to her sweater.

Frowning, Heather ran a finger over the rough wood. "This place is falling apart."

"I'll say." Growling under her breath, Moya straightened. "In the mating room, the cushions were so old that when Daniel got *enthusiastic*, the stuffing poofed out with each...um..."

Heather snickered. Her brother had probably roared with laughter. "Did it help the mood?"

"*Not*." Moya's brown eyes danced with laughter. Brushing paint flakes off her ice blue sweater, she dropped onto a bench that creaked in warning. "You know, it's great to have you at our Rainier Gathering for a change, but is there a reason?"

Heather stiffened. She usually attended the North Cascades Territory gathering and then would run up to Elder Village to see her mother. "Cold Creek would remind me too much of Mama."

"I'm sorry, so sorry about your loss." Moya reached out to squeeze her hand.

"Thank you." But Mama's loss wasn't the sole reason for avoiding Cold Creek.

The North Cascades were where her friend Vicki and her cubs lived, including Sorcha, Heather's goddaughter. And Heather couldn't face them, not just yet.

Vicki totally deserved to be happy, to have such adorable cublings. So Heather would stay away until she could take joy in her friend's happiness, rather than feeling envy and grief.

She shrugged. "And Talitha was happy to have more females here as moral support for the newbies."

Being a lesbian, Talitha was only occasionally interested enough in a male to mate and didn't experience the overwhelming lust that often terrified females new to being in heat. Tonight,

Heather's disinterest in mating meant she had time to sit with the new females and supply advice and sympathy.

"She has a kind heart, our Talitha." Moya waggled her dark eyebrows. "So do you, even if you try to hide it. I'm glad she didn't ask me."

"You start too many fights—like tonight—which makes you a bad example." Moya's brothers had taught their sister to hit first and apologize later. Earlier, when two young males had harassed Moya after being refused, she'd smacked them down...with her fists. For a short nerd, she had an impressive right hook. "I'm surprised the Cosantir didn't toss you out."

"Pot, kettle, girl," Moya sniffed. "*You* knocked their friend on his butt when he tried to blindside me. And *please*. Pete doesn't toss anybody out these days. Everyone does just as they want with no oversight from our lazy-ass Cosantir."

"The worthless garbage-guts." Pete Wendell, the God-appointed guardian of Rainier Territory, was a spineless coyote.

Moya pushed away from the railing. "C'mon, let's walk."

"Does it seem like our imperious leader is getting even worse?" Heather winced as boards creaked under her feet on the wrap-around porch.

"Noticed, did you?"

She had. Rather than supervising the Gathering, Pete had spent the night drinking, talking with his cronies, and ignoring everything else. Occasionally, he'd exert himself and find a female who wanted to mate.

As they passed the living room window, shouting came from inside.

"Hands off, scat-for-brains. She's *my* female."

"Yeah, like you can even get it up."

Heather shook her head. "You know, in the North Cascades, Calum has rules about bullying and brawling—and he enforces the rules."

"No wonder you prefer to go to Gatherings up there, despite the drive. Calum's the Cosantir?"

"He is." As they rounded a corner, Heather looked toward the north. Realizing her hand was on her belly—over her empty womb—she forced it down. "Although being in a car for hours makes me itch, avoiding this kind of turmoil is worth it."

"I bet. Last month, Talitha got hurt when she couldn't get out of the way of a brawl. Pete didn't do a thing."

"No surprise there. Why couldn't we have someone like Calum in charge?" Heather detoured around a smiling female who was flirting with an older male. Neither noticed her or Moya.

"Or no one at all would be even better."

That would be a disaster. Heather gave Moya a disbelieving look.

The little brunette had a problem with males in authority. All of them, all of the time. And since Cosantirs were essentially thought-melded to Herne, they were *always* male.

Moya scowled. "Fine, the Daonain need their Cosantirs. Unfortunately, unless the God calls another, we're stuck with Pete."

"'Fraid so."

Moya eyed Heather. "Hey, could you, maybe, ask Calum to tell the God about our worthless Cosantir? You're friends, right?"

"We are." As cubs, she, Daniel, and Tanner had often hung around with Calum and Alec. "As it happens, I asked him already."

Heather shook her head at the memory.

The Wild Hunt bar had been empty.

Waiting for her friend, Vicki, she sat on a barstool while Calum—who owned the bar—inventoried his stock and listened to her complain about Pete and how much of a mess the territory was. "Calum, why doesn't the God remove Pete? He's not what a Cosantir should be."

"Herne might not have even noticed, depending on how open Pete keeps the channel between them." Calum leaned an arm on the bar top. "Time

flows differently for deities. To them we are..." He paused. *"I think of it as the Gods being landlords who live far away and hire managers to maintain their properties. The Gods might drop in if in the area, but otherwise, they don't bother with their rentals unless they get a call about a problem."*

"How disappointing." She shook her head. "But they do check on us, right?"

"Indeed. Yet what they consider frequent checkups in eternal time might be decades to us mortals."

She had been disheartened at his words. How could Rainier Territory survive more years of Pete's indifference?

"Hey, earth to Heather." Moya waved her hand in front of Heather's face. "Well? What did Calum say?"

"Oh, sorry. After he told me the God might not notice how crappy Pete is, I asked him if he couldn't get Herne to remove Pete—since Calum's a Cosantir too."

Calum's expression had changed to disappointment...in *her*. "His answer was—and I quote—'My charge does not include oversight of another territory. If a Cosantir's clan is dissatisfied, it's up to the shifters there to take action.'"

His answer had made her feel as if she'd tried to shove her responsibility off onto someone else. Which was exactly what she'd tried to do.

"Huh. He's no help, telling us to deal with it ourselves. How typical." Moya growled. "Yo, Calum, just watch—I'll run right out and perform the ritual to call upon the Gods. *Not.*"

Moya sounded more bitter than cautious. Heather tilted her head. "Why are you down on the ritual?"

"Girl, shifters *die* doing that shit. My cousin wanted lifemates of her own so bad she went to the Gods to ask." Moya's mouth twisted. "We found her body a couple of weeks later. I think she got so tired she became careless."

"I'm sorry."

Moya sighed. "Me too. And her littermates were devastated.

Anyway, I guess Pete is safe from getting his whiskers clipped—at least from me."

A movement out on the front lawn caught Heather's attention. "What's going on down there?"

In the shadows of the shade trees, someone stood at the end of the long private drive. No one was on guard there, which was negligent. Other territories posted sentries to ensure humans didn't blunder into their activities, because while in the mating heat, none of the shifters were observant or careful.

"Huh, it's our mangy-tailed Cosantir," Moya said.

Three much shorter people joined Pete beneath a tall tree. Females, maybe? No, they had no curves. So cublings, probably teenagers.

Two of them handed something to Pete. The third showed empty hands.

Pete slapped the youth hard, knocking him into the tree trunk, making the youngling cry out in pain.

By the Lady, the mangy-tailed weasel had struck a *child*.

Outraged, Heather shouted, "Don't you hurt that cub!"

Even as she stepped off the porch, Pete motioned, and the younglings raced away, back through the gate.

Pete stomped toward the house, a growl in his words. "What are you doing out here? Females should be in the house. Mating."

As he climbed the steps, then swept past them into the house, fury filled Heather, and she raised her fist. She'd knock the patronizing words right back down his throat.

"No." Moya gripped her hand, fingernails digging in like claws.

Heather stopped, appalled at her action. The Cosantir was the avatar of the God. To disrespect the God was...unthinkable.

And the God would probably strike her dead. There was that too.

A Cosantir had many gifts from Herne, including the power to kill a shifter with a touch.

Biting back angry words, she followed Moya inside.

The living area was in an uproar.

As they joined Talitha, Moya asked, "Fairy farts and demon dung, what is going on?"

Slender and graceful as a willow tree, Talitha shook her head. "Caleb wanted a female who was going upstairs with Jens. The female had turned Caleb down, but he attacked Jens anyway."

Caleb was a big beefy male, outweighing young Jens by a hundred pounds at least. Punching Jens with a huge fist, Caleb knocked him down—and then stomped on his leg.

The sound of the breaking bone and scream turned Heather's stomach.

And infuriated her. The Law of the Fight forbade maiming and crippling. Like the others in the room, she turned to see what the Cosantir would do. Banishment was the minimum penalty.

Standing by the fireplace, Pete shrugged and walked away.

She stared, unable to believe the Cosantir would just ignore this. Others around her grumbled their displeasure in low voices.

"Now, you fucking cockroach, let's finish this." Caleb grabbed Jens' collar, and the young male yelped in pain.

Anger roared through Heather like a fire, burning away any hesitancy. These were her people, her clan...and no bully beta would keep her from protecting them. Turning, she grabbed the small armchair, hefted it up, and threw it with all her might.

It hit Caleb right in the nose. With a shout of pain, he released Jens and staggered back.

"Leave Jens *alone*." Heather grabbed another chair, and she planted herself in front of the young man.

Hands in fists, Moya joined her, then Talitha, followed by other shifters, forming a line.

Heather's eyes stung as she realized she wasn't alone. There were still honorable Daonain in Rainier Territory.

With a frustrated growl, Caleb strode away.

As shifters who knew first aid tended to Jens, Heather leaned against a window frame and looked out at the setting moon behind the trees. The first glimmers of sunrise limned the leaves in gold.

The Gathering was over. Until next full moon.

She had an ugly taste in her mouth from the violence. This couldn't—*mustn't*—continue. But it would if no one enforced the Laws of the Daonain.

There were too few shifters to lose any to crippling and death from stupid fights. And Gatherings should be a time of joy, of mating—not fear.

This was all wrong.

She realized she was touching her belly again. Just two weeks ago, she'd promised her unborn she'd keep them safe. They didn't need her protection, not any longer.

But what about the babies who weren't hers? What about the cubs to come, like those her brothers, Moya, or Talitha might eventually have? What about the youngling Pete had struck?

She shook her head. *I can't take on all the weasels—let alone the Cosantir*.

But...this mustn't continue. The Territory needed a guardian who would actually guard.

A mountain storm of frustration swirled inside her. What could she do? But when the storm died, the wind sweeping the sky clear, there was only one solution uncovered.

The ritual to call upon the Gods.

A chill ran up her spine. Shifters who called on the Gods often died. But...who better than her? She wasn't pregnant any longer. Her mother was gone; she had no mates. Not even a damn job.

Her brothers had each other...and they'd understand why she needed to do this.

Herne the Hunter needed to be told about his Cosantir, about Pete. The task was up to her.

And if she didn't survive, at least she'd have tried.

CHAPTER FOUR

Gods, I hate cities. Outside the windows of the sterile, chemically scented building, the roar of traffic, horns and sirens, and the babble and shouting of humans never stopped. There were people *everywhere*.

A week. Niall scrubbed his hands over his face. He'd endured almost an entire fucking week of being in Calgary, only returning home to Glenbeinne on Tuesday night to see his brothers, then last night for the full moon. That was way too much city for any Daonain.

How often had he been tempted to shift to cougar and start shredding noisy humans?

He glanced down at the computer monitor. *Finally.* Here was an end in sight.

Really, he loved his work. What could be more fun than tracking down how someone stole a high-tech company's specifications on a new military drone?

Trouble was, he'd prefer to work in the silence of his own home.

Ah, well. "Trevor, come and look at this code."

The new grad hurried over. "What'd you find?"

Niall ran a finger over the suspect lines on the display.

"Whoa, score!" The skinny young human bounced like he'd caught a breakfast bunny. "Jesus, I don't think I'd have caught the redirect." His gaze held more than a hint of hero-worship.

Sydney hurried over. The blonde was the other rookie Niall was mentoring this week. It was the new hires' first official job.

Lucky me.

Actually, he'd had fun teaching the two youngsters. They were good kids, bright and enthusiastic.

Reading the lines of code, Sydney gasped. "It's a jump to a different subroutine."

"Exactly. Next step is to find the subroutine and what it does." But not today. Niall pushed his chair back and stood up.

Sydney looked up at him, eyes wide. "I still can't get over how big you are. It's like working with the Witcher. Only you have better hair."

A foot taller, he looked down at her and snorted. *Young things.* "Good to hear."

Trevor waved his hand to get attention. "Okay, so if we—"

Hunter of the forest, give me patience. "Trevor." Niall set a hand on the boy's shoulder. "It's seven o'clock on a Friday night. Time to quit. You two head back to your flat, and I'll meet you here on Monday."

Both stared at him in open shock.

"No way," Trevor shook his head vigorously. "We're onto the problem. It's—"

Why the fuck wasn't Niall's littermate here? André knew how to say no diplomatically. Niall, being a cahir, far preferred direct action like breaking spines and disemboweling opponents.

Thumping new hires wasn't considered acceptable.

Use your words, Niall.

"No."

They waited for him to say more.

So he elaborated. "Go home."

No matter how eager these cubs were, if he had to stay in the city one minute longer, he'd go feral and bite someone.

This is far enough. In the dense forest, Heather pushed past thick bushes into a small space. She turned in a circle, seeing only leaves. She listened, hearing only the wind in the evergreens and a distant trickle of water. She sniffed. The sharp resinous tang of conifers and the dry dusty fragrance of the needles underfoot. Good enough.

After stripping, she bagged her clothes and car keys, tying them up in a tree.

In her mind, she turned toward the back and the door. Mentally pulling it open, she stepped through into the blinding glow.

Tingles ran over her body as she shifted, falling forward onto her front paws. As with all trawsfurs, the encompassing warmth of the Mother swept up from the earth, filling her with love. The memory of her own mother sent grief right after it.

Mama had given the best hugs.

I'd wanted to do the same for my own babies. But her dream wasn't to be, was it?

Instead...instead, she had work to do. With a disgruntled whine, she shook her thick wolf's fur to escape the lingering tingles of her shift. A few blinks let her eyes adjust to the ground being several feet closer. Her ears automatically perked forward, catching the sounds her human ears couldn't hear.

The first few seconds of a trawsfur were a sensory overload, especially when it came to her nose. *Everything* had a scent.

Pushing out of the bushes, she started down the animal trail. The thick duff of the path was soft and cool beneath her paws. She caught the tantalizing scent of deer, then the more pungent stink of dung left by a bear.

Far, far away, she could see the sparkle of snow on the higher peaks. Her goal.

Herne and the Mother of All didn't have phones, didn't get letters, didn't live anywhere on this planet or dimension or wherever.

Only the Cosantirs had an open line to the Gods. The rest of the Daonain had to work to gain their attention, like a loudly squeaking mouse might catch a human's notice.

According to the Elders, there was only one way for a normal shifter to make a request. The body's needs must be burned away until nothing but *will* remained. High in the mountains, a focused spirit would be a glowing beacon for the Gods. However, exhausted, starving, dehydrated—it was easy for a shifter to make a fatal mistake.

A growl escaped her. The territory must be made safe for cubs.

She would do this.

Tail up, ears pointed forward, she set off at the trot a wolf could keep up for hours. Or, in this case, days.

Thank fuck, I'm home.

Two hours later, in Glenbeinne, their tiny human-shifter town nestled in the Canadian Rockies, Niall unfolded out of his pickup and stretched. To eradicate the city stink, he pulled in a big breath. He could smell someone's fresh-cut lawn, the aroma of basil and garlic from the Mancinis down the street, and the sweetness of late-blooming roses next door. His favorite flower.

Yeah, he was home and not in that putrid city teeming with humans.

He didn't hate people; he just didn't want them around most of the time. And spending a week in Calgary—all humans, all the time?

Just claw me now.

André's SUV was still gone, but Madoc's was in the drive. Good enough. Unlike strangers, his littermates weren't abrasive, and they knew when to leave him alone.

Gods, I really need to be alone for a while.

Then a car pulled in behind his, and Jillian jumped out, cell phone in one hand. The female didn't eschew human technology. It'd been one of the reasons she'd attracted him at the Gathering last night. "Niall, you're here!"

However...he hadn't given her his number or his address. "Jillian. What are you doing here?"

She tucked her phone away and lunged forward to hug him. "I wanted to see you. We had so much fun last night."

"The effect of the full moon." Rather than hugging her back, he put his hands on her shoulders and gently, but firmly, moved her back.

"But...I like you." She brightened. "We should go out. Do something fun."

"No." He'd barely spoken to her last night. She didn't know him well enough to *like* him or not. It appeared Jillian was another of the females who chased the Gods-called.

Her showing up at his house wasn't welcome in the least.

"Jillian, we had fun at the Gathering. I'm sorry, but I have no interest in more."

At her unhappy expression, guilt poked at him like a gnome with a stick, then he suppressed it. Back when he was newly called to be a cahir, he hadn't understood how females might want him just for his status or his genes. His littermates had talked him through several heartbreaks before he wised up.

Now, other than mating at the mandatory Gatherings, he kept his distance.

"But...but I'm sure we're destined to be mates."

Sure we are. He stepped away from her. "I don't want a mate, Jillian, and neither do my littermates. Go home."

· · ·

Inside the living room, Madoc spotted Niall and a female outside. *Another* female.

Shaking his head, Madoc settled down in his oversized chair and rested his legs on the leather ottoman. By Herne's holy antlers, his feet hurt. Why did restaurant kitchens have such hard floors?

He couldn't wait to get his paws onto soft forest trails for a week or so.

Outside, a car door slammed loudly enough to reveal the female's emotions.

His poor brother. Despite having learned to say no to unwanted attention, Niall still felt guilty after each incident. The poor cahir could kill a feral shifter with less remorse than telling a female he wasn't interested.

Brows pulled together, Niall padded inside the house. He and André were both cougars and never made any noise—unlike Madoc.

After fetching a beer, Niall took his usual chair, one as big as Madoc's. "I feel like I kicked a puppy."

Madoc raised his bottle. "You did good, bro. Shake off the guilt...unless you invited her here?"

"Not hardly."

Madoc almost laughed. Females never seemed to realize some cahirs weren't sociable. His littermate could go for days without seeing another person and be perfectly happy.

This female had probably hoped to be invited into the house in hopes Niall's brothers would also fall for her. Females were rarely invited to move in unless all littermates were interested.

Considering how different Madoc, Niall, and André were, they'd never find a female they'd all agree on. Madoc didn't mind. The last thing he wanted was a female in his life.

Sure, he knew—in his head—not all females were dishonorable. Some had integrity. Loyalty. Steadfastness. His heart disagreed.

Niall rubbed his face, his color paler than normal.

"You look rough. Did Calgary get to you?"

"Major, yeah." Niall shook his head. "I fucking hate cities."

"How'd you get stuck with cub-sitting anyway?" As a cook in human restaurants, Madoc was used to working with young adults. But Niall normally worked alone. These human younglings had probably come as a shock.

"The person who mentors new hires had hip surgery, and the manager dumped the job on me."

"You poor bugger." Madoc chuckled. "Are the newbies competent?"

"Aye, they're talented. Barely twenty-two years old and all enthusiasm about their first project." Niall's slow smile appeared. "They're cute as baby salamanders in their first fire. By the God, they wanted to work the rest of the night. I had to order them to go home."

Madoc grinned. "Because you needed to get your tail out of the city?" In all reality, it was good Niall had left. Cahirs didn't do well away from the Gods' territory, let alone being surrounded by metal and concrete.

"I really did." Niall scowled. "I found the first piece of code inserted by the thief, but it'll take hours to dig the rest out. I'll have to return there on Monday."

"Monday in the city." Madoc shook his head. "Sucks to be you."

Niall gave him a sour look and drank more beer.

"You hungry?" When his brother's eyes lit, Madoc rose and headed for the kitchen.

Niall followed, taking a seat at the island. "What're you doing home anyway? Don't you have work?"

"The restaurant's getting remodeled, so everyone's off for ten days." Madoc gave his brother an assessing look. Yeah, he'd lost a few pounds while in Calgary. Meat and potatoes, then, for a good helping of calories.

He tossed a thick steak under the broiler. The potato salad he'd made yesterday would work, and he'd add a sliced tomato for an added vegetable. "I came home to change, then I'm heading up to Jasper. Fur and four feet. Fresh fish and clean air."

Banff National Park was closer, but Jasper had far fewer tourists.

"Sounds perfect." Niall finished off his beer. "Is André going with you?"

"No. He's at a law enforcement conference in Vancouver, remember?"

"Yeah. I forgot, eh?" Niall ran his finger around the top of the beer bottle. "Did he make a decision on what to do next?"

"Not that he said." Madoc slapped the very rare steak onto the plate and set it in front of Niall.

As his brother enthusiastically dug in, Madoc smiled. Feeding people made him happy as a bear cub in a berry patch.

As for André... Tapping his fingers on the island, Madoc tried to order his thoughts. "He doesn't want paperwork and keeps turning down desk jobs, which means he does mostly enforcement. What he should look for is a job where he can work with people—not arrest them."

Niall's brows drew together, then he nodded. "You might be right. Let's tackle him together to consider something outside of law enforcement."

Madoc grinned. It'd take them both to out-talk André. Their brother had skills. "Next time we're all home, we'll give it a shot."

Pulling out a notepad, Madoc scrawled out a note with a detailed description of his plans for Jasper. After an idiot hunter had winged André one deer season, they'd started leaving information before heading into the forests.

Finished, he set a saltshaker on the paper. "You should join me this weekend."

"I might." Niall tipped his head back with a sigh. "More tech than trails makes for an unhappy shifter."

Madoc tossed the beer bottles into the recycle bin. "The place I'm going has some fine trout."

"Trout, eh? So...how can a bear catch fish without a pole?"

For fuck's sake. "Don't you get start—"

Snickering, Niall finished, "They use their bear hands."

After swatting his gnome-brained brother off the stool, Madoc headed for his bedroom. Fifteen more minutes and he'd be on his way to the wilderness.

A couple of hours later, the loud ring of Niall's cell was a jarring sound in the silent house.

He eyed the phone. Ignore it? No, it might be André or Madoc.

Rising, he crossed the room and checked the display. Trevor—one of the two rookies he was mentoring. "Yeah."

"Criminy, Niall, Jesus, you won't believe what we found!" Trevor was so frantic his voice squeaked like a squirrel plucked off a branch by a hungry hawk.

"*Found?*" How could they find anything? They'd left the company when he had.

"Um, yes. I mean, you know, the code. We couldn't wait. We brought copies home. And the subroutine pointed us right to the leak!"

Cubs. Niall gazed at the ceiling in exasperation. "Go on."

"Their subroutine automatically emails copies of research data. Sydney researched the destination URL and traced it to a local company." Trevor was almost shouting. "But listen to this! The company is under investigation for ties to terrorists."

Terrorists? Fear blasted an icy bullet through Niall's tranquil night. Whoever had inserted the code into the software had been damned competent. Surely, they'd set up flags in case their tweaks were discovered? "Tell me you're doing your research from an anonymous location. An internet café or—"

There was a pause. "Uh, we're at our apartment. Why?" The cubs shared a cheap flat near the downtown area.

"Okay, then I want you to—"

"I know, I know," Trevor said impatiently. "We already forwarded everything to CSIS and you."

Gods, no. The Canadian Security Intelligence Service was an excellent start—but the younglings' information might not be seen for hours.

Niall growled under his breath. They were as clueless as cubs after First Shift. "Trevor, hackers often set flags in case someone cracks their code. And after that, they'll have several ways to find *your* location. You two get to somewhere safe—a police station or a hotel or a friend's house. Then let me know where you are. I'm on my way."

"Seriously? Why—"

Niall's snarl silenced the youngling. "Do it *now*."

The two-hour drive southeast to Calgary seemed to last forever. Niall's worry increased as the minutes ticked by.

Once in the city, he felt concern crawl up his spine. Why hadn't Trevor called with their new location? He dialed the boy, then Sydney. Both calls went to voicemail.

With a grunt of irritation, he tossed the cell phone onto the passenger seat and stepped on the gas. *Young humans.* He'd tear them a new one if they were ignoring his calls.

Just be all right so I can yell at you.

After parking in a lot half a block away from the younglings' building, he jumped out of his pickup and heard fire alarms.

Fuck. Slamming the door, he sprinted down the street to their building.

Residents were streaming out the door. The cubs weren't in the crowd.

He raced to the back of the building. No scent of the younglings.

Growling at a human who blundered into his way, he pushed through people exiting through the back door, then ran up to the second floor.

Their door was locked. Not too hot, though.

He kicked it in.

Smoke rolled out, along with the tang of fresh blood. Fire burned in the corners. More flames climbed the curtains and over the furniture. Trevor's body lay on a burning couch.

Niall pulled him off and saw his throat had been cut.

Ah, gods, *why?* Grief was a hard stabbing pain. Turning, he looked around for the girl. One by one, he checked the rooms, stopping only to cough. The smoke was growing thicker.

Sydney lay in a bedroom. The fire scorching the mattress hadn't reached her lifeless body yet.

Tears burned his eyes. This was all *wrong*. They were so young. Barely out of the kitten years.

What kind of species kills its own young?

Fury mingled with anguish—and guilt. If he'd stayed in the city and kept a closer eye on them, this wouldn't have happened.

This is my fault.

And the fault of the terrorists. By the Gods, they would *not* survive this kind of travesty.

He returned to the bodies, sniffing, taking in scents from Sydney's arms, from Trevor's shoulders. The three killers were male and had held the kids in place to kill them. Their smells lacked the fragrance of the wild. *Humans.*

The smoke and heat grew intolerable. There was nothing left to do here.

He reached for his cell phone to report the murders, but...

Herne help him, he'd left his phone and wallet in the half-ton. Someone else would have to report this.

Once outside, Niall pulled in hard breaths of the somewhat cleaner air. In the distance, he heard sirens. The firefighters would be here shortly.

Slowly, he sifted through the scents of the crowd on the sidewalk. The killers weren't present.

As he turned to leave, the wind shifted, and he caught the scent of his prey coming from farther away. He closed his mouth to muffle the snarl rising in his chest.

Over there... Three men stood just inside a shadowy alley between one apartment building and another. Watching what they'd done.

Keeping his gaze on them, he cracked his neck.

Time to hunt.

Mustn't give the prey any warning. He'd attack from the rear. So he turned and strolled away from them. Once out of sight, he jogged around the building to the other end of the alley they stood in.

Silently, he snuck up behind them.

A blow to the back of the neck knocked one out, a punch to the side of the head dropped the second man.

Niall kicked the third, and the sound of ribs breaking was a muffled crunch. Good, this one was still awake.

Grabbing their jackets, Niall dragged all three behind a row of garbage bins.

"What..." Holding his ribs, the one still awake gasped, "Who—"

"Let's talk." Wishing he had the mind powers of a Cosantir, Niall started the questioning, ignoring the way his gut clenched. He was a cahir, a protector. Hurting someone was...wrong.

It would also be wrong to leave murderers free to prey on the innocent. *Think of them as ferals, cahir.*

The man confessed as did the other two when they roused. Before he returned them to whatever gods humans worshipped, they gave him the location of those who'd ordered Trevor's and Sydney's deaths. Apparently, the terrorists were selling the stolen drone information for weaponry. At a warehouse near the edge of the city. Tonight.

After the exchange, the terrorists planned to relocate since Trevor and Sydney had revealed their existence.

But at this moment in time? Both terrorists and buyers would be at the warehouse.

Perfect.

The murderers' vehicle was parked by the trash bins, keys in the ignition. Niall tossed their bodies into the trunk. He'd drive their car to the warehouse and wipe it down. After dealing out justice, he'd head into the forests.

If he survived.

There would be no added strength from Herne for this battle. The God would not be with him here in this concrete jungle and not while seeking justice for humans.

Nonetheless, the terrorists would rue rousing the ire of a cahir.

He had failed to protect younglings entrusted to his care. Trevor. Sydney. He saw them again, faces filled with laughter, with enthusiasm, then all animation dissolved in death.

They had been murdered...and this would be more than vengeance. The Law of Reciprocity demanded payment for the lives cut short.

Maybe the gods of the humans would accept his offering.

By his hand, the terrorists would come to an end and take no more lives.

CHAPTER FIVE

How far have I come? At the summit of another mountain, Heather slowed. Far, far below was the winding dirt road and her Jeep hidden behind thick brush.

Was it the third or the fourth day? Before leaving, she'd told Moya she'd be out of town and asked her to check on Greystoke every few days. He had a cat door, but he was more a pampered kitty than a hunter.

By the second day, her hunger had peaked and died. The scent of prey, of shrews, of birds, of mice could be ignored. Thirst burned in her throat and was set aside. The climb grew steeper. The burn in her leg muscles turned to pain.

Onward. Upward.

The thick conifers thinned out to straggly bushes and scrubby trees with a sharp pine scent.

It rained. Again.

She wished she could call on the Mother of All, always the more loving of the Gods. But Cosantirs belonged to Herne, so her appeal must be to the Hunter.

She shivered as an icy wind cut through her drenched fur and swept the clouds from the black night sky. The pads of her paws left bloody tracks on the jagged rocks.

Pain could be set aside.

Her mind was quiet, emptied of anything except her need. *Cubs must be protected.*

Hours later, she scrambled onto a high ridge whipped by pine-scented breezes. The light of the waning moon shone down like a soft benediction.

Long below her, dark forests rolled away into the night. Almost hidden by the mountains, the glaciers on Mt. Rainier glowed white.

Grief touched her. She had no one to share this memory with, no younglings to bestow the story upon. How she had longed for cubs and mates.

No. She pushed the emotions aside. She was here for the need of others. For her clan.

Planting her paws on the hard rock, she lifted her muzzle and sang. Sang her gratitude for love and life and friends and an amazing mother and littermates. And then, in long mournful howls, she sang her request.

It was a true call to the Gods, birthed in her spirit, free of all else, so her appeal could soar upward.

Please.

There she stood, mind empty, soaking in the moon glow, bathed by the cold winds. She would wait until her strength gave out, and she fell from the rocks.

Time passed.

The approach of the Gods roared in her blood, shaking her as if she were downstream of a massive waterfall.

The loving, bright touch of the Mother warmed her and retreated, leaving the darker, deeper hum of the God.

Herne had come to her call.

Her mind held only her need: *Your Cosantir in Rainier Territory has lost his way. We need help. The cubs must be kept safe.*

She was touched by the God, her spirit stroked as she might caress a child, and then Herne's attention turned away.

She didn't know the God's decision or if her plea would be answered.

But she had been heard.

It was enough.

CHAPTER SIX

Bang. Bang. Bang.

André snarled. What in the God's green forests? Was there construction outside the conference hotel in Vancouver?

No, wait, he'd arrived home in Glenbeinne late last night.

Was Madoc hammering on something?

With a frustrated groan, he sat up in bed. *Ah, not Madoc.* There was someone pounding on the front door.

With a jaw-cracking yawn, he rose.

The pounding continued.

"Coming," he shouted and pulled on a pair of jeans and a faded black denim shirt. Shirt unbuttoned, barefoot, he stalked to the door.

A glance through the peephole showed a couple of Mounties—human ones he didn't recognize. He opened the door.

"Constables, is there a problem?"

They gave him an assessing look, undoubtedly noting his disheveled appearance.

"Ah, Sergeant Crichton. Sorry to wake you, sir. Would Niall Crichton be at home?" The dark-haired one was probably in his twenties. Just a youngster.

What had Niall been up to? "No, he's not." He stepped away from the door. "Come on in. Would you care for coffee?"

"No, but thank you." As they followed him into the living room, one glanced at his notepad. "Might I ask if you've heard from Niall since Friday?"

Worry set up residence in his gut.

"I'm not sure. I was at a conference in Vancouver and camping afterward." He patted his back pocket and grimaced. "In fact, my phone's still in the car. Let me get it."

The sidewalk was cold on his bare feet as he retrieved his mobile phone from the SUV. He automatically took a moment to listen for problems in the neighborhood. There was the snipping sound of the next-door neighbor cutting roses. Farther down the street came thudding sounds and calls of teens playing driveway basketball. Their summer break would be over soon.

On the way inside, he checked for messages and missed calls. "Sorry, he hasn't been in touch."

"Would you know where he might be?"

Seeing the worry on the young constables' faces, André frowned. "In Calgary, I believe. He was mentoring new graduates at a company there. Why are you asking?"

"The programmers he was overseeing were murdered Friday." The tallest Mountie's expression was grim.

André stiffened. "Niall would never hurt—"

The other one held up his hand. "No, no. We know it wasn't him. The victims placed a call to his phone maybe fifteen minutes before they were killed. We have a record of him putting petrol in his vehicle in Glenbeinne a few minutes later. I'm assuming he was on the way to Calgary."

Brawd, what trap did you put a paw into? "If he went to Calgary, then where is he? Do you think he walked into something dangerous?" Killing a cahir would be bloody difficult, even in a godsforsaken city.

"We...don't know." The two men exchanged glances, then one

sighed. "The victims sent information to Mr. Crichton's cybersecurity company as well as CSIS showing that the systems of the research company had been hacked by terrorists."

"It sounds as if the programmers were silenced." What a messed-up world it was where younglings weren't safe. "What about my brother?"

"He hasn't been to work or called in. Doesn't answer his phone. He hasn't used his credit card since the gas station. We can't locate his mobile phone. Someone has checked your house here every day since the murders. He hasn't been home."

"That's not good." They'd been thorough—and probably wouldn't have shared this much information if he hadn't been a fellow law enforcement officer.

André rubbed his face, feeling the scratch of several days of beard growth.

"Perhaps your other brother might know something?" the shorter Mountie asked.

André glanced at the kitchen, as if the bear might be there cooking. But wait, hadn't there been a message from Madoc on the phone? He checked. "No. His restaurant's closed for remodeling for a couple of weeks, and he headed into the mountains on Friday. He didn't plan to return for a week or so."

The two constables looked frustrated.

André eyed them. "Have you located the terrorists?"

"Yes, we did." The taller one's gaze darkened. "Their center of operations was a warehouse. It burned down Friday night. From the number of bodies and melted cartridges covering the floor, it looks like there was a bloody war. It appears as if the terrorists were packing up, perhaps to relocate after being discovered by the programmers."

"Who attacked them?" *By the Gods, Niall. Did you go after the murderers?*

"No telling. Possibly someone higher up discovered the

terrorist cell had been exposed and snipped off the weak link. Whoever it was did a good job of it."

Fear made a cold slide through André's veins. "Do you think my brother might've been there?"

The taller Mountie shook his head "Your brother's a software engineer. Does he even own a weapon?"

Fangs and claws are weapons. "No."

"As we thought. There's nothing registered in his name."

He swallowed past a dry throat. "The bodies... Is there any chance my brother is one of them?" If Niall had attacked, had he been killed?

"No, Sergeant." The man's gaze held sympathy. "Your brother is extremely tall. Although the fire has delayed identification of the warehouse victims, I can tell you none are your brother's height."

"I see. Thank you." As relief swept like a cool wind through his fears, he realized he could feel the brotherhood bonds tying him to both his littermates. He would've known if Niall had returned to the Mother.

Wherever Niall was, he was still alive.

And André would find him.

CHAPTER SEVEN

I failed.
Failed as a cahir, as a male, as a protector, as a mentor. Niall snarled, the sound wet and ragged. Vaguely, he realized his humanity was fading away, the cougar uppermost.

Just as well. He was a fucking failure.

And he'd killed—slaughtered—humans. So many. The terrorist murderers had died under his fangs and claws. His aching head filled with the sounds of their screams. The rivers of blood. The feeling of ripping guts out.

He'd torn them to pieces, then trawsfurred to two legs and burned their building down on top of them.

It'd been a funeral pyre. Humans liked those.

Stupid humans.

He realized his paws weren't moving. Somehow, he'd come to a stop, head hanging, tail on the ground. It must have rained; his fur was soaked.

Trying to remove the irritating wetness from his whiskers and ears, he shook his head—and pain exploded in his skull. As if he could escape the hurt, he broke into a lurching run again.

The forest around him kept blurring around the edges. How long had he been traveling?

Days maybe. He no longer knew.

After the killings and the fire, he'd run. Somewhere. Bleeding, hurting. He had a foggy memory of riding on top of logs—a truck—for hours before hearing the mountains call to him. When the truck stopped, he'd tried to slink off. Shouts and screams had assailed his ears. At least no one at the rest area had shot him. Fuck knew, he had enough holes already.

The forest had taken him in. And he just kept...moving.

Sooner or later, his body would give out. He flinched at the thought of his littermates. Of the breaking of the bond, of their grief.

He'd failed them too.

The forest grew thicker as he continued downhill. The rain was coming down harder, hurting his aching head and the gashes and bullet holes over his body. The trail changed to something very hard under his paws.

A light flashed, catching him in a spotlight, and there was a shrieking sound. *Brakes.*

He tried to spring away. Failed again.

Something hit him, flinging him into the air. Pain exploded in his leg, searing through him until darkness swept him under.

By the Gods, Niall, where are you?

As time passed, André took leave from the Mounties. He notified the territory's Cosantir so the clan could watch for any sight or rumor of the missing cahir.

Meantime, André conducted his own search, utilizing every resource he could lay his hands on. How bloody ironic the shifter who was best at internet searches was the shifter who was missing.

Reports drifted in. Bodies from the warehouse were identified—no Niall.

Wouldn't it figure this would be the time Madoc had taken his furry ass into the mountains? The bear often roved far and wide. André didn't have days to sacrifice to locate him in the wilderness.

Instead, he kept on with the search. He'd gone to Calgary. In a parking lot near the young programmers' apartment, he found Niall's pickup. His wallet and dead phone were inside.

Had Niall been on foot? The terrorists' warehouse was near the edge of the city. Surely a cougar would've been noticed.

Maybe Niall hadn't been at the warehouse?

André sighed, setting his wish to one side. Too many of the terrorists had slash marks—something an oversized cougar might do.

The cahir hated to kill, but the humans had murdered Niall's charges. Just thinking of the younglings' deaths infuriated André. His brother would have felt the same.

Yes, Niall had ended the terrorists as thoroughly as he would ferals.

André tapped his fingers on the desk. When his brother returned—and André would accept nothing less—he needed to be kept out of this mess and free of suspicion.

Hmm.

Everyone knew computer nerds were wusses. Making a couple of calls, he told law enforcement and Niall's boss that his brother was distraught, fearing for his life, and had left the province to stay with friends.

Part was the truth.

Because Niall certainly wasn't anywhere close to home. Where had he gone after attacking the terrorists? Bullets had been fired. How badly had he been hurt, and why hadn't he come home?

Yesterday, as a cougar, André had crisscrossed the forests closest to Calgary. Surely, a wounded shifter would have sought the wilderness.

He found no scent of Niall.

Shaking his head, he returned to searching through the wildlife sighting reports. One after another.

He stopped at one. Early Saturday morning, several people had seen a cougar jump off a logging truck outside Chilliwack. Bloody, limping, the cat had run off into the forest toward the south.

The area around Chilliwack and Abbotsford was outside the Gods' domain. An injured shifter entering the forest would instinctively head for the closest Daonain territory.

That would be the North Cascades, over the border in Washington.

Seriously, brawd? You went into the United States?

André packed and loaded his vehicle. *Dammit, Madoc, I need you here.*

When he'd called the bear's phone, he'd heard Madoc's cell ringing in the house. *Didn't it just figure?*

Ah, well, his brother should be back tonight or tomorrow. Pulling out a pad, André wrote out a note.

As he left the house, he realized he was rubbing his chest. The bond to Niall was growing weaker. Either his brother was losing strength, or he was far, far away.

Maybe both.

Thud.

The impact shook the Jeep. As the screech of brakes still screamed in Heather's ears, she stared in horror at the limp body near the front of her Jeep. The headlights mercilessly showed rain-soaked golden fur and a white muzzle.

Oh no, no, no. I hit a cougar.

At least, it wasn't a Daonain. A shifter would have heard her car and moved off the road. Wouldn't have been on the road to begin with.

Still. I hit some poor, big cat.

She rested her head on the steering wheel for a moment and tried to get her thoughts to work. Over the interminable days, she'd staggered down the mountain, falling all too often, which was pitiful for a four-legged animal. She'd been so dehydrated she'd stopped at every stream for the whole first day. An unwary marmot provided enough food to revitalize her. A bit.

I'm so tired.

Climbing the tree to her clothing had hurt so bad, and then she cried at finding the bag soaked from the rains. Wet clothing was even worse than wet fur.

But once in the car, the heat was wonderful. Almost enough to make up for the rutted gravel road and scant visibility. *Stupid, wet Washington State.* Where else could there be fog and a heavy rain at the same time?

Thank the Mother she'd been driving slowly.

Okay, girl. Chin up. She cautiously eased out of her car, hoping the injured cat wouldn't attack.

As she drew closer, her eyes widened. That was one huge cougar.

"Sorry, my friend," she crooned and eased forward. "I need to see how bad I hurt you." Where was the nearest wildlife rescue?

Over the petroleum stink of her car, she scented blood, cougar...and then the wild fragrance of a male shifter. "Oh no."

Fresh blood streaked the pale golden fur just below his hip—the leg was broken. She dropped to her knees, hoping he was conscious enough not to savage her. "Hey, kitty, you're...*really* hurt."

There was blood everywhere—old and new. So many wounds. Scrapes, slices, and a lot of round holes. From bullets? The putrid stink of infection oozed from some. "Somebody shot you up good, kitty."

The cat's eyes didn't focus. There was a deep gouge across his head. No wonder he hadn't dodged her car successfully.

She shook her head. He was way past her ability to care for him.

"Kitty, hey."

The cat's breathing was too fast.

"Cat, I'm going to take you to a healer, but we have to get you into the Jeep."

A disoriented shifter was never taken to a hospital. There was too much risk of them shifting in front of humans. Ailill Ridge was the closest shifter town, but Rainier Territory couldn't keep a healer. Because Pete treated everyone like shit.

The North Cascades had one, and since Donal rarely left his territory, she'd have to take the injured shifter to him.

She firmed her voice, making it a command. "Up you go. Now."

Her words took an eternity to get through, then with a chuff of exertion, the cougar rolled and rose onto his paws. Three paws. His back leg was definitely broken, and she had to close her lips over the apologies trying to spill forth.

Gods, he was brave. He had to be in an incredible amount of pain as he slowly crawled into the back of her Jeep. Stabilizing his leg, she helped boost him in. He settled there, laying his head on his paws with a low moan.

"Good boy." She stroked her hand over the matted wet fur. "I'll get you to Donal, and he'll get you fixed all up."

The cougar rubbed his big head against her hand. His eyes closed.

She held her breath, terror ripping through her, until his ribs moved up and down. Not dead. Just sleeping.

"Hang in there, cat. Please."

"You were right, Heather. He'd have died if we hadn't met you halfway."

A male voice rasped over Niall's ears. Feeling the heat of a person too close, he snarled, unsheathing his claws.

The whole world rocked beneath Niall as the male jerked back.

"By Herne's holy prick, if you scratch me, I'll cut your tail off." The resonant voice sounded familiar. And the curse was reassurance the male was Daonain.

At least, I'm not in the hands of humans.

Blinking, Niall tried to focus his eyes without moving, because, by the Gods, there wasn't one place on his body not hurting.

As his eyes cleared, he realized he was in the load space of an SUV. Slowly, a memory surfaced from his foggy thoughts. He'd been coaxed into the vehicle by a female with a beautiful voice—not high or shrill, but warm and very feminine.

Had she left him?

A lean male with long black hair stood under the raised back hatch. A sniff affirmed he was a shifter with a hazily familiar scent.

Niall turned his head carefully.

Leaning against the back was another male, tall, big-boned, square jawed. Also a shifter. His blue eyes met Niall's. "If ye can see yourself fit to do so, changing to human would be good." A faint Irish accent made the words into a song.

Trawsfur? Bad idea. Niall's tail twitched in annoyance, in fear. Human bodies had no claws, no fangs. Were defenseless.

Yet, a confused shifter could be deadly to those trying to help, and face it, his thoughts were drifting like leaves caught in a stream. He couldn't risk hurting the innocent.

Closing his eyes, he turned his thoughts inward. Where was the door in the back of his mind? *There.* The glow was diminished to such a pale thread he knew his body was failing.

With an effort, he mentally opened the door and stepped through. His body transformed.

Fuck, that hurt.

And now he was naked and injured and damned vulnerable with only strangers around him. He sucked in a breath, trying not to panic.

"I'm Tynan." The Irish-accented male studied him. "And you are?"

What's my name?

It came to him slowly. "Niall Crichton." His voice came out hoarse and ragged. "Where am I?"

"At the edge of the North Cascades Territory." At Niall's blank look, Tynan added, "Washington State."

Niall frowned. State—like in the *United States?*

I left the fucking country?

He and André had been down here last June. They'd gone home after the festival, right? Yes, yes, they had.

Images of the last few days drifted through his head, yet nothing connected. "I don't know how I got here," he admitted.

The black-haired male gently touched a painful area on Niall's head. "I'm not surprised. This is from a bullet. You're lucky you still have brains in your head, cahir."

Tynan scowled. "Too fecking blunt, Donal."

"Just the truth, brawd." Donal frowned at Niall. "The hemorrhage in there would've killed you if the crack in your skull hadn't let the blood escape."

Donal must be a healer. The presence of the Mother was unmistakable.

"Not enough leaked out though, which is why you almost died," Donal finished.

Healers were either wonderfully sympathetic or blunt to the point of rudeness. Donal was not in the sympathetic category. His irascibility seemed vaguely familiar.

Niall cleared his dry throat. "Almost?"

"I fixed the bleeding and relieved some of the tissue damage—or you wouldn't have woken. Now it's time to mend your fractured skull." Donal set both hands on Niall's head. "Ready?"

"Aye, go ahead." As the healer started, Niall gritted his teeth at the painfully itchy feeling under his skull. *Don't move.*

It lasted forever.

"Done. So, Niall, how in Herne's fucking forests did you collect so many bullets?" Stepping back, Donal turned his attention to Niall's busted leg.

Tynan handed Niall a bottle of water. "My question as well. Are there humans shooting at shifters?"

Niall frowned, trying to remember. Images like photos in a scrapbook teased his memory without lining up into a coherent story. "I—I'm not really sure."

Donal patted his uninjured leg comfortingly. "Give it time. Most of it should come back in a day or three."

Thank the Gods.

"I loosened the thigh muscles, brawd." Donal leaned on Niall's hip, pinning him down. "Straighten out the break for me, would you?"

"Brace yourself." Tynan gripped Niall's leg, pulling firmly.

Burning pain stabbed through Niall's leg as the bones moved. "Fuck, damn, hell, *shit*!"

Tynan snorted. "You've been around humans too much, cat."

"The bone's lined up well. Don't either of you move." Donal bent his head.

As the healer did whatever healers did to knit bones together, the pain deep in his leg changed to an impossible itch, like someone scratching at a tight scab.

An intolerable amount of time later, Donal straightened with a sigh. "Now, let's clean out all those pesky perforations from bullets. At least most of them are through-and-through. Heather, can you bring over my medical bag?"

The female who appeared was the one who'd coaxed him into

her car. Tall and leggy with red-brown hair. Scratches and scrapes marred her fair skin.

She smiled at Niall, then blinked. "You're a *cahir*."

She must have spotted the blueish, blade-shaped scar on his cheek—the God-given mark of a clan protector.

"Aye."

"No wonder your cat was so big."

"Sorry if I scared you." He hissed in pain. The sadistic healer was using a massive, irrigation syringe to forcefully hose out a bullet hole. The stink of infection and old blood hung in the air. Thank the Gods, blankets and towels were catching the mess.

"I'm sorry I hit you." Her eyes gleamed with tears for a moment.

"I was standing in the middle of the road." He managed a rueful smile. "No question about it being my fault."

Tynan's eyebrows went up. "*A-boat*? You're Canadian?"

Why couldn't Americans pronounce *about* properly? At least the Yank hadn't said "*a-boot*." But Niall could only nod as Donal started probing for a bullet. *Fuck.*

"Mother's breasts, but that looks painful." Heather sat down at the edge of the loading area next to Niall and took his hand in a firm grip. "Hang on to me, cahir. You have a lot of wounds to tend."

He closed his fingers around the warm, sturdy hand, grateful for the anchor to a world that kept turning gray and foggy. "Thanks."

Her scent was oddly familiar but not her voice. Yet he could swear he'd heard the healer speak before. Why was he so confused?

She squeezed his fingers, stopping the drift of his thoughts. Her eyes were a striking bluish-green and soft with sympathy.

"I like you," he told her.

And she laughed, low and melodic.

No, he hadn't heard her laugh before. He would've remembered.

As Donal packed up his medical bag, Heather gently removed her fingers from Niall's grip. Even though the huge cahir had been half-conscious and obviously hurting, he hadn't crushed her hand.

His clear green eyes opened, and he murmured, "Thank you."

She watched him for a minute. He was one big, brawny cahir. Blood streaked his wide, muscular chest and the ridged abdomen. His flaxen-blond hair reached his upper chest and was so tangled it made her cringe to think of the combing it would need.

"You're bleeding." Donal walked up behind her, sniffing audibly. "Your shirt's wet so I didn't notice before. Let me see your back."

She frowned. "You're spent, healer. I'll be fine."

"Aye, my energy is low, but if nothing else, I can clean it up."

Stubborn male. With a sigh, she rose, stripped off her shirt, and let him tend to the nasty gouge from her fall. And accepted his teasing—and Tynan's lecture about being more careful on the trails.

As she pulled her shirt back on, she eyed Niall, then asked Donal and Tynan, "Do you need help getting him into your car?"

Donal rubbed his neck, looking unhappy. "Ah, see, there's a problem with us taking him home."

"What kind of problem?" Feeling her legs wobble, she leaned against the car. Exhaustion, lack of food and sleep... She was a wreck.

"Margery is in Elder Village checking on their health."

Elder Village. He must have seen the grief she couldn't conceal for he patted her arm in sympathy.

"Anyway, with her gone, I'm swamped." Donal smiled ruefully. "I shouldn't have taken time to come here, but..."

"But we're friends, and you didn't want to let me down. Thank you, Donal. I'm so, so grateful." The way the cahir had been breathing, she'd known he was dying.

"You're welcome. However..." Donal frowned. "He needs someone to tend to him."

"But—"

Donal raised his hand. "All the wounds are closed, and his fractures are mended. However, bones take time to heal completely. He needs to keep weight off his leg and his tail in bed for a few days."

She glanced behind her. In the back of her Jeep, the cahir was sound asleep. After such an intense healing, it wasn't any wonder. "But Donal, I—"

"His cracked skull is fused, the blood leak stopped, but the tissues are inflamed, which means he'll be unsteady and unsafe—again, for a few days."

What a crow-cursed mess. *I'm all packed and leaving for parts unknown.* She crossed her arms over her chest and scowled at Donal.

He took a careful step back. "I'm sorry, sweetie."

No, girl, you can't bite his boy bits off. "It's not your fault. And I do understand. He's a stranger, so you'd have to hunt for someone to take him in." Taking time the busy healer didn't have.

Niall deserved someone who cared about his well-being. Normally, she might be wary of taking in a big stranger, but he'd been very careful not to hurt her hand when he was in pain. His gentleness revealed a lot about his personality.

More, he was a cahir—one of the God-called warriors who risked their lives to protect the clan.

She could put off leaving until he was back on his feet. "If he can't put weight on his leg, how do I get him into my house?"

Taking the words as acceptance, Donal smiled in relief. "I have a spare walker in my car."

A walker? "Now, won't *that* make the big, bad cahir look ever so macho."

"He'll feel like the village granny." Tynan chuckled.

Donal shrugged. "His balance might be off for a few days, and a walker's safer than crutches."

"A walker it will be." Heather loaded the walker, accepted the blanket Tynan handed her, and tucked it around Niall. He didn't even stir.

Getting all those injuries healed? The male would spend the next few days sleeping.

"You've really had a rough time of it, haven't you?" She gently smoothed the long blond hair away from his strong jaw.

Well, she'd take care of him and send him on his way.

And then she and Lord Greystoke would hit the road. There were places to see, things to do.

Since she was alive and all.

CHAPTER EIGHT

What in the Horned God's lands had Niall gotten his tail into? After a fantastic week in the mountains, dining on fresh trout and nibbling on buffaloberries and blueberries, Madoc had returned to an empty house.

And a mess.

Sitting at the dining room table, he scowled at the long note André had left. Friday night, Niall's trainees were murdered. Someone had slaughtered the killers. Niall was missing. André had gone to look for him.

The careful laying out of the facts with no speculation included told its own story. Madoc crumpled the note in his fist. André obviously believed Niall had exacted justice on the murderers.

Good for you, cahir. But where are you?

Rising, Madoc glanced around, trying to remember where he'd left his demon-spawned product of human technology.

Ah, there. At least he'd plugged the device in before leaving.

The phone showed a myriad of texts and emails. Nothing from Niall.

The restaurant had emailed. The place would be closed for another week.

André had sent several updates on his location and copies of the cougar sightings he was following.

Worry tightened Madoc's gut as he went through the reports. The cahir was bloody when first spotted. According to the sightings in the US, his condition had grown worse. If Niall had been fit, he'd never have been seen at all.

And the States, brawd? Are you insane?

It only took a few minutes to pack for himself and Niall, then toss the bags into his Honda CRV.

"Are you going away again?" His elderly neighbor stood beside her mailbox.

Madoc halted and smiled at the white-haired woman. "Yes, ma'am. We'll all be gone for...ah, for a while."

She patted his arm, startling him.

At his stare, she laughed. "No, I'm not afraid of you, big as you are. I know which one of you works in a restaurant and has been dropping off baskets of food for me."

Caught? By the Gods, no bear should be seen when he didn't want to be. "I woke you?"

Her creaky laugh was merry. "I never heard a sound. My son-in-law installed a security camera after someone stole Christmas packages off my doorstep."

He'd shown up on some security camera? If Niall, the lover of all human technology heard about this, he'd twit Madoc about being seen for weeks.

The woman patted his arm again. "Don't worry, dear. I won't tell anyone you have a kind heart. And I'll keep an eye on your house while you're gone."

Madoc smiled. "Thank you, ma'am."

He could only hope his injured littermate had found someone as equally kind.

Niall lowered himself onto the living room couch with a sigh of relief. Despite being healed yesterday, his leg ached like a beaver was gnawing on his thigh bone, and his skull didn't feel much better.

Herne help him, he was weak. A hot shower had sapped away his strength, but at least he was clean.

Sighing, he rested his throbbing head in his hands, and his wet hair fell forward in an ugly mess. Annoyed, he tried to brush it back, and his fingers caught in the tangles.

Something else he'd have to deal with...or he could go for an easy fix.

Hearing the female across the room, he lifted his head. "Might you happen to have scissors I could use, please?"

"To cut your hair?" Amusement filled her pleasingly throaty voice. "Your plan seems extreme. I'll comb it out for you."

He frowned. No one had ever combed his hair after his mother had taught him how as a cub. It seemed an...intimate... sort of activity. Like being groomed by another cat.

But his shoulders and arms had caught quite a few bullets. Maybe he'd been dragged from the brink of death, but he was still damned sore. Help, as humiliating as it was to need it, would be good.

The female... He eyed her. "I'm sorry, but my memory is still erratic. What is your name again, please?"

Her lips quirked. Not a young shifter, this one, but not even close to old. The faint laugh lines beside her mouth and eyes indicated someone who enjoyed life. Someone who, rather than being insulted he couldn't remember her name, instead, found it funny.

"I'm Heather Sutharlan, and you're in Rainier Territory." She walked over, cup in her hand. "The territory is in Washington State in the United States, in case you don't remember yesterday."

"Not a lot." He'd definitely been a lackwit. And had been sleeping since then. In between the nightmares. "Thank you."

She set the cup down on the coffee table in front of him. As she straightened, she winced with a grumpy expression that reminded him of Madoc when the bear was in a mood.

"Did you hurt your back?"

"Well, yes, but an injury isn't the problem." Her frown deepened. "After Donal finished healing you, he insisted on bandaging me up."

Cup in hand, Niall froze. "I didn't—did I scratch you?"

"Oh no, not at all." She sat down across from him. "I'd been, um, hiking and got a bit scraped up."

The cahir in him knew there was more to the story than he was getting. She had dark circles under her eyes, and her cheeks were slightly hollowed, as if her hike hadn't included any food. The skin on her face, neck, and hands had vivid scratches and bruises. "Did you fall off a cliff?"

"No, ah, yes. It was a...long...hike."

No further explanation was coming, but all right. It wasn't his business. Not unless something threatened her, in which case he'd be more than happy to lend his claws to the resolution. If she'd been in her animal form, the fall must have been serious. Thick fur usually prevented deep scrapes.

Shifters, especially cats, rarely fell. He considered how she'd been moving—straightforward walk, efficient, but not silent. "You're a wolf?"

She nodded, even as she moved her shoulders and frowned again.

Ah-hah.... "The healer's bandage isn't comfortable?"

"The pixie-brained idiot," she huffed. "I tried to get it off, but my shoulders were banged-up, too, and I can't reach it. Since it got wet in the shower, it's uncomfortable."

"Should be easy to fix. Bring me your first-aid kit and sit here." He motioned to the spot in front of his legs.

She hesitated, then rose.

A minute later, she handed over the first-aid kit and knelt between his legs, facing away. After unbuttoning her oversized flannel shirt, she tried to shrug it off her shoulders and failed.

"Poor wolf." He slid her shirt off and winced at the long scrapes and purpling bruises across her back. "Hold on."

Gently, he pulled up the tape. The deep gash under the white gauze bandage looked nasty. "Why didn't Donal heal this instead of putting a dressing on it?"

"He was out of energy. He managed to close it enough so I didn't need stitches."

Niall sighed. He'd been the one to run the healer out of power. "Sorry."

"It's not your fault." She paused. "Unless all those bullet holes were because you robbed a bank or something."

"No robberies. Just some murderous humans." And a balancing of the scales. As his memory returned, so had some of the uglier moments. He'd killed...so many. Bending his head, he concentrated on removing the rest of the bandage.

The red scrapes stood out garishly on her creamy skin. Soft skin. Warm. She had understated curves he wanted to trace with his hands.

Wouldn't *that* go over well. He'd end up dumped outside, tail in hand.

With a silent sigh of disappointment, he sat back. "Unless you want more of a barrier, even the deepest one could be left open with just some ointment."

"I'm all for no bandages."

Heather sat still, head bowed as the cahir put some ointment on his fingers and ever-so-gently applied it to the scrapes on her back. He was being very careful—and very polite, considering she'd caught the whiff of interest in his scent.

Finishing, he wiped his hands and picked up his coffee.

After pulling on her shirt, she fetched her comb and sat beside him. "Okay, tell me if I pull too hard. I don't want to reduce a kitty to tears."

He snorted, then smiled. "Do your worst."

Starting with the ends, she carefully worked through the long hair. Now clean, it was even paler than she'd realized.

Seeing someone getting the attention that should be reserved only for adorable gray felines, Greystoke jumped onto the couch to give Niall a disgusted stare.

The cahir chuckled and held out a finger politely for the cat to sniff. "I'm surprised a wolf has a cat for a companion."

"Lord Greystoke manages to tolerate me when I'm in fur, even if he's quite insulting about it."

"Greystoke. Like in Tarzan?" Niall grinned and *wow*—as if a square chin with a cleft wasn't enough, the male had a dimple in his right cheek. Females probably followed him around just to stare at his face.

It was good she had more control.

"I loved the Tarzan books when I was growing up." Still did.

Niall glanced at the books lying on the coffee table and then simply stared. "You're a Daonain shifter, and you're reading romances with *werewolves* and *elves*?"

"I love them. It's so funny what humans think of us. I'm still wondering how to partially shift like some of the heroes."

"Ooookay then." His appalled expression resembled Greystoke's when she ate a salad in front of him. "You know, somehow you don't look like the starry-eyed romantic type."

She snorted. "It's the flannel shirt, right? Not a ruffle in sight."

"Ah, maybe?" Wasn't it cute how the big cahir flushed?

"Two people falling in love is fun to read about." *Just not to live through. Never again.* "And when it comes right down to it, romance—or the continuation of a race or a clan or a family—is the motivation for just about everything. Otherwise, what's the point?"

"Interesting." When his gaze went unfocused, she realized he was thinking about what she'd said, not automatically turning his very macho nose up at the mere idea of romance. "Maybe that's why so many of my SF books have romance thrown in."

Tangles eliminated on the ends of his hair, she moved upward and felt her sore muscles pull. Huh, it was just as well she hadn't tried to leave today. Taking a few days to heal her bruises would be smart.

After standing, she kept combing. "I wanted blonde hair like this when I was little. I thought it looked like moonlight."

He reached up to tug a lock of her hair where it had fallen forward. "No moonlight in yours. It looks like all the colors of fall. Much more interesting."

To her surprise, she could feel her cheeks warm—and so she concentrated on the next snarl in his hair.

Deciding the stranger might be tolerable, Lord Greystoke graciously moved closer so the male could pet him.

"You're a good little cat," Niall murmured, gently stroking the gray fur. He smiled over his shoulder at Heather. "As a cub, I wanted dark hair so I could match my littermates."

"And they probably wished they were blond." With her fingers, she worked a mat out of one tangle.

"You know, I don't think they did. André's always been happy with who he is. And although as a cub, Madoc wanted to be bigger, he didn't care about hair."

"Did he get bigger?"

"Oh yeah. Turned out bears take a while to get their size on."

"They do. My brothers are bears." Heather tried not to notice how the cahir's shoulders stretched the black T-shirt. "That's whose clothes you're wearing—and why they *almost* fit you."

The sweatpants were short by a few inches.

His laugh was deep and masculine. "Then I'm very grateful your brothers aren't wolves."

CHAPTER NINE

The aroma of steak and eggs was simply too tantalizing to ignore. *Time to rise and shine, furface.*

Carefully, Niall sat up in bed, grumbling under his breath. He used to roll out and onto his feet without even thinking about it. Hopefully, he'd be back to normal soon, eh?

At least he was awake. For the last three days, he'd done nothing but sleep. He'd be awake long enough to eat and talk a moment with Heather then find he'd dozed off mid-thought. When Heather loaned him a Tarzan book, he kept drifting off and having to re-read pages.

Thankfully, his nightmares had decreased so he could now get a couple of hours sleep before he fell into blood and death.

He scrubbed his hands over his face. Nope, he wasn't back to normal yet.

Today, confused or not, he *had* to call André and Madoc. By the Gods, if they had any idea what had happened, they'd be trying to find him. Even if they didn't know, they'd wonder why he hadn't checked in.

He swung his legs out of the bed. The hardwood floor was

cold beneath his feet. It could be worse—up in Canada, it would be about ten degrees colder.

Must be nice to have chilly winters rather than *freeze-off-your-paws-and-tail* winters.

He'd never know since he'd be headed home soon.

Meantime... With a scowl, he pulled the Gods-bedamned walker in front of him. Last night, Heather had called the healer with a report, getting the okay for Niall to abandon the granny-support tomorrow. Donal had spat out a few insults about cahirs' tendencies to overrate their strength and ignore good advice.

Niall half-grinned.

The healer wasn't wrong.

Trying to be honest, he might still be a bit incapacitated. The healer had reduced the inflammation, so his headache was gone, but the memories of what happened after he'd entered the warehouse were mostly flashes of blood and screams. So many screams.

And he remembered all too well the sight of Trevor and Sydney. Lifeless.

His guilt was accompanied by a blast of rage so intense he shook with it. Then he shook his head at the pointless anger.

The perpetrators had been sent back to whatever gods ruled the humans. *Move on, cahir.*

A short while later, clean and ready for the day, Niall entered the main room of the cabin.

On a windowsill, Greystoke watched him with golden eyes.

Yesterday, Niall woke up on the couch with the cat sleeping on his chest. Startled them both. But Lord Greystoke had politely accepted his apologies. Progress was being made.

In the kitchen, Heather was broiling steaks and apparently hadn't heard him come in.

Leaning on the walker, he studied her. An inch or two taller than average. Thick hair the dark red-brown of a fox in summer.

Not overly curvy; not thin. Madoc would say she had a sturdy build.

His brother had no romance in his soul.

No one looking at her would take her for a male. She had smooth, lean muscles—and a perfect heart-shaped ass. He liked watching how her shoulder-length hair swung with her efficient movements.

Even her feet were pretty.

Glancing over her shoulder, she raised her eyebrows. "Are you coming to breakfast or going to stand there and watch?"

The female wasn't rude, but she went straight to the point.

"Sorry." He moved into the room. When she pointed to a dining room chair, he obeyed and sat. Yesterday, when he'd insisted on helping in the kitchen, the walker had rendered his efforts a failure. If he hadn't had a concussion, she might've smacked his head.

He leaned back in the straight-back chair. "Good morning, wolf."

"Good morning, cat. How are you feeling?" She set a bowl of scrambled eggs on the table.

He rubbed a hand across his chest and shoulders in assessment. "Good enough. The wounds only ache slightly, mostly from the bruising. Want me to cut some firewood?"

"Absolutely not." Her eyes were the azure-blue of Moraine Lake's glacier-fed water, and her husky voice was nearly as cold. "You'll obey the healer, cahir."

So bossy. "You remind me of my aunt—who's a cahir."

Heather's mouth dropped open. "A female?"

"Aye. When her tie with the moon's rhythms ended, she accepted Herne's call to protect the clan." He grinned. "She says it's far more fun than raising cubs."

"Well." The interest in the female's gaze was obvious. The God might get another female cahir when the time came, but not for many years in the future. She frowned. "I can't imagine fighting hellhounds though."

"There is that small downside, aye. Have you had trouble with them here?"

"Some." Her eyes grew sad. "Last December, we lost five shifters to one. Then in July, one killed three before the cahirs managed to kill it."

At least the cahirs had managed. The scaled demon-spawn hellhounds had razor teeth and almost no vulnerabilities. Even bullets bounced off. The scent and taste of the Daonain would send a hellhound into a killing spree until it found no more prey.

Niall rubbed his chin. It'd be fun to talk hunting techniques with the cahirs. Get some pointers. Hellhounds were still relatively rare in Canada. "Any chance of getting in touch with your cahirs?"

"I wish." Her mouth thinned for a moment. "They had a disagreement with the Cosantir and left."

His jaw dropped. "You have no cahirs in this territory at all?"

"No. I heard our Cosantir shorted their pay as well as ordering them to do things they found offensive." She turned back to her cooking. "No Gods-called stays here long. The banfasa we had fled too."

He frowned. Just what kind of a place was this?

Heather brought the steaks to the table. "I love that your aunt is a cahir. Do you have other family?"

The aroma of the steak was turning him ravenous. "Aye."

She set down a pitcher of orange juice. "Does anyone know how badly you were hurt? Where you are?"

Niall winced, his appetite fading. How would he ever explain to André and Madoc what had happened—let alone how many humans had died under his fangs and claws? "I have brothers, and they'll be...irritated."

"You know, when I say something like that, it means my

brothers will be angrier than a gnome finding an empty garbage can."

"We speak the same language, aye." Niall snorted. The female had an understated sense of humor, didn't she. "I'll have survived a shoot-out only to die at the claws of a bear and a cougar."

"So big, so blond, so dead." Grinning, she dished up the food.

"I do need to call them." He automatically reached for his mobile phone and found nothing. "*Fuck*."

She raised eyebrows that were a shade darker than her autumn hair.

"My phone and my wallet are in my half-ton. Which happens to still be in Canada." Outside Trevor and Sydney's apartment building.

"Really?" Her eyes narrowed. "You crossed the border as a cougar—up in the mountain range?"

"Yes."

"You covered some rough terrain."

He gave her a rueful smile. "I actually don't remember much of the trip." He pulled his plate closer. "Thanks for feeding me."

"Not a problem."

With a loud meow, Greystoke padded up to Niall's feet, then rolled onto his back, showing off his lighter gray belly fur.

It looked very soft.

After taking a bite of steak, Niall bent down.

Heather cleared her throat in warning, and he paused. "Niall, you're a cougar. Don't you recognize a trap when you see one?"

He grinned. "Sure, but springing a trap is half the fun." He stroked Greystoke's belly, once, twice, and then all four paws closed on his hand.

Greystoke's forefeet held him while the hind paws—with claws thankfully sheathed—pretended to shred Niall's fingers.

Niall lifted his hand with the clinging cat still attached. "I'm doomed."

Heather rolled her eyes. "You know, it's a wonder any male survives to adulthood."

Niall just laughed. It was true enough. "He's a great cat."

As if pacified by the compliment, Lord Greystoke released his vanquished opponent.

Returning to his breakfast, Niall shot a glance at Heather. "Not many shifters own cats."

"Cahir, one does not *own* a cat." Heather's tone was dry. "One can only strive to exist in harmony with them."

"Ah, got it. Was he a present, then?"

Greystoke moved a few feet away to indulge in a grooming session. Chastising the Daonain minion named Niall had apparently disordered his fur.

"No." Her expression turned soft. "I found him raiding the garbage in a human town. Starving. He couldn't have been much past his first year. So I brought him home."

The female had a tender heart—and a personality that wanted to make the world a better place. "Poor wolf. With me here, you're surrounded by felines."

Her eyes widened. "*Noooo*, I hate being outnumbered. As a juvenile, I ran with my bear brothers and their two friends who were cats."

Two male bears, two male cats—and one little female wolf. He bet she'd been the cutest of pups. "Poor baby."

"It was horrible." Even as she pouted, her eyes were filled with laughter. "I was either getting knocked off my paws or getting pounced on."

"Ah, I can just imagine." Did Madoc ever feel outnumbered by two cougars? He'd have to ask.

And the thought of his littermates reminded him. "Might I borrow your phone to call my brothers?"

"Sorry, there's no cell service out here."

Fork midway to his mouth, he stopped. "But you have electricity."

"I do." She shrugged. "But I keep technology to a minimum in my home."

Now, didn't she sound like his mother and fathers who had hated everything they couldn't understand? Especially human technology.

He glanced around the room. "No television?"

"No, cahir. No computer either."

She lived in a fucking electronic desert. Eyes narrowed, he reassessed the room. The comfortable furniture was covered in dark blues and greens with colorful pillows and throws. There were full bookcases and a basket of knitting stuff. It was a cozy retreat, and it'd drive him crazy rather quickly. "Seriously, no computer?"

"None."

"I can't check my email or anything?" He patted his chest half-seriously. "I feel withdrawal symptoms coming on."

She snorted, then shook her head. "Give me your brother's number, and I'll call them when I'm in town."

"Notifying them would be great. André's number is..." He frowned. "Is..." There was a frightening blank in his head. He tried for Madoc's and found nothing. His hand closed into a fist. "I can't *remember*."

"Easy, cahir." Her voice dropped to low and soothing. "Donal said you'd be foggy for a while. Give it time. Meantime, I have a friend who likes computers. I'll have Ryder do an online search for your brothers and drop a line to them. Okay?"

The frustration still hummed like an irritating noise in his head, but he found a smile for her. "Yes. Thank you. Seriously."

It'd be a fuck of a lot easier if he could do it himself though.

So...was the lack of electronics from hatred for the human technology or simple ignorance? "Heather, have you ever *used* a cell phone? Computers and phones and the internet can be fun, even for shifters. They're not that difficult; I could show you—"

Her annoyed huff silenced him. "Did you just *assume* I don't know how to use human technology? Really?"

"Uhhh...maybe?"

She rose and set her plate in the sink. "Okay, techno-addict, I need to head out and get us some groceries." She added in a dry voice, "I'm afraid you'll just have to crack a book to get your entertainment."

She disappeared into her room, not waiting for him to respond.

Niall stared after her, replaying his words in his head. Hell, he hadn't even waited for her to answer his question before just...yes, *assuming* the answer.

With a grunt of exasperation at himself, he rubbed his stubbled face.

The humans he worked with would say he'd just shoved a paw —no, a foot—in his mouth. He'd never quite understood the term until this moment.

Her irritation died quickly as she cleaned up for town and grabbed her shopping list, which she'd prepared with Niall's input last night.

The dining area was empty. The male possessed a modicum of self-preservation and had retreated to his bedroom.

Picking up her car keys and stuffing her wallet into her pocket, Heather called, "Niall, I'm heading out. Back in a few hours."

Maybe his remark had hurt more than normal because, even if she wasn't *interested* in him or any male, he was impossibly sexy. Every time he moved, heavy, ripped muscles flexed and made her want to touch. And he was a cahir. Like fast food, they came in super-sized packaging. Bigger and stronger than other males. Faster. Brave and protective.

His shoulder-length, wavy hair was a pale blond against tanned skin, and she already knew how soft the strands were. He had sharp cheekbones and a square jaw with a compelling dent in it. His eyes were the sharp green of emeralds in sunlight—and she had to admit the intelligence in them was just as attractive as his body.

Well, mostly intelligent.

In the car, she glanced at her laptop case on the passenger seat.

Have I ever used a cell phone? She growled under her breath, unplugged her phone from the charger, and shoved it into her back pocket.

Yet... She frowned. Patronizing wasn't like him. He was always polite and appreciative of whatever she did for him. And he'd been stunned silent when she offered to comb his hair. Had no one done anything personal for him before?

Even when he was obviously hurting, he never whined. With the hated walker, he'd only growled a time or two under his breath.

She liked him.

Which meant she'd just have to find out why her lack of tech caused him to act like a cat whose tail had been stomped on.

To make up for the hours in a car and being among humans, André had spent his nights running the forest trails, snacking on rodents, bathing in streams, and curling up in comfortable hollows.

Which meant it was time to get a hotel room and enjoy a hot shower. He ran a hand over his stubbly growth of beard, then through his collar length hair. Longest it'd been in years. Thankfully, the RCMP had relaxed their dictates about hair length.

As he crossed the footbridge into the center of Ailill Ridge, he checked his mobile phone. During the search for Niall, he'd kept Madoc appraised of his locations, and the bear was on his way to this town in Rainier Territory. They'd probably catch up with each other today.

Pocketing his phone, he started sniffing for any trace of his brother in the small downtown pedestrian square.

On the way south, he'd stopped in Cold Creek to speak with Calum, the Cosantir of the North Cascades Territory. As it happened, the healer there had reported tending a shot-up male werecat three days before.

André could still feel his sense of relief. Niall had been alive. Had been healed. Unfortunately, since the healer had been in the mountains for a birthing, André hadn't been able to speak with him.

Using his powers as a Cosantir, Calum had checked his territory and said Niall wasn't within his lands.

And Calum would know.

André had met the Cosantir months ago when mercenaries attacked a Daonain Beltane festival, and Niall and André helped save Calum's mate. Quite a fight. Calum's mate, a retired Marine, had been picking off the mercenaries with a rifle. When mercs shot at her from behind, two female wolves attacked them, risking their own lives.

Such magnificent courage.

He and Niall had helped—and had been disappointed not to meet the little wolf they'd helped save, but they'd left for home before she woke. Then again, she'd been so injured and dazed, it was doubtful she'd even remember them.

Now, here he was in the States again. What in the God's green forests had drawn Niall down this way?

Continuing to walk, André checked the various scents. No trace of his brother.

He glanced around the picturesque, pedestrian-only square of the old mining town. A creekside park filled with tall shade trees and picnic tables ran along the east end with a bridge to the parking lot.

The west parking lot was concealed by ski, bike, and fishing shops as well as a wilderness tour business. The Bullwhacker Bar on the southwest corner was strategically positioned to lure in the tourists for after-adventure drinks.

After sniffing down the last side of the square, André gave up. If Niall was here, he hadn't been to town.

But perhaps someone had seen or heard of him.

He spotted a muscular male with dirty shoulder-length black hair and a dark beard scruff leaning against a building.

Getting closer, André took a discreet sniff and caught the faint untamed scent of a Daonain. *Perfect.* "Pardon me. Can you tell me where the Cosantir of this territory is?"

To André's surprise, the male sneered. "Who's asking?"

What happened to manners? André tilted his head. "André Crichton from Canada."

"Huh." The shifter appeared disappointed André provided no excuse for a fight. But brawling on the streets was unacceptable. Fighting could endanger females and cubs—and reveal the existence of shifters.

"He's over there." The male pointed down the square toward a balding male. "Pete Wendell. You be fucking respectful to the Cosantir, or I'll—"

"Thank you." André walked away. *Mustn't hit him. I'm a member of the RCMP. We don't kick yowling fleabags.*

Pity, that.

André slowed as he approached Pete Wendell, who was talking to a couple of cubs.

This unfit male is a Cosantir? In the North Cascades, Calum was so powerful the air around him shimmered, and all Cosantirs gave off a hefty sense of the God—or so he'd thought.

This Pete Wendell had the merest trace.

As the male took something from one of the cublings, André frowned.

The two youngsters were about twelve, around the age of First

Shift. Dirty, underfed, wearing torn clothing. Maybe the Cosantir was giving the lads money?

As the boys ran off, André caught the male's attention. "Cosantir?"

"Yeah."

Two rude males in five minutes. This town was setting a record. "My brother was injured and apparently is somewhere in your territory. Do you know where he is?"

"No. Sorry."

André took a calming breath and smiled pleasantly. "Well, might you point me in the right direction to locate him?"

Wendell's mouth twisted as if he'd seen maggots in his freshly caught kill. "You want me to waste my evening scanning my entire territory for an idiot shifter who got himself hurt?"

It'd taken Calum less than ten minutes. "Yes. I'd appreciate your help, please."

Wendell snapped, "No," and walked away.

The anger boiling inside André required a stern effort to be reduced to a simmer. Punching the flabby fleabag would be suicide; the God's guardians could kill with a touch...although such a weak Cosantir might need to perform a ritual to even access the God's power.

Fuming, André pulled out his phone to update Madoc.

"André!"

And there he was.

Smiling, André pocketed his phone and opened his arms in time to get caught up in a hug. A burly bear hug, no less, complete with a vigorous back pounding.

It felt good. Losing track of Niall had shaken them both.

"Have you found our idiot cat?" Madoc growled.

"The Cosantir here refused to look. We'll need to ask around if someone has seen him."

Madoc jerked his chin toward the grocery store. "Niall eats even more than I do. Let's try there."

The short, white-bearded store clerk had a nametag displaying "Murtagh". He nodded when they stopped at the checkout counter. "Good afternoon, gentlemen. Might I help you find something?"

André smiled, catching the scent of a Daonain. "We're hoping you can. Our littermate was hurt in another territory—badly enough we fear he's not thinking straight. We're trying to find him."

"You think he's here?"

André spread his hands. "The Cosantir in the North Cascades thought he was probably in this territory."

"Niall's a cahir," Madoc added. "Eats a lot."

"Ah-hah." Murtagh tugged on his beard. "A cat, perhaps?"

"Aye." Hope rose.

"As it happens, Heather just bought a ton of groceries. Said she has a wounded werecat at home who cleaned out her pantry."

A wave of relief almost blinded André. "Perhaps you could give me Heather's phone number?"

"Sorry, no can do. Her cabin doesn't have cell service." Murtagh picked up a pencil. "But I can write you out directions to her place."

"It would be very appreciated. Thank you." Hope rose. Someone was looking after Niall.

Still... André barely kept himself in check. He wouldn't feel right until he saw his brother for himself.

Impatience had Madoc tapping his fingers on his steering wheel. In the passenger seat, his littermate was navigating using the grocer's directions.

Madoc rolled his window down, breathing in the scent of the surrounding forest. "Gotta say, this is beautiful territory. The mountains have good bones."

"Aye. And Mt. Rainier is stunning."

They both glanced southward where the massive mountain dominated the horizon. Gray-brown volcanic rock vied with the reduced late-summer snowpack.

"Be fun to make a run up Rainier, wouldn't it?" Madoc grinned. "Bet the streams would teem with fish."

"*Bears*." Chuckling, André pointed. "Turn here."

Easing his SUV onto a rutted dirt road, Madoc drove slowly. Fir trees grew close enough to the road the branches brushed his vehicle with a welcoming sound. It was a great forest.

The road ended in a clearing with an older, one-story log cabin with a wood shingled roof. Sturdy, dark red shutters matched the red door.

As Madoc hurried toward the building, a pixie chittered in annoyance, and a fir cone hit his head. He hardly noticed.

Because on the small porch, Niall had risen to his feet.

Whooping in joy, Madoc strode forward.

"Madoc. André." With a wide grin, Niall limped down the three steps, leaning heavily on the railing.

Madoc wrapped his arms around the big cahir, feeling the rightness of being together with his littermate again. A second later, André hugged them both.

"Thank you." Niall's deep voice was husky. "For coming. I've needed you."

Madoc stepped back in surprise. Niall rarely confessed to a weakness. "By the Gods, how badly were you shot up?"

André kept one hand on Niall's shoulder. "And why didn't you come home?"

"I was damaged." Niall pushed his hair back to reveal a long healing gouge above his ear. "One bullet cracked my head. The bleeding inside messed up my thinking. I just...ran."

Madoc's gut clenched. They could have lost him too fucking easily.

"I don't know why I came south." Niall's face was thinner, the cheekbones sharper. "I never even stopped; my paws just kept moving me southward. It's a good thing Heather hit me with her car."

"She what?" André growled.

"Hey, rain and fog—and I was planted in the middle of a gravel road. By the time she saw me, it was too late. Thankfully, she was going slow." Niall shook his head. "She has guts, loading a wounded cougar into the back of her Jeep. I'd have died of the brain bleed if she hadn't hauled me to the healer."

Madoc's gaze met André's and revealed the same shock. Their littermate had escaped death by a whisker.

And, even if the physical wounds were healed, the cahir looked...haunted. Unhappy.

"Come," André said softly. "Let's get you home."

Niall hesitated. "Heather's not here. I'd like to..."

"Will she be back soon?" Madoc asked.

"No clue." Niall sighed. "If we're leaving, we'd best be about it."

"It would be wise." André set a hand on his arm. "The female might not appreciate finding strange males on her doorstep in an isolated location."

"There is that." The cat chuffed. "Trust a cop to think of stranger-danger."

Madoc let out a breath of relief. He'd feel a lot better once Niall was safe at home. "Why don't you leave her a note?"

"Good plan." Niall started back in then paused. "Ah, bros? What's my phone number?"

Niall had hoped to see Heather before they left. Apparently, it wasn't to be—and André had a point. Madoc and André were strangers.

Needing to reach out to her in the only way he had left, he left a thank you note. Somehow, someway, she'd become a friend.

On the way out, he stopped to give Greystoke a few scritches under the chin. "Watch out for her, cat. Who knows, maybe she'll miss me."

He knew he'd miss *her*.

After climbing into the passenger seat of Madoc's red CRV, they headed down the mountain. And the pain began...

Cursed rutted road. The first bump jolted his leg like a hammer's blow. He gritted his teeth. The next few ruts and jolts, he managed to endure without swearing.

Far too soon, he was sweating as the pain continued. The metal in the bloody car started to nauseate him.

And, oh Gods, the itching...

"If we hurry, we can be into the North Cascades by—" André stopped abruptly. "Change of plans, Madoc. We're staying in Ailill Ridge. I saw a bed and breakfast there."

"What?" Madoc glanced in the rear-view mirror at André, then over at Niall. "Brawd, you look like you spent the night drinking mead."

"I wish. At least I'd've had the enjoyment of a fun evening first." Niall swallowed, then forced a smile. "Spending the night here might be wise."

The trip to town took an eternity.

Finally out of the car and inside the bed & breakfast, he limped up the stairs, following his brothers and the striking manager. He'd been a gnome-brained fool to leave his walker at Heather's. His bad leg felt like a dwarf was pounding on it with a mallet, and his skin still crawled from the metal in the vehicle.

Unfortunately, the only unoccupied bedrooms left were a suite on the top floor. After a quick assessment, André turned to the female. "This will do quite nicely."

Tall and slender, the stunning manager had hair as blonde as Niall's. Her pink suit—and her stance—showcased all her assets.

"Excellent." She nodded at André.

Niall made it the last few steps into the room.

The female's gaze swept over him, lingering on the blue-tinted facial scar. She gave him a brilliant smile. "Cahir, my name is Gretchen. Do call me if there's *anything* I can do to make you more comfortable."

At Madoc's muffled laugh, Niall shot his brother a glare, then smiled briefly at the woman. "Thank you, Gretchen."

As she went down the stairs, he found a chair and, with a muffled groan, stretched out his aching leg. *Thank all the Gods.* "Fancy place."

"Too fancy." Madoc's sour look at the overly ornate furnishings made Niall grin. After spending his teen years in the Yukon Territory, the bear preferred simple and functional, from clothes to furnishings. He was usually in jeans, flannel shirts, and either soft suede boots or high-top running shoes.

"You'll just have to deal with it," Niall told him.

"I'm not the only one who'll be dealing with problems." Madoc smirked at him. "Once again, you've got a female rubbing all over your gods-blessed cahir self. Better you than me."

When Niall grumbled, Madoc grinned, then motioned at Niall's leg. "Why are you still hurting so much? I thought you saw a healer."

"I did. First, he fixed the bleeding and tissue damage inside my head, then my busted skull. That would've been a good day's work." Niall sighed. "But he also had to extract all the bullets, correct the infections I'd picked up, and then—"

"Fix your fractured femur?" André finished.

"Exactly."

"You tapped out the healer all by yourself?" Madoc shook his head.

Niall chuckled. "I'm just that good."

"If you didn't have a cahir's extra strength from Herne, you'd be good and *dead*," André murmured. "At least your animal instincts sent you out of Calgary and back to the God's forests."

Niall winced. If he'd stayed in the city, he'd have bled out. Herne's powers didn't extend out of his territories. "Right."

"You're also lucky it was a *shifter* who hit you with her car," André added.

"By the Gods," Madoc muttered. "A human would've just figured you were an animal and left you there...or if you'd shifted to human, they'd have taken you to a hospital."

Niall shook his head, remembering what Donal had said. "I was on borrowed time. I would've been back in the Mother's arms long before I reached any hospital."

The lines in André's face deepened, making Niall regret his words.

Madoc pointed at Niall and grinned. "Only you would get picked up by a tender-hearted female. What does she look like, anyway?"

"Ah..." Niall's heart lifted at the thought of her. "Totally not like Gretchen—not cold, glossy perfection. Heather has a warm beauty. I'm guessing she's around our age. Sunset hair, blue-green eyes the color of a glacier-fed lake."

His brothers stared at him.

"Ah..." He cleared his throat. "You'd like her, Madoc. She's a jeans-and-flannel shirt sort of female."

André tilted his head, studying Niall as if he'd grown a tail. "Since we'll be here a few days, perhaps we'll have a chance to meet your female."

Niall frowned. "Not mine, brawd. There's—"

"You think it'll take a few days before he can leave?" Madoc asked.

"I fear there's another problem." A corner of Andre's mouth tipped up. "We have your passport, bro, but I get the impression you didn't go through customs on the way into the US."

Niall blinked. "No, I didn't." And the borders now matched arrivals and departures. "I'd better return the way I left and avoid the border guards."

"The North Cascade Range is some rugged shit." Madoc eyed him. "André's right. You're not up to steep terrain yet."

"Mangy furball," Niall muttered, insulted, even if it was true. Time for revenge. "So what do you call a bear with a bad attitude?"

Madoc's glare promised pain.

"The bearer of bad news."

André laughed then had to dodge the pillow Madoc threw at him.

Sobering, André turned back to Niall, "We also have the problem of the dead bodies you left behind, brawd."

At Niall's wince, André softened his voice. "At the moment, everyone believes you found the two youngsters. Fearing you'd be next, you holed up somewhere far away."

Niall blinked. "I what? Why would they think that?"

"Ah, well"—André examined his fingernails—"I might have said you sent word about fleeing."

"Huh." André had always been the canniest of the three of them. "It's not a bad misdirection."

"A believable one." Madoc fetched bottles of juice from the small refrigerator and handed them out. "Wimpy computer nerds aren't known for going after killers."

But Niall *had* gone after the murderers, and despite killing them all, Trevor and Sydney were still dead.

If only he'd stayed with the youngsters. But *no*, he'd wanted to be home. To be out of the city. Leaving them to be murdered.

I failed them. Niall closed his eyes against the memories.

"Brawd. Look at me." André's grip on his shoulder broke through the darkness, and Niall opened his eyes and met his gaze. "It'll get better. Give it some time."

Niall pulled in a breath. His brother had been a cop for decades—long enough to have had to kill in the line of duty—and his dark eyes held that knowledge. That empathy. "Thanks."

Taking a chair, André rested his elbows on his knees. "At this time, the investigators believe one of the terrorists' customers killed them during a buy gone bad. There's no evidence you were there—good job, by the way—but it's best if you stay away until the furor dies down. Law enforcement *and* news reporters want to interview you."

Reporters? "By Herne's wiggling worm, there will be no interviews." Niall turned to Madoc. "Maybe I'll go visit our uncle up in Yukon Territory." It was where his brother had fostered after First Shift.

"It's isolated enough. For now, we'll stay put here and see how things go in Calgary."

"You have to work," Niall protested.

"Nope. The restaurant's still closed for remodeling for...let me check the latest." Madoc pulled out his phone, checked his emails, and let out a laugh. "Another couple of weeks, and I have another email from someone down here named Ryder reporting you're at Heather's place and giving her mobile number and email."

She had a mobile phone *and* email? He'd really stuffed his fat, furry paw into his mouth all right.

But...Niall grinned. She'd been as good as her word. And hey, now he had her email.

"I took a leave of absence, as well." André toasted Niall with his bottle. "You two have followed me with every new posting. It's my turn to follow you."

The cold emptiness inside Niall receded. His littermates were here. Together, they could take on anything.

Since Niall was safe to be on his own for a few hours, Heather had swung by Espresso Books to use their internet, deal with her email, and contact Ryder, then had a lovely visit with her mother's best friend, Ina, before doing the grocery shopping.

Now, back at the cabin, she looked forward to teasing Niall about human technology and assumptions. He really was so much fun—and could laugh at himself, too.

But when she walked in, he wasn't in the main room. Probably taking another nap.

Or maybe hiding and trying to figure out what to say. Silver-tongued, he was not. Although she liked his unvarnished speech. He didn't bury the truth under a lot of horse manure.

After greeting Greystoke with strokes and snuggles, Heather fed him and unloaded groceries. Considering her laughable cooking skills, what should she make for supper? Would Niall have a preference?

As she crossed the dining room toward the bedrooms, she spotted a note on her kitchen table.

Heather,

My brothers showed up right after you left. We're heading back to Canada.

Sure you are. She rolled her eyes. This morning, Niall had bumped his knee on the coffee table and turned white. There was no way he'd be able to tolerate a bumpy ride. The interstate wasn't too bad, but there was a lot of rough road before then. *Niall, you idiot.*

Thank you for getting me to a healer and caring for me these past days. If there is anything I can do for you in return, please call on me.
 Niall

A number was scrawled across the bottom. At least he'd remembered his phone number.

She huffed a laugh. The male could barely walk and thought she should call on him for her problems? Still, Law of Reciprocity or not, it truly was a sweet offer.

But the truth was, she'd never see him again.

She rubbed her chest against an unexpected ache of loss. Another person gone out of her life. And one she'd really come to like.

They'd discussed everything from his favorite sci-fi shows to her paranormal romances, argued about Canadian and US politics, and bonded over annoying littermate stories. Now, just as she found out they both enjoyed human technology, he was gone.

She looked around her cabin. Why did it feel so lonely, so empty?

Gods, she was going to miss him.

Safe trails, cahir.

She pulled in a slow breath. "Hey, Lord Greystoke."

The cat paused in his grooming, one hind paw in the air. His ears pricked forward.

"Our houseguest is gone, so we can get back onto our interrupted travel schedule."

Greystoke considered her a moment, then glanced at the kitchen.

"Yes, yes, don't worry. I won't forget your crunchies."

By leaving, she wouldn't have to deal with her too-empty cabin. Yes, it was time to travel.

A bubble of anticipation rose inside her. She'd get to see the beautiful places her friends had talked about. Find a new home, a new clan. Discover a new job and new goals.

She froze at feeling...happy. Somehow, the darkness that had filled her days had lifted. When?

Perhaps after almost dying during the Call to the Gods? Oh. She felt again the fear as her paws slipped. As she fell. How she'd realized she wanted to live.

But there was also Niall. Having him here had reminded her

of all life still had to offer—friendship and conversation and laughter.

She was ready to move on and live again.

And going forward, she'd simply avoid any emotional entanglements. Easy enough.

She let out a short laugh. The Gods must have agreed and helped by removing Niall from her life.

Fetching her phone, she pulled up her travel checklist. In all reality, it was just as well Niall had kept her from leaving. More paperwork had turned up for the sale of the Cle Elum office building.

Plan out the next few days to finish the paperwork. Get her packing done. Drop any perishable food off with Ina. "Looks like we should be able to leave on Saturday."

As she tucked her phone away, she saw the almost-healed gashes on her knuckles. At least the coming trip would be less perilous than the previous one.

Danger or not, she'd accomplished what she'd set out to do. The God had heard her plea.

And there was another reason to be leaving. Until and unless the God acted and removed the Cosantir, there was very little anyone could do to fix things.

So, much as she'd like to see what happened when Herne finally acted, she'd probably be halfway across the country by then.

Smiling, she pulled out a map, and her eyes were drawn to the so-very-close border to Canada. Where Niall lived.

No, absolutely not. Scowling, she looked to the east instead. Perhaps she'd start with the Sawtooth National Forest in Idaho.

Or—*ooooh*—Idaho had hot springs.

CHAPTER TEN

Following his brothers out of the B&B, Niall took a deep breath. The days had been warm and dry, and the air held the dusty scent of evergreens mixed with the less-appealing odors of humanity—petroleum, cooked food, along with the artificial perfumes of soap, deodorants, and that odd, sticky spray humans used on their hair.

He wrinkled his nose.

Then again, it smelled far better than Calgary, and here, in a Daonain territory, his strength was enhanced by the God. "I've made a decision—I'm never going into a city again."

Madoc slapped his arm—and wasn't it nice his shoulder no longer hurt. "'Bout time you came to your senses. You should have told your company to take a long leap off a high cliff."

"Yeah." Niall followed André across the brick-paved square toward Espresso Books—a combined bookstore and coffee shop. "That won't be a problem in the future." Yesterday, he'd sent an email, tendering his resignation.

The cybersecurity company's carefully worded acceptance held an apology for what he'd been through, gratification he was all right, and understanding for his disinclination to return. Not expressed was their undoubted relief at losing an employee who might be a source of unfavorable publicity, not to mention investigations and trials.

André dropped back to walk beside him. "It's a shame. I know you liked your job, brawd."

Niall shrugged, stuffing his hands in his pockets. It was odd. He knew he'd loved working cybersecurity, yet ever since Trevor and Sydney were murdered, that life seemed...distant. All he wanted right now was to disappear into the wilderness. To bury himself in his animal's head and forget the grief, the deaths, the guilt.

And he couldn't right now, so he'd have to use other techniques. Talking with his brothers was helping, probably more than anything else. He'd had to tell himself he'd been through this before. Violence, even for a cahir, was a shock to the system. He was working on taking care of himself—eating healthy, sleeping, and starting to get out and about...like today.

Silently, he followed his brothers into the coffee shop portion of the place and did a quick scan in hopes Heather might be there. But she wasn't.

The twenty-something, freckle-faced barista looked up from messing with a machine. "Hey, Madoc. The usual three or just you?"

"Corey." Madoc held up three fingers. "Please."

Niall grinned. Of course the coffee shop guy would know Madoc. Hating Gretchen's weak brew, the bear had been making frequent coffee runs. He was still grumbling about the lack of Tim Hortons in the territory and insisting the American Starbucks couldn't compare.

They chose pastries to go with the drinks, and Madoc paid.

Niall poked at the bills—all the same dull green no matter the denomination. "Boring. What do Americans have against color?"

André laughed and led the way to a table.

Taking a seat, Niall realized nothing hurt. He was definitely stronger. "When can we head back to Canada?"

André took a sip of his coffee and considered Niall with a frown.

Even if not wolves, littermates tended to defer to one sibling. André had always been their alpha. Leadership suited neither Niall nor Madoc, and André couldn't stop exuding authority if he'd tried. Being a Mountie fit him as closely as did his fur.

"You're better," André said finally, "but not steady or strong enough to manage the Cascade Range over the border. Not yet."

Well, fuck.

"Can we, at least, get out of this messed-up territory?" If Niall had been a wolf, he'd probably have whined.

"Did the cat and dog fight wake you up last night?" Madoc chuckled.

By the God, it had. From the screeching, hissing, and growling, a couple of werecats had been brawling with werewolves. "Hearing the scat-for-brains fighting in the center of *town* set off every cahir instinct in my body. *Humans* live here. Do these shifters care nothing about the Law?"

"It's perplexing, aye?" André's brows drew together. "Animosity between feline and canine Daonain should never have been allowed to reach open battle. I almost went down to break it up, but the presence of a foreigner would probably have upped the violence."

"And a Mountie can't arrest someone in this country." Madoc rubbed a finger along his short beard. "This kind of idiocy should be handled by shifters in the territory or the Cosantir. Where is he—hibernating for the winter?"

"He does seem rather ineffectual. And the shifters appear disinclined to act." André smiled slightly. "However, we've met some good Daonain here. The grocer was helpful, and of course, there's Niall's female, Heather."

"Not mine." He'd be getting teased about her for years...and he didn't even care. "But it's a shame you poor males missed out. You'd like her."

André took a sip of his drink, studied Niall for a long moment, then smiled. "I think you can tolerate the drive to Cold Creek. We can relocate there where the dog and cat fights won't bother you."

"Good." Madoc swallowed the last of his pastry. "Head for the North Cascades in the morning?"

Three fists thumped the table, signaling a consensus.

"How long did you take leave for?" Niall asked André.

"A month." André looked up as two elderly women entered the shop. "I also requested a new posting."

Guilt trickled into Niall's gut. "Because of me."

"Partly. It seems expedient to remove us from the area." André motioned with his cup. "But I enjoy exploring new areas. We all do."

Madoc chuckled. "After having parents who never settled anywhere, you'd think we'd be the opposite. Isn't that how it's supposed to work?"

Niall shrugged. "We never gave permanency a chance after leaving our twenties."

Upon becoming adults, Daonain males were encouraged to wander from territory to territory for a time. It broadened their horizons—and more importantly, stirred up the gene pool.

"My fault," André admitted. "In law enforcement, it's best to be unbiased, not swayed by relationships. Attachments aren't wise."

"Logical." But not entirely the whole truth, Niall knew. André avoided entanglements with anyone except his brothers in much the same way Madoc avoided females outside of full moon gatherings.

Then again, he himself had never wanted to settle down with anyone or anywhere.

They had each other. It was enough.

. . .

André led his brothers out of Espresso Books, thinking of a cat-vs-wolf fight in Quebec. His grandfather, the Cosantir, had given the four miscreants a choice: be shaved of their fur or be banished. They'd chosen to be shaved—and had never set a paw wrong again.

The Cosantir here lacked imagination. Or maybe he just didn't care.

He damned-well *should* care. This territory was a disaster—hungry cubs on the streets, violence between shifters. Niall had mentioned they had no cahirs and no healer, probably because shifters who could choose their location wouldn't *want* to live here.

"Let's get Niall used to walking again." To avoid the tourists clogging the square, André headed into the creekside park.

"Yes, let's." Grinning, Niall led the way down the sidewalk running beside the water.

The large stream probably was a raging torrent in the spring, but this late in the year, the water flowed smooth and quiet. A footbridge crossed over from the parking area to the park.

André watched three, long, sleek undines play tag around the bridge pillars, darting in and out of the sunlight. "I haven't noticed many OtherFolk around, have you?"

Perhaps because of the inadequate Cosantir?

"Rather a thin population. A sprite here and there. A gnome behind the grocery." Madoc grinned. "Maybe they all moved to Canada."

Niall gave him a laughing look. "Next, they'll demand we give them hockey sticks."

"Pixie vs gnomes for the Stanley Cup." André snorted. "All the gnomes would be suspended within minutes."

After they'd walked a while, Niall's gait slowed. Without discussing it, André simply turned and headed back.

Niall scowled. "Okay, I get it. I'm not ready to challenge the Cascade Range yet."

"Nope, you're not." Madoc slapped André's shoulder. "Why don't you get your running in. We'll meet you at the footbridge."

Niall wasn't the only one who needed to stretch his legs. "Sounds good." André broke into an easy jog. Maybe tonight they could shift and run some forest trails.

Passing the square, he kept going, ticking off minutes in his head until the time came to turn and head back. As he neared the bridge, he saw his brothers weren't there yet.

Loud laughter from the stream bank caught his attention. Another brawl about to happen?

No. A group of males and females were gathered in a circle under a tree. A high-pitched squeak sounded. Had they caught a mouse?

André veered toward them and checked the scent in the air. They were all shifters.

In animal form, a shifter might enjoy a good chase and rodent snack. But these Daonain were in human form—and torturing animals was despicable.

Shouldering a male to one side, André joined the circle, ready to rescue a rodent.

It wasn't a rodent; it was a *pixie*. A young one, even smaller than his hand.

A black-haired male dangled the sprite by her long, green hair then tossed her to a beefy, brown-haired male. The little being let out another pained squeak.

Rage roared through André with the force of a summer wildfire. "By the God, you will *stop*." As the idiot shifters jumped in surprise, he struck the male's forearm with the edge of his hand.

The shifter's grip loosened, and André swept up the pixie. He glanced down, relieved to see no obvious damage. "One second, sprite, and you'll be safe."

She didn't try to escape his gentle hold.

Moving to the tree, he reached up and set the young pixie on a low branch. With a happy leap, she disappeared into the foliage.

Now for the beetle-headed boggarts. He turned toward the shifters.

Two looked down in shame. The rest were openly unrepentant. Sneering, even.

What was wrong with this clan? "Take out your aggression on other shifters, not the OtherFolk...assuming your Cosantir lets you live after your behavior today."

"Our Cosantir?" The beefy brown-haired male let out a laugh. "Pete wouldn't get upset over this—not even if the stinking pixie went toes-up."

André crossed his arms over his chest. "Have you forgotten all you were taught as cubs? Tormenting OtherFolk is against the Law of Respect. If your Cosantir won't deal with you, then—"

"Back off, stranger." The voice came from behind him.

"I will not." André turned and recognized the soft-looking male as the rude Cosantir he'd met his first day in Ailill Ridge.

Pete Wendell.

Wendell lifted his chin as if he had a crown on his head. In a way, he did. With the power of high, low, and middle judgment, a Cosantir could banish and even kill a shifter with a touch. "I said *leave*."

No honorable Daonain would walk away from the abuse of the OtherFolk—and Cosantirs *must* act when the Laws were flagrantly disobeyed. "What kind of a Cosantir are you? Your people deliberately harmed a pixie, and you don't care...or are you afraid they won't listen?" Anger flaring even higher, André set his feet. "Are you toothless or simply incompetent?"

Wendell's face darkened. "You fucking asshole. *Burn*." He slapped his hand on André's shoulder.

André stiffened, knowing right down to his bones he was going to die here. The power of the God flared...and continued to grow until the light around him was so bright he had to close his eyes.

And then the fire sank inside him, searing along flesh, veins, down to his bones...and deeper. Flames burned through his defenses until his very soul lay open and exposed.

He heard his name called, but the voice inside him could be heard by no ears. His name—and a call. *The* Call. There were no words, yet he had no doubt.

Herne was calling upon him to be Cosantir of this territory. To serve this clan.

No. I don't belong here. This isn't my territory or my country.

Sensations and images filled his head. The ragged cubs, the sounds of werecats and wolves fighting, the pixie trembling in his palm, his request for help denied.

The territory needed a true Cosantir. The clan needed *him*.

Within the space of a breath, of a thought, he answered.

Aye.

Power surged through him, filling him until it spilled outward, past his skin and into the air around him.

Over the roaring in his ears, he heard an agonized cry. The grip on his shoulder disappeared.

André didn't move. Couldn't move. Could only stand and endure as the God made him into His Own.

Strolling across the pedestrian bridge toward the square, Heather tilted her head back, enjoying the sun on her face. She'd accomplished a lot the past few days. The business papers were signed. Packing was done. Cabin was ready to close for a time.

Now she needed to pick up some supplies for the road—and a box of lightweight kitty litter.

Tomorrow, she and Greystoke would be off for places unknown.

She smiled at the cloudless blue sky. Surely a herald of happier days to come.

Although, she had to admit, she missed Niall. The cabin seemed awfully empty without him. Oddly enough, in just those few days, Niall had turned into more of a friend than most of her previous lovers.

Maybe the shifters were doing things backward, what with mating first, then trying to be friends.

Should she go call upon the Gods and suggest full moon Gatherings be ended? She grinned, visualizing a lightning bolt hitting a little, red-furred wolf on a cliff. Nope, that idea was *not* something she'd be taking to the Gods.

Reaching the park, she noticed a group of shifters. *Ugh.* Obnoxious Brett and cockroach Caleb were there.

Being his usual overbearing self, Pete had just slapped a hand on a dark-haired stranger's shoulder.

She shook her head, veering away from the group.

Then, Pete stiffened. Back arching, he gave an anguished cry and staggered away from the stranger.

What in the Mother's name had happened? Reversing direction, Heather moved closer.

The dark-haired male stood motionless, every muscle rigid. His chiseled features seemed carved from the hardest granite in the mountains as his brown eyes darkened to an unfathomable black. The air around him shimmered in a palpable aura, one with the unmistakable presence of the God.

Heather froze.

"You asshole! What did you do to Pete?" Brett lunged at the stranger who obviously couldn't fight back.

"No." Stepping between them, Heather shoved Brett back.

"*Bitch.*" Brett swung. His fist caught her high in the face, knocking her sideways.

Pain exploded in her cheekbone. Regaining her balance, she

jumped back between him and the stranger. "Leave him alone, Brett."

He loomed over her, and her jaw tightened. He'd not get another punch in. She set her stance, ready to—

A huge blond-haired male gripped Brett's arm and threw him across the park, almost into the creek.

Heather's eyes widened. *Niall*.

The cahir's green eyes were blazing with anger.

Beside him was an equally furious male with shoulder-length brown hair, a short beard, and hazel eyes. Turning to the dark-haired male who Brett had attacked. "André, what..." His voice died.

Heather put her hands over her mouth to suppress the gasp.

Because André's eyes were the color of night—the color of a Cosantir's eyes when he channeled the power of the God.

Heather stared at Pete. The Cosantir—the *previous* Cosantir—sat, shoulders slumped. Any trace of the God had disappeared. He looked stunned, like he'd been hit over the head.

"By the Lady," Niall snapped. "What's happened here? André—brawd?"

André slowly turned his head toward Niall, and his eyes began to focus.

Niall called him *brawd*. Was he one of Niall's brothers? *Oh no*.

At the startled sound she made, André's gaze focused on her.

The punch of the God's presence was so potent she took a hasty step back. "Cosantir," she whispered, bowing her head instinctively.

He flinched.

Niall grunted as if he'd been struck, then he bowed too. "Cosantir."

"So it seems." André paused, his mouth twisting. "But why, I do not know." The resonant voice held a faint accent. "This isn't even my country."

Dismay closed like a vise on Heather's skull. The God had

called André to be Cosantir of her territory...and he wasn't American?

Of course, he wasn't, if he was Niall's brother. Niall was Canadian.

Oh Gods, she'd been the one to ask Herne for a new Cosantir.

What had Herne done? The male could never go home. Couldn't return to whatever job he'd done before. Would have to deal with this disaster of a territory, a place where he didn't belong and knew nothing about. His clan would be made up of strangers.

Even so, hope bubbled up inside her. She'd asked Herne for a new Cosantir...and the God had come through.

But seeing the pain in the new Cosantir's face, all she could think was: *I'm so sorry*.

André felt the power of the God inside him, pulsing as if his skin was too tight to hold it in.

He could still feel Herne's anger at the previous Cosantir who'd failed the God. Could feel his own anger at the circumstances binding him to this territory. In the States.

"*Gods.*" His knees started to buckle.

Slinging an arm around him, Madoc held him steady.

André pulled in a breath. He could always count on his brothers. "Thanks."

"Trust you to shoulder a whole new mess of trouble," Madoc grumbled.

André's eyes refused to focus, but he felt shock from the shifters around him. Some were furious.

The former Cosantir sat on the grass, his expression panicked.

As the shifters began cursing and shouting, André shook his head. Fire continued to burn inside him, shooting raw jolts of lightning through his soul. He straightened his spine and hoped he could still walk. "Niall, Madoc, get me out of here, please."

To his dismay, Niall answered, "Your will, Cosantir." Then his voice softened. "We got you, brawd."

Despite his brothers moving slower than a pair of drunken dwarves, Madoc managed to get them back to the B&B. Leaving them in their sitting area, he made a run to the coffee shop for donuts and coffee. André needed something to ground him.

By the time he'd returned, Niall had sprawled on the couch, keeping an eye on André, who rested in an armchair.

After setting out the food, Madoc handed André a lidded cup of coffee.

"Thank you, brawd." André's usually smooth voice was ragged.

Madoc waited until his brother successfully navigated a drink. "You all right?"

A muscle in André's cheek twitched. "Ask me tomorrow."

"Right." Madoc couldn't even imagine. Cahirs occasionally mentioned the horrendous hours after being God-called, but Cosantirs didn't. Maybe because the process was more spiritual than physical?

Leaving André to sip his drink and stare at the wall, Madoc handed Niall a coffee, then took the other chair.

Niall rubbed his chin. "A Cosantir. What the fuck was Herne *thinking?*"

"Maybe the God noticed how the arsehole named Wendell sucked at the job?" Madoc took a drink of coffee. "And here was André, someone already dedicated to law enforcement with the right mentality to be guardian of a territory."

"True enough," Niall conceded. "Yet..."

There was always a *yet*, wasn't there?

Good Cosantirs were profoundly involved with their clan, and that wasn't André's way. The three of them never formed deep attachments to anyone or anything besides each other—not to people, clans, or territories.

Madoc sighed. No more moving.

"A Cosantir and his territory are...one," Niall echoed his thoughts. As the bards would have it, the mountains were a Cosantir's bones, the streams his blood. The clan and animals in the territory were his heart.

"He'll change," Madoc murmured. He'd have to. So would they.

Because Cosantirs didn't move.

"No, Gretchen. We're here to talk with the Cosantir—not you."

The firm tone in the older woman's voice drew André out of the hole he'd fallen into. From the angle of the sun in the room, he'd been staring at the wall for a couple of hours. By the God, he felt like a slug squashed under a heavy paw.

Ah, right, that was essentially what'd happened, wasn't it?

Niall set aside his laptop, Madoc his book, and his brothers rose.

Three older people climbed the stairs and entered the sitting area. They halted, studying his brothers before their gazes settled on him.

And three clan Elders bowed their heads in respect.

Herne help me, I'm not ready for this.

He almost laughed because *Herne* was the one who'd dumped this duty on him.

Hands on the chair arms, he leaned forward to rise, hoping he wouldn't land on his ass.

"No, no, Cosantir. Please, stay seated." The short, thin female with chin-length, silver hair clucked her tongue. "I was present when the God called Calum to be Cosantir of the North

Cascades. It took Calum hours before his legs worked—and even longer to stop calling Herne foul names."

Calum? The incredibly competent North Cascades Cosantir hadn't wanted the job?

Oddly heartened, André relaxed. "In that case, would you please be seated?"

Madoc and Niall were already pulling chairs from the corners, setting them close enough for conversation.

"Thank you, cahir." The female sat, then told André, "I'm Ina Donnelly."

"Good morning, Ina." André turned his gaze to the short, white-bearded male he and Madoc had met once. "You're the grocer, yes?"

"I am. I own the grocery." The male put his hand on his chest. "Bernard Murtagh—just Murtagh."

The other male had steel-gray hair and wore a business suit. He bent his head to André. "Cosantir, welcome to Rainier Territory. I'm Friedrich Schumacher, and I own the bank."

André nodded in acknowledgment. "I'm André. My littermates, Niall and Madoc."

Greetings were exchanged.

The banker leaned forward. "Cosantir, we're interrupting your day because... Ah, before there are...complications, it would be wise to transfer the clan funds to your care." In most territories, Cosantirs managed the money and properties for the good of the clan.

André eyed the male. It was interesting the way he'd spoken the word, "complications." "Please explain."

The banker's jaw tightened into a grim expression. "We spoke with the previous Cosantir before coming here, and I'm afraid Pete refused to sign the paperwork transferring the money to you."

Niall stared. "Why?"

"He considers the account to be his." Friedrich's bulldog face was set in a disapproving mask. "I warned him over and over about using clan money as his own. In fact, in July, we transferred almost all the checking account money into the savings account which requires the Board's sign-off for withdrawals. However, at this point, he still has a legal right to the accounts and could cause problems."

Isn't this just a dog's breakfast. André rubbed his face. How in the God's green forests was he going to turn this territory around?

With an effort, he straightened. This was now his task, and he'd give it everything he had. His brothers would help because that was who they were.

Murtagh's voice held an apologetic note. "Pete always had a bit of an ego and maybe wasn't exactly energetic, but he was a fair Cosantir in the beginning. Around five years or so ago, he and Roger were courting a fine female when an avalanche killed her. He grew...bitter."

"Almost like he blamed the God." Ina shook her head. "He acted as if, being the Cosantir, he should be immune to loss."

"We all want that, don't we?" Murtagh sighed. "After that, he was different. Well, no one stays the same all their lives. Life changes us, aye?"

André exchanged glances with Madoc and Niall. Their parents had grown increasingly narrow-minded as the years went on. People did change and not always for the better.

Murtagh stroked a hand down his beard. "Truth to tell, he stopped putting in any effort. He liked the way things come easy as a Cosantir. Having the respect and no one questioning him."

The banker scowled. "And not having to earn his own way."

"Really?" Madoc tilted his head. "I didn't think the stipends for the Gods-called were especially generous. Don't most supplement their clan income?"

Since the Gods-called—healers, cahirs, Cosantirs, blademages, soulweavers—worked erratic hours for the clan, the territories provided stipends. Aside from healers, the amount was nominal.

Niall stretched out his long legs. "So Wendell grew lazy, stopped enforcing the Laws, and used clan money as his own."

"You have it in a nutshell, cahir." Ina smiled at Niall—then André. "We're most pleased to have you with us, Cosantir."

"Thank you." Heartened by her obvious approval, André studied the Elders. Apparently, along with his littermates, here were three he could count on.

He noted the folder in the banker's hand. "You three are here for a reason."

"Very good. We'll get right to it, then let you rest." Ina straightened in her chair. "The Board of Directors of Rainier Territory Company is hereby convened. I appoint"—she hesitated—"I'm sorry, Cosantir, might I have your full name?"

"André Crichton."

The banker spread the papers out on the coffee table and printed André's name on one.

"Excellent." Ina continued, "The three directors appoint André Crichton as CEO of the Rainier Territory Company to replace Peter Wendell. Mr. Wendell is removed from his post, effective immediately, and an audit of the company books will be conducted to ensure all is in order."

Murtagh snorted. "You and your fancy wording. Good job, Ina." He took a paper from the banker, scrawled his name, and handed it to Ina.

After adding her signature, she leaned forward and gave the paper to André. With his acceptance, the clan accounts would be under his control.

Financial matters weren't anything he enjoyed.

No choice. Running a territory required money. He signed.

"Does Wendell have a personal bank account?" Niall asked.

"He does." The banker shook his head. "But it has almost no money in it—Pete doesn't use it for anything."

André's jaw tightened. Wendell wouldn't take being cut off

from his usual funds well. Ina had spoken of an audit. "We're going to need an accountant. A Daonain accountant."

"Good luck." Madoc shook his head. "Shifters don't usually become—"

"Heather Sutharlan is an accountant," Ina interrupted. "She's one of those CPAs and has a business degree, as well."

Heather. Wasn't she the female who'd hit Niall with her car—and saved his life?

Niall leaned forward. "She's a CPA?"

"I don't figure she has time to help us out, Ina." Murtagh shook his head. "She doesn't like it here in Rainier Territory and has her own business to run."

"Actually"—Ina tapped her lips—"she sold the business. Just recently. But I think she's planning to leave on an extended vacation. Tomorrow, in fact."

"Perhaps we can get her to lend a paw first." André said.

"I'll ask her." Niall straightened. "First thing in the morning before she takes off. Can I borrow your car, André?"

André studied his brother who'd been so subdued since the deaths in Canada.

He looked more alive.

Smiling, André tilted his head. "Of course." It appeared he'd get to meet the female who had such an effect on the cahir.

A brother had to get his amusement where he could find it.

CHAPTER ELEVEN

The next morning, Niall drove André's SUV slowly down the tiny dirt road leading to Heather's cabin. Damned if it wasn't a relief to be in a forest and away from the craziness surrounding André.

By Herne's prick and pebbles, his brother was a Cosantir. Hard to wrap his tail around that one. He chuffed, thinking of André's displeasure about his change in circumstances.

But really, if Niall had been the God and had every shifter in the world to choose from, he'd have picked André too. The cat was compassionate, protective, a leader, and more than anything—a fixer. If he saw a problem, he wasn't capable of ignoring it.

Good pick, Herne. But fuck, this will really mess up my life.

His own change in circumstances hadn't really hit home until Madoc called a moving company to have their rental house packed and put into storage.

Niall sighed. He'd never wanted to live in the States. And to be the only cahir in a territory? That was just...wrong.

Reaching the cabin, he parked and walked up onto the porch. The early morning air was cold and crisp, filled with the scent of firs and cedars.

He envied Heather the location of her home, even if those bloody ruts in the road still made his leg ache.

The door opened before he could knock. She was barefoot and in jeans. Her green flannel shirt turned her eyes the stunning color of the forest surrounding them. And her faint feminine scent was as alluring as roses on a summer afternoon.

"This is unexpected." Her lips quirked up. "Are you like a hawk that keeps returning to the same nest?"

There was the sense of humor he adored. "I'll move back in anytime you want."

When her mouth dropped open, he chuckled. Of course he couldn't live here—not with the mess with André—but it'd be difficult to say no if she asked. He'd missed her—a lot.

She had a quiet, relaxed personality, a warm voice, and a delicious scent. Hearing her puttering away in the kitchen or humming as she worked on a crossword puzzle was startlingly companionable.

Then she'd turn around, and he'd see her perfect, heart-shaped ass, and he'd have all sorts of other thoughts about her. Like stripping off her tight jeans and...

Bad cahir.

Her eyes narrowed. "*Ooookay*, tell me why you're really here."

Stay on task, cahir. "The Cosantir has need of your help." He almost grinned because the statement was like bringing a grizzly to a coyote fight. No Daonain refused a Cosantir's request.

"But...but I'm leaving."

Several inches taller than she was, he could see the suitcases in the center of the living space. "I'm sorry, wolf." Or he would be if it really disrupted her life.

Admit it, cahir, you really want time to get to know her better.

"Right." With a wry smile, she gave him the proper answer. "As the Cosantir wills. What does he require?"

"He needs an accountant."

Her mouth dropped open in surprise, then her husky laugh

brushed like velvet over his skin. "Oh, because of Pete. The banker was always lecturing him about mingling personal and clan funds. Does the Cosantir want me to try to figure out the mess?"

Damn, she'd figured out the reason for his trip quickly. Her keen brain was incredibly alluring. "Exactly. Ina suggested you. I'll warn you: The paperwork looks to be a nightmare." He tucked a wayward strand of hair behind her ear, forcing down the desire to move closer.

She froze, looking up at him with those stunning blue-green eyes.

By the God, those tiny freckles sprinkled over her cheeks would tempt a saint. Slowly, he ran a finger along her jaw before stepping back.

Swallowing, she took her own step back. "I'm surprised Pete would give you any records—if he kept any."

"He didn't. The banker said Wendell kept the clan records and property keys in the realty office. Since Wendell isn't answering his phone and has made himself unavailable"—the previous Cosantir was not only worthless, but also a cowardly fleabag—"I... ah...broke into the realty office to get everything."

Her eyes widened. "I'm surprised you're not in jail."

It'd been closer than he liked to think about. Thank the Gods, the Board Elders had provided him with the legal paperwork, or a very aggressive chief of police would have arrested him.

The chief of police in a human-shifter town should never be a *human*. That was just wrong.

Niall smiled. "It seems the Rainier Territory Company owns the realty office, and Wendall hadn't bothered to rent it. He has no legal right to the building." The male was an idiot.

Heather laughed so hard she had to lean against the door jamb. "Your trespassing is so going to scorch Pete's tail."

Fuck, she had a seductive laugh. Would it get deeper, throatier if she laughed when they were mating?

Straightening, she glanced behind her. "It's going to take me a bit to unpack and get together everything I'll need. I take it the Cosantir wants me there as soon as possible?"

"Aye. I can drive you. Do you need to change or—"

"Thank you, no. I'd rather have my own vehicle."

He'd hoped to have her in the front seat of his car, to breathe her in, to be able to talk with her. Ah, well. This was one reason she was so fascinating. She didn't need him, wasn't clingy, stood on her own paws. "As you wish."

"Where?" The tiny muscles around her eyes tensed slightly. "At the B&B?"

"No, not there."

She relaxed...and now he wanted to know why.

"In the realty office?"

"No, André felt using it would be undiplomatic. There's a big building the clan owns over on the northwest corner of the square. It has a shamrock sign. He's setting up there while we sort things out." No one had turned off the power to the vacant building—spendthrift fools.

"You broke into the realty office and are working in the Shamrock? You're being very visible."

He snorted. "If nothing else, it'll spread the word about the change in Cosantirs."

"Interesting times is a curse in certain cultures, you know." Heather shook her head. "I'll be there within the hour."

"Is there anything you need to get started?"

Her nose wrinkled. "Property leases, receipts for maintenance, repairs, deposit records, anything like those."

"Of course. I meant paper, pencils, accounting books, or—"

"No need." She continued in a voice as dry as the Sahara, "As it happens, I have an excellent accounting program on my laptop."

Her laptop. *Ouch.* "Right. About that." He met her gaze, trying to show his contrition. "I'm sorry for assuming you were ignorant of technology."

Before she could respond, he continued, "Our dam and sires

were anti-human and rabid technophobes. Before they died, they basically disowned me and my brothers for our choices of occupations. So...I overreacted."

She frowned. "What occupations could upset them so much?"

"Ah, well, Madoc is a cook in human restaurants. André's with the RCMP—a Mountie."

Her eyes held understanding. "Both occupations would surround you with humans. And you?"

"I worked for a cybersecurity company."

"Oh Gods, you can't get much further from a technophobe." Chuckling, she headed into her house, saying over her shoulder, "You're forgiven. Tell the Cosantir I'll see him in town."

Niall was grinning as he headed back to his vehicle, and even the twig thrown by an annoyed pixie didn't bother him.

He'd been forgiven.

Now, he had to decide how much further he wanted to take it. Would she like his brothers?

An hour later, Heather entered Espresso Books and smiled at the low *bong-bong* of the bell over the door. It appeared Talitha had changed out the bell again.

Stopping just inside, Heather took a slow breath. Beneath the aroma of freshly brewed coffee was the fragrance of books. Old books and new books. The finest of perfumes.

Behind the bookstore counter on the right, Moya lifted a hand in greeting before returning to ringing up a pile of books for a customer.

Heather headed left toward the coffee section of the store. What with Pete's attitude toward record-keeping, this auditing project was going to require massive amounts of caffeine.

"Hey, Heather," Corey called as he handed over a tall drink to a woman at the pick-up window. "Whatcha want today?"

"Heather?" The masculine voice behind her was smoky-dark, like a warm midsummer's night.

She turned to see a male around six feet tall, all lean, hard muscles.

"Niall's Heather?" He held out his hand. Rich, dark-chocolate brown eyes held hers.

Her hand was in his before her brain had a chance to override an utterly instinctual compliance. And really, why would she want to?

The male's chiseled face with sharp high cheekbones and strong jaw was simply gorgeous. Brown hair a shade darker than his eyes curled over his collar.

He hadn't released her hand, and she was...staring. *Oops.* "Um, right. No, not right. I—I know Niall, but I'm not—"

When laughter lit in those dark chocolate eyes, she gave herself a mental slap and then, *oh cat-spit.* "You're the *Co*—" Remembering the humans in the store, she bit back the rest of the word.

In the park yesterday, she hadn't seen much more than the power blasting from him. Today, his aura was muted to a low shimmer, much like Calum's.

And she could see...*him.* "André, you're André."

"I am." When his lips curved, a tantalizing crease appeared in his cheek. "Madoc said you protected me before he and Niall arrived, and someone punched you." His words held a light French accent.

As his fingertips brushed over her bruised cheek, his eyes darkened slightly. "Thank you, Heather."

Her heart actually skipped a beat at the low caress in his voice.

No, girl. Being attracted to a Cosantir would be insane. As bad as wanting a cahir, right? She didn't have a good track record when it came to males—and she sure didn't need her heart broken. Again.

Pulling her hand from his, she gave him a polite smile. "It was an honor to be of service...André."

He studied her for a long moment, his gaze sweeping over her face, her hands, her shoulders. Reading her body language as he might if they were in animal form.

After a long moment, he inclined his head and stepped back to give her more space. "When you see what awaits you, Ms. CPA"—his smile widened—"you might rethink those words."

CHAPTER TWELVE

"What a complete pile of scat." After two days of wading through the mess, Heather's brain was about to explode. She scowled at the piles of paper covering the three tables she'd pushed together. Ragged receipts for years. Canceled checks. Leases.

She could tell exactly when the last accountant had left. Old Harold, a wolf, had been driven away by Pete's brother, the pack alpha.

Hadn't Harold and Pete been arguing about the clan finances back then? This was the reason. According to the books, right about then, Pete started using the clan funds as his own.

She scowled. If only Niall had shown up at her cabin an hour later, she would have already been on the road, having a lovely time. Well, after she had this nightmare of papers straightened away, the road would still be there, waiting for her.

I could have been soaking in a hot spring in Idaho right now.

And yet...

After so many years of frustration, it felt good to truly *do* something for her territory and clan.

A flicker of light and shadows had her looking up to see André crossing the room. His silent predatory gait suggested he was a werecat. He wore jeans and a dark blue chamois shirt. The rolled-up sleeves exposed corded, muscular forearms. "Good morning."

"Good morning, Cosantir." Although she'd never bowed her head to Pete, she couldn't keep from giving this Cosantir, who radiated such intimidating, controlled power, the sign of respect.

For a few seconds, he eyed the piles of papers, which had grown taller since he'd been in yesterday. "How are you managing to remain sane?" When he smiled, the flash of white teeth in his darkly tanned face made the temperature in the room rise several degrees.

Mother of All, he should have a warning label—*Hazardous materials. To avoid danger of meltdown, keep this male away from females with functioning ovaries.*

Laughing, she shook her head. "Progress is being made, really. I do have a few concerns, though."

"Go on."

"Many of the clan's properties aren't rented—probably because they need repairs. The few with occupants are..." How could she say this without sounding as if she was attacking the earlier Cosantir?

"Are...?" His dark gaze held the patience of mountains.

"I'm afraid Pete loaned houses to his friends without getting leases or rent." Brett and Caleb both lived in clan-owned houses. She'd always suspected they were staying in them for free. The records had confirmed her suspicions.

"Ah." André's beard-shadowed jaw tightened. "If you'll make up a list of addresses and the appropriate monthly rent, Niall will serve them notice their free ride is at an end. Please have the appropriate leases on hand in case they wish to stay."

Well.

His warmly resonant voice was decisive yet quiet. Completely in control. Then again, he'd been a cop. She needed to remember that. "I'll get the list to you today."

"Thank you, Heather. Next?"

"Remember the box filled with unopened mail?"

Madoc and Niall had emptied the realty office of every scrap of paperwork and covered the tables with boxes, each labeled with the originating locations like "Top Desk Drawer" or "Filing Cabinet Drawer One."

One was labeled "Box on floor." Niall said it appeared as if the mail had been simply tossed into the box.

"I remember." The disgust on André's face showed what he thought of the previous Cosantir's guardianship.

"No, no, there's good news. The mail held inquiries about the properties. If you get repairs done, we can get them rented out and income coming in."

Except there *had* been *some* income.

"Very good. I'll have someone assess what needs to be fixed." His perceptive gaze sharpened. "What else is worrying you?"

The Cosantir didn't miss much. She bit her lip. "The boxes—the desk drawers your brothers emptied—the cash in them totaled over fifteen thousand dollars."

"Cash." André straightened, his expression hardening, reminding her again he was a cop. "Thousands in cash doesn't sound...legal."

She wasn't sure. Shifters were rarely involved in drugs, prostitution, or gambling, the usual illicit sources of money. "Honestly, André, I don't think Ailill Ridge has any crime worth noting. Not...you know, big stuff."

"Good to hear." He smiled slightly. "Daonain do tend to be more about fistfights and speeding. Not human vices."

He would know, wouldn't he? She nodded.

"In any case, carry on." André tapped his fingers on the table. "I'll hire a crew for the property repairs."

"When you do..."

"Aye?"

"Could you also have them work on the Gathering House? It could use some help."

The Cosantir stilled like a cougar catching a scent. "Wendell neglected the site of the most important of our traditions?" The way his eyes darkened sent a chill up her spine.

Her mouth had gone too dry to speak. She nodded.

"Key, please."

After a quick search, she found the set in the pile and handed it over.

He glanced at the address, then turned at the clump of boots on the floor. "Brawd."

The brother named Madoc nodded to her, turned to André, and bowed his head. He'd undoubtedly seen the black of the God in his brother's eyes. "Cosantir?"

"We need to check the local Gathering House for needed repairs. Might I assume new furnishings are needed as well?"

Heather nodded, then hesitated. The Cosantir was already angry, but wasting money hurt her little accountant's heart. "Bear in mind that anything you purchase will... The males will fight and destroy anything breakable."

André turned to look at her, his now completely black eyes implacable. "No. They won't."

A shiver traced across her skin.

The clan had no idea of the difference between the new Cosantir and the old one...but they were about to find out.

CHAPTER THIRTEEN

Sack in hand, Madoc munched on a blueberry muffin as he left Espresso Books. Sweet and buttery. Just what he needed. By the God, he was exhausted.

Since yesterday, he'd been in and out of houses with the newly hired repair crew. They were a competent bunch of shifters, and since he was good with his hands and knew his way around repairs, they'd easily agreed on a list of what needed to be done... even after André had ordered each house be hellhound-proof.

Cosantirs took protectiveness to a whole new level.

House hunting for him and his brothers had fallen to Madoc, as well, but he'd found a place that might suit them all. Fuck knew none of them wanted to remain in the B&B. The blonde predator, Gretchen, had started rubbing all over André as well as Niall. She was a walking confirmation of all the reasons they avoided females outside of full moon gatherings.

Madoc didn't envy the Gods-called. Not after seeing the avaricious reaction of certain types of females to his littermates. His brothers would far rather chase than feel like prey. Him—he'd rather avoid all of it.

A glance up at the sun showed he had enough time to finish

assessing the properties if André's accountant had the remainder of the list for him.

It'd taken him longer than he'd planned, since he was also chatting with the locals about their concerns. André needed to know what was wrong before he could fix it. In the evenings, the three of them were having brain-storming sessions on how to get everything done. Madoc huffed a laugh. Even his fixer brother was going to be challenged by this territory.

The more Madoc learned from the locals, the more he realized how bad the previous Cosantir had been. Even worse, rather than hightailing it out of the territory, Wendell was still around, poking his whiskers out of his den occasionally. And bad-mouthing André.

Not that André would care about the yowling of an incompetent fleabag.

Taking another bite of the muffin, Madoc strolled across the square toward the Shamrock building. In the grocery, Murtagh saw him and lifted a hand in greeting.

So far, most of the shifters he'd met were good people. Lamentably, they didn't seem to have much of a clan-like cohesiveness.

By the God, sometimes he missed the simple, straightforward life he'd had where he would cook at the restaurant and in his own kitchen, hang out with his brothers, attend the monthly Gatherings, and wander the forests.

His stable routines had been overturned.

Cosantirs didn't leave their territory and usually served Herne until old age or death. And where André lived, so did his littermates.

Across the square was the town's small café. The place was family owned and staffed. They weren't hiring.

Although he preferred more versatility in a menu than eggs or burgers, at least it would've been a job.

Madoc shook his head. *What am I going to do for a living?*

At the end of the square, he reached the Shamrock building

where André's CPA was holed up. The door facing the square was propped open.

Stepping inside, he stopped to let his eyes adjust to the dim lighting. The room was huge. A door to the right probably opened to the smaller section of the building.

Typing on a laptop, Heather sat at a group of tables piled high with papers.

At tables near the left wall, two middle-aged females were flipping through brightly colored catalogs.

Heather looked up. "Hi, Madoc. André isn't here if you're looking for him."

"No, it's you I need to talk to." He smiled, enjoying the pretty sight of her. She had a nice sturdy build, and her gold-brown flannel shirt and jeans delighted his sensible soul. The red-brown, shoulder-length hair was long enough for a male's grip—but short enough it didn't get tangled in everything.

Was there a term for *sexy but practical*?

He placed his bag on the table. "For you—in return for a list of the rest of the properties needing to be checked."

An eyebrow lifted. Like her eyelashes, it was only a shade darker than her hair. She didn't wear makeup, not that her beautiful blue-green eyes needed any. Being sensitive to the scent and taste of chemicals, he appreciated her restraint.

Peeking in the bag, she squeaked in surprise. "Donuts!"

Made him grin.

"I totally won this trade-off." She pulled out a chocolate donut covered in glossy icing. "How'd you know my favorites?"

"Talitha was behind the counter and helped me choose. Said she knew you." Madoc motioned toward the two other females. "Did André hire more accountants?"

Mouth full, she shook her head and finished her bite. "No, those tables are for the Gathering House's decorating teams. Two or three shifters will pick a mating room and give me their specifications on how it should be remodeled—you know, like paint colors, cushions, and accessories."

Right. Madoc and his brothers had discussed the plan only last night. André was moving fast. "One of my crews is repairing the major damage at the house today. It might take a couple of days before the others can get in."

"Perfect." Heather motioned toward oversized wall signs announcing a clan meeting and work party on Friday.

"What about—"

A group of females of various ages entered and headed for Heather. Politely, he stepped out of the way.

One gray-haired female took the lead. "Heather, Ina left us messages about coming in to see you."

Heather beamed at them. "Thank you for coming. The new Cosantir was hoping you'd help sew new cushions for the mating rooms."

"*Finally*." A younger, redheaded female rolled her eyes. "Last month, I walked into a mating room where the seams on a down cushion had split open. It looked like a snowstorm."

The rest laughed.

She shook her head. "It's not funny. Can you imagine feathers in your hoo-haw?"

Madoc pretended to scratch his beard to hide his laugh.

"It's good we'll be making new cushions then." The gray-haired female looked pleased.

"Exactly. The decorating teams are giving me their plans for each room with examples of the cushions they want." Heather held up a sheet of paper. Attached was a paint strip with one color circled, along with magazine clippings showing three different cushions. "We can make a trip to Cle Elum and buy the fabric, stuffing, and any other materials."

The youngest female shook her head. "I can't afford to buy—"

"No, no, I explained badly," Heather said. "Clan funds will pay for the materials and your time."

The gray-haired one raised her eyebrows. "We'll be paid?"

"Yes. The Cosantir says if you have sewing machines and know how to use them, he considers you skilled labor." Heather grinned. "He *is* asking for volunteers to empty out the rooms and repaint them. It'll be a clan workday, and considering the amount of food he ordered, it might also end up being a party."

"Fun! I'm in—for both the sewing work and the volunteering." The redhead bounced on her toes.

The others chorused agreement.

"Perfect." Heather was beaming. "Can you visit the Gathering House and get an idea of the size, shape, and number of cushions needed for the rooms, so we know how much fabric to buy? I also need a way to get in touch with you. And when you'd like to go to Cle Elum if you want me to organize a van."

"We're on it." One woman pulled out a sheet of paper and wrote her name, phone number, and email on it, then passed it to the next woman.

Impressed, Madoc eyed Heather. Not only organized, but a rather effective force of nature.

Leaving the females to it, he idly looked around the room. Had it been a store in a previous life? Big with a high ceiling. Tall windows facing the square—with iron grillwork his cahir brother would approve of.

There was a long counter running along the back wall, with a room beyond. *Hmm.* Had this been a restaurant before? After handing their list of names to Heather, the group of women headed out, already discussing the best time for a shopping trip.

"Your turn and thank you for waiting." Heather handed him a paper with the remaining properties and addresses, then fished another donut out of the sack.

"No problem." He eyed the counter along the back wall. "What used to be here?"

"This part of the building has always had a restaurant. It recently closed."

Just as he thought. He wandered around the back counter. Yes, there was a good-sized kitchen back there. Nice set-up too.

Returning to the table, he asked, "Did it close because of a lack of business?"

"No, it was always busy. The owners were human and simply grew old." Heather shook her head. "Pete didn't make any effort to lease it again."

"Got it." Crossing his arms over his chest, he planted his feet and studied the room. It would work. Maybe.

When Heather made a tiny sound, almost like a laugh, he regarded her. "What?"

"My brother, Daniel, stands like that when he's trying to come to a decision." She grinned. "He's a bear too."

Huh. Well, many bears preferred to think things over carefully—and then move explosively. "I'm thinking I'll lease this building and open a restaurant."

No more boring menus.

She blinked. "Right. Niall did mention you're a cook."

"Aye, I can cook. Even manage the place. But I don't know scat about owning a business."

"As it happens, I do." Her sweetly curved lips tipped up in a very kissable smile.

By the Gods, mating wasn't what he should be thinking about. "And?"

"Now, you need to remember I plan to leave the territory soon. However, for the next few days, I can get you started on what you'll need to do."

The confidence in her gaze was just what he needed to tip him into the decision. "You're hired."

That evening, at Espresso Books, the bell on the door *ding-donged* pleasantly as Heather walked in two minutes before the bookstore would close. The coffee counter was already shut down.

She pulled in a deep breath of the book fragrance—the enchanting scent of adventure and new worlds to explore.

Behind the counter, Moya looked up from the book she was reading. "She's alive! There've been rumors you got buried under a mountain of accounting records."

Heather laughed. "With the mess Pete left behind, it was a close thing. But there's sunlight at the end of the trail."

"If you were dealing with Pete's leavings, you totally need a beer. I'll even buy the first one."

A night out? Heather hesitated. But she was feeling sociable for the first time in ages. Besides, Nikolaou, the human owner of the Bullwhacker, was getting on in years and could use more business. "Sure. It'd be fun."

"Yes!" Jumping to her feet, Moya pulled on a hoodie. The rich blue set off her black hair and big brown eyes.

Heather smiled. "Only you would find a hoodie with a ruffled hem."

"Girl, I embrace my femininity at all times, whether I want a male or not. Usually not. You only dress up sexy for Gathering nights." Moya gave Heather's flannel shirt a disapproving sniff. "Hey, I have something for you. Wait one moment." She disappeared into the back and ran up the stairs to her second-floor apartment.

Heather took advantage of her absence to peruse the new releases stand and made a sound of glee. A Wen Spencer, a Kingsolver, a Shea. Feeling like a dragon adding to her hoard, she shoved money under a mug on the counter and stowed the books in her tote bag. "I bought books," she called.

"Why am I not surprised?" Moya trotted down the stairs and handed Heather a top. "Wear this tonight. I bought it for your birthday, but you'll probably be in Wyoming or somewhere by then."

"Now, now, don't be envious, just because I'll be fancy-free, wandering through gorgeous scenery and exploring new places."

Moya's bottom lip poked out. "You're right. I'm totally envious."

Stepping behind a bookcase, Heather shed her shirt and donned the three-quarter sleeve, pullover sweater. It was a gorgeous teal color, soft as puppy fur, with a V-neck low enough to show the swell of her breasts. "This is beautiful. Thank you, Moya."

"Happy early birthday."

Grief was a sharp stab in Heather's heart. On previous birthdays, she and her brothers would trek up to Elder Village to spend the day with Mama.

Not this year. This year, she'd be far away from anyone she knew.

All alone in their B&B lounge, Madoc drummed his fingers on the end table. By the Gods, his littermates needed a good swat across their furry cat-butts.

Niall was in his bedroom, messing around on his laptop. More and more, he'd been disappearing into his computer as his mood darkened. Unfortunately, the reticent boggart wouldn't talk about what bothered him.

The cat needed to be in fur, but—as most shifters learned—their animal side didn't always pay heed to a healer's warning about taking it easy. Nope, it tended to be *leap, ow, and oh-shit*. And Niall was one of the worst of those, as they'd learned in the past when he'd re-broken a leg. This time, he was being careful, staying in human form—and getting increasingly grumpy.

Speaking of grumpy cats, so was André. All too often, his face would turn expressionless, and his eyes would darken as he went inside himself. Probably reading some mental Cosantir manual.

But too much introspection wasn't good for anyone, even Cosantirs.

Or bears.

Madoc was missing the comfort of a kitchen with an actual ache. Much like Niall with computers, cooking was his comfort zone.

Lacking that... It was time to get out of this B&B and have a carefree evening.

"Yo, André, Niall. Time to check out the nightlife in this place."

The grumbling sound from one bedroom was Niall. "Brawd, the nightlife consists of one rundown bar."

"Makes it easy to pick where we're going, doesn't it?" Madoc slapped his hands together. "You have five minutes."

Niall let out a put-upon sigh. "Fine."

André appeared in his doorway, a hint of amusement in his face. "I get the impression *no* is not a permissible response."

Madoc let out a low rumbling growl. Cosantir or not, his brother might well get his ears boxed.

With a chuckle, André held up a hand. "Message received. I'll be ready in five minutes."

Good enough. Rubbing his shoulders against the door frame, Madoc listened to his brothers cleaning up. And his fingers itched to be cutting up vegetables.

By the Gods, I need a kitchen.

Across the square from the Shamrock building, the Bullwhacker was a typical small-town bar. As they bought mugs of beer, Heather looked around for a table with a fond smile.

Aside from getting grungier, the place hadn't changed in all the years she'd lived here. There was one main room with a long bar and filled with wooden tables. An adjacent room held three pool tables and a dart board.

But why was it this full on a Thursday night?

Ah, them.

"Hey, Moya. Your brothers are here with their crew." Zorion and Ramón ran a construction business, and in fact, were the ones repairing the clan's properties.

Moya made a disgusted sound. "Wherever I go, there they are."

"I don't know—I think it'd be nice to have my brothers closer." As a young couple headed for the door, Heather grabbed their table in the center of the room.

As she sat, she noticed the construction workers—all wolves—were glaring at three werecats near the bar. "Then again, your brothers are rather quarrelsome. Does it seem like Ailill Ridge needs another bar just to keep the cats and dogs apart?"

"Gods save us, I didn't come here to watch a fight." Seated, Moya thumped her beer on the table hard enough to make it foam. "My brothers are idiots."

"*All* males are idiots." Heather drank some of her beer and wrinkled her nose at the blandness. She preferred the variety Calum had in his tavern. "I think it's because IQ and testosterone are incompatible, so when one increases, the other goes down."

"Are you saying my littermates are over-testosteroned?" Moya snickered, then tipped her head toward the door. "Is one of those your new temporary boss? The Cosantir?"

"Here?" Heather looked over, and her breathing caught at the sight of the three devastatingly virile males. Darkly chiseled perfection, André was a master of stillness and control. A blond, badass Viking, Niall moved like the predator he was. Then there was Madoc, a brawny, rugged bear whose sociable nature couldn't conceal his deadliness any more than his trim brown beard could hide the strong square jaw. "Yep. Him—and his brothers."

"Wow." Moya put her elbows on the table, her chin on her laced fingers. "Three new males in the territory. All yummy in different ways. Wouldn't three mates be cool?"

"Pixie dreams, girl." Heather shook her head. "Whenever I connected with a good male, his brother was either a walking disaster or didn't want *me*. Can you imagine getting *three* to agree on a female?"

"Oh, hmm, true." Moya pouted. "When we first moved here, I kinda hoped to catch your brothers, but see, Daniel thought I was adorable, but Tanner? *Pfft*—there's no chemistry whatsoever."

"There's a shame; I'd like having you for a sister." As for Heather with Moya's brothers, she sometimes had fun with them at Gatherings, but there wasn't any real zing there.

Heather watched the Crichton crew ordering drinks at the bar and glanced at Moya. "Want to meet André and his brothers?" A touch of envy hit because the males would adore her friend. Years younger than Heather, Moya had inherited her Spanish mother's curves, warm skin, and big brown eyes.

After a second, Heather added a cautionary question. "And will you be polite?" Moya got along with authority figures about as well as a salamander tossed in a lake.

Moya snorted, then watched the males for a bit. "This new Cosantir doesn't seem nearly as obnoxious as Pete. Okay, yes, I'll be good. It'll be fun to meet someone different."

Lifting a hand, Heather caught Niall's attention and motioned to her table.

With a pleased nod, he grabbed his brothers and herded them over.

Moya grabbed another chair from a nearby table.

The three males settled down at the table. Madoc, whose flannel shirt couldn't disguise the width of his shoulders, was to Heather's right. André, dressed in a long-sleeved Henley with pushed up sleeves was to her left.

Niall wore a dark hoodie over a dark T-shirt and sat beside Moya across the table. His long blond hair glowed in the dim bar lighting.

Heather frowned. Although he'd had days to recover, he still looked tired and...drawn. She wanted to pull him into her arms and give him a hug.

"It's good to see you all out and about." Heather hesitated. How to introduce them? Tradition would have her introducing someone *to* the Cosantir, but she'd come to realize André disliked being put on a throne. And this *was* a bar. So female first.

"Moya, this is the Crichton crew. André"—she set a hand on André's forearm and was disconcerted by the taut skin and steely muscles under her fingers—"and Madoc." She bumped her shoulder against his, and it was like hitting a concrete wall.

Gods, what do these males eat?

"Niall is beside you. Guys, meet Moya Moreno, owner of the bookstore part of Espresso Books."

Moya smiled at the males. "Welcome to Ailill Ridge."

"Thank you, Moya," André said.

Niall's way-too-sexy-for-words dimple accompanied his smile. "Thanks, Moya." Madoc turned to Heather. "Crichton crew?"

"It seemed appropriate after seeing the Moreno crew over there." Heather nodded toward the construction workers.

"Ah, them. They're a skillful bunch." Madoc lifted a hand to Ramón and Zorion and got chin lifts back. He turned to Moya. "Your littermates?"

"To my vast regret." Moya gave them her trademark pout. "We're all wolves, which means there was no escaping the overprotective idiots when I was growing up. Heather's lucky her littermates are bears."

"Are your brothers here, Heather?" Madoc asked.

"No, they're at the ranch and haying this week. I'm afraid they can't make the workday on Friday either."

"I bet it'd be fun to guard a sister and smack down pushy males." Niall eyed Madoc. "You should have been our sister—since you were the last one born. What do you think, André?"

André's lips quirked, but he gave Madoc a slow appraisal. "Aye, he'd make a fine-looking female. However...a bear?"

"I guess so much fur is un-girly, eh?" Niall grinned. "Hey, what do you call a wet bear?"

Madoc's guttural growl was so threatening, Heather jumped.

André winked at her. "I don't know, brawd. What *do* you call a wet bear?"

"A *drizzly* bear."

Madoc's huge huff of annoyance made Heather snicker.

Across the table, Moya had covered her mouth to try and hide her giggles.

As Niall grinned at their response, the haunted darkness disappeared from his eyes.

With Ramón, Zorion sauntered over to the table and bowed politely to André. "The Gathering House is all ready for your workday tomorrow. We have a few things left to do, but the house is safe, and the rooms are ready for painting."

"Excellent." André's pleasure showed on his face. "Thank you for your hard work. There will be food offered during the day; your crew is welcome to join in."

"Food is always welcome." Ramón grinned at Niall and Madoc. "If these two females start picking on you, you can join our table."

Moya swatted at her brother, and laughing, the two headed for the bar.

Heather had to smile. The Moreno crew were good guys...and not accepting of just anyone. It was interesting to see their approval of Madoc, Niall, and André.

So, if the Gathering House construction was almost finished, it was time to figure out the next house for them to work on. She turned to André. "When they're done at the Gathering House, maybe they should start on one of the—"

André put his hand over hers. "*Ma chère,* we will save work for work times. Tonight is for socializing."

The feeling of his warm, callused hand shot tingles from her fingertips all the way up her arm. She couldn't look away from the dark heat in his eyes. "Right. Of course. Socializing."

"I like socializing." Madoc rested a thick forearm on the table and grinned. "Looking at you and Moya, I bet it'd be fun to hear about how you met—and the resulting shenanigans. Especially if you knew each other as cubs."

Moya grinned. "My brothers and I only moved here a few years ago, so there are no cub stories. But...the way we met?" Her smile went soft. "It's so Heather."

The memory of that night probably wasn't a good one for Moya. "Girl, you don't have—"

"It was my very first Gathering, and I thought I knew what to expect, but..." Moya shook her head. "Mamá wasn't forthcoming at all about the actual mating act."

"By the God's green forests." Niall's expression darkened, and Heather knew Moya had roused every protective instinct in the cahir's body.

Moya glanced at him, and her mouth twisted into a wry smile. "Yeah, you get it. My very first male was all about the slam-bang, and it hurt, and I was crying when I left the mating room."

"Can you point the arsehole out?" Niall's tone was soft...and deadly.

"No, no, he was just young, and he learned. Boy, he really did."

Heather sighed. "Moya, I—"

Moya pointed at Heather. "Look at her turning red. She hates when anyone talks about how special she is."

The three males turned.

"She's toasty." Madoc rubbed his knuckles over her cheek, so very gently for such huge hands, and a disconcerting tingle of attraction ran through her.

When André squeezed her fingers, she realized his hand was still covering hers.

"Let's hear the rest," Niall prompted. He shot a smile at Heather, his green eyes laughing.

Moya waved a hand in the air. "So, there I am, a crying mess, and people are staring at me, making it all worse. Heather walks up, puts her arm around me, and asks me what happened. Gods, I totally clung all over her and told her the whole thing. She took me for a walk and told me everything Mamá should have. And probably a lot more. When we come back inside, she pulls her brother to one side and talks to him, then hands me over to him. And he was so, so gentle. Afterward, he took me around and made sure I met only nice males."

Daniel—and Heather—still tried to keep an eye on Moya. Despite her nonchalant way of telling the story, the brunette didn't entirely trust males, especially during a full moon.

"Heather is an amazing friend." Moya smiled over.

Heather glanced at André and saw him nod in approval. Madoc slung an arm around her shoulders, bending down to rumble in her ear, "Good job."

His intoxicating scent washed over her, all male with a tantalizing hint of citrus.

Niall smiled at Heather, his green eyes soft, then he shook his head. "I still want to pound—"

"No, Heather dealt with *him* too. She shoved him up against a wall and scolded him. And oh, his face turned bright red. I've not been with him since, but other females say he's turned incredibly considerate."

"Being lectured by a female on your mating failings probably hurts even more than getting pounded." Niall grinned at Heather.

The approval radiating from the three brothers warmed her more than a sunny spring day after the cold of winter.

And André was still holding her hand.

He had a strong hand, the fingers callused, the knuckles scarred. The capable, competent hand of an intimidatingly attractive male. One who she wanted to...

No, wolf. What are you thinking? You know better.

. . .

Realizing he was still holding Heather's hand, André tried to feel guilt. But no, he enjoyed touching the little wolf too much.

He studied her, enjoying the way the form-fitting sweater clung to her modest curves. He wanted to run a finger over the beginning swell of her breasts framed by the V-neck. And more... To stroke his hands over her soft flesh, breathe in the scent of her arousal, and grip her silky hair as he took her lips.

His jeans grew uncomfortably tight as he hardened.

Bad Cosantir. Remember what she told Niall? She didn't deal with males except at Gatherings, and didn't avoiding entanglements sound all too familiar? There was irony.

With a sigh, he released her and picked up his beer.

As his brothers compared notes over their first Gatherings, he thought about Moya's story. He could see Heather taking the female under her care, then—with that practicality he enjoyed so much, she'd set the young male on the right trail. She undoubtedly had a fair amount of experience dealing with pushy males.

He wished he'd been there to hear her lecture the idiot.

"Oh Gods." Heather was staring at the bar. "Here we go again."

André followed her gaze to where Moya's brother stood at the bar, holding a pitcher of beer, and arguing with someone in a red T-shirt.

The red T-shirted male shoved Zorion. The beer spilled. And Zorion punched the guy in the face.

Red T-shirt's friend jumped up from the bar stool and swung at Ramón.

André's eyes narrowed. Red T-shirt and his friend moved like werecats. "Is this a cat and dog fight?" he asked Heather, and his brothers turned to hear her answer.

"It is. The alpha, Roger, and his betas hate cougars, and their narrow-minded attitudes spread thru the pack." She gestured toward the fight.

Hissing, snarling, growling. Far too much like animals. This was unacceptable. André rose to his feet. "Cahir, if you would shut this down, please?"

Niall stood and bent his head. "Your will, Cosantir."

"He's not up to a long fight, brawd," Madoc warned. "Let me assist."

"If you would, please."

"Cosantir." Madoc's formality was a stab in his heart until his grin appeared. "Thanks. I wanted to play too."

Over at the bar, Niall picked the two cats up by their shirt-fronts and gave them a hard shake. "You are ordered to stand down."

They stared at him, started to swing, then apparently noticed his size and the mark of a cahir on his cheek. Cahirs only took orders from a Cosantir.

Both went limp in his grip.

André sighed as the humans stared at his brother holding up two grown males like they were kittens. He motioned for Niall to put them down.

His brother, of course, tossed them several feet in the process.

Behind Niall, Madoc caught Zorion's collar and put a hand against Ramón's chest. "André says no."

"Nobody tells us what to..." Zorion's voice trailed off. "Oh. Oh fuck."

Moya's brothers turned to look at André as did the wolves who'd risen to join the fight. On the other side of the room, the cougar contingent came to a halt.

With a sigh, André crossed to stand between the two groups, all too aware of the humans in the bar.

He pitched his voice to carry to sensitive shifter ears and no further. "You are in a public establishment." He looked at the humans around the room to make his meaning clear. "I assume you know the Law?"

To reveal the Daonain is death, ordered by a Cosantir, carried out by a cahir.

He opened to Herne, trying to control the surge of power. It often felt like he was an unmanned raft on a white-water river.

His quiet voice deepened to the bottomless depth of the God. "I enforce the Laws. And fights of this...nature...are intolerable. Have you forgotten who you are?" He might be less harsh if the combatants were young shifters, but at least half were past their foolish twenties. There was no excuse.

As he swept his gaze around the participants, faces paled as they grasped his warning.

Good enough. He glanced at his brothers. "Thank you. I believe the altercation is ended."

"Your will." Niall moved away from the werecats.

"Gnome-nuts, my beer is getting warm." Madoc grinned and headed back to the table.

As André followed, he heard the red T-shirted werecat call to the bartender, "Yo, Nik, give me a pitcher for Zorion here. I spilled his."

It was a start.

CHAPTER FOURTEEN

Beside the quietly flowing creek, André was sitting on a park bench behind a screen of huckleberry bushes. Leaning back, he tipped his head to the warmth of the sun. In his bones, he could feel how the cold would soon grip the land.

Forests always felt like home to a shifter. As a Cosantir, the sense of belonging had blossomed, as if he was bound to each tree, each river, each animal.

And when he opened his mind and scanned his territory, the shifters appeared as bright spots, like fireflies lighting the darkness. A greenish glow was Madoc; the slightly bluish one farther away was Niall. A dimmer glow was Murtagh, another was Ina. Soon he'd have names for more of the lights.

A golden glow he recognized was approaching.

"Heather." He opened his eyes.

She froze like a startled deer. "Please excuse me, Cosantir. I didn't realize you were here." She had a small brown bag in one hand, a drink in the other.

"Did I usurp your lunch spot?" He smiled to ease her concern. "Join me?"

After another second, she continued forward with the

comfortable confidence she normally displayed. "Were you napping?"

"In a way." He slid down to give her room. "I'm still adjusting to how it feels to be tied to the God."

"Ah, that." She opened her bag, took out a sandwich, and offered half.

He shook his head...as if he'd steal the female's lunch.

"Okay then." She took a bite of her sandwich, rummaged under an orange, then handed him one of two cookies.

Turning down such a treat was beyond him. "Thank you."

"Does having the power hurt?" Her worried gaze ran over him as if to ferret out any sore spots.

She really was delightful. "No. It's more like acquiring an extra sense and receiving a flood of information. I need to learn to filter it out." He touched the sleeve of her flannel shirt. "For example, we don't constantly pay attention to how our clothing feels. Not unless there's a problem."

"Got it." She chewed slowly, her gaze turning to the water before back to him. "Can't you just ignore it all?"

Interesting question. "It gives me information on the clan and the land, so...no." He shook his head. "When I was in law enforcement, I avoided becoming too close to the people I served. But here, I'm joined to the territory, and the people belong to me in a way I can't deny."

And no longer wanted to avoid, he was finding. Change was upon him, like it or not.

"Is that why you look tired?"

"Aye." He savored for a moment the sweet taste of the homemade cookie. "As a Mountie, I found carrying a firearm a rather uncomfortable responsibility. Now I carry the power of the God. If I lose control of my emotions, people could die."

She smiled at him and shook her head. "I haven't known you long, but I already know you're not the type to lose control."

Interesting. She hadn't even stopped to think about her assertion.

"Calum told me the Gods don't pay continuous attention to us, which is how Pete's guardianship started well but, years later, went sour."

Where was she going with this? He lifted an eyebrow. "And?"

"I daresay when picking a Cosantir, the God pays very close attention." She smiled at him. "I don't think he chose unwisely."

That was as fine a compliment as he had ever received. He bowed his head slightly. "Thank you."

Heather bit her lip. The more she learned about what a Cosantir had to endure, the worse she felt about what had happened to him. He'd lost his job, his home, and his country. His very mind and senses were affected. And, having watched Calum, she knew Herne would continue to demand a high price from him.

She had played a part in André's being chosen. Somehow, somewhere, she needed to share what she'd done with him. Hiding it would be wrong.

He was her Cosantir. And rapidly becoming a friend.

"By Herne's dauntless danglers, Madoc, this place is huge. You seriously want to live here?" Niall followed his brothers onto the three-story house's front porch.

Rather expecting to be hit by a fir cone or twig, he glanced at the nearest trees, but no fairies were there to chitter at the interlopers.

"Great view, brawd." He rested his hands on the porch railing to enjoy the sight. The building was high on a bluff with the town spread out below. The other three sides were surrounded by forest and the steadily rising mountains. Bathed in the heady scent of fir and cedar, he felt the mountain calling him.

"Yeah, and really, this is a good size for us." Unlocking the front door, Madoc motioned Niall and André in. The small foyer led to an open floor plan with a high vaulted ceiling. An interior balcony on the second floor overlooked the great room. "I'm thinking we'll be living here for years to come."

André flinched obviously at the reminder they couldn't leave. "Forgive me, my brothers."

"Brawd, you wouldn't have even been in this country if it wasn't for me." Niall shook his head. "I'm sorry too."

"Such sorry-tailed miscreants." Madoc slapped Niall's shoulder hard enough to sting. "In all reality, I'm looking forward to staying put. Belonging somewhere."

Niall leaned against a wall to study his littermate. "Seriously?"

"Yes, cat. Our parents never belonged anywhere, didn't want commitments to any clan—let alone to cubs. If they could have dumped us without feeling guilty, they would have."

"Aye." Niall sighed. None of them had received parental attention.

André moved his shoulders in acceptance. "We weren't neglected, just...not especially loved."

"The point is—we're not them." Madoc crossed his arms over his chest. "It's time to belong somewhere. Now the shock of being stuck has worn off, I'm pleased to get the chance."

Stay put? Niall felt a momentary dizziness, as if he'd reached a summit and suddenly saw an entire world spread out before him. *He could belong to a clan in more than name.*

And he wanted that more than he'd realized. "Okay. Okay then."

So...this might be a place where they'd live for years. He looked around more carefully.

Front picture windows gave an incredible view of the valley

below. The huge fireplace with a glass insert would be cozy during snowy winters.

"Down the hallway are rooms for offices or whatever." Madoc motioned toward the kitchen. "And the kitchen's great. I'll have fun in there."

Niall grinned. If the bear was having fun in a kitchen, it meant he and André would be eating well.

"Some of the rooms are furnished." Madoc took them up the stairs to the second floor. "The owners moved to an elder village near their offspring and didn't need much."

"Elder village." André raised an eyebrow. "The owners are Daonain?"

"Aye."

"Good security." The heavy doors were well constructed, and there were iron window guards, including cleverly designed sliding ones for the picture windows. "Someone was wary of hellhounds." Unfortunately, too many of the houses he'd seen in town weren't prepared at all.

Skimming a hand over the dark wood railing, Madoc led the way down the inner balcony. "This side and the back of the house have male shifter suites and smaller guest rooms." He opened the doors, showing three large suites, each with an outside balcony. "Once our furniture arrives, we could move this furniture into the guest rooms."

"Is there also a suite for a female?" André asked.

As in...for a mate? Niall blinked. They'd never found anyone the three of them were interested in. They hadn't even tried since none of them wanted a mate.

But things were changing.

"Aye, not that we'd need one." Madoc's short response answered Niall's concern. "It's across the way." The inner balcony formed a U-shape, and Madoc led them around to the other side and opened a door.

Here was a huge suite showing whoever had built the house

loved their mate. Floor to ceiling windows offered a spectacular view of the mountains. Furniture in creamy colors looked feminine—but was sized for males to enjoy too. Built-in bookcases bracketed the white marble fireplace. Why the fuck was he thinking of Heather's collection of shifter romances?

Speaking of romances... "That's one massive bed."

"Makes you wonder how many mates the female had." Madoc grinned. "The owner left the custom bedding too."

The adjoining room was a nursery suite with a playroom. For cubs.

No, don't even go there.

But maybe someday...?

He cleared his throat. "It's a good, secure location for the young and the female."

Madoc rolled his eyes. "Trust the cahir to think of protection. The attic on the third floor has the older cubs' rooms."

"You're right, it's a good house for us, brawd." André bumped Madoc with his shoulder. "Space enough to entertain, places to be private."

Niall looked out a window and longing hit him. The woods started at the back door and rolled away for kilometers. "Room to run."

By the God, he needed to shed his human skin. To forget about terrorists and younglings who'd died too young and all the blood.

He needed the forest around him.

CHAPTER FIFTEEN

Walking down the town square, Talam heard Sky humming a song behind him. The tune was kinda cool, almost like the wind in the alder trees by the stream.

Sky was always humming or singing. Talam glanced back, meeting his brother's blue eyes that were just the color of the sky like Mama always said.

Talam wrinkled his nose. *His* name meant earth in old Irish—because his eyes and hair were brownish. Talk about boring...but he kinda liked his name anyway.

As they passed the café, he caught the smell of bacon, and his belly twisted up something awful. When his stomach gurgled, his littermate laughed.

"Shut up," Talam growled, and the sound was almost like the one coming from his empty stomach.

At Sky's flinch, Talam hunched his shoulders. He was a shitty weasel to lash out.

Especially since his brother looked awful. His skin was always whiter than Talam's. Only today, he was almost the color of snow. An' maybe Sky was a finger or two taller than other twelve-year-olds—and Talam—but he was so skinny no one was scared of him. "Sorry, brawd. I got the grumpies."

Sky bumped Talam's shoulder in forgiveness. "It's cuz you're hungry. Me too."

"We need to find food." Talam put his hand over his stomach. "And if the Cosantir isn't gonna use us anymore, we have to start stealing our own money and food." None of the kids working for Mr. Wendell had seen him in the last week. Mateo said the Cosantir was holed up in his big house. And maybe he wasn't even the Cosantir anymore. Like that'd ever happen.

"We can't steal anything *here*. Mr. Wendell would get madder than...than the beaver when we messed up its dam."

Yeah, the stupid beaver had tried to bite them with those huge teeth. "We don't have a choice, Sky."

Yesterday, they'd tried to catch food in the forest. Major fail. It sure wasn't like they had guns like human hunters.

Maybe sometime this year, he and Sky would have First Shift and be able to snag mice and rabbits. Talam heaved a big sigh. Spit, with their luck, by the time they figured out how to be whatever animals they turned into, all the food prey would be hibernating for winter.

Didn't matter. They'd manage. They always did.

But...why'd Mama have to die? Anger made him want to bite something. Bite *her*.

And then he felt lower than the gnome peeking out of a storm drain.

It made a face at him, and he couldn't keep from grinning back. Ailill Ridge didn't have a lot of OtherFolk, but it had more than the human town of Cle Elum where Mr. Wendell had taken them sometimes.

The other kids said Cle Elum was where they'd be bused to middle school. If they were in school. Since Mama was gone, nobody knew to sign them up or anything.

And they hadn't wanted to be. Because...what if they shifted in a human town? Kids had trouble controlling their trawsfurring for a while.

Talam shivered. Just thinking about First Shift was scary. He'd heard the whispers; kids sometimes died.

Farther down the square, an old woman came out of Espresso Books. She had whitish hair, some wrinkles even. Mr. Wendell said old people were the best targets being how they were slow and didn't give chase. They usually carried more cash than the younger ones too.

Cash was what he and Sky needed.

"Brawd, look," he whispered.

Sky turned. "Okay. Let's."

Talam rubbed his palms on his jeans as he thought. Usually, he'd get the prey's attention, and his brother did the pickpocketing. Sky had fast hands.

But not today. "This time, you do the bump; I'll do the dip."

"I can—" Sky stopped and held out his hands. He was shaking. "Yeah, you're right. Sorry."

"Not your fault." It wasn't Mama's fault either. Not for dying. Not even for moving them here cuz she liked people and wanted to live in a bigger town.

She couldn't have known a hellhound would attack their neighborhood. And she'd... He swallowed at the ugly memory. Of the screams of the renters in the other side of the duplex. Mama had shoved him and Sky into the tiny root cellar. But it was too small for her. After smashing a bottle of pickles to make the wooden cover stink of vinegar, she'd run. And the hellhound had caught her.

Maybe she hadn't been a perfect mom, always falling in and out of love with stupid males, but they'd had food and a place to sleep and clothes. And love.

She'd saved them. And she'd died.

When his eyes burned with tears, he rubbed his arm over his face. He wouldn't start crying like some baby cub.

He and Sky had to take care of themselves. Since he was the older brother—by at least ten minutes—he'd make sure they had food today.

Stopping outside of Espresso Books, Heather smiled at Ina, who'd talked her into a coffee break before heading to the Gathering House's workday.

One coffee and a chocolate donut later, she was ready to paint some rooms.

She pulled in a breath, enjoying the fresh air. Around the square, the small maples were turning gold and red to herald the arrival of autumn. Only a few people were strolling around. Tourist season was almost over.

She glanced across the way to the dark windows of the realty office. "Have you seen Pete since he lost his title?"

"No. As far as anyone knows, he hasn't emerged from his house."

Pete and his brother, the pack alpha, lived near downtown in a massive house. Oftentimes, the current alpha female also lived there.

The alpha females in Rainier Territory never lasted long.

According to gossip, Roger and Pete weren't getting along, not since the shifters realized Pete's public posts about the June festival had brought the Scythe mercenaries down on them. Some of the wolf pack had died, and Roger blamed his brother. A lot of shifters did.

Pete really was an arrogant boggart-brain. Boggarts were the stupid—and vicious—cousins to house brownies...and Pete could be just as malicious as they were.

"I'm faster than you are." The shouting of young voices came from near the café.

"No, *I'm* faster." Two teenaged boys chased each other down the square. One barreled right into Ina, knocking her back a step. The shorter, bigger-boned boy grabbed her arms to steady her.

"Oh sorry, lady. Sorry!" The blond looked up at Ina with penitent blue eyes.

Ina smiled. "I'm fine, lads. Don't you worry..."

As Ina talked, the shorter, freckle-faced boy slid his hand into Ina's purse.

"Hey!" Heather made a grab for him and missed.

Wallet in hand, the boy sprinted toward the park, followed by the blond.

Niall was just leaving the park.

"Niall, stop those boys!" Heather yelled.

Moving faster than she'd have thought possible, Niall grabbed one boy by the back of his shirt and the other by his arm.

"Let go!" The short one tried to punch at him—and hit nothing.

Ignoring the struggling boys as if they were baby mice, the cahir strolled toward Heather. "You need them for a reason?" he asked, his deep voice easy.

"They're pickpockets." Heather grabbed the wallet from the brown-haired boy's hand and returned it to Ina. "The blond deliberately ran into Ina so the other could raid her purse."

"I'm afraid that's true, cahir." Ina shook her head.

Seeing the lads turn pale, Heather bit her lip, starting to regret involving the cahir. The boys had dirty faces and hair. Their clothing was equally dirty, as if no one had bathed them recently.

Where was their mama?

Heather put a hand over her belly. If her cubs had lived, they'd never be on the street stealing. Why were these two?

If they were hungry, she needed to make sure they had some food. "Can you tell me where your mother is?"

. . .

Not releasing his hold, Niall studied the two scruffy boys. The thought of children stealing...

By the Gods, they couldn't be older than twelve or thirteen. All bony arms and hollowed faces. Dirty hair past their shoulders. The slimmer one looked like an English-Irish mix with light-skin, blue eyes, and blond hair. The other was a sturdier lad. He had brown hair with a reddish hue, brown eyes, and freckles.

Shouldn't they be in school? Or maybe the fall session hadn't started yet in the States.

He frowned at them. "Answer Heather, please. Where is your mother or father?"

The boys hadn't washed recently, and the pungent teen sweat almost made him choke. He couldn't tell if they were Daonain. If they hadn't yet had First Shift, they wouldn't carry the scent of the wild.

"None of your business." The sturdy one nailed Niall's leg with a hard kick.

"Hey!" Still gripping the back of his shirt, Niall lifted the kid and gave him a shake.

"Leave Talam alone!" The other one went berserk, hitting and screaming.

Screaming. High and shrill. The panicked sounds from his nightmares were a knife through his soul. Had Trevor and Sydney screamed like this in terror and pain...before they died?

"Niall. *Cahir.*" The bite in Heather's voice pulled him from the black abyss.

He realized he was holding both boys up in the air. "*Fuck.*"

You fucking brute. He set them down carefully.

They'd been scared into silence but not hurt, thank the Mother of All.

"What the hell is going on here?" A male's booming voice came from far too close.

Turning, Niall saw a human had come from behind him while he was in a brain fog. Appalled, he relaxed his grip.

Yanking free, the boys fled.

Gnome-nuts.

"I asked what is going on." Chest puffed out like an aggressive turkey, the man moved into Niall's space.

Oh, right. This was the arsehole cop who'd wanted to arrest him for breaking into the realty office.

Hissing under his breath, Niall moved back. Knocking a law enforcement officer through a wall would annoy André.

Ina cleared her throat. "Niall Crichton, this is Ailill Ridge's Chief of Police—Chief Farley. Chief, Niall kept those two boys from stealing my wallet."

"Stealing?" Farley had a burly build like Madoc's. His weapon's belt held an American cop's usual mix of firearms and handcuffs. "I'm sure you must be mistaken."

Heather's irritated snort showed her opinion of the cop's statement, and her irritation diffused Niall's initial desire to punch the idiot.

Her voice was very even. "Chief Farley, I saw the boy pull Ina's wallet from her purse—and then he and his buddy ran."

"Oh, hey, I'm sure it's just kids being kids." The Chief flipped his hand in dismissal.

Kids.

Trevor and Sydney hadn't been much more than kids. Niall swallowed. His mouth tasted like metal, and the air felt too cold. "Hardly." He pulled in a breath from a chest that didn't want to let air in. "They were stealing and—"

"Listen, you." The cop poked his shoulder with a hard finger. "I run a quiet town here. We don't have problems and don't need outsiders causing any."

Don't hit the human, cahir. Gods, the way he felt right now, he'd likely break the cop's neck.

I need to get out of here. Into the forest. Into fur.

He unclenched his jaw. "Well, then, I'll be on my way." Turning, he walked away.

"But..." At Heather's protest, he almost stopped. *No.* Staying wouldn't be smart.

He walked faster. Heading for the south of town.

For the forest.

As André strolled down the sidewalk toward the Gathering House, worry chewed at his gut like a hungry shrew.

Niall had planned to meet him at the Shamrock building. He hadn't shown—and wasn't answering his phone.

André sighed. The cahir wasn't back to normal, at least not mentally. Not surprising after the murders of his trainees and then dealing with their killers. From the pictures of the warehouse, it had been a slaughter.

How much did those deaths weigh on his brother?

Where are you, brawd?

André blinked, because he had a way to know, didn't he?

Stepping under a shade tree, he let everything go, opening himself to the God so his internal sight would reveal the location of shifters in his territory.

Two near him. The house he was heading for was lit up like a wildfire with the numbers of Daonain there, and he wasn't experienced enough to separate them out. He sent his gaze farther out, and...*there*. Niall's slightly blue light was moving fast somewhere in the mountains to the south.

He'd gone to seek the solace of the wilderness.

Be safe, my brother.

After a moment, André released the sight and refocused on the present.

Time to concentrate on the clan and getting them to pull together. With any luck, this would be a positive, joyful day for everyone.

A few minutes later, he went through the gate and had to stop and stare. It appeared a lot of people had started early.

The Gathering House was a two-story clapboard with ornate Victorian trim and a wide wrap-around covered porch. The building would have been beautiful if maintained properly.

It would be beautiful again. Much had been accomplished in the past few days.

As he strolled up the lawn toward the house, he saw the Moreno crew was working on replacing a broken window. Madoc and a couple of females were sanding the porch floorboards. The front door was open, and there were shifters on ladders, painting the interior.

Under a female's watchful eyes, several elementary-school-aged younglings were kicking a soccer ball around. Badly. Seeing their frustrated expressions, he paused to coach them on using the inside of their feet to pass the ball. They picked up the technique quickly.

Smart cubs. Good cubs.

As he continued up the lawn, one of the females on the porch started singing. After a few beats, Madoc's booming bass accompanied her, and they were soon joined by others, inside and outside.

André smiled. This was what he'd hoped for.

"You!" A male's angry voice carried above the song. "You stole my powers. Ripped them right out of me."

As the singing came to a stuttering halt, Pete Wendell stomped across the lawn. Since last week, his face had thinned, and the lines around his mouth were deeper. "You stinking piss-ant; you'll pay for what you did."

"Yeah." Brett, the black-haired, stocky male who'd tormented the pixie, was right behind him. "You're a fucking *thief*."

André sighed. "No, I'm not." He'd figured this confrontation was inevitable, but the timing was unfortunate.

"You stole Pete's powers," Brett shouted, spittle flying.

Seriously? Did the male lack the wits the Mother had gifted

him? "A Cosantir's powers come directly from Herne. There can be no theft."

"Oh, like we'd believe a foreigner. Pete wouldn't hand off his power." Brett's mouth twisted into a sneer.

"Never," Pete asserted.

"I don't know how you did it," a beefy male shouted, "but you give them back."

If only I could.

But no, even if he could, he wouldn't. The more he learned of the territory, the more he saw how badly Wendell had done.

André eyed the three males. How to diffuse this situation?

"Brett's right!" Another male crossed the yard followed by three more. "You're a stinking foreigner, and you don't belong here."

"Yeah, go home, *Canuck*." Brett's tone made the word into an insult.

This wasn't good. If they attacked, it was likely the God would respond—and take over. From what he'd seen in the past, Herne had no problem with ending a misbehaving shifter's life.

Killing off my own clan? Unthinkable.

André kept his voice even. "I'm sorry the God decided your previous Cosantir was—"

Shouts and jeering drowned out his words.

Daonain crowded onto the porch and the lawn to watch.

When Madoc came down the porch steps, André motioned for him to wait. Better to handle this without assistance.

When Brett stalked forward with a long branch in his hand, André almost rolled his eyes. Did the fool think he could escape a Cosantir's power by using a branch?

Before André could speak, a very familiar female yelled, "If you're upset with the change in Cosantirs, blame *me*."

Heather stood on the top step of the porch, her red hair blazing like dark fire in the sunlight. She planted her feet and crossed her arms. "You beetle-headed maggots, *I'm* the one who performed the Call to the Gods and asked for a change."

"Holy cat-spit." Moya stared at Heather. "Seriously? You performed the *ritual?*"

"And nearly died, yes." Heather's brows drew together. "We needed a Cosantir who could lead the clan and protect it, not one who used the title to prop up his overblown ego."

Merde. The female had unsheathed her claws, hadn't she?

Then, what she'd said sank in. *She'd* called on Herne to replace Wendell. He had a second of anger, the urge to blame her for upsetting his entire life.

And yet...good for her. Her territory needed help, and she'd stepped forward to do something about it.

Impressive.

As the shouting increased, Heather met André's surprised gaze. And guilt assailed her. She had no remorse for calling on the Gods. No, she'd done what was needed.

The guilt was because she'd done the ritual and planned to wash her hands of the territory's problems. The new Cosantir could deal with everything, and she could go back to being uninvolved, right? Her suitcases were still packed so she could leave as soon as Pete's accounting was straightened out.

Closing her eyes, she faced herself in an internal mirror and didn't like what she saw. Not at all.

This is my territory. My clan. And I am better than this.

A louder shout drew her attention to where Pete's cohorts were still trying to incite a battle.

She had a pixie-like urge to throw things at the caterwauling fleabags. Would a hammer to the head knock some sense into them?

A male's shout rose over the others. "Let's kill the thief and see if Pete gets his powers back."

The appalling idea—kill a Cosantir?—silenced the entire crowd.

"Has your brain gone missing?" In the quiet, Murtagh stepped out of the crowd. "Look at André. Pete *never* carried that much power. Anyone trying to kill our new Cosantir will be returned to the Mother, no ifs, ands, or buts."

Duffy joined Murtagh. The short police officer was in his eighties. Unlike the human Chief of Police, Duffy was a shifter—and had always despised Pete. "Have you thought about why we are here today? Maybe because the Gathering House is filthy and falling apart. It's a disgrace, an embarrassment to our clan."

Pete reddened. "There wasn't any money to—"

"No money, because our territory funds have been going into your pockets, Pete," Heather snapped.

"We know who's the real thief." Talitha stood beside Moya, face red with outrage. "There you are in a big house filled with pricy furniture. Buying expensive gifts for the female of the month...yet you don't work at any job."

"How long has it been since Pete enforced any of our Daonain Laws?" Quinn, a short, gray-haired retired teacher asked in a quiet voice that carried across the lawn.

"Far too long." Maeve, Murtagh's mate, shook her head. "He hasn't protected our clan—not the females or the cubs."

"Pete's stupidity was the reason the Scythe attacked the festival last summer." Sinead's voice rose to a shriek. "Why my mate was shot and almost died."

Several people called agreement.

Because it was true. Even knowing the Scythe were hunting shifters, Pete had openly posted festival flyers around town. The happy weekend had turned into a bloodbath.

One where Heather had killed. The taste and smell of human blood and their deaths still haunted her.

Swearing, Pete and his friends shoved through the crowd. Leaving.

At the gate, he turned to glare at André...and then at her. The depth of hatred in his eyes shook her.

A minute after the gate clanged shut, Madoc clapped his hands together and said loudly, "Well, I hear the sandpaper calling my name. The porch won't sand itself."

Jolted, the shifters headed back to work, although Heather could hear discussions breaking out everywhere.

Okay, I'm done. Inside, she cleaned her paint brush, gathered her stuff, and headed for the door.

As she feared, the Cosantir was on the porch. With a cub leaning against him to help with sanding the railing, he chatted with some shifters on how to secure their homes against hellhounds.

When the group left, she bit her lip, not knowing where to start. "Cosantir."

He turned. "Heather." His smoky baritone was soft. "You performed the Call to the Gods?"

"I did." She sighed. "I didn't think about how Herne chose someone. I just told the God how the Cosantir here had lost his way, and I asked for help."

Under his dark gaze, she straightened her shoulders. "I think Herne selected well. And I'm thrilled Pete is no longer the Cosantir."

Their conversation wasn't exactly private, and several other shifters murmured agreement.

She shook her head. "But I'm sorry this turned your life upside-down."

"I doubt Gods understand human conventions like countries and borders." The wry humor almost broke her heart.

How would she react if the God dumped her in Canada and said she could never go home?

As she regarded him, she could feel the power coming from him like heat waves. Herne definitely had his hand on this Cosantir. "André, Cosantirs, cahirs, healers are named the Gods-called, not the Gods-forced. Did Herne not give you any choice at all?"

André rubbed the back of his neck then admitted ruefully, "I was shown the mess the territory was in and agreed to take it on."

Because the kind of person the God would pick wouldn't be able to refuse.

After a second, he added, "Because I'm still chafing at the bit doesn't mean you did anything wrong. Heather, only a very few brave souls call on the Gods, especially to help their clan, rather than themselves. You do your territory proud."

The wholly unexpected compliment made her eyes prickle with tears. She'd been afraid he'd hate her for her small part in forcing him here to live.

But André had too much compassion.

Now it was time for her to take the next step. And this was the right time and place to share her thoughts.

Because, from the quiet inside, she knew everyone was listening.

It just sucked she had to start with a confession of her self-centeredness. She raised her voice. "When I made the trip to the Gods, I figured I'd done all I needed to do. The God would call in a new Cosantir, and I could wash my hands of the territory's problems. Unload everything on him."

She pulled in a breath. *Mother's breasts, this is hard.* "And today, I realized I spend my days working on my business, being with my family or alone in my cabin—I do nothing to help my clan here in Rainier Territory. I'm a slacker."

There was silence.

Farther down the porch, her friend Moya made a sound like she'd been kicked in the stomach. "Me, too, girlfriend. Me too."

Heather faced André. "You've been working constantly since Herne dumped our territory in your lap. But"—she looked around at the others on the porch, in the yard—"Calum, the Cosantir in the North Cascades, doesn't do it all himself. His *whole clan* pitches in to help."

Turning back to André, she spoke into the heavy silence. "So, as you fix our clan, Cosantir, I'll be right there working beside you."

His gaze warmed.

She looked around at the other Daonain. "I'm glad we have a Cosantir who will use my help—and that of the rest of us—to make this territory a good one again."

The shout of agreement shook the porch.

Shifting to cougar had been an exquisite joy, and when the wave of love from the Mother filled his soul, Niall had opened to it like a flower greeting the dawn.

For hours, he'd run through the pine-scented forest. He'd splashed across rippling streams that chilled his paws. Two unwary field mice had made a crunchy noon snack. Finding the perfect ledge, he'd napped, the sun warm on his fur until a scolding tree fairy wakened him.

And then he'd run again, leaping over downed trees, springing across creeks and gullies.

The sadness of the past sloughed off like a winter's fur in the spring. Green leaves and evergreen needles brushed against his sides, cleansed him, made him new again.

Eventually, he remembered his duty to his clan. To his brothers.

And he returned.

It was early evening when he headed down the sidewalk toward the Gathering House. A relieved breath escaped him at the sound of conversations and music. He wasn't too late.

Guilt tightened his shoulders. He'd totally let his brothers down today, running off like a little cub into the forest.

And he'd also failed his Cosantir. *Gods, André. You're my Cosantir.*

Life could sure be weird—and Niall would make the best of it. Since the Cosantir was his littermate, he might not get slapped into the next life right away for screwing up today.

André *would* remember they were brothers...right?

At the fence gate, a blond male in his twenties held up a hand. "Sir, could you wait a—oh, cool, a cahir. Yeah, um, go right in."

"I'm Niall. Did André put you on guard duty?"

"I'm Jens." The male drew himself straighter. "Yes, the Cosantir assigned me to make sure no humans get past the gate."

"Did he send you something to eat?"

"Oh no. Guards are only working here for an hour at a time; he didn't want us to miss the fun." Jens looked down. "He's sure different from Pete."

"So I hear. But André's a guardian from his whiskers to his tail." Looking back over the years, Niall knew his brother had always been one. Just...now he had the power to go with it.

Of course, the ability to fry a shifter might be a problem if one was a straying brother. When pissed off, Madoc would simply swat Niall into the nearest creek.

André, though... Fuck, with him, it only took a look for Niall to feel the guilt.

Time to face the music. "Nice meeting you, Jens."

"You, too, cahir." Jens opened the gate and let him through.

Striding across the long expanse of lawn, Niall realized it might not be easy to find André. There was a crowd at the food and drink tables. Scattered here and there were families sitting on blankets, eating and talking. More shifters filled the porch, some still working.

Like sparkling bubbles in a brook, laughter floated out from inside the house.

As Niall passed four young adults sprawled on blankets, a male was telling another, "...really thought Brett was gonna kill the Cosantir."

Niall halted so fast he almost tripped. What the fuck?

"If he'd tried..." The female sitting on the blanket was probably barely out of her teens. "What would have happened?"

Niall snapped out, "He would have died."

Startled, they all jerked around to stare up at him.

"Herne will kill anyone who attacks a Cosantir." His anger turned his voice into something harder than granite. "Whatever the God left, I would shred and piss on the bloody remnants."

Two of the young adults cringed lower to the blanket, two tilted their heads to expose their throats.

"Hey, brawd, get up here," Madoc shouted from the porch.

As Niall strode toward the house, relieved sighs came from behind him. By the God, by the fucking God. As he moved away, the anger raged so hot it was a wonder the grass didn't burn beneath his feet.

Madoc greeted him with a swat on the shoulder and quick sniff of the air. "You spent time in fur?"

Niall nodded.

A simmer of power announced the Cosantir's presence as he joined them. "Do you feel better?" His eyes narrowed, undoubtedly seeing the fury still steaming from Niall.

"It helped." *Until a minute ago.* "I hear someone named Brett tried..." He growled under his breath. "Cosantir, I regret not being here when I was needed."

"Easy, brawd. I was in no danger." André gripped his arm. "There was no need for a cahir."

Niall's muscles started to loosen. Tactful or not, André never lied.

With a smile, André added, "Although more hands are always welcome, you've worked double-time since I was called. You were due a day to yourself."

The understanding in his littermates' faces made his throat

tighten. "Thanks, my brothers." He glanced at Madoc. "Later, you'll give me the whole story about what happened."

Madoc grinned. "It's a good tale. You'll like it."

Seeing the bear wasn't worried, Niall was able to relax completely. "I'm starving. Is there still food?"

"Aye." André's expression was pleased as he looked around. "I think everyone brought something to share."

"What's that female up to this time?" Madoc's gaze was on something behind Niall.

Niall turned.

Heather was climbing the porch steps. She handed a guitar to her friend Moya. "Here, I brought this for you."

Her friend narrowed her eyes. "I didn't ask for my guitar."

"I knew you'd want it so you can stay on tune when you sing."

Niall grinned at his brothers. "She's as managing as you are, André."

Madoc nodded. "Very manipulative. Of course, André's smoother about it."

André gave them both a dour look...but didn't deny the charge.

"I'm not going to sing, Heather," Moya protested.

"Sure you are." Heather smirked. "Didn't you tell me how music pulls people together?"

Moya eyed her suspiciously. "*Yeeees?*"

"As it happens, André is trying to pull the clan together. Aren't you going to help our Cosantir?" Heather turned toward André.

Niall could see the amusement in André's eyes, but his brother merely inclined his head in agreement.

"Oh." Moya bowed her head slightly to the Cosantir, then shot a glare at Heather. "I guess I'm singing."

"The two of you together are frighteningly effective," Niall said under his breath.

André smiled slightly. "Let's be grateful the redhead is on our side."

With a light strumming of the guitar, Moya started singing.

After a minute, Niall leaned against the wall and simply listened with a happy heart.

Moya had a hauntingly resonant voice. The ballad, *Chosen of the Gods*, told of the first days of the Daonain after the Fae withdrew from the world. Unlike the other half-bloods, the children of the Wild Hunt—the shifters—couldn't reproduce with humans at all. Seeing their plight, the Gods intervened, and Herne chose the first Cosantir to watch over the clan.

All over the grounds, people had stopped to listen. When Moya reached the chorus, Heather added her voice—a lovely contralto—and motioned for people to join in.

Within a minute, the air filled with the sounds of the Daonain lifting their voices in a heartfelt refrain of gratitude to the Gods.

And to the Cosantirs who were a gift from those Gods.

CHAPTER SIXTEEN

"This is our territory," Talam shouted at the other teen. Brown-haired and brown-eyed, Mateo was dirty and skinny like the other orphans in town. And, at thirteen, he was bigger than Talam.

Talam's heart pounded furiously, but he held his ground. Sky stood behind his right shoulder, ready to fight.

Mateo glared, but his littermate, Alvaro, retreated. They might be bigger, but they already had three of Ailill Ridge's streets and most of the square. They weren't desperate.

Not like Talam and Sky.

"Fine. Just stay out of our area." Mateo stalked after his littermate.

With a soft whine, Sky leaned against Talam's shoulder. "That was close."

Talam was shaking almost as much as Sky. "Yeah. I'm glad they didn't really want to fight." Most of the kids working for Mr. Wendell had ended up kinda friends.

"I guess they're hungry too." Sky sighed.

"We could check behind the café. In the dumpster." Talam watched Mateo and Alvaro move near an older woman and start mock-fighting with each other. It was one of the pickpocket tricks Mr. Wendell had taught them.

Alvaro bumped into the woman and knocked her back a step.

The move was smooth and—

The huge shifter who'd caught Talam and Sky yesterday was heading straight toward Mateo and Alvaro.

"*Hsst.*"

Mateo glanced over, and Talam jerked his chin toward the cahir.

Making a clicking sound, Mateo warned his littermate and then yelled, "Yeah, try 'n' catch me, mutton-head brawd," and ran away.

Holding his hands up, Alvaro smiled sheepishly, "Sorry, lady. I'm clumsy, yes?" and darted away. Within seconds, both kids disappeared around the corner.

The huge shifter stared after them, then his sharp gaze turned to Talam and Sky. His thick brows drew together.

He looked really mean.

With a squeak, Sky took off running, Talam right behind him.

Herne's majestic maypole. Niall frowned as the younglings ran. Was there not one, but *two* pairs of pickpockets in town?

Seriously?

Foot up on a bench, he braced his arms on his thigh and took the time to think. He sure hadn't when he caught the boys last time.

His time in the forest had been what he needed to gain some distance from his guilt about the trainees' murders. When he'd trawsfurred, the sweet brush of the Mother's love was reassurance he would be welcomed back when his days were totaled. He hadn't realized how much he'd feared that his actions had been unforgivable.

Today, his brain functioned on all levels, and rather than two murdered trainees, he actually *saw* these cubs. They were far too thin. Too scraped up and dirty. Clothes in rags.

If they were Daonain, the clan had failed them, and André needed to act. If they were human, he'd see what the local government had in place to help the lads.

Of course, he needed to capture the cubs first. It was a shame the Chief of Police wouldn't help.

Still frowning, he walked into the Shamrock.

At her tables, Heather stomped down to a stack of papers and tossed a new one on. She looked about as irritated as he felt. And wasn't it interesting how just the sight of her lifted his mood?

"Problems?" He walked around the table to stand beside her.

"Would it be bad of me to staple a few of these receipts to Pete's tail?" She tilted her head, looking up at him. "You look a bit grumpy yourself."

"Aye. I saw your little pickpockets again—and possibly two more. I told André about them last night, but damn, rounding them up will be like trying to catch pixies."

"As a cub, I never did catch a fairy." Her smile died quickly. "I'll keep an eye out for the boys. See if I can talk to them."

"Good. I'll do the same. Maybe leave them some food or something."

Her smile blossomed, and she hugged him. "You're a good male, cahir."

"Nice to hear." He inhaled, breathing her in. How could anyone resist a female who smelled so feminine? No artificial perfumes—just Heather. Her feminine scent was enticing, even without the faint rose fragrance from her homemade soap and shampoo.

Without thinking, he put his hands on her shoulders and rubbed his chin on the top of her lush hair.

She stiffened.

"Uh..." He grinned and lifted his hands. "Will you hurt me if I say I love your hair?"

Her expression held disbelief at his limp-tail comment, then she laughed. "Cahir, behave. I know you Gods-called are swamped by females. Grab one of them if you need your wood scratched." The words sounded like a denial, but her eyes held a...challenge.

Well, now.

He held her gaze, even as he carefully tucked a lock of hair behind her ear. Was he misreading her? "I'm not interested in them. You however..."

Her pupils dilated slightly, her scent changing, growing more compelling with a faint hint of arousal.

Ah, the interest was mutual. And she *had* hugged him, after all. Leaning down, he brushed her lips with his. "I miss living with you, *a thaisce*."

She stared at him with those gorgeous blue-green eyes. Obviously unsure what to do—which was quite unusual for the infinitely practical lass.

A sound from the front caught his attention.

André stood in the doorway. He tilted his head, leaned against the door jamb, and waved for Niall to continue.

I can do that.

Fingers sliding through Heather's hair, he cupped the back of her head, holding her as he truly kissed her. Her lips softened, opened, and he took it deeper.

When her arms curled around his waist, he flattened her against him. Was there anything headier than a strong female who wanted him?

But this wasn't the time or the place.

Reluctantly, he lifted his head and placed light kisses over the freckles on her cheeks and nose. "We'll continue this at another time," he murmured, running his hands over her back and ass, learning the feel of her.

She pulled in a breath and retreated a step. "No. No, Niall, I can't."

Can't? Not, "don't want to"?

If he'd had his cat ears, they'd be perked forward. How long had it been since he'd had the joy of truly *chasing* a female? He looked over Heather's head to his brother, who had silently crossed the room. "André, I like this one."

His littermate smiled faintly. "I can see why."

She backed away from them both, eyes wary—and cheeks flushed. Her scent held no true anger, just interest.

Oh yes, he really did want this one. For himself *and* his brothers.

This was so wrong. Heather backed away another step, trying not to breathe in the intriguing, heady mix of scents. The testosterone-laden fragrance was making her knees weak. Her breasts felt too full, her nipples hard and rubbing against the fabric.

She shook her head. *Stop it.*

She couldn't deal with falling for a male, then having her heart and life shattered. Again. *No, no, no.* She'd already decided to avoid romantic entanglements.

It would be wise to be clear about her boundaries.

Straightening, she kept her tone easy. Casual. "Thanks for your interest; however, I only want friends in my life. Aside from Gatherings, I'm not interested in anything more."

Niall looked as shocked as if she'd dug claws into his pride 'n' joys.

André, though, gave her a long, evaluating look. "A female always has a choice. Although I do wonder what prompted your decision."

Oh spit. The Cosantir had the curiosity of a cat shifter coupled with a fearsome intelligence.

"Wondering is a waste of your valuable time. Let me show you something more important." She motioned at the table. "I finished the audit of the clan's assets."

Edging around Niall, she started handing papers to André.

"These are my audit findings for the last years of Pete's guardianship. I sent copies to the Board of Directors."

She handed him more. "Here is a list of properties with a status on each one."

More papers. "And this list is an evaluation of the current investments with my recommendations for changes."

"Nice." Niall read over André's shoulder. "Good suggestions."

She handed over the last of the stack. "These contain information about how I reached my findings for the audit."

André flipped to those pages. His flicker-fast smile appeared. "You surveyed other territories for information on what their Cosantirs normally receive for their personal funds?"

"Seriously?" Niall read for a bit. "You Cosantirs come cheap, brawd. My cahir stipend is higher."

"Cahirs have to be able to leave their jobs to deal with ferals or hellhounds—and you might be injured," André said mildly. "Cosantirs have a less stressful calling. We may need to raise the cahir stipend to attract more cahirs. One warrior isn't nearly enough."

"A raise would be nice." Niall grinned.

Having watched Calum's work for the benefit of the North Cascades Territory, Heather wasn't convinced. "You know a lot about a Cosantir's work."

André shrugged. "I fostered with a grandfather who was Cosantir up in Quebec."

So he knew what he was getting into. "I've not traveled much, not the way males do during their wandering years. I know Calum owns a bar, but how do other Cosantirs supplement their stipend?"

"Many either inherit a business or run one of the clan's businesses," André said.

Heather grinned. "Because none of you take orders worth a damn?"

"Precisely." André's smile flashed.

"They tend toward community-centered occupations—like downtown businesses," Niall added. "A bar is unusual."

"Calum is fond of the ambiance in Irish bars. His tavern is as family oriented as you can get in the US." She had to admit she loved the Wild Hunt.

"Logical." Niall frowned at André. "What are *you* going to do for a job, brawd?"

"I haven't decided yet." André shrugged. "It's not as if we need money right away."

Heather's eyebrows lifted. Were they rich? She closed her mouth rather than asking.

"She has question marks in her eyes." Niall teasingly tugged a lock of her hair. "Our mother was a bard and...*mmm,* rich. We still get royalties from the songs she sold to various human bands. And I must admit, cybersecurity jobs also pay the big bucks."

André returned to studying the papers. "Even if we count the cash found in the realty office, Pete will still owe the clan money."

"I'm afraid so. He and Roger also need to pay rent on their house since it belongs to the clan." Heather shook her head. "Pete spent a lot of money in the last few years—and almost none of it for the clan."

Niall scowled. "It's depressing to know he started off as a good Cosantir."

"True. Yet it's heartening when the reverse happens. People *can* turn their lives around and move toward the light." André bumped his brother's shoulder. "Wendell's fall is a fine reminder that vigilance is required to remain on the right side of the line. Even for cahirs with pretty hair, eh, brawd?"

Heather eyed the Cosantir. He'd reassured his brother, delivered a lesson, and teased him, all in the same breath. Cat-scat, no wonder the God had chosen him.

. . .

Finished with his chores for the day, Madoc walked into the Shamrock building and was pleased to see his brothers already there.

"This is a comfortable building," André was telling Niall. "Maybe we should—"

Walking up behind them, Madoc slapped his hands down on their shoulders. "Keep your furry feline paws off my building."

"Excuse me?" Niall's light eyebrows rose. "What do you mean —yours?"

"Mine. Paperwork is complete." Madoc looked at Heather who was sitting at the tables. "Ready to help with the next part?"

"I'm done with the clan account audit, so yes. Absolutely."

She really was a nice female.

André turned in a circle, his gaze lingering on the counter in the back. "Was this a restaurant before?"

"And will soon be again." Madoc rubbed his hands together like a raccoon with a new treat. "I'm figuring one different menu for each day of the week. Say, barbecue on Sundays, pizza on Saturdays. And so on."

Niall scowled.

Madoc stiffened. Did his brother hate the idea of a restaurant? "What?"

"Now I'm really fucking hungry for pizza. Thanks, brawd."

"Flabby feline." Madoc shoved his asshole littermate hard enough he bounced off the wall.

The cahir just laughed.

"Did you get the warehouse in back too?" André glanced at the rear.

"Yep. And the small section off to the side. I guess it used to be a store." Madoc smiled. "I bought it all, but I only need the restaurant part. You and Niall can have the other room and the warehouse for whatever you want."

"I don't need either, thanks." Niall shook his head. "I'll have a room at home for my office for cybersecurity work. I can get contracts, maybe even with the clans. It's obvious the Cosantirs need instruction on security."

Madoc hadn't been with his brothers when the Scythe mercenaries attacked the festival, but from what he'd heard, it should never have happened.

"Good plan." André eyed the door to the side section, then turned to look at the back of the room.

"What are you planning, Cosantir?" Heather asked.

"I think I will take the other section and the warehouse."

Madoc blinked. "Both?"

"Aye. Come and tell me what you think." André led Madoc and Niall through the arched double doors and into an adjoining room a quarter the size of the restaurant.

"That used to be a gift shop," Heather called.

"And will be again." André called back. "Yesterday, I learned our shifters have a wealth of craft and artistic talents. A gift shop featuring commissioned local crafts will bring in money for our clan members. I'll run it as my business."

"Huh." Niall grinned. "I can set up an online store and catalogue for you."

"I'll take it."

Madoc turned in a circle, imagining shelving, paintings, woven products. "The local fruits will make some fine jellies and jams."

"Perfect. As for the other building..." André led them back through the restaurant's kitchen and out the back door. The warehouse was only a few steps away.

Inside, Niall looked around. "It's just open space. Lots of it. What are you planning?"

"Remember how we talked about a community center one night?"

Madoc nodded. Their brainstorming sessions had ranged far and wide. "You going to run with it?"

"Aye." André crossed his arms over his chest. "If we divide up the space, this could be a place to work on their crafts, teach new skills, and come together during the long winters. We might even manage a basketball court or gym in the back to keep bored younger shifters out of trouble."

"I like it." Madoc grinned. "The people dining in my restaurant will end up in your gift store or the community center. The ones who come in here to do their knitting will be smelling food until they're enticed into the restaurant. Very sneaky, cat."

"I try." André nodded his satisfaction. "If we all win, the clan thrives."

Heather could hear them talking. Madoc's rumbling bass, Niall's smooth baritone, and André's resonant, accented tones. They were planning their futures around the good of the territory.

The three brothers worked together so well.

A homesick ache ran through her. Mama was gone. She hadn't seen Daniel or Tanner in a while. As cublings, she and her littermates had played together all day long. But these days, her brothers were immersed in their ranch.

Like almost all Daonain females, at coming of age, she'd moved into her own place—the cabin left to her by her grandmother.

At the time, it'd felt wonderful to get away from Daniel and Tanner. Shifter brothers tended to be overprotective of their sisters and would growl if their sister brought one or more males home.

Of course, the same happened in reverse. Since females were territorial of the den, brothers bringing home a female didn't go over well.

Heather loved her cabin, really, but it sure got lonely sometimes.

The business she'd owned had kept her busy though. Busy enough she hadn't realized how much more satisfying it was to work with other shifters. Here, she didn't have to watch her words or actions about a life hidden from humans.

The past few days here had been eye-opening. Being part of the town and the clan. Knowing her work made the clan stronger. And then, to be able to help Madoc with his restaurant opening... it made her day.

And face it, when Niall kissed her, she'd had a wayward notion it would be so, so nice to be with him. And André. Yes, all three.

When Madoc's big bass laugh boomed through the open door to the warehouse, she grinned.

The Crichton brothers were certainly different from each other. André with his incisive intelligence and well-reasoned but compassionate decisions. He was like her in wanting to fix problems.

Niall was like her, too, in his love for organization and technology. Yet Herne had seen his protective instincts and called him to be a cahir.

Madoc was intriguing. He was more reserved with her than she would have expected from the sociable male. And only with his brothers did he seem to fully relax. But...he seemed such an easygoing bear. How could he handle his cougar brothers?

She liked all three of them.

She grinned. After Pete's fiscal irresponsibility, gossip circulated about their buying a big house...and where the money for it came from. She'd enjoyed dropping the information that the brothers were quite well off and didn't need the clan's money. It was just one way she could ease their path.

Next week, they would move to their new home. By then, she'd have all the clan business tidied up and would pack up all these boxes for André's office there. She'd miss working with him.

Ah well, such was life. She'd soon be immersed in getting

Madoc's restaurant opened. Wasn't it interesting he'd planned to have different menus each day? Like a pizza day.

Her stomach growled. *Great.* Like Niall, now she had a craving for pizza.

As the male walked into the kitchen from the warehouse, she heard Madoc's deep laugh and then a singsong, "*Ooo,* cahir."

Niall growled. "Don't start."

"*Oooooo,* I hear Egypt is calling for their missing river, the Ni—"

A loud thump ended Madoc's warbling.

At the hearty sound of masculine laughter, Heather grinned and shook her head. The big bear could obviously hold his own.

CHAPTER SEVENTEEN

The moving van had rumbled away, the crew pleased with their hefty tips. Madoc stood on the porch of their new home and looked down on the town below. His town.

Had it only been a little over two and a half weeks since he'd first seen Ailill Ridge?

Now he and his brothers had bought a home so quickly it made his head spin. Paying in cash meant there were no pesky lenders to appease.

Once inside, he crossed his arms over his chest and surveyed how their stuff looked in the great room.

Not bad. Being big, he and Niall preferred oversized furniture, and the beige suede couches, chairs, and ottomans were a good match for this huge room. Far better than in their small rental houses.

Under his direction, the movers had unpacked the kitchen, and it was ready to be used. The kitchen was the heart of a home, after all.

Earlier, Niall had bought groceries, so Madoc started country ribs on the grill. The air coming from outside held a spicy-sweet fragrance.

They'd eat out on the patio in the sun to celebrate their new home.

Niall came down the stairs and over to the kitchen. "You sound happy, brawd."

Madoc realized he'd been humming. "The house feels comfortable. Like it fits us." Even more than other animals, bears needed a den. "We can make this a real home."

He hadn't realized it'd bothered him to move so often.

"Yeah, bear, we will." Niall slapped his shoulder before striding toward the side hallway. Probably to unpack in the back corner room he'd chosen for his office.

A musical chime at the door announced company.

Surprised, Madoc crossed to the foyer and swung the door open.

No one was there.

No, wait. A Jeep was parked in front of the porch with someone rummaging in the back. A someone with a very fine ass.

Taking a step back, the female lifted a box into her arms. It was Heather.

Madoc went down the steps quickly. "Let me help."

"Oh, good." She handed it over. "The boxes were heavier than I expected. I paid a couple of youngsters to load them into my car."

"We could have—"

"No." She picked up a smaller box and walked inside with him. "The boys were thrilled to work, and I'm sure they need the money."

Leaving the front door open, he led the way to the room between Niall's office and André's den. The dark mahogany file cabinets André had ordered were set up, along with two matching desks. "André is calling this the business room."

Heather ran a finger over one glossy surface. "He has excellent taste in office furniture."

"We all like wood furniture, but for André, the darker, the

better." Foolish cat. A warm medium-brown walnut was nicer, more like the woods on a sunny day.

Madoc opened the connecting door to the adjacent room. "André claimed this room, too...and Niall dubbed it *The Cosantir's Den.*"

Two walls held floor-to-ceiling bookcases—and André owned enough books to fill them. Rich brown leather chairs and a small couch were set in a circle around a dark blue oriental carpet.

Heather smiled. "What a nice man cave."

"I think so." André's voice came from the open door to the business room, and Madoc saw Heather startle. Then flush.

Interesting. He'd seen André holding her hand at the bar a week ago. Was his brother making moves on the practical accountant? That would be a first.

André set the box he was carrying on the desk, then walked into the den. "I wanted a location where people could discuss clan concerns."

Heather nodded. "Calum's bar has a cozy sitting area for the same reason."

André motioned toward the boxes from her Jeep. "I thought you planned to bring everything over in a day or so."

"I was, but"—she smiled at Madoc—"the flooring guy for the restaurant wants to start tomorrow."

The floor refinishing was the final step of the remodeling. Anticipation rose inside him. By the Gods, he missed cooking for customers. "Ready to help me hire staff?"

"Absolutely. I know some of the cooks and servers who previously worked here are eager to return."

"Then, after everything is set up, can you give me time every week to keep the books up?"

She frowned, hesitated, then nodded. "Yes. Yes, I will."

Resting his hip on a chair arm, André considered her. "Why the hesitation? I thought you'd decided to stay."

"After getting you guys settled, I thought I'd see about a software job—not return to being a CPA." For a moment, she looked so lost Madoc wanted to hug her. "But I don't know why I didn't think about it. Before Shaquana and I designed the small business software, I loved accounting."

"But there's less money and less prestige in it?" Madoc guessed.

Her smile was rueful. "I think that's it."

"Then, Ms. CPA, the clan would also like to hire you to keep the books—and keep me honest." André nodded at the business office. "One of those desks can be yours when you're here working."

"I'll take it." She smiled at him. "Be warned. If you toss receipts onto the floor, you'll see my fangs."

Amusement in his gaze, André bowed his head in pseudo-submission.

She really was cute, wasn't she? Madoc grinned. "So accountants are higher in the clan than the Cosantir."

Her blue-green eyes sparkled with laughter. "Higher than restaurant owners, as well."

"Yes, *ma'am*." He bet if they'd been in animal form, he'd have had his furry ass nipped.

She knew how to tease. How fun was this? Now he wanted to play. "Can I bribe you to overlook crappy filing?"

"Maybeee..." She looked interested.

"Stay for supper; I've made barbecue."

When her eyes lit up, he knew he had another person to feed, and his happiness was complete.

Late that evening, Heather sat on a cushioned patio couch, snuggled under a fuzzy blanket Niall had unpacked. After dancing in the firepit earlier, the salamander had buried itself in the glowing coals. In the forest, a light breeze rustled through the trees, and she sighed, enjoying the quiet of the night.

The brothers had disappeared into the house to finish cleaning up—and said that, as a guest, she wasn't permitted to help.

The Crichton crew were fun to be around. The way they teased each other—and her—made her homesick for Tanner and Daniel.

Madoc was an amazing cook, and she'd simply inhaled the barbecued country ribs, fresh corn, stuffed potatoes, and biscuits. *So good.*

Her cooking abilities extended to excellent breakfasts, a handful of very unadorned dishes, and a mean mac 'n' cheese. From a box.

Madoc, it appeared, was a genius in the kitchen.

After supper, they'd brainstormed plans for the territory, something the brothers apparently did most evenings. What they wanted to do for her clan was simply amazing. Swept up, she contributed her own dreams for the territory. And to her surprise and pleasure, they folded her ideas into their plans.

Then they'd talked about Canada and what they loved about their country. André's accent had thickened when he'd spoken nostalgically of his fostering years in Quebec. Niall had spent his teens with two uncles in British Columbia, apparently having a wonderful time.

Madoc, though, reported he'd been in the Yukon Territory—and didn't say anything else. His closed expression hadn't invited questions.

Maybe if she got to know him better, he'd share. It bothered her to see the big, laidback bear looking unhappy.

Reaching for her glass, she noticed it was empty. *Whoa, doggie.* Her head was buzzing, and when she tilted her head back, the stars danced like fireflies in the black sky.

Uh-oh. How many times had she emptied her glass over the

course of the evening? Madoc had made the rounds several times. So had Niall.

Sitting up, she felt as if the couch, which had legs, was rocking. Yep, she'd had too much to drink.

Foolish wolf. Now what? She shouldn't drive, couldn't stay here, and her dignity wouldn't let her beg a ride all the way to her cabin. Besides, the males had been drinking too.

The door opened, and Niall stepped out onto the patio.

"All finished with clean-up." He sat down beside her, slinging an arm over her shoulders. His fingers rubbed gentle circles on her upper arm. "It's sure great to be out of town. This is a brilliant location, don't you think?"

Think? How could she think with how close he sat? His touch was sending a tingling warmth up her center.

She really shouldn't have had those last two or so glasses of wine.

What were they talking about? Oh yes. "You found a fine location, especially the way your property backs up to the national forest."

"I haven't had a chance to check who else lives along the outskirts near us. Do you know?"

"Most of your neighbors are shifters. The pack house is a couple of streets over on the other side of Nugget Creek." She motioned to the right.

"Yeah?" Catching her hand, Niall kissed her fingers, sending more heat streaming through her. "Did you ever live in the pack house?"

"Ugh, no. The alpha, Roger, and his betas are too aggressive for my comfort." Which was why she didn't go on pack runs any longer. She paused. "Ah, in case you didn't realize, Roger is Pete's littermate."

"Oh, great." Niall frowned. "Didn't Roger have a problem with his brother stealing from the clan?"

How could she say this? "Roger is alpha because he's stronger than any other wolf, not for his mental abilities. Despite being slug-lazy, Pete's smarter. Although they share a house, they don't spend much time together. In fact, Roger's mostly living at the pack house these days."

When Gretchen dumped Roger for Pete, she'd probably added to the wedge between the brothers. The B&B manager loved to play one male against another.

Considering how she went after Gods-called males like a starving coyote after raw steak, Heather was surprised André and Niall had escaped her clutches.

Or maybe they hadn't. What did Heather know?

Heather shook her head. She shouldn't sneer at Gretchen for lusting after André or Niall—not when she was doing the very same thing herself.

With Niall's rock-hard body beside her, all she could think about was putting her arms around him. Running her hands over all those muscles. Licking the hollow at the base of his throat.

Kissing him.

She huffed in annoyance at herself.

"Hey, whatever you're thinking about, it can't be that bad." He squeezed her fingers.

"I do *not* want to talk about it." She took her hand back and —*bad wolf*—leaned into him a bit farther.

"All right. We can talk about something else." Niall tipped her chin up, and his gaze roamed over her face. "Gods, you're beautiful." His thumb stroked her cheek.

"Hardly. I—"

His lips cut off her protest.

When her mouth opened under his, he took it deeper, pulling her closer to him. With a solid grip in her hair, he pinned her just like a cat would while he slowly explored her mouth.

She flattened her palms on his hard chest, feeling the blazing heat of him through his shirt. The world began to spin around her as she surrendered to his lips, his hands.

No, wait. This wasn't the full moon, and she didn't want to get involved. Not with any male.

Fighting the surging desire to pull him closer, she pushed.

His arms loosened immediately. "Fuck. Sorry, *a thaisce.* I forgot."

"It's all right. I—"

"Yo, Niall, I need help lifting this." Madoc's shout drew the cahir to his feet. He paused, looking down at her.

"Go on." She waved a hand. "I'll enjoy the fire a bit, then take myself off."

He stroked a hand down her hair, then disappeared into the house.

With a sigh, she drew her feet up and curled herself into a corner of the couch. What was she thinking, letting him kiss her? *Bad wolf.*

Mating at non-full moon times was the quickest way known to end up in a foolish attachment. And then getting left. As she always did—by family, by males...by babies.

She touched her belly. Her babies hadn't even been with her long enough for her to have a rounded belly. And why that lack should hurt didn't make any sense.

A tear slid down her cheek. *Stupid alcohol.*

The cushions sagged as someone sat on the couch. Firm arms pulled her close, so she leaned against him. "What's the matter, *ma louloutte?*"

The soft French accent, the smoky resonant voice identified André.

"Cosantir, I'm sorry." She tried to sit up.

"It's André, and I asked you a question." He kept his arm around her waist and stroked her hair from her damp cheeks. "Do *not* try to tell me nothing."

The word died on her lips.

His hand paused. "Did Niall upset you? Was he too—"

"No." Shifters rarely pressed themselves on a female if they couldn't scent she was interested, not unless they were being aggressive. What was the point since a male couldn't maintain an erection if the female wasn't aroused? "I just... It was a long summer."

Leaning against the other armrest, he drew her against his chest. "Is long an American word for painful?" he asked softly.

Painful. So very painful. "Yes," she whispered as her eyes brimmed with tears again.

"Can you tell me what happened?" He rubbed his cheek on top of her head.

How could he be so nice when she'd caused him so much misery? "It's noth—"

The low hiss stopped her short. "Tell me."

The alcohol, her sadness, the firm command overcame her defenses. "My mom returned to the Mother...and then I lost my babies."

His muscles tensed with surprise. "You had cubs?"

"No. Yes." Her breath caught. "Th-they weren't born yet. I had a miscarriage."

As more tears trickled down her cheeks, he was silent, slowly stroking her shoulders.

"I'm sorry. I cannot even imagine how the losses must have hurt." The low voice, filled with sadness for her, was as soothing as the hand rubbing her back.

She sank into his sympathy, let it lift her on a wave of safety.

His winter-crisp, masculine scent wrapped around her, and before she realized what she was doing, she raised her lips to his.

He gripped her chin as his mouth came down on hers, possessing her firmly, taking and giving until she felt him tense.

"No, *ma chère*, we will not do this." His cheek rubbed over hers, then he kissed her forehead. "However, if you're still of the same mind when sober"—he nipped along her jaw—"you will not escape so easily."

His withdrawal was like cold water in the face. What was she doing?

"I'm sorry; you're right." She pushed herself upright, and he released her. "I need to go home."

Rising, he helped her to her feet and gripped her waist with strong hands to steady her when she wobbled. He chuckled. "No, you won't be driving tonight."

"But—" They were all exhausted. She couldn't drag anyone out to drive her home.

"We'll make up a bed in a guest room, and you will stay the night." His voice brooked no refusal. "It's not as if we don't have plenty of extra rooms."

They'd shown her the house. It truly was huge. Her laugh came out a gurgle. "All right, thank you."

"Better." He hugged her and kissed the top of her head. "Madoc will make us all a fine breakfast in the morning."

CHAPTER EIGHTEEN

"I didn't realize wolves hibernated like you bears," Niall called to Madoc.

Still half asleep, Heather took a seat at the kitchen island. Even glaring at the stupid cat would take too much work.

A masculine chuckle sounded and then a cup of coffee was set in front of her. André brushed his hand over her hair.

"You're my favorite," she told him.

He grinned.

Madoc laughed as he set a block of cheese in front of her. "Drink the coffee—and grate the cheese."

Niall was shredding potatoes for hash browns. André had taken over getting biscuits in the oven and cooking bacon, while Madoc whipped up scrambled eggs and sausage gravy.

The bear supervised everything with the ease of a master chef. His open enjoyment at cooking had them all smiling.

She breathed in the aromas and sighed happily. Shifters who spent enough time in the forests didn't have to worry about cholesterol. *Thank you, Mother of All.*

They'd barely finished cooking when the doorbell rang.

"I'll get it," Madoc called after putting a platter of eggs on the dining room table.

Coffee in hand, Heather turned to see who'd come.

"Good morning, Madoc." Dressed in a skintight red top, Gretchen breezed past the bear with a long box in her hands. "I knew you would be busy unpacking, so I brought you some of the B&B pastries."

Just claw me now. Heather glanced toward the back door. Maybe she could escape?

Curiosity in her eyes, Gretchen looked around and spotted her targets. "André, Niall, good morning to you."

Then she noticed Heather. Her eyes narrowed. "I see you've hired kitchen help, Cosantir. Although she's a bit long in the tooth for manual labor."

Whoa, the li'l doggie has her fangs out.

Heather smiled sweetly. "No need to have a tantrum, youngling. I'm simply here for breakfast. You may still try your hardest to get one of them to fuck you."

Beside her, Niall choked.

Gretchen gave a squawk like a goose being nipped. "You...you bitch."

Heather gave her a puzzled stare. "Why yes...as are you. Did you forget we're both wolves?"

André's cough sounded far too much like laughter.

Face a dark pink—which, naturally made the blonde only more attractive—Gretchen turned to him. "I'm sorry to have interrupted your day, Cosantir. I hope you enjoy the goodies."

Her pursed lips made it clear she'd provide other goodies if he only asked. A second fuck-me-now look went to Niall.

Niall smiled politely. "Thank you for the food. Have a good day, Gretchen."

After shooting Heather another malevolent glare, the female flounced out of the house, hips swaying enough to dislocate a hip.

Unhappily, Heather looked away. *Why didn't I keep my mouth shut?* Bickering in someone else's home was simply tacky behavior. No matter the provocation.

After closing the door, Madoc scowled at his brothers. "It was bad enough wading through females when the lure was solely Niall. With two of you, the numbers will probably double."

Heather was starting to feel unwelcome. She glanced down at her front—yep, still female. Had he forgotten she was here?

"Brawd, I hope not." Niall grimaced. "The lip thing she does. Doesn't she realize it's called a duckface?"

Madoc rolled his eyes. "Beats the puckered one that makes her mouth look like a butthole."

Gods, what a visual. Heather tried to stifle a laugh. *Mother's breasts, what expressions do I use without knowing?*

"You held your own." Niall tugged a lock of Heather's hair. "I like it."

Still frowning, Madoc nodded his agreement.

"We all appreciate the way you cleared the house." Stepping closer, André cupped her face between his hands. "Are you feeling all right this morning?"

"I am."

His eyes were dark and gentle. Concerned. "No headache?"

She wanted to lean into him so much that she stepped back. "No. Really, I'm sorry about overindulging. It's not something I usually do."

"We've all been overworking since Herne tapped André." Niall finished wiping down the countertop. "You included. We were due for a night off, eh?"

Madoc leaned against the long island and rested his muscular forearms on the dark gray-blue granite top. His hazel eyes were almost green in the morning light as he eyed Heather. "You don't look old."

Her breath hissed out, then she laughed. He really did remind her of her blunt brothers.

Talk about being forced to face one's fears. "I'm in my fifties."

"So are we." Madoc looked puzzled. "Since when is that old?"

André's gaze traveled from her head to her bare toes, his smile wicked. The heat in his gaze said she was desirable, whatever age she was.

She could feel her cheeks heat.

Niall bent down to brush his lips over hers. "Say the word, and we'll put you on your hands and knees to check how creaky your joints are getting." His hand ran up her back, pulling her closer as he whispered in her ear. "The three of us can test your endurance. Flexibility too. Being able to bend is very important to us aged shifters."

Hands and knees. All three of them. Her toes curled, and desire flooded her like a tsunami.

Gods. She pushed the cahir back a step. "Behave, cat."

Scenting Niall's interest and clearly hearing the murmured words, André considered his littermate. The cahir was used to females falling into his bed. After leaving his twenties, he'd never pursued one.

Until now. He was unquestionably interested in Heather.

André agreed. He wanted her in his bed...or, better yet, in a bed like the one upstairs in the mate's suite where he and his brothers could share her. Could satisfy her over and over and then take their own pleasure.

But she was determinedly moving away from Niall.

Meeting André's gaze, whatever she saw made her cheeks pinken enough her freckles disappeared.

Yes, he liked seeing her blush too.

But he shouldn't push. Her strong personality covered a tender heart. One that had apparently been badly hurt.

She'd had tears on her face last night.

He turned to his brothers. "We haven't had a chance to

explore the forest behind the house. After breakfast, shall we enjoy a four-legged morning?"

Niall and Madoc thumped their fists on the island in agreement.

André smiled at Heather. "Join us, *ma louloutte.*"

A while later, Heather was still bemused at the affectionate term loosely meaning *my wolf*. Ah well, better than being called a cabbage or some other weird food endearment, right?

Thank the Mother she'd taken French classes in college.

Following the males downstairs, she realized the house had a shifter portal. The underground tunnel emerged in the forest.

As they all stripped down, Niall stepped out first to ensure the area was secure. "All good."

Leaving her clothing on a convenient bench, Heather followed the males up and out into a well-concealed clearing.

Mmm. She wouldn't have been female if she hadn't delighted in the sight of broad shoulders, strong back muscles, and very fine asses. And face it, the view from the front of their more-than-substantial packages was just as nice.

After a long stretch, Madoc shifted into a bear. No hump, nice straight profile. He wasn't a grizzly, just a really big, black bear, probably five hundred pounds or so.

She smiled at the sight. Then realized his lustrous brown eyes were watching her warily. What did he think she'd do—scream or something? Her brothers were nearly the same size.

"Aren't you splendid." She moved to stand beside him and stroked his fur.

In an open test, he rubbed his huge head on her hip, almost knocking her over.

"Pushy bear." Bending, she gave him a vigorous scratching.

Aside from a beige muzzle, his fur was a dark chocolate color and thick.

When she dug her fingers into his soft undercoat, he moaned in happiness.

She laughed. "You're lucky, dude. Black bears are common enough around here you won't have to worry about being seen."

Niall frowned. "What about wolves and cougars?"

"We have lots of cougars. Wolves, though, are rare this far south in the Cascade Range. The pack tries to stay out of sight and not attract biologists who'll try to tag us like cattle."

Humans were so annoying.

As the chill wind swept over her bare skin, she shifted to wolf, cherishing the rich feel of the Mother's blessing sweeping from her paws upward.

She was loved.

Taking a moment to adjust to four legs and a tail, she swiveled her ears to catch suspicious sounds, then lifted her nose to sniff out the scents on the breeze. *All good.*

Lowering her head, she realized Niall and André hadn't shifted.

"Fuck me, she's *'pretty wolf.'*" Niall stared at her. "André, she's the wolf who attacked the mercs last summer."

André's eyes narrowed.

She stared back at them, memories churning in her head. Was he talking about the ghastly night last summer when the Scythe attacked, and she killed... *No, don't think of death.*

Her part in the battle ended when she and Margery attacked two mercenaries trying to kill her friend, Vicki. One merc had hit Heather with a rifle barrel. *Gods, the pain, the dizziness.* Everything had hurt, and her eyes had refused to focus. But something huge and blond had killed her attacker, then a panther killed the second soldier and trawsfurred to a dark-haired blurry form.

These two?

She took a step forward and sniffed. Her memories were fragmented, but her far more sensitive wolf's nose remembered their scents. Niall's earthy fragrance like the forest in the autumn. André's, a crisp mountain breeze.

It was them.

She shifted back to human and simply knelt there, her legs not wanting to hold her up. "You... It was you. You two saved me and Margery."

Niall had carried her to the healer.

His hearty laugh filled the clearing. "No wonder I keep thinking you smell familiar."

"I noticed, as well. Admittedly, we were all covered with the stink of guns and blood." A crease appeared in André's cheek as he smiled. "You look much healthier, pretty wolf."

"Thank you." She looked at him, then at Niall, knowing she and Margery would be dead if they hadn't come. "Thank you both."

"You're very welcome." André touched her cheek, then stepped back and trawsfurred into a sleekly muscular cougar.

Niall tugged her hair, then shifted. Yes, he was one huge cougar. André had tawny fur; Niall's was pale gold.

Two cougars and a bear. *Cat-scat.* Just like when she was a cub, she was totally outweighed and outclawed.

With a huff of exasperation, she shifted back to wolf.

Niall, the jerk, promptly swatted at her, claws safely sheathed.

She dodged and darted around him to nip his rear leg. As he leaped away, André curved a paw over her neck and proceeded to rub his furry cheek on her head, marking her with his scent.

When Niall bounded closer, undoubtedly to do the same thing, she leaped away, spotted a deer trail, and led the way out of the tiny clearing, tail held high.

Hah, boys, take that.

And then André sprang over her, far too easily, and took the lead.

Bad cat.

Somewhere around noon, Niall sprawled in a grassy meadow beside André and watched the wolf playing with an oversized bear.

She wasn't a delicate female, but nicely muscular. He liked how she was built—what Madoc would call *sturdy*. Her fur was a beautiful reddish-brown, her ears dark brown. Her muzzle, belly, and feet were white as was the cute tip of her dark tail.

André had a slight smile on his face. "She's got some moves."

The wolf dove in to nip the bear's hind leg and sprang away before Madoc could bowl her over.

"She does." Niall nibbled on a stalk of grass. "Her two brothers are bears."

"Experience, then. But it takes stubbornness to persist in playing until the skill is gained."

Niall grinned. "I'd say she qualifies for the stubborn label." Something else he liked about her. She was the very opposite of a pushover.

One of Madoc's sweeping blows sent her flying a few feet. But the bear was being careful, as Niall knew he would be.

Undeterred, Heather found her legs, lunged forward in a feint, and nipped Madoc's shoulder.

She was simply delightful. "I like her."

André glanced at him. "So you've said. As I recall, after saving her, we asked Calum if we could keep her."

Niall burst out laughing. "We did, didn't we?"

"Full moon is in a few days." André's gaze was on the bear and wolf.

"Is it now? I might actually look forward to it for a change." Because Heather would be there.

"My thought as well."

Niall considered Madoc. He was playing with Heather despite his initial wariness. Because Madoc was always wary around females. "He won't ask her to mate at the Gathering, even if he's interested. He waits until they come after him."

"I know." Andre's jaw was hard. "Whatever happened during his fostering left more scars than we realized."

"By the God, André, our teen years were decades ago."

"Aye, but what happens during the years of fostering sinks deeper than any other time. It's as if First Shift leaves us open to imprinting trauma and cultures and languages, the way hatching imprints a duckling on its mother."

"Never thought about it like that." But Niall could see the truth. It was why shifters never lost the accent from wherever they'd fostered after First Shift. Why André still sounded as if he'd lived in Quebec all his life rather than just his teens.

So... It appeared the trauma Madoc suffered then had sunk claws-deep in his soul. Yet there was hope.

"Look at them play. He never plays with females." Niall smiled slowly. "I wonder if she'd be interested in taking on the two of us under a full moon."

"I'm not invited then? You wound me, brawd."

Niall rubbed his shoulder against André's, knowing his brother wasn't serious in the least. André preferred a one-on-one for a new female. If and when he and Niall paired to take a female, André would already know exactly what to do to please her.

"I look forward to a time we can enjoy her together," Niall said. "You and me."

And maybe, if hopes came true, the three of them might possibly win her favor.

CHAPTER NINETEEN

On Friday, Talam entered the electronics store with Sky beside him. On the way to the human city, Mr. Wendell had stopped at a campground so everyone could shower. Clean and dressed in new jeans and T-shirts, Talam and Sky were playing "good kids".

From the corner of his eye, he watched Mateo and Alvaro enter the store.

The two were playing the "bad boys" part of the scam. Their T-shirts and jeans were torn and muddy. Mr. Wendell had rubbed grease in their hair, and they'd streaked their faces with dirt.

"Yo, check this shit out," Mateo yelled to his brother and held up a remote.

"Let me see." Alvaro shoved past a couple of older humans. "Good shit."

The two boys rambled through the store, noisy, pushy, touching everything.

Like wolves defending their hunting grounds, the human guards headed right for them.

Talam nodded to Sky. *Time to move*.

Casually, Sky moved over to the phones.

Talam positioned himself to block the high mirror so anyone looking would only see him. Although the store clerks should be watching Mateo and Alvaro.

Quickly, Sky shoved phones into his pockets and the bag inside his jacket. All the storage places were lined with special stuff so the alarms at the front didn't get set off. "Done."

As they sauntered toward the front, Talam picked up a cheap calculator.

At the register, he paid for the calculator with the money Mr. Wendell had given them. Then, holding his breath, he followed Sky through the tall scanners.

Nothing alarmed.

Out of the store and in the mall, he almost let out a scream of victory. *Yes!* His heart was still pounding like crazy.

"Mr. Wendell's gonna like all this stuff we scored." Sky grinned big.

"Yeah. And we'll get lots of money from him for it." Talam headed for the parking lot where the Cosantir waited. They'd unload and then get sent to the next store.

Hours later, in the van returning to Ailill Ridge, Talam sat beside Sky. The other two sets of brothers in the van were also quiet. They were all stuffed from the burgers and fries Mr. Wendell had bought them in Cle Elum.

Mr. Wendell had been happy with their work.

Talam winced. What they did wasn't really work—it was stealing, and they were thieves. His shoulders hunched. Mama would hate what they were doing.

He pressed his lips together. It was steal or starve. Same for the other cubs.

A few times last week, they'd found sandwiches left on picnic tables in the park. So they'd had some food at least.

When Mr. Wendell called the boys back to work for him last weekend, they'd all jumped right into his van. And he'd had new clothes and food waiting for them.

We don't have a choice, Mama.

When Mr. Wendell drove down an alley behind the town square, there were construction guys going into the back door of the Shamrock building. People had been coming and going there for days. "What's going on at the Shamrock?"

Sky leaned forward to hear.

Mateo turned in his seat to look back at them. "Those new guys bought the Shamrock. Want to get the restaurant going again."

Talam exchanged looks with Sky. "Is one of the males a cahir?"

"Uh-huh. And one's the new Cosantir."

Talam frowned. He and Sky hadn't believed the territory had a new Cosantir.

"If Mr. Wendell isn't the Cosantir, what is he now?" Sky asked. "I mean, is—"

The van skidded to such a hard stop it rocked violently. When Mr. Wendell turned, his face was bright red. And the expression on his face made Talam shiver.

Oh cat-scat.

"Get *out*," Mr. Wendell yelled at him and Sky.

Clumsy with fear, Talam followed Sky out the sliding side door and stood there. "Mr. Wen—"

"I'm Cosantir and will always be Cosantir." Mr. Wendell was so mad he was spitting. "You two pukes can starve. I'm done with you."

Sky made a sound like a whimper.

No, he mustn't. Talam swallowed hard. "Sky didn't mean—"

Mr. Wendell's eyes were filled with hate. "And if you try to steal here in *my* town, the Chief of Police will break you into little pieces."

Shaking, they backed away. 'Cuz Cosantirs could kill people, and maybe he really was still one.

"Shut the fucking door."

Giving them a sympathetic look, Mateo closed the sliding door.

The van sped away so fast it threw loose rocks at them.

Staring after it, Talam couldn't find enough air to breathe. Their only way of making money to live on was gone.

"I'm sorry, Talam." Sky's eyes were filled with tears.

"Not your fault he's gone fairy-headed about being a Cosantir."

"But what are we going to do? How can we eat?"

"We have money from today." Talam patted Sky.

When their money ran out, then…he had no idea.

CHAPTER TWENTY

It was the equinox, the time when night equaled day. There was no clan celebration planned as in other territories, so Madoc had visited the grocery store to get the right foods for the harvest menu he'd planned—a nice butternut squash soup, roast chicken and wild rice, and a sweet apple crisp to finish.

Carrying the sacks, he glanced around the square, keeping an eye out for Niall's pickpockets. The cubs hadn't been in the square recently, and the last time Niall had seen them, they'd apparently been in decent, clean clothes.

Madoc shook his head. He, André, and Niall might've been emotionally neglected as younglings, but at least they'd always had food, clothing, and a place to sleep. It hurt to think of cubs not having even the necessities, so yeah, they'd all watch for those lads.

Passing his restaurant, Madoc couldn't resist popping inside. Nose wrinkling at the stink of chemicals, he smiled as he surveyed his place. Only two more weeks and there'd be a grand opening.

The September sun slanting through the big windows and open door gleamed on the newly refinished hardwood floor. The tables and chairs, stored in the warehouse, would be brought in next week. He had interviews set up for waitstaff and cooks and a cleaning crew. Yeah, it was all coming together and much quicker than he'd hoped for...thanks to Heather and her knowledge of how to start up a business, her lists, and the people she knew.

He had hoped she'd be competent with money and paperwork. She was all of that and more. Even better, she was a comfortable person to be around. Half of the miracles she'd achieved were simply because people liked her.

He liked her. Who would have thought?

Okay, he did have trouble getting past her being a female. But during their play as wolf and bear, he'd learned a lot about her personality.

It was difficult to disguise one's nature when in animal form. She played hard, all in, and was as competitive as an opponent could wish. Yet, when knocked off her paws, she always jumped up and leaped back in, her jaws open in a wolfy laugh. No, she didn't get angry. She played fair, not biting too hard, not going for his eyes or ears. But she'd also played smart, using her smaller, quicker shape to score on him.

Yeah. She might actually be good people.

Maybe...

Moonlight filtered through the forest canopy, so bright the evergreen needles seemed to sparkle. Saturday, two nights before the full moon, Heather brought up the rear of their tiny pack of three wolves. She liked this position. If she wanted to fall back, she could—or she could jaunt forward and nip Talitha's tail.

Just for fun.

When teeth closed on her tail, the pale gray wolf spun, shoved against Heather's shoulder, and nipped her flank. With a pleased yip, Talitha danced forward to catch up with Moya.

Although younger, Moya loved to lead. Heather's friend in

Cold Creek would consider Moya to be officer material and Heather a sergeant. According to Vicki, sergeants were the practical noncoms who got shit done.

Sounded about right.

She lifted her nose, sniffing the lovely fragrance of the forest after a rain. The sharp tang of conifer needles mingled with the scent of damp earth and moldering leaf litter.

The trail wound up and up until the trees gave way to rocky outcroppings. Moya led them onto one ledge that looked out across the lower lands to the north. Behind them, the mountains piled higher and higher until topped by the moonlit whiteness of Mount Rainier.

Heather stood between her friends and drank it in. This, her world, her territory was heart-stoppingly beautiful. Lifting her muzzle, she sang her gratitude for the earth, for the Mother of All, for the moon. Her friends' howls joined in, twining with hers in a beauty all its own.

As Heather's last howl trailed off, she could hear the distant response of the Rainier pack.

Moya snarled...as usual.

With a wolfy laugh, Heather bumped her shoulder against Moya's and nudged her toward the path down.

Grumbling, Moya headed off.

In a clearing not far from Heather's place, they trawsfurred and dressed before walking down an animal trail to the cabin.

"The fire is ready, if you'd light it, Moya." Heather walked around the cabin, lighting candles here and there. The scent of cloves and cinnamon filled the air. "Talitha, can you get out the food while I open the wine? Isn't Eileen joining us?" Talitha's mate was a cougar and didn't join them for pack runs, no matter how small the pack was.

"No, she wanted a solitary celebration this time." Talitha loaded up a tray with the desserts she brought. "She's such an introvert."

"Balances you out," Moya called.

When Heather set the wine bottle on the woodstove hearth, the fire was crackling cheerily. Greystoke abandoned his window perch to stake out a corner of the cushions and blankets.

"Happy Mid-Harvest, Heather. You know, your whole cabin feels like an altar." Already sitting on the blanket pile, Moya was finger-combing twigs from her butt-length hair.

"Thank you." Heather glanced around in pleasure. Tall vases with sprays of blazing red and yellow foliage filled the corners. The coffee table had a basket of apples in honor of the abundance of the Goddess, circled by antlers for Herne the Hunter. Colorful gourds and dry corn filled a basket next to the woodstove.

Sitting on the opposite side of the blanket pile, Talitha accepted a glass of wine from Heather. "It really does. I do miss the seasonal celebrations the clan used to have."

"Me too." Heather took the center spot in front of the fire. "Those days may come again. The Cosantir was appalled there was nothing planned for the equinox."

"Really?" Moya looked intrigued. "He'd arrange a celebration?"

Talitha snorted. "Cosantirs don't arrange things. He'll ask someone—say, Heather— to put something together, and five minutes later, she'll have everyone working their tails off."

"Oh." Moya nodded wisely. "That sounds about right."

Heather snickered. Because André *would* probably give her the job. Only… "The difference here is André, Madoc, and Niall would be working alongside everyone."

"Yes, they're not unfamiliar with hard work." Talitha nodded approval.

Moya scrunched up her nose. "I'm reserving judgment. So far, the new Cosantir seems better than Pete—and Roger too. That's not a very high bar, though."

Heather eyed her friend. Moya never spoke of her past before she and her brothers moved to Ailill Ridge. Even then, she'd had a bottomless hatred for authority figures. Pete, Roger, and the pack betas had solidified her feelings.

"Roger hasn't been bothering you, has he?" Talitha asked in concern.

All three of them had problems with the alpha.

Unable to dominate Heather, the alpha disliked her. He'd even stopped pushing her to rejoin the pack.

In her late thirties, Talitha had a wife—and Roger hated lesbians. He avoided her entirely.

Moya, though, was only twenty-four and downright cute. Since the Daonain had a shortage of females, he kept trying to bully her into staying in the pack.

"The alpha-hole and his betas have been subdued ever since Herne ripped Pete's powers away. I think they were shocked."

"We all were. At least Pete hasn't shown his muzzle after the clash at the Gathering House. And I must say, the work day was great." Talitha raised her glass. "To the new Cosantir, who is pulling this clan together, shifter by shifter."

After a moment, Moya surprised Heather by joining in. "Yes, to a Cosantir who uses charm rather than bullying."

André was winning Moya over? He really did have godlike powers.

Heather lifted her glass. "To the Cosantir's health—and the health of the land and the clan."

Someday, she'd tell André the first toast of their equinox celebration had been to him.

Smiling, she popped one of the small apple cake bites in her mouth.

Reaching over Greystoke, who swatted her trespassing arm with a furry paw, Moya picked up her small hand drum. Setting it in her lap, she tapped out a slow rhythmic beat.

Heather filled their glasses again and lifted hers. "As the warmth and light turns with the season into cold and dark, we give thanks for what we've gathered, what we've learned, and what we've stored to help us in the months ahead."

After they drank, Heather smiled at Moya.

"As the earth is dying, we celebrate the dark aspect of the Mother, the crone who welcomes us home before our rebirth." Pausing her drumming, Moya lifted her glass.

After they drank, Heather turned to Talitha.

Talitha's gaze was on the young salamander, dancing in the flames. "This is a celebration of balance. Without dark, there is no light; without winter, there is no spring; without death, there is no life. We thank you for the gift of balance, Lord of the Hunt and Lady of the Harvest."

After another sip of the fruity, sweet wine, Heather set the glass on the hearth.

The slow, steady drumming was an echo of her heartbeat as she watched the salamander pirouette in the fire.

So much had happened in the past season. So many losses. Shifters falling to mercenaries and a hellhound. Her mother, her unborn babies. Her business too.

And she'd almost died during the Call to the Gods.

Now, here at the point of balance, she could look ahead and see...hope.

Hope for her work. Thanks to the Mother, she had the mind and skill to veer off the trail to a new occupation, one where she could make a difference.

Hope for the territory after so many years of frustration. And she'd be a part of bringing the clan closer together.

Hope for...well, not for love. She wouldn't venture down that trail again.

But she'd been blessed with friends, like book-loving feisty Moya, warm-hearted Talitha, and quiet Eileen. And friends in Cold Creek—who were undoubtedly having a much bigger celebration.

New friends had come into her life too. Niall, a nerd with a warrior's body and spirit. Madoc, who probably never met a stranger...unless, of course, she was female. And André, who had the heart to watch over them all.

Yes, I am blessed.

CHAPTER TWENTY-ONE

"What do you think, Greystoke?" Two nights later, on Monday, Heather stood by her bed and contemplated her choices. "Should I go with gold to set off my hair or turquoise for my eyes?"

Sprawled beside the array of tops, her cat yawned.

"Yes, yes, I know. You have zero interest in sex and couldn't care less about the bizarre mating practices of other species." She glanced at the window. The sun was heading for the treetops. She needed to dress and head for the Gathering.

Choices, choices.

Vicki or Breanne or any of her Cold Creek friends would have opinions. How many times had the group met before a Gathering to dress and talk? She missed their all-female mini parties.

Since Espresso Books wouldn't close until right before the pre-Gathering clan meeting, a mini party today had been out of the question.

Just as well, since Heather was running late after spending the day at the Summerlands Ranch outside of Ailill Ridge. Her brothers sure could make a hash out of their bookkeeping. At least they'd been too busy with moving cattle to the winter pastures to interrogate her on what she'd been doing. Her littermates could sniff out whenever she was attracted to a male—and then she'd get teased mercilessly. *The benighted fleabags.*

"I think we'll go with the gold." She picked up the sleeveless, form-fitting top. A front panel laced-up from below the breasts to a scoop neck. On someone with big breasts—or if the laces were too loose—it would be more porn than sexy, but her girls weren't very big.

Anticipation rose inside her. She'd told André and Niall she would only mate at Gatherings. Would they be interested?

She huffed a breath of a laugh. Madoc sure wasn't.

Such a confusing male. So open and sociable, and beneath it all, he was as wary around females as a cat walking past a wolf pack. He'd relaxed some around her, but no, he wouldn't be joining her in a mating room.

Which was a shame because he had a gorgeous body. All those big bones were covered with thick, rock-hard muscles. The short beard didn't soften his strong, rugged face. Would his long, brown hair be soft to the touch? And what about the curling hair on his chest? She wanted to touch.

Honestly, Heather, get a grip.

It was sure obvious the full moon would rise soon. Anticipation was already shivering through her.

She'd see the three Crichton brothers. Soon.

But would any of them want her with every fertile female in the territory trying to catch their attention?

Word of mouth about the clan meeting before the full moon rising had been quite effective, André thought as he walked through the Gathering House.

The open downstairs was packed with Daonain. More crowded the second-floor balcony overlooking the main floor.

Everyone was checking out the renovated space and touching the new furniture in wonder.

It was good to meet more shifters, to be able to name the sparks he saw when he mentally scanned his territory.

He blinked. *My* territory? When had he started to consider Rainier Territory as his own?

Herne was probably laughing his antlers off.

André smiled ruefully, the last of his bitterness gone. They'd become his clan, and they needed him. Somehow that made all the difference.

In the living area, André stepped onto a sturdy coffee table so everyone could see him. It was time to start making clear how things would change.

"Daonain." The closest shifters stopped talking, but the rest... *Gods, what a babble*. He drew from the power given to him, and his voice deepened. "*Silence.*"

The room went still.

Taking in the shocked expressions, he wondered how long it had been since Wendell had acted like a Cosantir?

"Daonain, if we haven't met yet, my name is André Crichton. A little over two weeks ago, Herne called me to be the Cosantir of this territory." He shook his head with a smile. "I must admit, I wasn't pleased. My littermates and I are from Canada. We had jobs there. Lives. But...I accepted the call."

Several faces showed anger. Some held surprise. To his relief, the majority appeared relieved.

"Please meet my brothers. Madoc." He motioned to Madoc, who stepped up beside him long enough to nod to the crowd.

"And Niall, a cahir."

As Niall did the same, André said firmly, "Rejoice, Daonain. The clan increases."

The shifters echoed back with the traditional response, "The clan increases."

"For the last week or so, many of you have been working to

restore our Gathering House to what it should be." André tapped the coffee table under his feet. "As you can see, the Wainwright brothers build very sturdy furniture."

The crowd's laughing agreement made the Wainwrights stand taller.

"The Moreno construction crew did the major repairs. The town's sewing circle worked on the cushions, and everything else was done by volunteers. They all did a magnificent job, don't you think?"

Led off by young Jens, cheers filled the room.

"I'm not sure everyone knows, but a change in Cosantirs involves more than merely power. Cosantirs also manage the clan's properties and finances. To ensure everything was in order, a local CPA, Heather Sutharlan, has audited the accounts. Until moonrise, she will be in the front corner if you want to view the records and findings." André pointed to a corner of the living room, hoping he hadn't just staked his favorite redhead out like prey for the beasts.

To his surprise, Madoc sauntered over and leaned against the wall next to her.

When she gave the bear a startled look, André shot his brother a smile.

Grinning, Madoc shoved the sleeves of his flannel shirt up, as if preparing for blood.

Not what André wanted to happen tonight. Which led him to the next subject.

"A Cosantir's duties are to enforce the Laws. *All* the Laws." André sighed and grimly continued. Because it was clear the clan needed to be reminded of the basics.

"Exposing the Daonain to humans will lead to death." And it was a shame Wendell hadn't been returned to the Mother for his careless postings last summer.

There were nods of agreement. The attack by mercenaries

had been a brutal reminder of the consequences of humans learning about them.

"Be respectful of the OtherFolk in the territory. We all serve the God of the Hunt and the Mother."

He received more nods.

"Please do remember that the Law of the Fight forbids death or permanent maiming."

To André's surprise, several people turned accusing stares toward Brett, the greasy-haired friend of Wendell's.

The male scowled, then glared at André. *Interesting.* The male would be one to keep an eye on.

Now to bring up André's own rules, which would be more difficult to enforce. "Brawling will no longer be allowed inside the Gathering House. We are not mindless animals, like wolverines, to attack each other without thought. Go into the nearby forest clearings to fight."

Although most of the shifters appeared to be smothering cheers, there were far too many males either glaring—or smirking in open defiance.

One sneering male took the prize for stupidity. "What are you going to do—kill us for a brawl?"

"*Non.* No need to get carried away." André smiled slightly. "Belligerent animals will simply be tied up and left on the porch until morning. If the scent of females in heat leaves a brawler in discomfort, I daresay he'll be wiser next moon."

The male's jaw dropped in horror.

A redheaded female burst out laughing. "Exploding balls, I love it!" Spreading her fingers outward, she mimicked the blasts. "Boom, *boom.*"

Everyone around her cracked up.

Smothering his own laughter, André tried to remember the next item on his list.

Ah. "My brother Madoc is opening a restaurant in the Shamrock building and will be hiring. In the adjoining section, I plan to open a gift shop featuring local arts and crafts." He smiled at the females and male who'd made the mating room cushions. "Very few Cosantirs in the world don't have a secondary job. This will be mine."

The buzzing in the room rose. Yes, he'd taken a direct stab at Wendell.

He waited until the whispers died down. "We plan to turn the Shamrock warehouse into a community center with various areas for crafts, cub-care, and possibly an area for our teen shifters."

Happy whispering indicated the center would be popular. *Excellent*. The clan needed ways to come together.

"Finally, the clan owns several properties around the town, many of which are in disrepair and vacant. We'll be fixing those up and renting them to generate funds. If any of you are in one of those houses for free, you need to vacate the premises or pay rent, starting on the first of October."

"What about the communal house?" an overly thin female called. "Will you open it up again?"

"What?" In the corner, Heather rose to her feet. "It's not open? When did it close?"

The underweight female turned. "In July. A waterpipe broke and flooded the place. Pete had the water shut off and kicked everyone out."

Heather's face held enough anger to set the house on fire.

André met her gaze. "Is the house on the list of ones to fix?"

She checked her tablet. "It is. Move it to the top?"

"Yes, thank you." André looked at the female who'd asked the question. "We'll get it open as soon as possible. If you're in need or know someone who is, leave their names with Heather. My phone number is posted on Heather's table. You can call me to keep updated on when it will open."

As the female stammered her thanks, he saw several older shifters looked appalled. Because Cosantirs weren't usually available by phone.

Times change.

But perhaps he should avoid making the traditionalists *too* uncomfortable. "When the gift shop opens, I'll be easy to find and would prefer to talk with you all directly." He smiled at one of the older shifters. "But at this time, my days are as mixed up as a brownie's on cleaning day, and I can be difficult to locate—as my brothers can attest."

Madoc snorted in the way only a bear could—and set off laughter.

"So, if there's a problem, the phone might be the route to take."

The traditional shifters nodded, obviously relieved he wouldn't transform the world into one they would no longer recognize.

"Finally, I want you all getting your homes secured against hellhounds." He shook his head, hating to even mention demon-spawn on this night of joy. "The territory has already lost shifters to the demon-dogs. Let's lose no more. Install window guards and sturdy doors—and check your neighbors are doing the same. On the night of the dark of the moon, be inside a secure home from sunset to sunrise. Yes, my people, this is a curfew."

He could see from some expressions that achieving compliance would be a work in progress. Hopefully, there would be time. This was a start, at least.

"Thank you all for coming early to this Gathering...and in the Gatherings to come, we'll continue to have clan meetings first."

Before stepping down, André watched as the patterns in the room changed.

Heather's table was soon surrounded. People waiting were introducing themselves to Madoc.

Shifters he hadn't met moved forward to greet him and Niall.

A few groups of males acted like wolves whose prey had been stolen.

They'd be the ones to watch.

By the time the moon was up, those who wouldn't be participating in the Gathering had left.

The air in the house slowly filled with the scent of females in heat. With the fragrance of arousal. Shifters were making their choices and going upstairs to the mating rooms.

André gave Niall an assessing glance and was pleased to see his color was good. The darkness had released his spirit, and his enthusiasm for life had returned.

Niall caught his look and snorted. "You're worse than a mother bear with a sick cub. I'm fine."

"Yeah, see? Didn't I say André should've been a bear." Laughing, Madoc thumped André's shoulder.

Shoulder stinging, André dodged the next blow. Bears—always showing their affection with painful swats. "It's good you're fine, cahir, since Gretchen is watching you like you're a new-killed rabbit, and she's hasn't eaten in a week."

"Oh yeah? I'm not the only one she's watching, oh sparkling new Cosantir." Niall bumped his shoulder against André's. "Maybe I'll tie you up and leave you for her."

"You're not very brotherly." André watched more shifters climb the stairs to the mating rooms. A female walked between two young males who appeared more than delighted. It brought back fond memories of his first few years as an adult.

"Then, let me be brotherly. Madoc and I will take the first shift of preventing trouble," Niall said.

Since it would probably take two shifters to discourage fighting, they'd decided to take turns. Once André knew his people better, he'd find others to help keep the peace.

Madoc waved his hand toward the room. "Go find someone to enjoy."

"You don't want to mate right this moment?" André shook his head. "I'm shocked."

Madoc scowled; they all knew he found Gatherings annoying. Yet, he was popular. The females liked his size and the deadly look of him. "Laugh all you want, cat. *You* are going to be overrun with females wanting to break in their new Cosantir."

André's wince made his brothers grin.

Niall nudged Madoc's shoulder. "As long as they break him in and don't break him."

"You two aren't as funny as you think." Huffing a laugh, André headed off to do his duty. Even Cosantirs had to obey the Laws.

Behind him, Niall was saying, "So, Madoc, why don't bears like fast food?"

Madoc growled. "Don't start that scat."

"Because it's hard to catch."

André glanced over his shoulder in time to see Madoc shove his littermate into the wall, and Niall's roar of laughter turned to a pained yowl.

André grinned. By the Gods, he loved his littermates.

Turning, he moved away. Looking around, he could feel his blood heat as he took in the scent of the females. Of their arousal. Their soft feminine voices stroked over him.

He knew exactly who he was going to look for first. But before he reached the center of room, females surrounded him. Not one was a redhead.

All right, Cosantir. Duty before desire.

As the night went on, André traded guard duty with his brothers, who had no trouble finding females. More often, they were dragged upstairs by the more forward of females.

It was Madoc and Niall's turn at guarding. And André had done his duty several times as an unmated Daonain.

Now, he could indulge his own desire. He surveyed the room, his senses open.

Then he heard a familiar voice, low and throaty with a clear enunciation that pleased the Canadian in him immeasurably. He followed the sound, ignoring flirtatious looks and side-stepping one bold female who stepped into his path.

There.

His redheaded problem-solver stood with Moya. The brunette's lilting voice highlighted the beauty of Heather's contralto tones.

André stood for a moment, realizing he'd wanted Heather from the first time he'd seen her. Tonight, he didn't have to set his attraction to one side. Not on the night of a full moon.

Tonight, he could openly appreciate her as a lovely female. She was slender with understated curves that begged for his hands... for his exploration.

By the Gods, the golden, low-cut top she wore was simply a trap. The lacing was loosened far enough to hint at the inner curve of her breasts...and roused the male in him. As did the gorgeous thick hair spilling over her shoulders in all the colors of autumn. Her fair skin was much lighter than his, and...those freckles.

When he was a cub, his mother had told him freckles were the tiny handprints of pixies. Science be damned, he still felt that way.

Hearing her laugh, he moved closer. His quarry was telling Moya about being *caomhnor* to a cub named Sorcha.

"Would you believe Vicki told me I should be stern with Sorcha." Heather laughed. "As *if*. I told her discipline was up to the parents. As *caomhnor*, I provide love, attention, and presents. Lots and lots of presents."

Moya laughed. "Or, as the humans say, you get to spoil the youngling rotten."

"Exactly." Heather grinned. "The next time Vicki annoys me, Sorcha is getting a drum set."

What a precisely aimed vengeance. A laugh escaped André, and the two females jumped as if they'd forgotten they were at a Gathering. He did like older females. Younger ones couldn't set their raging hormones aside long enough to do anything except mate.

"Cosantir," Moya greeted with a slight tip of her head.

"Moya, it's good to see you."

She blinked as if surprised he'd remember her name.

"Your first clan meeting went very well." Heather lifted her glass of cider in a salute. "Congratulations."

"Thank you." He smiled. "So far, no brawling."

"Not with your brothers prowling the room." Moya turned to Heather. "Did you see Niall when some creepazoid insisted you were lying about Pete? The cahir got all pissed off—he even hissed at the guy. So protective."

André grinned. "It's why we still think of her as Niall's Heather."

As Moya laughed, Heather choked on her drink. "*Excuse* me? I've told you I am *not* Niall's." The snotty tone was delightful.

Smiling, André held out his hand. "Perhaps you might join me upstairs, and we can discuss who possesses you...while indulging in other activities."

André's smoky-dark voice was a velvety caress, and Heather's hand was in his before her brain had a chance to object.

And really, whyever would she want to?

He kissed her fingertips, kept her hand in his, and guided her up the stairs. Escorting her into a vacant room, he closed the door behind him.

She looked around. "This is nice." The design team for this room had gone for a *twilight-in-summer* ambiance. The floor cushions were a shadowy green. Dark red floral fabric covered smaller pillows. Brass sconces on the sun-colored walls gave only enough light to convey the slanting rays of the sun.

Along with a faint odor of paint and new fabric was André's

personal scent, like the cold, clean wind off the glaciers on Rainier. She breathed him in and felt her body wake. Soften.

He nibbled on her fingers, his steady, perceptive gaze on her face. When he nipped the base of her thumb and a streak of heat shot through her, his eyes crinkled.

"We will have fun, you and I." He pulled her firmly against him. He was taller, maybe six feet, and all lean, hard muscles. His blue cashmere, collared sweater had a V-neck, showing the hollow at the base of his throat.

Unable to resist, she ran her fingers over his taut skin, tracing the line of his collarbone, the striations of muscles over his chest.

His grin flashed white in his olive-toned face. "Yes, we are both of an age to appreciate the opening notes of the dance as well as the finale." His lips brushed hers, his tongue teasing over her lower lip, before he took her mouth with a firmness that melted everything inside her.

His fingers curved inside the laces of her shirt to stroke the insides of her breasts and make her yearn for more.

"I wanted to unlace this downstairs, but I think I'll simply remove it all." With a swift move, he pulled her shirt over her head, eyes lighting in open appreciation of her bare breasts.

With an arm behind her back, he studied her as his hand cupped one breast. His palm was warm and callused as he fondled her.

As heat ignited every cell in her body, her knees wobbled, and he chuckled. "Let's get more comfortable, and then we will talk."

Talk?

He efficiently stripped her of her shoes, jeans, and briefs, then discarded his own clothing.

"What do you mean talk?" Her body was on fire. They could talk later. Much later.

His laugh was wicked as he stretched her out on the cushioned floor and knelt between her spread thighs.

In the faint light from the wall sconces, she could see the shadows dance over the sculpted musculature of his chest and ripped abdominal muscles. *Must touch.* When he leaned forward to kiss her again, she stroked the taut velvety skin of his chest, down his stomach. When she curled her fingers around his magnificently erect shaft, his appreciative growl sent quivers up her spine.

He brushed his lips over her cheek, then kissed her slowly. Thoroughly. Leaving her boneless. Her hands were behind his neck, her fingers in his wavy, dark hair. Soft hair.

His cheek creased. "When I called you Niall's Heather, I realized I'd never thanked you for caring for my brother. For taking him to a healer and tending him afterward." His hands moved over her breasts, teasing the nipples, sending electric shocks straight to her pussy.

"I..." Oh Gods, she needed him inside. "I hit him with my Jeep. Of course I took care of him until he was better."

"Not everyone would. Thank you for saving his life." His perceptive eyes were the color of the darkest chocolates. Smiling slightly, he pinched her nipples, rolling them to almost the point of pain.

Her back arched as heat flared like a wildfire in her pelvis. Her moan didn't sound like her at all.

"Ah, you are fun. Let us see if you taste as divine as you sound."

Her thoughts fled when his lips closed on one nipple. His tongue was so hot and wet her toes curled. He moved to the other, teasing and sucking.

"André." Her voice was a husky groan.

Then he moved down, kissing and nipping her belly, then her mound. He opened her labia, exposing her with a hum of satisfaction.

She tensed, waiting...waiting.

Slowly, he licked over her pussy, nibbling the folds, circling her clit, delving deeper inside until everything woke into pleasure and throbbed with need.

It was full moon, and her body was making urgent demands. "Inside. I want you inside me."

"Of course you do." His French accent had increased, and his deeply masculine voice held amusement. "And I will be...eventually."

When she tried to pull his hair to move him, he captured her wrists. With one hand, he pinned both wrists to her stomach as he continued to torture her so skillfully that everything spiraled out of control.

Without even a warning, a violent storm of sensation roared through her veins in an explosive release.

"Gods." Her ears were ringing as she gasped for breath. When she tried to pull her hands free from his grip, he released her.

But he didn't move to cover her with his body.

"André?"

"I fear I am not yet satisfied, *ma louloutte*." Lips quirking, he regarded her for a long moment as she tried to get her breathing under control. "That was too much fun to stop at one."

Then he bent his head, his tongue tracing a circle over her clit, lightly, slowly.

"What are you doing?"

"*Mmmm*. Everything." With terrifying skill, he drew her right back to a crescendo of need, then slid his fingers inside her.

The stunning pleasure of the intimate penetration sent her over into another convulsing climax.

This time, it took her a minute before her eyes would focus. Had she ever had anyone simply *play* her body like this before? "André."

"*Oui*. I'm glad you remember my name." He nipped her inner thigh, sending off more aftershocks. "One more time, for my own enjoyment. And yours."

He didn't stop until another long rolling orgasm left her sated and limp on the cushions, her full moon heat thoroughly quenched for the moment.

Chuckling, he lay down beside her, his arm over her stomach, his hand on her breast.

"You haven't... Don't you want to get off too?"

"I will, pretty wolf." André licked his lips. The taste of her was pure decadence. But she'd probably hit him if he took her to another climax. "I certainly will." He covered her lips with his, coaxing her into responding. Her kisses were as exquisite as her voice.

He smiled down at her, pleased by the unfocused look in her stunning eyes. It was the perfect time to get a candid answer to his question.

Nipping her lower lip, he pulled back enough to ask, "I was wondering, do you enjoy being shared with littermates?"

"I... What? Um, yes, maybe, sometimes?"

Pressed against her side with one hand cupped around a sweetly small breast, he could feel her quivering response as well as hear it. "Why only sometimes?"

She blinked, obviously trying to order her thoughts. *No, no...* He didn't want a polite answer; he wanted raw honesty. So he took a beautifully reddened nipple between his fingers and rolled it... and watched her thoughts fragment. "Tell me, Heather."

"Tell...oh, sharing." She swallowed. "Like one-on-ones, really, the act can be horrible. Or boring."

Ah, yes, he understood, having experienced both. But never from the receiving end, which would add a paw to the horrible side of the scale. For him, sharing a female with his brothers had always been wonderful. He also liked one-on-one, as it held a different kind of intimacy. And let him concentrate and observe without any distractions. "Can having two or three be better than one?"

"Yes, sometimes," she whispered and didn't elaborate.

If she thought his curiosity was satisfied, she was quite wrong. He licked a line along her collarbone, enjoying the slight saltiness of her skin. "What makes it better?"

When she didn't answer, he smiled and slid a hand down the tender skin of her belly.

"Heather, what makes being shared better?" Breathing could reveal as much as skin—and hers hitched when his fingers stopped at the edge of her pussy, just above the swollen knot of nerves. Was it bad how much he adored sensually tormenting her?

Her hips tilted up as the full moon heat started to take her again.

He didn't move. Simply waited, holding her gaze.

She swallowed. "There can be so many sensations, like a deluge, and everything else goes away."

Ah, this one would, of course, live too much in her head. He found the same joy at losing himself in physical pleasures. "You don't achieve the same results with one male?"

Because he thought she had already with him.

"Yes, but with two males, it lasts longer."

Of course. And there was his answer. He and his brothers could give her this pleasure.

He slid his hand down, his finger grazing her clit for her reward. His reward was the joy of her indrawn breath.

Then she gave him another tidbit: "I've never been with more than two at once."

Hmm. If she liked two tonight, they'd see about giving her three in the future, wouldn't they? Smiling, he moved on top of her and took her mouth.

It was time. He couldn't monopolize her time all night, much as he'd enjoy it.

Propping himself up on one arm, he slowly entered her. "This time, we will end together," he whispered.

· · ·

By the Mother. Heather tipped her head back, stunned at the delicious pleasure. Her tissues were swollen, and he felt...divine. Rather than the usual shove-it-in style of many males, this was a slow, sensuous slide. Filling her, inch by inch, in a slow, merciless invasion.

Intimately joining their bodies together.

His gaze trapped her as he seated himself fully. "You feel even better than I'd imagined...and I have a very good imagination."

When she couldn't find any words, his white teeth flashed in a quick smile.

"Now, *ma chère,* let us dance." He ruthlessly wrapped her legs around his waist, removing any hint of control from her.

And then he started to move, slowly increasing to deep, driving thrusts. Taking her and making her his. Part of her was animal, and the wolf responded to the full moon, submitted to his domination, to his relentless strokes.

Her mind blanked out as the sensations grew and grew. Until the hot glide of flesh on flesh filled her world, building to a crescendo, and sending her into a soul-shattering climax.

This time, he joined her with a deep purr of male satisfaction as he poured himself into her.

A while later, they'd showered in the sparkling clean, tiny bath. Heather couldn't stop smiling. "The whole Gathering house feels so much nicer."

"I'm pleased. We did good work, yes?" He dried her back, stroking his hands over her bare skin in open affection. Staying connected.

As they walked down the stairs, his fingers tangled with hers as if he was unwilling to release her yet.

The happy warmth simmering inside her disappeared downstairs when she heard the shouts and growls. A high yelp sounded before two loud thuds.

"Sorry for the noise, people," Niall called out in a cheerful voice. "Go on with the fun."

She followed André to the center of the living room where Niall held a male down while Madoc handcuffed his ankles, then his hands behind his back.

To her surprise, her brothers Daniel and Tanner were doing the same to another male. They froze at the sight of André.

"Cosantir." Daniel bowed his head, followed by Tanner.

"Very nice work." André nodded to them, then looked at his brother. "Cahir, if you would dispose of our little shrews outside?" He made a sweeping gesture toward the door.

"Your will, Cosantir." Niall grabbed a downed male by a collar. Madoc did the same, and they dragged the poor idiots out to the front porch.

Laughter followed the red-faced handcuffed males.

"You came up with quite the punishment." Tanner shoved his hands into his jeans pockets.

"Isn't it though?" Heather shook her head. So much embarrassment combined with sexual frustration would make any male think before starting a brawl.

André was a scarily effective Cosantir.

From nearby, Moya said, "I knew there would be at least one fight tonight."

"This is why a lot of us females go to Cold Creek for Gatherings." Normally soft-spoken, Talitha had raised her voice. "There isn't any brawling allowed in the Wild Hunt tavern."

"Last month, a male asked me why there are fewer and fewer females here for full moons." Moya raised her voice as well. "Well, *duh*."

Several young males looked stunned, as if a bear had swatted their brains out.

Heather bumped a shoulder against Daniel. "Dudes, nice work."

Daniel gave her a quick squeeze.

"Hey, sis." Tanner did the same from her other side, making her feel like a dwarf between giants.

She realized André was watching, smiling slightly.

"Cosantir, may I introduce my brothers, Daniel and Tanner? They have a ranch northeast of here, not far from Ailill Ridge."

Her brothers bowed their heads and said together, "Cosantir."

André tilted his head. "Thank you for helping with the fight."

"We've had plenty of practice." Daniel grinned. "The ranch hands are always getting into it."

"Actually," Tanner said, "since we weren't available to help fix up this house, we'd like to take a shift as...as whatever you're calling security people."

"Bouncers," Heather said, "is what they're called in human nightclubs."

"A bouncer. Sounds like a dwarf on drugs." Daniel grinned. "I like it."

"I'll take you up on your generous offer." André glanced toward the front door. "My brothers would undoubtedly like to be off at the same time."

"We're on it, then." Daniel eyed André. "I have to say, dumping idiots on the porch is a terrifying solution. Were you the alpha of a wolf pack?"

"No. Unlike this lovely wolf"—André's appreciative gaze swept over Heather and made her stomach quiver—"I'm a cat. I was with the RCMP. Canadian Mounties frown on brawling."

"And so...the handcuffs." Tanner grinned.

"More are available in the locked kitchen drawer." André pulled a set of keys from his pocket and handed a key to Tanner.

"We're glad you're here, Cosantir. Consider us on bouncer duty until you relieve us." Daniel squeezed Heather's shoulder. "See you later, sis."

As they moved off to patrol the crowd, she could hear Tanner saying, "He's fucking efficient. Nice."

Laughing, Madoc and Niall came back in.

Lurking by the door, Gretchen snagged the cahir's arm. "Oh Niall," she cooed, hanging on his arm. "No one here is as strong as you are."

Turning slightly, she smirked at Brett and Roger who sat on a nearby couch.

When the two wolves glared at Niall, Heather realized she hadn't seen Pete at all. He must have driven to a different territory for the full moon.

"Cahir." Gretchen rubbed her breasts on Niall's arm. "Let's go upstairs." Again, she looked over at Roger and Brett to see if they were watching.

"Honestly," Heather muttered. "She causes a lot of the fights here."

"Some females always do." André took her hand. "But she won't be as successful in the future. Fighting outside without witnesses isn't particularly satisfying, especially once it snows."

Heather laughed. "There's that."

Seeing Madoc, Gretchen reached for him too.

Madoc dodged—and deserted his brother, crossing to join André and Heather. "Sucks to be a cahir or Cosantir." He grinned at André. "You should have known better; if the God calls, just say no."

André rubbed the back of his neck. "Brawd, why didn't you share your wisdom before I answered?"

Madoc's laugh was a bass rumble like Moya's Harley motorcycle.

As Heather's heat began to rise again, tingles of awareness sparked to life inside her. The bear had an intriguing scent, and his shoulders were tantalizingly broad. Although appealing laugh lines framed his mouth, his eyes spoke of a painful past.

A high, angry squeal sounded when Niall tossed Gretchen

onto Roger's lap. The cahir stalked across the room to Madoc and glared. "Abandonment in the face of danger? You were no help."

Whoa, doggies. Niall was stunning when he was annoyed.

He turned his attention to her. "Why didn't you rescue me, cruel female?"

She sniffed. "Like the way you rescued me after André pounced on me in the forest?" After bowling her over, the big cougar had lain across her, grooming her neck fur...and Niall simply watched with a cat smirk.

"True, I was bad. And far be it from me to deny a female her revenge on a full moon night." A dimple appeared in Niall's cheek even as he held her gaze.

The floor beneath her feet no longer felt quite solid, and a worried...aroused...sound escaped her.

"Sounds like an invitation to me." André took her right hand and placed it in Niall's. "My brother, for you."

Niall gripped her hand firmly.

Then André took her left hand and gave it to Madoc. "And for you, brawd."

What?

Her breath thickened in her throat as a sultry heat rose within her.

Madoc was watching her carefully. Lifting her hand, he brushed his lips against the inside of her wrist and inhaled.

Undoubtedly, he could scent her interest. But he still waited, one eyebrow rising.

Niall kissed her fingertips. And waited.

Two at once. Was this why André had asked her earlier about more than one?

And she'd answered him, hadn't she.

She straightened her spine despite the quivering deep inside her. "Yes," she said to Niall, turned to Madoc and smiled. "And yes."

Before entering the mating room, Madoc and his brother had already silently established it was Niall's turn to mate. It seemed only fair; Niall had been interested in Heather from the beginning.

So, while Niall took the enticing female, Madoc simply enjoyed himself. She kissed beautifully, and her breasts were beautifully formed, the rosy-pink nipples sweet on his tongue.

And the little sounds she made in her husky voice made him harder than he'd ever been in his life.

She gave herself to them freely, with no demands, no artificial poses. When he sucked on her nipples, her hands were in his hair, holding him to her. When Niall thrust harder, driving her up, her fingernails dug into Madoc's scalp, making him chuckle.

And her scent... As a bear, he was, perhaps, ruled overly much by his nose. He licked under her breast, inhaling the bouquet of all she was, and felt her quiver.

"Now, brawd," Niall murmured.

Teasing her by rubbing his beard-covered chin over her swollen breasts, he took a nipple between his fingers, pinching firmly. Closing his lips on the other nipple, he pressed it gently between his teeth.

Her head went back as she climaxed, her hands gripping his hair hard enough to hurt. Gods, this one was fun.

It was a shame females never wanted a second male after the first, at least, not during full moon when it took a while for their heat to rise again. Usually, a female would rise after her climax, shower, and leave the mating room. Practical shifters, females were.

But...Heather was pulling Niall down on her other side, cuddling with both of them.

Cuddling.

She was on her back, her head pillowed on Madoc's biceps, her lush hair a coolness over his arm.

Stroking over her incredibly soft skin, he tried to get over his surprise.

He'd enjoyed sleeping piles of shifters before, of course he had. But only when in fur. This... He put a finger under her chin, turned her head toward him.

Although she'd already reached her release, she let him kiss her. No, more—she welcomed his kiss. And his touch.

He couldn't stop, as if his hand was drawn to her skin like a magnet to the North Pole. Her nipples had gone from tight peaks to soft and flat, as languid as the rest of her body.

Yet she didn't rise and shower. Didn't leave.

He stared at her for a moment.

Niall met his gaze, equally perplexed. Then his brother simply smiled in a *let's enjoy it* kind of way.

Despite his aching cock, Madoc was in complete agreement.

Her lips were reddened from his kisses. Enjoying the sight, he ran a finger over her lower lip and was startled when she kissed it. *Well, then.*

His fingers stroked over her, learning her. Her forehead was high, her eyebrows perfect arches. Her eyes were closed. Her long, thick eyelashes were slightly darker than her sun-lightened hair, maybe the same color as the freckles dotting her cheeks and nose.

"No makeup," he said to Niall, then wanted to smack himself for breaking the moment.

"When I stopped wanting mates, it didn't seem worth the effort." She opened her eyes, and he was still stunned at their mesmerizing blue-green color. A corner of her mouth tipped up. "On Gathering nights, most males don't see past a top that shows a bit of breast."

A laugh broke from him. "You know males too well."

"Mmm." She took his hand, pressing small kisses to it, shocking him right down to his paws.

She was...sweet. Where had the infinitely practical Heather gone? This one—he didn't know how to deal with this one.

Moving his hand to her cheek, he kissed her again. By the God, he liked kissing her.

Then he ran his fingers down her neck, over her collarbones. The silky skin stretched over her and made lickable hollows.

Her breasts—he'd already explored them thoroughly, and Niall was staking his claim there.

Dropping lower, Madoc stroked over the slight curve of her belly and used his teeth lightly on the tempting softness. When he flattened his hand over her mound, she pulled in a startled, excited breath in the most adorable of sounds.

And then she laughed and rolled on top of Niall. After kissing him, she rose onto hands and knees, moving down the cahir's body until she straddled his thighs. She turned to look at Madoc —"Come and play, bear"—and waggled her ass.

He went into shock—but his cock shot right to attention.

His brother looked as nonplused as Madoc felt. No female ever allowed them seconds.

Niall took her face between his hands. "Heather, are you sure?"

"I don't say things I don't mean." Her lips quirked as she smiled at them. "You two kept touching me; now I'm all hot. Do something about it, won't you?"

Madoc's voice came out more of a growl than human. "I can do that."

Heather braced her hands on Niall's broad shoulders and enjoyed the thick muscles beneath her palms. Between her knees, she could feel his thighs moving apart, making room for his brother—and spreading her apart at the same time.

She shivered as the cahir's big hands cupped her dangling breasts. The two had more than satisfied her the first time, as if to drive home what she'd told André about the wondrous nature of having two at once. It was very rare she reached the amazing place where her world expanded to encompass the universe.

Afterward, even though satiated, she was pleased to simply cuddle and kiss—and willing for more. But then the slow exploration they'd done afterward—especially Madoc—had driven her right into a needy burn far sooner than should have happened.

And how amazing the hard-faced bear could be so gentle. So obviously unaccustomed to the simple enjoyment of leisurely touching. Whoever had made him so uncomfortable with relationships should be dumped in a pile of horse dung.

Between Niall's legs, Madoc knelt behind her. And rather than driving into her, his hands massaged her bottom. "So smooth."

His bass had gone even deeper to a subterranean growl. The calluses on his hands were slightly abrasive, an added sensation, like a counterpoint to Niall's fondling of her breasts.

Then Madoc's fingers slid through the wetness between her legs and up to her clit. The exquisite sensation blazed a trail of fire right through her body. "*Gods.*"

As her arms went boneless, she tried to straighten up.

Niall's hard hands caught her shoulders, holding her in place. His eyes filled with mischief. "I trapped our pretty wolf. Make her howl."

There was a low laugh behind her, then Madoc gripped her hip, holding her ass still as his fingers explored her pussy, her clit, up inside, teasing until her whole lower half throbbed with need.

"Gods, please." Her breath burned in her lungs as she trembled, realizing Niall was holding her up.

"That's a good howl," Madoc growled. And she felt him replace his hard fingers with his shaft at her entrance. Slowly, inexorably, he sheathed himself, the fullness almost unbearable.

She stretched around him, the friction painfully delicious, and he didn't stop. He was impossibly thick in girth, and she panted, straining to accommodate him.

Then she felt his groin pressing against her buttocks as he sheathed himself completely inside her. A shudder of need shook her.

Rather than thrusting, he reached around her to slide a finger up and down over her clit.

"Oh, oh!" The overload of brutal pleasure heightened as she clenched around the huge penetration within.

And then he was pulling out, sliding back in, his finger keeping up the same rhythm as his cock.

The deep driving thrusts continued in a devastatingly controlled rhythm. And everything in her simply let go, overwhelmed by the multitude of sensations—Niall's hard grip on her shoulders, pinning her in place, the fingers stroking her clit, the long heavy thrusts.

A mind-shattering climax crashed over her.

She heard the rumbling sound of pleasure behind her, then Madoc gripped her hips and hammered into her, hard and fast, before plunging deep, joining her in pleasure.

God, Gods. She was panting as if she'd run over a mountain or two. But everything in her felt like a glorious molten pool.

Madoc closed his arms around her. His chest was against her back, and his hair spilled over her shoulders in a cool wave.

Carefully, Niall moved her arms and eased her down onto his chest. Somehow, he rolled them all onto their sides, so she was held between the two males. Her head was pillowed on someone's biceps. Madoc was still deep inside her, and she could feel him press a kiss to the back of her head.

With a sigh and a wiggle, she closed her eyes.

Can I stay here forever?

CHAPTER TWENTY-TWO

After the Gathering, Heather slept most of the morning away rather than dragging herself out of bed to go to work. There were benefits to not owning a company.

It was a gray, drizzly day, typical of late September weather, and she was grateful for her waterproof hoodie as she walked down the square to Espresso Books.

Inside, she waved at Talitha, who was manning the latte machine.

Moya was sitting at a table close to the book section and already had a coffee, as well as a plate of pastries, for Heather.

"Perfect. It's cold out there!" Heather took a seat and picked up her coffee. "I so need this. Are you dragging too?"

"Totally." Moya smiled. "Although last night was wonderfully different. There was only one fight, and I can't believe what a difference the remodeling made. I swear, some of the younger females went upstairs extra times just to try out the various rooms."

Heather laughed. "I was in two. One looked like summer and the other felt like an Arabian palace."

"I dragged the Cosantir's brother—Madoc—up to what I've

dubbed the purple room." Moya grinned. "He has a great laugh, doesn't he?"

The stab of possessiveness was totally unexpected—something she'd never felt before and shouldn't be feeling at all, not for a mating under a full moon. What was wrong with her?

But at least Moya would have been far sweeter with Madoc than someone like Gretchen. And Madoc deserved all the sweetness in all the world. She smiled at her friend. "He does. They all do."

"Mmm." Moya nibbled on a scone. "After the Cosantir, I saw his brothers taking you upstairs. You go, girl."

"Thanks, I guess." After hearing the way her voice had gone stupidly breathless, she bit into a donut to prevent herself from talking. Even now, she could feel André's hand on hers, giving her over to his brothers. How Niall hadn't released her. How the two had...

The slow welling of heat inside was disconcerting, as was the knowledge she wanted them again, wanted their hands on her. Wanted to hear Madoc's deep growl, see André's wicked smile as he forced her into another orgasm, enjoy Niall's hard hands, so very gentle on her breasts.

Gods help her.

"But... I wondered." Moya's brows drew together. "Were they... Why did you want two at once?"

Ah. Sometimes Heather forgot her friend was in her midtwenties, younger than Vicki, even. Whatever Moya had lived through in her teens must have been ugly—and then her introduction to sex had left her cautious. "You've never been with two males?"

"Uh-uh." Moya grimaced. "I have enough trouble dealing with one, even when in heat."

Heather reached across the table and patted her hand. "It's getting better, though?"

"It is." Moya crumbled a few pieces of her scone, then her

smile appeared again. "So what is it like with two? Why would you do that?"

Laughing, Heather told her about the overwhelming fun of mating with two.

"But you were up there for a long time. Why? I thought once you get off, you come back downstairs."

Her innocent friend. Heather shook her head. "If the mating wasn't particularly great, yes. However, if it was wonderful and if I like the males, then it's nice to let the second one have a turn." With Madoc and Niall, the way they'd simply...enjoyed...touching her afterward, they'd driven her right into *demanding* a second round.

What a lovely round it had been too. She felt her cheeks heat.

"And the Cosantir?" Moya grinned. "Was he god-like?"

"Totally." Heather laughed. Because...it wasn't a lie.

"In that case—" Moya stopped as a customer with an armload of books crossed to the bookstore counter. "Oops, excuse me for a minute."

As Moya greeted the female, Heather leaned back and sipped her coffee, thinking about the previous night.

So amazing and intense. The Crichton brothers were simply irresistible. Why did she have to like them so much? And want to be with them again?

No, girl. A mating during Gathering was a simple act with no ensuing entanglements or expectations. And that was the way she wanted it.

Dreams were for the young. She knew better than to hope for more than last night—especially with males like them. Even if Niall and André hadn't been Gods-called, the three would be popular with females. They were intelligent, perceptive, generous in mating, and physically...simply stunning.

Which meant if they'd wanted a mate, they'd already have one. So there was that.

It was good she'd made it clear she didn't want anything more than an occasional mating during Gatherings. There were no expectations on anyone's part.

She rubbed her sternum to try to relieve the ache beneath... because she wanted more. *Don't be a fool.* If she got involved with them and the relationship didn't work out—they never did—she'd be shattered past any hope of mending.

"So what are you in town for?" Moya asked.

Heather jumped, then laughed. "Merely a bank run. Then to the Cosantir's house for more work on the clan's accounts."

"I love that you're finding work here. This is where you belong."

Heather half-smiled, thinking of the numerous job offers she'd received since selling the company. Yet it'd been easy to say no to them. Because she had more interesting projects on her plate. "Did I tell you Madoc hired me to help with the restaurant? We've made so much progress it'll open on the sixth."

Moya's happy squeal drew everyone's notice.

Looking around, Heather called, "I told her the Shamrock Restaurant is re-opening a week from Saturday."

Everyone cheered. She wasn't the only person to enjoy food she didn't have to prepare, let alone clean up after.

Smiling, she returned to their conversation. "Since I'm staying put, I'm going to see about finding a few more clients."

Moya's eyes became glassy with tears for a second. "I'm so glad. I didn't want to tell you how much I would miss you if you left."

Heather put a hand over her friend's. Despite what she'd thought, not everyone had left her. She had some really wonderful friends.

Hearing the chime over the pounding rain, Madoc opened the front door, and there was Heather on the porch.

Her hair was drenched, and raindrops glistened on her eyelashes. "You look like a drowned pup."

"Such a compliment." Her laugh was husky and far too appealing, reminding him of how she'd sounded the night before. Right before she'd offered herself to him.

Gods, she was enchanting. Niall's bite mark showed on her neck. The cat liked to use his teeth. Her lips were still slightly swollen, and he wondered if her nipples were as well.

No, bear. Females were different in real life than on Gathering nights. In fact, they had completely separate personalities at various times.

He'd learned the hard way.

Shutting the door behind her, he took a few steps back to establish an appropriate distance between them. "André's in his office."

She cocked her head, a wrinkle forming between her eyebrows. "All right. Thank you." Her tone was pleasant, her smile polite.

He watched her walk away. Surely he hadn't seen hurt in her eyes.

They'd had fun last night; he'd be the first to admit it, but that was all there was to it.

Unsettled, he headed for the kitchen, needing to cook. Maybe he'd make some molasses cookies. For himself.

A few days ago, he'd treated Niall to Nanaimo bars. The cahir loved the chocolaty-yellow custard bars. Then he'd made *pouding chomeur*, a caramelly upside-down cake for André.

But there was nothing like the smell and taste of chewy molasses cookies like the ones his sire's sister made when he was a cub.

As he gathered the ingredients and started, he tried to work out what felt like a horde of foxtails under his fur.

Last night had been a Gathering—and he'd mated with females. Nice ones. Nothing new there.

He'd shared a female with his brother. Nothing new, either, yet the mating with Heather still lingered in his mind, like an elusive scent on a breeze.

Why? Because he'd already known her before the Gathering?

Automatically, he started measuring ingredients into the mixing bowl. Sugar, butter, eggs, molasses...

That couldn't be it. He and his brothers usually stayed in a town for two or three years. He'd mated with several females more than once.

He set the vanilla down, frowning. But had he ever *talked* to them? More than what was needed to undress and have sex?

No.

They'd talked more than he was used to last night. Had laughed together.

His brows drew together. Before and after the mating, she'd been as comfortable to be with as...as molasses cookies were to eat. Because he'd worked with her on the restaurant business. Had eaten with her. As a bear, he'd played with the little wolf.

He'd mated a female who wasn't a stranger.

And he liked her.

A cold sensation crept up his spine. He'd made that mistake with a female before.

CHAPTER TWENTY-THREE

In the town square, Niall tried to spot the youngling pickpockets. As far as he could tell, they stuck to the side of the square near the park.

For a while, whenever he'd seen them, they looked better. Still underweight, but cleaner. Clothing decent. No air of desperation. Not thieving.

But now, it appeared they were back to dirty clothes and hair. And scoping out targets.

Did they have an alcoholic parent who went on a bender at intervals?

He wished he knew if they were Daonain or not. Surely if they were clan, someone would be looking out for them.

Well, waiting for them to show themselves wasn't working. And they looked hungry. Time to try something else.

A discarded lunchbox in their garage had given him this idea. After a washing, he'd filled it with granola bars, juice boxes, and jerky. The stuff would keep even if not found right away.

Now, to see if he could find where they ran to when leaving the square.

He canvased the long stretch of park beside the creek. And

there, beneath the pedestrian bridge, he spotted what might be the cublings' nest.

Propped up against a concrete abutment, ragged plywood formed a lean-to. There were a few ratty blankets and a backpack with clothing spilling out of it. A sagging box probably held their few treasures.

Their scents were fresh, and he smelled no one else. Yes, this was their spot...and they obviously had no adult caring for them.

Fuck this heartless world. The cubs were homeless.

In a nearby alder tree, a pixie watched him suspiciously, like he was a jay robbing another bird's nest.

He set the lunchbox inside the lean-to, and guilt stabbed at him. This felt an awful lot like he was baiting a trap. Yes, he was.

But he sure couldn't help them if he couldn't talk with them. And after the way he scared them the first time, they'd run if seeing him.

And by the Gods, they were quick.

This wasn't going to be easy. But...he'd do his best to see them safe and happy.

CHAPTER TWENTY-FOUR

Walking into the Shamrock, Heather almost did a dance of joy. The dark hardwood floor gleamed as did the brass lamps on the walls. The tables and chairs were in place. Dishes had been delivered. The staff had been hired. And the whole town was delighted to have the restaurant open again.

The scrumptious aroma coming from the kitchen made her stomach growl.

Since the restaurant would open this Saturday—four days away—Madoc had been testing his menu to ensure he had everything he needed, and all the equipment worked. *Mmmm.* Today must be pizza day.

Talking him out of a slice or two shouldn't be difficult. The male loved to feed people—even her.

No, the disgruntled thought wasn't fair to him or her. He didn't dislike her. He simply treated her with the same distant politeness he used with any female younger than an Elder. As if he'd never kissed her, never played with her breasts, never been inside her.

She couldn't even resent his behavior since it was the same way she wanted to treat all the males in all the world.

Yet, when he walked out of the kitchen, her heart still sped up, even though it'd been well over a week since the full moon.

By the Gods, she had fewer brains than a pixie.

His courteous smile didn't reach his eyes. "Heather, what's up?"

"Nothing for you. I have to drop off some paperwork for André." She returned his smile. Politely. "I just came in this door to see how everything looked over here."

"Ah."

"The restaurant is beautiful, Madoc. From what I'm hearing, the place will be crowded on opening night."

Feeling her eyes prickle with tears, she strode quickly across the room, escaping through the shared double doors to the gift shop.

She almost ran into André.

"Heather, how—" His smile died. Setting her bag on the floor, he pulled her into his arms. "*Ma chère*, what has hurt you?"

The sympathy in his dark resonant voice almost undid her, and she blinked hard to hold back the tears. "N-nothing."

He made a French sound in the back of his throat, a huffed noise disputing what she'd said.

"No, really. I'm fine. It was a...a female moment."

"I see." He looked past her, through the open door to the restaurant. "I suppose we can leave it at that. For now."

She started to relax.

"And you say you feel fine. I'd have to agree—you truly do feel fine." He drew her closer, right up against his hard body, illuminating exactly what he meant.

Her hands closed on the steely bulge of his biceps, and she found herself totally breathless at how good it felt to be held.

All week, he'd been moving closer, holding her hands, stroking her hair, touching her face. Whenever she saw him, the flirtatious dance made her senses tingle and heated her body.

And here she was in his arms and couldn't think of anywhere

else she wanted to be. Except, no, she wasn't going to do this. "André." She tried to put a protest in the word—and realized it came out throaty and entreating.

He cupped the back of her head and...kissed her. His firm lips moved lazily over hers. When she parted her lips, he took advantage, sinking deeper, kissing her with an unshakable insistence that melted her bones.

"Well, well, well." Niall's smooth baritone came from behind her. He'd come through the gift shop's second door—the one to the busy square. "Stealing kisses should put you in a good mood, brawd."

"It did." André rubbed his cheek against her hair. "But my cahir, I would hate to be selfish."

Leaving the door open, Niall prowled forward, his green gaze trapping hers. "Well, if you're sharing, I haven't had a kiss from our pretty wolf for an entire week."

Without a word, André handed her over to his brother, who pulled her up against him.

Niall's arms were unyielding, his mouth disconcertingly gentle...and his kiss just as passionate.

Leaning against her from behind, André nibbled on her shoulder.

Sandwiched between the two powerful males, she quivered as heat engulfed her.

"Want to come home with us?" Niall asked. "Be with us tonight?"

"N-no. No." And her breathy answer lacked any conviction. So she made her voice firm and loud. "No, I'm heading for Cold Creek. I'll spend the night with my friends."

From behind Heather came a familiar high voice. "You... You..."

She turned far enough to see Gretchen in the doorway. The blonde's eyes burned with fury before she stomped back out, slamming the door behind her.

"I suppose it's somewhat indiscreet to be kissing our accountant in a place of business." André chuckled and nipped the back of her neck before stepping away.

"Rules, so many rules." Eyes dancing with laughter, Niall kissed her lips and released her. "How about tomorrow night, *a thaisce?* Shall we continue then?"

"Yes." She blinked. "No, I mean no. We can't do this." This was insane...yet the need to step back into their arms made her tremble.

"But"—Niall frowned—"we did do this."

"No, we shouldn't. Won't." *Gods.* She grabbed her tote bag and dropped the paperwork from it on the desk. "I'll...I'll see you tomorrow, André, like we planned. Nine at the communal house." Moving fast, almost running, she escaped the gift shop.

Niall's voice drifted out behind her, "I like her, brawd," followed by André's low chuckle.

In front of the café, Talam scattered the crumbs from his peanut butter sandwich on the bricks. The birds would like them.

Next to him on the bench, Sky did the same. "Who do you figure left the sandwiches—Heather or the cahir?"

"Probably Heather. She looks like a sandwich sorta person." Talam didn't know why, but the red-haired female had left food at their den a few times.

She was nicer than the big cahir who'd try to catch them after, like they were stupid or something. The pixie always warned them, and they'd stay away until he gave up.

He brought good food, though.

Talam turned sideways to keep an eye on Mr. Wendell. The Cosantir—no, the *old* Cosantir—had come out of the bar and was glaring at the Shamrock restaurant across the square.

Would he be getting kids together to take to a city?

Talam sighed. Even if he did, they wouldn't get to work. He'd seen them and turned his back.

Why'd the male have to get so mad? They needed to work. Bad.

Their money ran out a few days ago, and it wasn't easy to pick pockets here. There weren't any big stores, either. And even if they lifted stuff, where could they sell it for money?

The sandwiches had helped, but he was really hungry and so was Sky.

A slamming door at the Shamrock made Talam jump.

Gretchen stomped away like someone had toasted her paws over a fire.

"Whoa, she's really pissed off," Sky whispered.

"Yeah." Talam glanced at Sky. "We sure won't try to pick her pockets."

Sky snorted. Yesterday, they'd been scavenging in the garbage cans behind the B&B, and she'd yelled and thrown rocks at them when they ran.

"Gretchen," Mr. Wendell called. "Were the mangy fleabags bothering you?"

"It was *Heather*!" The blonde crossed to talk to him in a screechy voice that made Talam's ears hurt. "The disgusting, old, bat-eared bitch was coming on to the Cosantir. And now she's off to spend the night in Cold Creek, and she'll probably fuck every male there too."

"Heather." The way Mr. Wendell growled the name made Talam's stomach twist in fear. "She brought Crichton here, and I lost everything. It's *her* fault."

Gretchen kept ranting. "I heard she was going to leave Rainier Territory, but nooo, she's staying. Why doesn't she just *leave*? She makes me so mad! Maybe I should run her over with my car or burn her house down or..."

Giggling, Sky wiggled his fingers over his head.

Talam choked. Because his brother was right—she was waving her hands in the air like a drunken gnome.

When Mr. Wendell stopped talking, Gretchen snapped something at him and stomped away.

Talam rolled his eyes. Back when he or Sky got stompy, Mama'd say they were *"obviously cublings in need of a nap"* and would send them to bed for an hour.

He missed her.

Still in front of the bar, Mr. Wendell was staring at the Shamrock again. When he smiled really mean, it made Talam's stomach feel all shivery.

"Want to go back to our den?" Sky whispered.

Talam scowled. "He's gonna leave soon." They couldn't pick any pockets with him around.

Instead of leaving, Mr. Wendell motioned them over. Was he going to let them work again?

They ran over as quickly as they could.

"Mr. Wendell, sir." Talam tried to look really respectful.

"I'm not one to hire wagtails back, but you were good workers before." Mr. Wendell's eyes narrowed. "I'm going to give you one last chance. I have a special job requiring two workers."

"Sure. We'll do it. Sir." Talam said fast. He glanced at his brother, whose bony wrists stuck out of the ragged shirt. Sky needed food. So did Talam, but Sky really needed it. And it was getting cold.

"Good." The male pulled out a ten-dollar bill and handed it over. "Get something to eat. I need you strong. Then I'll pick you up in the usual spot at five tomorrow morning."

Before sunrise? Talam stared.

Mr. Wendell pulled a cheap watch out of his pocket and handed it to Sky. "This is your only chance. Don't be late."

"We won't." As the male walked away, Talam glanced at his littermate. "Are stores even open before the sun rises?"

That evening, in the Wild Hunt Tavern in the North Cascades Territory, Heather was sitting on a couch near the fireplace and mostly ignoring her friends. Because she had Sorcha in her lap.

Smiling, she handed a small chunk of banana to her favorite girl in all the world. "Here you go, my cubling. I still can't believe you'll be a whole year old in November."

Chortling, Sorcha waved her banana-filled hand in the air, then popped the fruit in her mouth.

So adorable. Rosy-pink cheeks and fluffy, golden hair. Just this month, Sorcha's blue eyes had changed to the same green as Alec's. She also had his sociable nature.

"You are the bestest of babies." Heather's squeeze set off a stream of giggles. Yes, this was what Heather needed. Babies and friends...and no captivating males to confuse her.

A roll of thunder sounded, and rain lashed the big picture windows, making Heather glad she'd arrived before the storm began. Since Calum had started a fire in the huge fireplace, Heather and her friends had taken over their favorite sitting spot near the hearth. Emma and Breanne were on the opposite couch from Heather's. Darcy and Margery were in chairs.

"All right, Heather, time's up." Vicki carried a tray of drinks from the bar, followed by her mate Alec. "Trade you a beer for a baby."

"Nope. That's a poor exchange." Pulling Sorcha closer, Heather kissed the pink cheeks. The baby waved her little arms and let out an infectious peal of laughter.

Everyone grinned.

With a sigh, Heather relinquished her charge to Alec who was cub-watching tonight. He already had black-haired Toren in one arm. Sixteen-year-old Jamie was carrying her half-brother, Artair.

Vicki kissed each cub, then dropped onto the couch beside

Heather as they left. "I can't believe I'm raising three babies and a teenager."

Picking up a beer, Emma raised it in a toast. "In a couple more years, you can hand the littlest ones over to me during the days. I'll teach them how to surf the internet."

Vicki gave her a sour look. "This is all I need—a squad of juvenile computer hackers."

"Actually, if you need an instructor for that, you want Niall." At the interested looks, Heather added, "He's the new cahir in Rainier Territory."

"A computer hacker?" Calum's voice behind her made her jump. The Cosantir was a cat-shifter and as silent as André and Niall. *Sneaky-pawed cougars.*

She turned. "He worked cybersecurity in Canada and knows the business from both sides."

"A Canadian." Calum's eyes narrowed. "The one who Donal treated a month ago? He's still here?"

Whoa, she knew more than Calum for a change? "Did you not hear about Rainier's new Cosantir?"

"I heard, aye." His lips curved slightly. "The God seemed quite chuffed with his new conscript."

Gods actually *talked?* Remembering the unnerving touch of the God on her soul, Heather shuddered. *No, absolutely no.* "As it happens, André Crichton is the new Cosantir, and Niall is his brother."

"Wait." Vicki held up her hand. "Niall and André. From the festival? Weren't they the ones who helped you and Margery when the mercs tried to blindside me?"

"*Mmmhmm.* Their third littermate, Madoc, also came."

"Interesting." Calum raised an eyebrow. "What do you think of your new Cosantir?"

Under his perceptive gray gaze, she felt her cheeks heat. "He's...well, more like you than Pete. Careful, organized, logical."

No, the description made him sound like a CEO. André was far more. "Brilliant. Compassionate."

The females around her leaned in.

"He even unsheathed his claws about the brawling at Gatherings." Grinning, she told them about the two fighters left on the porch all full moon night. "At dawn, Niall released them, and I tell you, they walked bow-legged all the way off the property."

Her friends hooted with laughter.

Calum's grin flashed. "Excellent discipline. I might have to give it a try." He set a hand on her shoulder and murmured in her ear. "To formally call upon the Gods took courage. I'm proud of you."

He walked away, leaving her open-mouthed. How did he know?

"So…" Breanne leaned forward. "What do these new males look like?"

Margery wrinkled her nose. "They're probably as flabby as Pete." The curvy brunette had no love for Pete, who'd trapped her in Rainier Territory. The old Cosantir had figured a banfasa—the Daonain equivalent of a nurse practitioner—was the next best thing to having a healer.

Last spring, Heather had helped her get out of Ailill Ridge. One more thing Pete blamed her for, right?

"No, no, I want to hear. What do they look like?" Emma bounced a little. The bard had an insatiable curiosity.

"*Weeeell*. The Crichton crew certainly aren't out of condition." Heather couldn't suppress a smile. "As a cahir, Niall is as big as Alec, but with clear green eyes and gorgeous platinum-blond hair down to here…" She held her hands to her upper chest to show the length.

"Oooo, yum," Darcy said. "And the Cosantir?"

"He's the dark to Niall's light. Seriously ripped." She shot Margery a grin. "Not even close to flabby. Dark hair, darker eyes, and his voice is like warm whiskey."

Emma sighed. "I adore my males, but...wow."

"What about the third brother? I take it he's the runt of the litter?" Darcy asked.

"Madoc—a runt?" Heather's laugh died as she remembered his overly polite smiles and talk. "Niall and André are cats. Madoc's a bear, almost cahir-sized, but brawny."

"Blonde like Niall?" Vicki asked.

"No, thick, wavy brown hair"—Heather marked the length by patting her shoulders—"warm hazel eyes. He's sociable. Everyone likes him."

"You *like* those brothers, don't you?" Margery looked simply delighted.

She did. She hadn't realized how much until trying to describe them. *Aaand*, she'd better shut this down fast. "Sure—but as friends and, you know, full moon fun. Nothing more."

"Full moon fun, hmm?" Vicki had an evil look in her eyes. "Did you...indulge?"

Honestly, at Heather's age, she should have some control over when she turned red, wouldn't one think?

"She did!" Bree squealed, spilling her drink.

Heather threw a peanut at her. "It was just at a Gathering."

Vicki tilted her head. "I don't remember you turning red before when talking about full moons and past indulgences."

"Exactly." Bree pouted. "Remember when she told us she'd *had* my mate—she didn't bat an eye."

Heather sniffed. "You're acting like a batch of cubs. *Teenaged* cubs."

Heh, she knew the way to change the subject. "Margery, I told Niall I knew a male who went to Canada to find a shifter-counselor. Would you believe it was André and Niall who told your littermate they had a shepherd in their territory?"

Margery's mouth dropped open. "Oliver? Have they seen him?"

"Yep, when he came to the Lammas celebration in August. He's not drinking, is seeing a shepherd, and has a job doing trail maintenance in one of the national forests."

Happiness lit Margery's face. "He's doing all right."

"So it seems. André said he's coming out of the shadows. He's gained weight and muscle. Niall said Oliver was smiling a lot—especially at the females who were enjoying having a new male in town."

"He sent me a letter in August, but..." Margery huffed. "He said nothing more than he was doing all right."

"*Males.*" Darcy made an annoyed chuff. "Communication isn't in their vocabulary."

Looking over Darcy's shoulder, Heather saw the tinker's lifemates, Owen and Gawain, at a nearby table. Undoubtedly having heard Darcy's raised voice, they were watching closely.

Probably to make sure it wasn't them who'd pulled her tail.

Emma grinned and made a guess. "Your brothers?"

"Yes. One whole letter. Patrin and Fell are somewhere. Doing something. And alive." Darcy growled. "I don't even know what they're planning to do or where they'll live when they get done chasing the Scythe."

Chuckling, Heather caught the gazes of Darcy's lifemates and raised her voice. "Darcy, your brothers need a good nip on the tail to teach them to communicate."

Darcy huffed, crossing her arms over her chest. "Exactly."

Owen grinned in relief; Gawain winked at Heather, and they turned back to their own conversation.

Beside Heather, Vicki had obviously followed her gaze, and she let out a huff of a laugh at the big, deadly males, so worried about putting a paw wrong with their mate.

What would it be like to be loved so much?

Heather shook her head. She'd known it from the other side. Opening her heart wasn't going to happen.

Even for the Crichton brothers? *No, girl.* Maybe André and Niall were interested, but Madoc certainly wasn't. She wasn't going to risk everything to have it all fall apart.

Friends, though—friends are worth every risk.

Downing half her glass of beer, she smiled at Emma. "So bard, have any good tales about your Ben, Ryder, and Minette?"

CHAPTER TWENTY-FIVE

In the back seat beside his brother, Talam shivered. His clothes were still wet from the downpour earlier. Their den wasn't very rain-proof.

The van bounced crazily as Mr. Wendell drove down a dirt road filled with ruts and holes.

When the vehicle stopped, Talam undid his seat belt. Peering out the window, he saw a log cabin with a light burning over the porch. Black forest surrounded the clearing.

"Where are we?" His voice cracked on the last word.

"This is the job." Mr. Wendell pointed to the house. "You're going to burn that place down."

What? The shock held Talam silent, but beside him, Sky squeaked like a mouse getting eaten.

I don't want to burn anything. After a second, Talam asked carefully, "May I ask why, Mr. Wendell?"

"A bad person—a human male—lives there and needs to be driven out of the territory to keep our females and cubs safe. So we'll burn his house down and make him move." Mr. Wendell's voice was sharper than the lava rocks on the high slopes.

A bad human like the ones who'd killed shifters last summer? What had Mateo called them—Scythe mercenaries? If it was one of them, they might hurt the females and little cublings in town.

Talam swallowed, wanting to ask more questions. Wanting...proof.

Because Mr. Wendell sometimes lied. Like how he'd promised all the boys fifty dollars apiece, then only gave them half. Or saying he'd never abandon them in a human town, but when a storekeeper caught Farlan and Padraig, he'd left. Driven away. Those two had never come back to Ailill Ridge.

"I don't think we should," Sky whispered. Talam could feel him shaking. "It's not right."

"I don't give a *fuck* what you think." Mr. Wendell was getting louder and louder. "You're going to burn the fucking cabin, right the fuck now. If you ever tell anyone I was here, I'll shift to bear and rip you into tiny pieces. Got that?"

Fear shot through Talam so hard he almost pissed his pants.

"Yes, sir," Sky whispered as he gripped Talam's hand.

"Yes, sir." Talam added, real fast, "But everything's wet. Nothing will burn."

"It will." Mr. Wendell pointed to the back. "Take the tire iron and the bundles of clothing. Put three bundles on the porch, up against the wall. Break the windows and drop the other two inside. Then come back here."

Talam wanted to say they wouldn't do it. Sky was right. They shouldn't burn someone's home.

"Move!" When Mr. Wendell raised his fist, Talam jumped out. Sky followed.

"I don't want to," Sky whispered over the sound of the rain sprinkling the trees. At least it wasn't pouring down like earlier.

"Me, neither." Mr. Wendell might've promised money and to use them as workers again, but...Talam didn't want to work for him anymore. Not never.

Opening the back of the van, he grabbed a twine-wrapped bundle of what looked like old clothes. It was huge, coming to his thighs, and he staggered as he carried it onto the porch.

They got the first three bundles placed on the porch. But then...

Breaking somebody's window felt wrong. Mama wouldn't want him to do this; she'd be really upset. He didn't want to do this.

A scary growl came from the car, and he flinched. Mr. Wendell would hurt them if they didn't finish this job.

Holding his breath, Talam swung the heavy tire iron. The glass broke with a horrible crash. He and Sky hefted up the bundle of fabric and pushed it through the window.

Almost crying, he busted out the other front window and helped Sky shove in the last bundle.

They ran back to the van.

"Good." Mr. Wendell still sat in the front seat, and Talam scowled. The male wasn't going to help at all? "Leave the tire iron on the ground. Get those containers and pour the gas onto the bundles. Use it all."

The big red containers were really heavy. It took both of them to hold a container up and pour gas onto the giant bundles on the porch and inside.

They ran back.

"Toss the containers in the bushes." When they returned, Mr. Wendell handed them each a box of matches. "Light one, toss it onto a bundle. Don't get too close."

As they ran back onto the porch, Talam's stomach was twisting so hard he almost threw up. *This isn't right; it just isn't.* "I'll light the ones inside."

"Okay."

Talam leaned in one window, lit a match, then remembered Mr. Wendell saying not to get too close. After taking a few steps back, he tossed the match.

PHOOM! Flames exploded from the bundle.

"Scat!" Heart hammering, he watched for a second. At the other window, he lit the next bundle—standing much farther away.

"I'm done." He turned.

His brother had already fired the first bundle by the door. Now, Sky was trying to light the one at the end of the porch, but the wind kept blowing out the matches when he tossed them.

He was too close. "Sky, stay farther—"

The match lit, flames exploded up and out, and Sky *screamed*.

"No!" Talam tore across the porch. Grabbing his brother, he yanked off the burning jacket and slapped the little flames out off his shirt.

Sky was crying, half screaming. Spotting a birdbath, Talam pulled his brother there and splashed cold water onto his face and chest. And hands. Patches of his skin were horribly red and black.

"It's okay, Sky, you'll be—"

With a popping sound, the porch light burst leaving the area in darkness except for the burning cabin.

"C'mon," Talam helped Sky to his feet. "Mr. Wendell probably has—"

Over the noise of the crackling fire came the sound of a car starting. And moving away.

"He *left* us." Talam swallowed hard. Mr. Wendell had left them here—miles and miles from home.

In her Jeep, Heather yawned and opened the window to let in more of the cold dawn air. A couple of hours on Vicki's couch hadn't been nearly enough sleep, but she'd had one too many beers to risk driving back right away.

Some tiredness was worth it to see her friends in Cold Creek. Although if she'd been thinking, she'd have rescheduled the communal house meeting with André to later today. As it was, she'd have barely enough time to feed Greystoke, shower, and change her clothes.

Ah well.

Slowing, she turned the car onto her tiny dirt road, squinting against the slanting rays of sunrise.

The long night drive had been pleasant. She'd had time to think. And to enjoy the moist air after the rain. Soon, the snows would come to strand her in her little house for days at a time. Snow tires could only overcome so much, after all.

But this year would be—

Is that smoke? She sniffed the air. No one lived close enough for her to smell their fireplace or woodstove, and after last night's rain, there sure wouldn't be a wildfire.

She stepped harder on the gas pedal.

Smoke thickened as she sped down her muddy dirt road fast enough to slide around the curves. The flickering light through the trees set her heart to pounding.

Her cabin was on *fire*.

No, oh gods, no. In the middle of the clearing, she stomped on the brakes, and the Jeep skidded to a stop. Shutting it off, she ran across the stubby grass.

The whole front of the cabin was on fire all the way to the wood-shingled roof. Flames shot high into the gray sky.

Greystoke. He was inside. Trapped.

Panicking, she tore around the house to the back. It wasn't yet on fire. Fumbling her key, she unlocked the back door and rushed in, snatching up the small cat carrier from the laundry room on the way past. "Greystoke. *Greystoke*, where are you?"

No answer.

But he hid when he was scared. He'd be under something.

The acrid smoke dulled her nose as she tried to scent him out. Flames licked up the living room walls. The feral crackle and roar had every instinct screaming to run. Surely, Greystoke would have retreated from the fire.

She ran into the bedroom.

He wasn't under the bed. "Where are you? *Please*."

The closet door was ajar. *There* he was, huddled in a corner.

She grabbed the back of his neck and tucked him in the carrier. "Shh, it's okay, Greystoke."

No it wasn't.

Something crashed to the ground in the main space.

Gods, the roof was going. Sweat poured down her face, her back.

Jump out the window? No, the iron grillwork would take too much time to open. The back door it was.

As she raced through the kitchen to the laundry room, a ripping, cracking noise came from overhead. Burning timbers fell all around her. Bending, she raised her free arm to protect her head and jumped over a flaming, fallen rafter.

There was another ripping sound, and something heavy slammed into her from above. The sharp snap of her arm breaking shook her body. A log rafter scraped and burned down her back, driving her to her knees.

No! Screaming defiance, she regained her feet and threw the carrier through the back door with all her strength. *Live, Greystoke.*

More timbers hit her, and she fell again. *Get up.* She was burning.

On three limbs, she crawled out the door, fell down the steps. Burning, hurting, she rolled in the wet grass, screaming as her broken arm caught. But the flames went out.

Dragging her arm, she crawled away from the house. *Pain, so much pain.*

When the black swallowed her, she was so very thankful.

The clan's communal house was a fucking mess.

Lumpy, sagging couches and chairs. Stained, filthy bed mattresses that Madoc wouldn't dream of touching. The interior paint was faded and chipped, and there were fist-sized dents where shifters had punched the walls. The rugs were ancient. Half the windows were broken and covered with plywood.

At least the boarders had tried to leave the place clean.

The kitchen smelled of new wood and tile where the water-damaged floor had been ripped out and replaced. Good job there.

Finishing his walk-through, Madoc stepped outside to report to André, who'd inspected the outside with Niall.

Off to one side, Niall was talking on his phone while André stood silently staring down the cul-de-sac street.

Seeing Madoc, André raised his eyebrows. "What did you find?"

"Needs new furniture and carpeting. Appliances are ancient. A few drywall repairs are needed. The residents will need to paint the interior."

"Then we'll make it happen." André glanced at the street again.

"You expecting someone?"

"Heather was supposed to meet us here an hour ago. She's not answering her phone."

"It could be because she doesn't have cell service at the cabin." Niall pocketed his phone and joined them. "Calum's mate said Heather left around four so she wouldn't be late for our meeting. She was going home first."

Madoc frowned. "Why didn't she come directly here?"

"She has a cat," Niall said.

Seriously? Madoc almost laughed. A wolf with a pet cat? *Interesting.*

André rubbed the back of his neck. "So, the question is—did she make it home?"

As if he could see through the dense forest, Madoc looked toward the mountains where her cabin was located.

A thin line of darkness rose into the clear morning air. Madoc stiffened. That was *smoke*. With everything drenched from the rain last night, the forest couldn't be burning. "Yo, look there." He pointed.

Niall turned. "By the God."

Madoc didn't remember seeing many other homes in her area. The smoke could well be coming from Heather's place. "André, we need to—"

"We will." André thought for a second. "I'll drive. Niall, you're with me. Madoc, lock up and take your SUV."

"Meet you there." Madoc ran to shut up the house.

The drive seemed interminable, although Madoc's bones vibrated from the speed he was taking on the rutted roads. He'd even caught up to André.

As the SUV emerged into the clearing, his heart sank. Even knowing her cabin must be the source of the smoke, he'd still hoped.

Only partial walls stood as the heaviest bottom logs hadn't caught. The roof had collapsed, leaving smoldering coals. And her Jeep was here.

Parking next to it, he jumped out.

Niall shouted, "Heather!"

They all stopped to listen. No answer.

Gods, please don't let her have died in there. Madoc's heart felt as if it would crack.

André motioned to him, then Niall, sending them around the house from different sides.

A minute later, Niall shouted. "Back here!"

Rounding the corner, Madoc sped toward him, fear clamping his throat closed.

She lay, belly down, eyes closed. Her shirt was scorched off her back, exposing blackening burns.

He stood, paralyzed, then saw the slight movement. She was breathing. *Alive.*

The relief almost buckled his knees.

The red coals of her cabin pouring out heat had kept her warm—and perhaps from going into shock. However, they needed to move her. "I'll get your first aid kit and blankets."

When he returned, André had turned her over to do a quick assessment.

"How bad?" Madoc asked, setting the first aid kit down.

"Burns, mostly on her back and arms. And one arm's broken." He used a splint from the kit, curved it around her arm, and secured the straps. "Cahir."

Carefully, obviously trying to find unburned areas of skin, Niall lifted her. When he transferred her to Madoc's blanket-padded arms, she moaned in pain.

By the Gods. "It's all right, little wolf. We're here," Madoc whispered.

As Niall wrapped the edges of the cotton blankets around her, she opened her eyes and looked around blindly. "Greystoke. Where—"

What did she mean?

"We'll look, Heather. Hang on." Niall glanced at Madoc. "Her cat."

Herne help them. Madoc couldn't imagine telling her of the death of her pet. He glanced around, desperately hoping to see a small feline. But...wait.

Holding her carefully, he caught Niall's gaze and jerked his chin toward an odd-looking box. "What's that?"

Niall jogged over to check. "Thank the Mother, it's Greystoke." He knelt. "Hey, buddy."

A low complaining meow came from the box.

"Looks fine to me," Niall called.

"Did you hear him?" Walking carefully toward their vehicles,

Madoc tried to smile reassuringly, but fuck, she looked bad. "Your cat's all right."

She blinked as it apparently took a few seconds for his words to penetrate. Then she relaxed. "Thanks, bear."

"Let's get her to..." André opened his car door, then stopped. "This territory has no healer."

"Cold Creek does. We can take her there." Niall stowed the meowing cat in André's car. Then sniffed the air.

A second later, he'd stripped, shifted, and was nosing around the remnants of the porch, then the yard.

"What's he scenting?" Madoc asked André.

André's voice came out a low growl. "The fire started in several places, and the window glass is *inside* the house. It was broken from the outside."

"Arson." Madoc's mouth tightened, and he glanced at Heather. Eyes closed. She hadn't heard them. "You think he's picking up their scent?"

Shifting to human, Niall grabbed his clothes and joined them. "I recognize the scents—two boys, only twelve or thirteen years old. The trails go back and forth to where a car was parked at the edge of the clearing...and then down the drive."

"Cubs did this?" Madoc stared at him.

Niall glanced at André. "They're the pickpockets I told you about. The ones I've been trying to find."

"Ah."

"One boy keeps falling. Might be hurt." The cahir looked furious—and worried.

A hurt cub. All Madoc's instincts were to find the child, no matter what he'd done. But Heather needed healing.

André tilted his head to study the sky. "It's going to rain soon. Their trail will get washed away."

"Their trail went down the drive. If their ride left them..." Niall spoke slowly. "It's too far to town for younglings."

"Aye." After a minute, André said decisively, "One to take

Heather to the healer. One to track. One to drive the other car to pick up the tracker and younglings."

"I'll track. I have the scent." Niall gazed toward the road, obviously ready to get moving.

André turned to Madoc. "Brawd, my bond with the territory is too new. As Cosantir, I can't leave yet."

Madoc nodded. "I'll take her. Flatten out the passenger seat so I can keep an eye on her while I drive."

While giving directions to the healer's clinic, André reclined the seat.

Gently, Madoc settled Heather on her side.

As he started up the vehicle, her tiny groan made his hands tighten on the steering wheel. He'd never felt so fucking helpless in his life. Her eyes opened. "Madoc?"

"I'm taking you to the healer. Can you hang in there? Please?"

Even though her brow puckered with what must be fucking horrendous pain, her lips tilted up slightly. "Sure, anything for a bear."

The pain in his chest felt like he'd torn a muscle.

Anger raged through Niall. The two cubs had progressed from picking pockets to burning down houses? What was the world coming to?

But they're cubs. Need help. They might not be Daonain. He didn't know. Didn't care. They were still only younglings.

André had tossed Niall's clothing into his SUV and was following him down Heather's private road out to the bigger gravel one.

In cat form, Niall padded down the road, following the scent trail. At least the children had chosen the flattest part of the road and walked side-by-side.

A thought hit him.

He sniffed his way from one side of the road to the dense undergrowth on the other side, then trawsfurred.

André got out of his car. "What did you find?"

"There's only one trail—the cublings leaving. No trail for them arriving."

His brother's eyes darkened. "As you thought. Someone drove them here and abandoned them."

"Seems like."

"This is getting murkier than a dwarf's treasure cave." André's frown grew. "Move out, brawd. Let's get to the end of this trail."

In agreement, Niall shifted back and picked up the pace once out on the road. The cublings were taking the most straightforward way home.

He broke into a lope, checking frequently for their scent. They'd dodged into the brush a couple of times—probably to avoid being seen.

Talam's brother fell more often, leaving imprints of hands and knees. There was the stink of pain and fear sweat, the gut-wrenching odor of burned skin. The cub was definitely hurt.

And there they were, ahead of him on the edge of the gravel road.

Probably having heard André's car, Talam turned and spotted Niall. Like little mice, they disappeared into the brush.

Sorry, cublings. Mice might be able to hide from a cat. You can't.

Bounding forward, Niall dove into the forest after them.

Talam dodged through the trees—the boy had skills—then realized his littermate had fallen. Spinning, the lad sprinted back to stand between his brother and Niall.

Hiding would be the normal reaction to facing a cougar. The cub had courage.

Talam's brown eyes met Niall's. His small hands closed into fists. "Take me. Leave Sky alone—he had nothing to do with anything."

Ah, he recognized Niall was a shifter. So they were Daonain. That made things easier...in a way.

Niall trawsfurred. "How badly is your brother hurt?"

"He—the burns. They're bad."

So were *Heather's*. Anger flared...and died. With a sigh, Niall knelt beside the blond cub.

Sky's chin, neck, chest, and hands were badly burned. His blue eyes were filled with tears, his lower lip quivering, but he didn't make a peep.

"It's to the healer with you, cub." Niall scooped him up gently and led the way out of the forest to where André was waiting.

Years as a Mountie had been no preparation for tangles like this. Even worse, he'd lost the emotional distance he'd maintained as a law enforcement officer. As a Cosantir, the clan was not only his to guard but also to nurture.

What hurt them...hurt him.

Pulling up in front of their house, André set the SUV to idle and got out.

In the corner maple, a pixie chittered annoyance at the vehicle, visitors, and the stink of wood smoke. André glanced at her, grateful that sprites rarely threw things at Cosantirs.

After removing the carrier with the unhappy cat from the back, André opened the rear door. The distressed lad there had barely spoken, nothing more than to tell André their names. But there was time to get more information from him. "Talam, you're staying here with me."

Reluctantly, the lad slid out of the car, shooting a worried look at his brother in the passenger seat.

Niall had already moved to the driver's seat.

Setting a hand on the open window, André told him, "Bring

Heather and Sky back here when the healer is finished. Heather will need someone helping her for a while."

"Yeah." Niall's exhalation held a growl. "Especially with her home in ashes."

"What? No!" Standing beside André, Talam stared at Niall. "That wasn't *Heather's* cabin. We wouldn't—"

"He said a bad human lived there. A man." The burns on Sky's chin were ugly, and he winced as he spoke—but he didn't stop. "He *said*."

Talam had gone pale. "We wouldn't burn down Heather's house."

Niall eyed the cub. "You didn't want revenge on her because she caught you pickpocketing?"

"We weren't mad." Tears were in Talam's eyes. "She's nice. She leaves us food sometimes like you do."

"Oh?" André studied his brother...who hadn't mentioned anything about food.

"I couldn't find them, but I did find their nest," Niall admitted.

And apparently, so had Heather. Naturally, his brother and a soft-hearted female would feed the cubs.

"Head on out. We'll have food and beds ready." André closed the driver's side door, then thought to add, "Don't break my car, brawd."

Niall's mouth tipped into a cat's smirk. "Just a dent or two... this time. No worries."

Gnome-brained cahir.

As Niall drove away, André picked up the pet carrier and looked at Talam. "Let's get the cat settled."

With Sky in Niall's care, his brother wouldn't run. Silently, the cub followed André into the house.

André kept the boy busy as he set up the corner guest room next to his. A plastic-lined box with dirt, a can of tuna, and a dish of water should work for the cat until they could get better supplies.

He'd opened the door to the carrier, but the gray feline was still huddled in the back. Talam sat down to pet him. "He smells like smoke. Was he...was he in the cabin?"

André nodded, guessing Heather's injuries had happened when she'd tried to rescue the cat.

The boy's eyes filled with tears, and André heard him whisper, "I'm sorry, cat."

André watched a minute. He'd been furious at Heather's injuries. But the cubs hadn't known whose cabin it was, and their open horror and guilt at their actions had washed away his anger with them.

Mind clear, he saw the young pickpocket was protective and loyal to his brother. Had a sense of empathy for the little cat. Had a conscience.

Why had this cub been left on his own?

"Let's give Greystoke time to sniff around and settle in." André waved the cub out of the room and closed the cat in.

As they headed downstairs, Talam bristled with anxiety. The youngling needed a shower and food, but perhaps they should talk before the lad made himself sick.

"Let's sit for a minute." At the dining room table, André gave Talam a glass of milk and a couple of Madoc's molasses cookies before getting himself a coffee.

Watching André with wary, brown eyes, the cub didn't touch the food.

André wanted to pat him on the head and tell him everything would be fine, but it would be a lie. "Now, please explain why you burned down Heather's cabin."

"We didn't know. Mr—" The cub jerked straight and shut his mouth tight. After a moment, he said, very carefully, "Sky and me, we got told how the human in the house was bad, and we needed to burn it down so our females and cubs would be safe. So the man would leave the territory."

Someone had fed the boys a carefully thought-out lie about a bad human and a danger to females and cubs.

"It appears someone lied to you." André took a sip of his coffee as he studied the cub. Big-boned, dirty brown hair. Filthy, threadbare clothing. Admittedly, youngsters this age were gangly, but the hollow cheeks spoke of near starvation. "Is this someone a friend?"

"*Ha*." As if shocked at the angry sound, Talam cringed. The lad was exhausted, his mind not working quickly.

All the better for André.

Talam took refuge in drinking his milk. After a sip, he half-drained the big glass. "Um. It's... He's not a friend. He hired us for this an' promised he'd let us work..." Stopping abruptly, he finished the glass of milk instead.

So an adult male hired the boys to burn the cabin. Someone who apparently hated Heather. Could Niall have missed his scent at the cabin? "Did your employer ever get out of the car?"

Talam shook his head, eyeing the cookies.

André pushed the plate closer. "They're good. Madoc makes them for us."

One bite and the first cookie disappeared as fast as the milk.

"Talam." André kept his voice soft. "I need to know who paid you to burn Heather's house."

Shoulders hunching, the cub slid down in the chair and shook his head. And started to tremble. It seemed he was more frightened of the man than of André. Had the criminal threatened the *cubs*?

André could get the answers. Coercing a mind lay in the realm of a Cosantir's powers. Unfortunately, the effect was like taking a baseball bat to a brain. As with erasing large amounts of memory, what remained after a coercion might not be the same.

Well, finding out the male's name wasn't urgent. They could wait and possibly gain information another way.

Would the cub be able to look Heather in the face and still refuse?

Meantime, he had other questions.

"It seems as if you've been living rough. Do you have parents in the area, Talam?"

"Uh-uh. We're gather-bred. And a hellhound killed Mom."

André sat back. Hadn't Niall mentioned something about hellhounds here? "In July?"

"Uh-huh."

"Who's been caring for you? Didn't anyone realize you're on your own?"

Talam shrugged. "We just moved here when school let out. 'Cuz Mom liked humans and wanted to live in a bigger town."

And their lazy slug of a Cosantir hadn't bothered to see if a murdered female had cubs? André growled.

The youngling tensed.

"Nay, lad. I'm not angry with you." André rubbed his neck. How many pieces of this territory were broken? "I'm not happy you and Sky were left to fend for yourselves."

Talam didn't look as if he thought it was unusual. Instead, he nibbled at the second cookie, obviously trying to make it last.

"After you have a shower, I'll make us sandwiches. And there are more cookies for later." André chuckled as the treat disappeared in two bites. "Talam, are there more cubs who aren't being cared for?"

Talam was watching André carefully, obviously trying to decide if telling him would betray his comrades.

André shook his head. "Youngling, I'm not going to punish children who are only trying to stay alive. Part of my job as Cosantir is to be sure our cubs are safe and taken care of."

"You're really the Cosantir?"

"I am."

Talam shook his head. "I heard the other one says he still is."

And how could a cub possibly know who was lying?

With a sigh, André opened to the power within, knowing his eyes would be turning black, and the air around him would shimmer.

The cub's eyes went wide.

Cutting off the flow, André felt Herne's faint amusement. Because, unlike with a territory, the God remained very aware of his guardians as long as the Cosantir didn't close off the channel. Was that what Wendell had done?

Turning his attention back to the lad, André leaned forward. "Tell me about the other cubs, Talam. Let me help."

Heather woke as Madoc lifted her out of the car. Clenching her teeth, she managed not to scream at the pain. The fire was out; why did it feel as if she still burned?

It hurts so bad.

"Hang on, little wolf," Madoc crooned as he climbed the steps onto the covered porch and kicked the door several times. "Yo, need the healer!"

"By Herne's holy prick, use the doorbell or—" Donal's annoyed voice broke off. "Heather?"

Her scorched throat only allowed a whisper to escape. "Donal."

"Bring her in here."

"Heather, oh no." Margery appeared. Her friend had the softest, calming voice. "Where all is she hurt?"

"Busted up left arm. Bad burns across her back." Madoc's deep voice sounded like her brothers', and his open concern made tears fill her eyes.

"Lay her on her uninjured side until we see what's what." Margery patted the long exam table. "Here."

Madoc laid her down carefully, and it still *hurt, hurt, hurt*. Removing the blanket jostled her arm, and tears streamed down her face.

Pulling off the remains of her shirt and bra was even worse. She clamped her teeth together to keep from screaming.

"What happened?" Margery asked. "Oh, and I'm Margery, banfasa, and he's Donal, healer."

"Madoc from Rainier. Her place burned down."

"Oh Gods. Her cabin?" Margery's distress sent sorrow spiraling through Heather again.

My cabin. Gone.

Drying his hands, Donal ran an assessing gaze over her. "By the Gods, you look as bad as Darcy did when she showed up here."

"Let's take a look at the break first." Donal scowled as he examined her aching arm.

Owww. At her whimper, Madoc closed warm fingers around Heather's other hand, and she gripped the comforting hold with all her strength.

Far too soon, Donal drafted the big bear to pull on her arm. Two different places in her forearm had been broken and lining everything up took *forever*. She didn't scream...not quite, but tears filled her eyes until the whole room blurred.

"That's it." Donal set his hands on her. "Don't move."

Madoc's powerful hands held her forearm in place.

Donal coaxed the bones to fill in the break, mended the ripped flesh, and scoured away any potential infection. She knew how healing worked, but the wretched, scratching feeling still felt horrible.

"Done." Donal stepped back. "Wear a sling for five days and no using your arm until after that."

She might have argued, but he touched her burned back, and she yelped instead.

"Gods, Heather," he muttered. "Cleaning and healing this is not going to feel good."

The mere thought made her want to cry—and Margery looked as if she'd join in.

The worst part of being a Daonain was not receiving pain killers. Narcotics on top of pain meant a shifter could lose control, trawsfur, and attack the nearest person.

"I need someone to..." She swallowed hard. "If you touch my back again, I'm liable to hit you, Donal."

"Let me help," Madoc said quietly.

"I can do—" Margery paused, then smiled at Madoc. "Yes, your help would be good."

Sitting beside the exam table, he put his hand behind her neck, his other on her butt, and pulled her against him so her arms were trapped against his hard chest.

Under the acrid stink of smoke, she caught the fragrance of citrus...and his own masculine scent. The one she'd smelled the night of the full moon. When she buried her face against him, he made low rumbly sounds.

And his gentle hold was unyielding as the cleaning and healing of her burns went on and on.

Slowly, far too slowly, the searing fire in her back lessened and eased to a lingering ache. And a ghastly memory.

"I hate burns." Donal sounded as grumpy as a badger with frostbitten paws. "You can let her go, Madoc."

Madoc loosened his arms and sat back. "You did good, little wolf." He helped her sit up,

"Thank you."

He smiled his answer, then glanced at Donal. "Her voice sounds better."

"I fixed her throat and lungs." Donal shook his head. "Next time, don't breathe the smoke."

"*Donal.*" Margery hit him, then handed Madoc a damp washcloth.

With two fingers under her chin, Madoc wiped her face. Who knew the bear could be so gentle?

When she winced at an unexpected pain, he frowned and tipped her head to the light. "Donal."

"Ah, hold still, girl. One more scorch." Donal touched Heather's face, and her cheek stopped hurting. Until her seared back had been healed, the smaller burn hadn't even registered.

"Anywhere else?" Donal asked.

Heather shook her head.

Taking Heather's hand, Margery smiled. "You'll ache for another couple of days, but you won't have any scarring. Would you like a shower to get the rest of the dirt off?"

"Yes." Every breath with the nauseating stench of smoke brought the memory of her cabin burning. "Please."

CHAPTER TWENTY-SIX

Seated at the small table in the kitchen, Heather took a sip of hot tea and felt her world starting to pull together. "Thank you, Margery. For everything." For the shower and the loose clothing and for trimming the scorched spots from her hair. Even for helping her figure out the sling for her arm.

"You're welcome." Margery bent and wrapped an arm around her shoulders. "You're the reason I escaped Pete and Ailill Ridge—and found Donal and Tynan. Anything I can do for you, I will."

"Heather, you look better." Madoc stood in the doorway, smiling at her. Then his dark brows drew together, and his jaw turned hard, transforming him into one deadly male. "You're cold."

When he disappeared, she stared at the doorway. He'd looked so angry because she was cold?

A minute later, he returned and wrapped a fluffy blanket around her, resting his hands on her shoulders. "Better?"

She'd lain there in the cold grass, knowing she'd die there, all alone. But he and Niall and André had come for her. He'd brought her here, held her, and even seen that she'd been cold. The sense of being cared for made her eyes prickle with tears. "Thank you."

He gave her shoulders a squeeze, then sat beside her and accepted a glass of iced tea from Margery. "Thanks."

Donal took a chair across the table, looking tired.

"Did I thank you for the healing?" Heather asked. "And are you all right?"

"You're welcome." Donal shot her a reprimanding scowl. "But don't break any more bones. I hate fixing those."

She almost laughed at Madoc's startled look.

The bear had probably never run into such a brusque healer.

"Of course, my favorite healer." Heather bowed her head. "I'll avoid falling rafters in the future."

"Do that."

"Bad healer," Margery muttered, cuffed the back of his head, and handed him an iced tea.

Unrepentantly, he grinned at her.

Heather smothered a laugh. The banfasa was totally perfect for Donal.

Margery refilled Heather's cup from the tea pot, poured some for herself, and sat beside Donal. "If your cabin's gone, Heather, you'll need a place to stay."

The loss was a stab in the heart. Her wonderful little cabin, inherited from her grandmother. Her home. Memories and mementoes. Photos and the last blanket her mother had knitted. All her clothes. Her favorite books. Her colorful dishes.

And... *I'm homeless*. She blinked hard. There would be time later to mourn. "I'll—"

"You'll stay with us." Madoc's hand closed over hers.

"No, no, we have extra room *here*." Margery frowned at Madoc, then added with a pout, "Breanne wants you to stay at the lodge. Vicki says you belong at her place and...would you believe she said Sorcha is missing you? Honestly, adding a cub as a bribe is cheating."

Even as she chuckled at Margery's grumbling, Heather treasured her friends' generosity.

"Is that how it works? Bribes? Or maybe even hostages?" Madoc's hazel eyes lit with mischief. "So little wolf..."

She eyed him warily. "Yes?"

"*We* have your *cat*."

A while later, she finished her tea, listening as the others quietly talked.

Having so many friends who cared for her had eased the lost, shaky feeling inside. Knowing Greystoke was safe with André, and she'd see him in a few hours gave her something to look forward to.

A hard knocking on Donal's front door made her jump. Someone called, "Is the healer here?"

Was that Niall's voice? Was he hurt?

By the time she'd pushed to her feet, Donal and Madoc had ushered Niall into the clinic room. To her surprise, the cahir held a gangly cubling who had ugly burns down his front.

She frowned, recognizing him. One of the two young pickpockets.

Niall set the boy down on the table and backed out of Donal's and Margery's way. Seeing Heather, his face lit. "Pretty wolf, you look so fucking much better."

She huffed. "I bet."

Looming over her, he ran a hand down her hair, his green eyes gentle. "By the Gods, you had us worried." Ever so carefully, he pulled her into a hug. And right there was where she wanted to stay, encircled by his arms and supported by his strength.

Cheek pressed against his shoulder, she frowned at the odd feeling of leaning on someone. On a male. Had she always been stronger than her lovers?

"Hey, brawd," Madoc asked. "Is this one of the two cubs?"

"Aye." Niall hesitated, then stepped back and set his hands on her shoulders. "Heather..." His face had gone grim.

"What's wrong?"

"Your cabin... The fire was set. Deliberately."

What? No. His words blanked her mind like a brisk wind sweeping the sky. "But...why? Who would do such a thing?"

Madoc moved closer and tucked an arm around her waist from behind. Supporting her against his hard frame.

"We don't know why yet, but"—Niall motioned to the cub on the exam table—"Sky and his brother Talam set the fire."

He wasn't making sense. None of this made sense.

Gripping Madoc's forearm to keep herself upright, she stared at the boy. Yes, those were burns Donal was examining. "He's just a cub. How did he even get there?"

"It appears someone hired the lads, drove them to your cabin, and gave them the stuff to start the fire. Then he abandoned them there. I found the boys trying to walk back to town."

Her mind scrambled, leaving her feeling much like when she'd slid off a cliff, her claws unable to find any purchase on the unforgiving granite.

Someone hated her enough to want to destroy her home. *Why?*

And who was it?

The boy knew. Anger flickered inside her, feeling...betrayed. She'd wanted to help the cubs. Had left food for him and his brother.

And he'd burned her home.

Her hands clenched into fists.

The youngling didn't notice, wasn't seeing anything.

Margery had cut his shirt up the back and was gently trying to pull it free so Donal could get to the burns, but the boy was terrified. Shoulders hunched, arms in front, he was guarding the burns on his front torso. Standing to one side, Heather saw the cub's stomach was sunken, every rib visible.

Tears made trails down the ash and dirt on his pale face. So young. So scared.

Cubs shouldn't be scared. This was wrong, so wrong.

Unable to help herself, she walked over and set her hand over the cub's clenched fingers. His hand was freezing. "Hey, youngling. Need someone to hold onto?"

Madoc watched as the youngling realized who had spoken. Bursting into tears, Sky told Heather over and over they hadn't known it was her house. They'd never have burned it if they'd known.

Heather hugged him carefully, then looked over. "Niall, can you hold Sky from the back so Donal can work?"

When Niall took hold of the lad, Heather stayed where she was, holding the boy's hand, leaning against him.

Caring.

Joining them, he took the cub's other hand. Cold, shaking. "Easy, lad. It'll feel better soon," he murmured.

"'K," Sky whispered.

Heather gave Madoc a nod. It'd hurt her to learn someone had deliberately burned her home. Madoc had seen the anger in her face. He'd have been angry too.

But she'd set those emotions aside. Because the boy needed her.

A female—this female—had a nurturing heart.

By the time André had Talam fed and washed and into one of his T-shirts, the lad was drooping.

André started to put him in a guest room, but the big brown eyes looked so forlorn. He'd guess the littermates rarely left each other's side.

There were calls to make, ones the boy didn't need to hear, but... Come to think of it, there was another unhappy soul here. "You know, I think Heather's cat needs some company. He had a frightening time of it."

When Talam didn't speak, André opened the door to Heather's room.

"Can you nap here with Greystoke? Having you with him will let him feel safe."

The cat was a small gray ball on the bed.

"Okay," Talam whispered and crawled up beside him.

After grabbing a blanket from the closet, André tucked it around the lad who was already half-asleep, curled around the purring feline.

Meantime, he'd get things moving.

With two more pairs of cubs at risk, the communal house needed to be reopened immediately. They'd wanted to wait until the boarded-up, broken windows were replaced, and new furniture obtained. But the plumbing and floor repairs were complete, so it was livable.

After the full moon, he'd given Ina the list of those who needed room and board so she could see whose needs were the most urgent. She'd know which shifters would be able to watch over the cubs.

When André called to request a meeting with the board Elders, they showed up so quickly it made him uncomfortable. He doubted he'd ever get used to this kind of instant obedience.

Ina was the last to arrive.

"Cosantir." She bowed her head as he let her into the house.

"Thank you for coming, Ina." He showed her into his study, grateful he'd planned enough furniture for it. Drinking the tea he'd provided, the grocers, Murtagh and Maeve, sat on one couch, Friedrich in a chair.

As Ina found a seat, André poured her a cup and moved the

plate of cookies closer to her. "You're going to need the caffeine and sweets, I fear."

As they did, he took a seat and poured his own cup. "Thank you all for coming. I'm afraid we have a problem." He explained about Talam and Sky and the other homeless cubs—and how Talam had shared enough to realize someone was using the boys to steal.

The board members were appalled.

They should be. "I must ask: How did this not get noticed? Sky and Talam lost their mother during the hellhound attack in July."

Murtagh and Maeve exchanged glances. "We noticed... Ah, there was stock missing, usually after cubs had been in the store. And we wondered why they weren't in school when it started up. But some families prefer to homeschool."

Maeve added, "Sometimes the cubs looked fed, sometimes not." The Murtaghs' three children were grown, he knew. Their daughter lived in another territory; the sons were here and lifemated to a good female.

"I'm afraid I only saw the two—the ones who tried to lift my wallet," Ina said. Her cubs—three males—were also grown and had moved south to Gifford Territory.

"We reported the matter to Pete. Must've been the end of July?" Murtagh looked to his wife for her nod. "He told us he'd take care of it."

"We thought he had, Cosantir." Maeve's brows drew together. "We often saw him with cublings in his car and talking to them in the square."

Pete. André's jaw tightened until it ached. He had a suspicion about who'd "hired" the cubs to steal. But the boys would have to name him, and so far, Talam wasn't talking.

"Heather and I talked about the younglings. She's been trying to catch them so we could get them help." Ina shook her head. "I'm sorry, Cosantir. I wasn't very observant."

Friedrich sighed. "I admit, I don't notice much outside financial matters."

André nodded his understanding. In all reality, Friedrich had probably grown tired of butting heads with Wendell.

"What do you need from us, Cosantir?" Ina asked.

"We need to get the cublings off the street and away from whomever is using them. I want to open the communal house. Then... Ina, will you choose shifters who can act as parents to these boys. Parenting can be their contribution in return for room and board."

Ina gave her top a determined tug. "I will be happy to find the right people."

"Don't choose only females. I want two strong males in the house," André added.

Murtagh nodded approval. "In case the unknown male tries to get to the younglings?"

"Exactly. We'll set up bunkbeds in one room for all the boys." André looked at the board members. "Among you, you know almost everyone in the territory. Who else was killed during the festival or hellhound attacks? And who left someone behind? Who needs help and isn't getting it? I want to know—whether it's from physical problems, inability to find a job, or domestic problems."

The four of them bowed, Friedrich speaking for them, "Your will, Cosantir."

André rubbed the back of his neck. "Normally, a Cosantir is chosen after having lived in the Territory for years. Instead, I'm new to you all, and I'll need to rely on your help. Once I know everyone, I hope things will get better."

By the God, things had better improve. This was intolerable.

Niall parked André's car in the multi-car garage and walked around to unbuckle the sleeping cub. Healing drew from the body's stores, and Sky didn't have any to spare. He'd probably sleep much of the next two days.

"Talam?" Sky rubbed his eyes and froze, looking up at Niall.

Niall sighed. "I don't bite, cub. Relax. We're here."

Wide eyes. The child was too scared to ask where *here* was.

"This is the house I share with my brothers. Talam is here too."

"Oh. Is Heather...is she gonna be all right? Where will *she* stay?" Tears filled the blue eyes.

"Right here with us until she figures out what she wants." Niall ruffled the fine blond hair. "Since she'll have her arm in a sling for a few days, maybe you cubs can help her if she needs something requiring two hands." Waiting on her would be a cub-sized fulfillment of the Law of Reciprocity.

Sky sat up straight, jaw determined. "We *will*."

As Niall helped the cub out of the car, Madoc's red SUV pulled in. "Let's go. I'm starving—and we want to get to the food before the bear eats it all."

Niall opened the garage door to the kitchen and ushered Sky in.

"There you are." André prowled in from the living room, his gaze dark with whatever he'd been up to. But he smiled at the boy—and André's smile could charm a pixie out of her hole. "Sky, you look better. Your brother's been worried about you." He raised his voice. "Talam, your littermate is here."

"Sky!" The dark-haired boy charged into the kitchen, barefoot and dressed in jeans and a green T-shirt. He skidded to a stop, looking his brother over carefully. "Are you okay?"

Sky grabbed him into a hug. The way they clung to each other, trying not to cry, made Niall's eyes dampen.

André nodded in understanding. An unsupervised childhood

filled with close calls meant they knew exactly how traumatic it was when a littermate was injured.

"Something smells good." Niall felt as if his stomach was plastered against his backbone. "Do we have enough food?"

"Remembering how much we ate at their age, I took Talam shopping. We found clothes for them and Heather, then bought groceries and cat supplies. Food is ready when anyone is hungry."

Thank fuck. "I'm starving. And Sky will be too." Post-healing required food and rest.

Behind him, Madoc and Heather came inside.

Talam froze.

After a long moment, the boy approached Heather. His small body tensed as if he expected to get hit. "I'm sorry. You brought us food, and we...we burned your house, and you got *hurt*." The cub's eyes filled with tears before he burst out crying. "I don't know how to *fix* it."

"Oh, youngling. It'll be all right." Tears in her own eyes, she curled her good arm around the boy, pulled him close, and let him cry.

By the God, she had a forgiving nature. It helped she knew the cubs had been misled.

As he watched them, he had a feeling the male who'd used the children might well feel her fangs in his throat.

Niall would help.

When Talam let go of Heather, André moved forward. After wiping her cheeks, he pulled her into his arms, careful of the sling, then kissed the top of her head. "I'm pleased to see you looking better. We have a room all ready for you. Are you up to having a meal?"

Niall's eyes widened. Had he ever seen André acting so...tender?

Shifting weight from one foot to another, Niall studied his brother. And tried to decide how André felt. How *he* felt.

Brothers were for companionship and family. Females were for full moons, for fun mating. Nothing more...right?

Yet he wasn't sure of that age-old truth any longer.

Therein lay the problem.

He watched as André stepped back and took Heather's hand.

"Greystoke is in the same room you had last time, and he seems fine. Eating well too." André grinned at Niall. "Don't worry, cat; we restocked your cans of tuna fish."

Talam giggled and whispered to Sky, "He said the cahir likes tuna sandwiches."

Rather than laughing, Sky lifted his chin and loyally told Niall, "I do too."

"Good lad. However, from what I'm smelling, we're having sloppy joes tonight. It's what one of our aunts made when she wasn't sure when her males would get home, since the stuff can simmer forever on the stove." Niall grinned. "Let's get the table set and some food dished up."

After snuggles with Greystoke, Heather came downstairs and soon discovered the awkwardness of having only one hand. Washing one hand was weird.

Trying to hold a bun filled with loose ground meat with one hand? A disaster.

Sitting beside her, André chuckled. "Let's try this." He cut her bun into quarters.

She shot him a grateful look. "I foresee a few days of frustration."

"We're gonna help," Sky told her. "Me an' Talam."

Mouth full, Talam nodded.

Before she could say she'd manage, she saw the warning in Niall's expression, then the need to atone in the cubs' faces.

Well, now. "Thank you. I can see I'll really need your help."

Niall winked at her.

She turned to André. "Is there anything interesting being planned?"

"You'll be sleeping for the next couple of days," Madoc reminded her. "You need to finish healing."

She'd go crazy if she didn't have anything to do. "Bear, you're not helping."

Her glare, which made most males back off, bounced right off his thick hide. He grinned.

André set his plate to one side. "It appears there are four more younglings being used to steal. Niall, Madoc, I'd like you to round them up."

"Used to steal? Some boggart was *using* them?" Heather stared at André, then the cubs. By the Mother's breasts—she'd seen cubs stealing from a store in Cle Elum. "Here?"

"In all the surrounding human towns, apparently." André's voice was grim, and the cublings shrank slightly.

"Four cubs to find, hmm? We'll do our best," Niall cracked his neck as if ready to begin immediately. "What then?"

"We'll open the communal house and have the new residents foster the boys until permanent homes are found."

Noticing the cubs' worried expressions, Heather kicked André's ankle. When he glanced at her, she tilted her head at the two.

He frowned, then understanding lit his eyes. He was as intuitive as she'd hoped. "Talam, Sky, because what Heather called a boggart is still loose, it's better if you stay with us."

Talam relaxed. "Thank you, Cosantir."

Leaning toward his brother, Sky whispered, "Is he really a Cosantir? Mr.... Uh, *he* said *he* was."

"Yeah," Talam whispered back with a cautious glance at André. "This one really, really is."

Had the boggart lied about his authority? Until André proved he was... Heather narrowed her eyes. "André, what did you do?"

His wicked grin took him from being darkly handsome to completely captivating.

She blinked. *Don't go there, girl.*

"So," she said brightly, "what all has to be done for the communal house."

The discussion ranged from there.

By the time the meal was finished, Heather was exhausted.

André put his hand on her shoulder. "Come, *ma louloutte*, let's get you to bed."

At the foot of the stairs, he looked as if he was going to pick her up, and she scowled. "Don't you dare. I'm tired, not incapacitated."

His low laugh was incredibly male. "So stubborn." Although he let her climb the stairs, he wasn't more than an inch from her all the way up.

She hadn't really looked at the guest room on her previous visit. The pale blue walls and white trim created a serene ambience. The queen-sized bed's old-fashioned patchwork quilt was in shades of blue—with her snoozing cat in the very center, of course.

An overstuffed chair with a footstool and standing lamp made the area seem like a refuge. A breeze through the half-open window carried the fragrance of the forest—comfortingly familiar. "This is lovely, André."

"I'm glad you like it." He opened the small closet where built-in shelves on one end held clothing. "Margery texted me your sizes, so Talam and I made guesses on what you might like."

She saw jeans and flannel shirts. And, *hmm,* the briefs looked exactly like what she usually bought. Her eyebrows lifted.

He chuckled, not embarrassed in the least. "I did undress you at the Gathering."

"So you did."

"And I will again now," he murmured, carefully removing her

sling. Disconcertingly skillful, he removed her baggy shirt, then the loose sweatpants.

Nudity wasn't anything shifters noticed, yet she heated as his appreciative gaze swept over her.

"You're as lovely tonight as you were at the Gathering." His voice was like a wide, deep river, flowing smoothly but not hiding the strength of the current. He touched her cheek. "Since Talam and I forgot to buy sleepwear, I brought one of my shirts, old enough to be soft. Or do you prefer nothing?"

At home, she rarely bothered with nightclothes, but in a house full of males and cubs? "The shirt, please."

Thankfully it was a button-up rather than a T-shirt that would require lifting her incredibly sore arm. But, being André, he'd undoubtedly taken her injury into consideration.

Picking up the shirt, he helped her into it. When the backs of his hands brushed her breasts, her heartrate increased.

He tilted his head, caught her wrist, and breathed in. "*Ma chère*, you honor me. But I fear you need sleep more than you need my attentions. However, if you decide I'm wrong after you rest, my room is next door."

His smile was so wicked she couldn't help but laugh. And be tempted. "I'm afraid you're right. I need sleep." Her smile faded. Even more, she needed time alone to mourn the loss of her beloved home. Her refuge.

André rubbed his knuckles on her cheek. His deep voice softened. "If you need a shoulder to cry on or someone to hold you while you sleep, come to me. Or go to one of my brothers. They feel the same."

Niall would. Madoc probably not. But they really were wonderful males.

"Thanks, André." She hugged him, then went up on tiptoes and kissed his cheek.

After the Cosantir took Heather to her room, Talam and his brother were sent to bed. Excited for Sky to see their room, Talam led the way up the stairs. He paused at the second floor. "These have the males' rooms down this side. Heather's is past the corner." Talam had a little glow remembering how comfy the room looked.

At the third floor, he opened the door to their attic room. The ceiling was slanted, the walls were light green, and a poufy plaid comforter in greens and blues was on the big bed.

"Wow," Sky whispered. "For us?"

"Uh-huh." Talam opened the closet and bathroom doors. "We got clothes, too, and toothbrushes and stuff."

And it felt good.

When the human landlord heard Mom died, he'd showed up with foster home people. Talam and Sky had run, leaving everything behind—because the other boys had warned them of what happened if humans found out kids didn't have parents. Mateo and Alvaro had barely managed to escape the human foster home before their First Shift.

Having First Shift where there were humans... Talam shivered.

"Hey, André bought us books too," he told Sky. "Moya at the bookstore—we've seen her around, you know, the female with black hair?—she picked out some we might like."

His brother's eyes widened. He loved to read even more than Talam. In the last town, they'd gone to the library all the time.

Sky moved closer and whispered, "Did you tell them about Mr. Wendell?"

"Uh-uh." Talam's stomach hurt. "We *can't*."

"Yeah." Sky scowled. "Yeah. I know."

As his brother brushed his teeth and washed his face, Talam changed into pajama bottoms.

Once in bed, they bickered about which books they wanted and started to read. The room even had lamps on the nightstands.

Talam heaved a sigh, barely able to believe it. They were in a safe place, in a real bed, in clean clothes, with a full stomach.

And the healer'd fixed Sky's burns. He was all right.

A few tears slid down Talam's cheeks.

With a huffing sound, Sky turned in bed, so his head was on Talam's stomach—and kept reading.

Laughing and crying, Talam made his stomach bounce so he could hear his brother giggle. And, picking up his book, he wondered, *does happiness have a scent?*

My cabin is gone. And someone hates me. With Greystoke in her lap, Heather sat by the window in the guest bedroom. Past the rain trickling down the glass, the world outside was as dark as her mood. She'd tried to sleep, but...couldn't. Couldn't get past the sight of her home burning, of the gut-wrenching pain of her arm breaking, of her flesh burning.

Of lying in the dirt. Alone, so alone. Waking to realize no one would come.

But André, Madoc, Niall—they'd found her, cared for her. Insisted she stay with them. Had saved Greystoke too. Would they have any idea how much their rescue meant to her?

She rubbed his ears to hear his rough purr. "I love you, Lord Greystoke."

The long sleeve of her shirt slid down over her hand, and she rolled it back up. André's shirt. Along with the faintest laundry fragrance, it carried his scent from when she'd hugged him.

They'd come for her. She shook her head, trying not to let the knowledge sweep her away. To make more of it than what it was.

But in the depths of her, countering the hard, ugly belief that males always leave, she had...this. These three brothers had found her and cared for her.

Tipping her head back, she watched clouds scud across the

black sky in front of the last quarter moon. It must be late. The forest stretching out to the south was silent except for the hoot of an owl and the soughing of the wind.

In a house filled with people, why did she feel so lonely?

André woke to the faint sound of footsteps outside his bedroom. Was one of the cubs up? Maybe they were hungry...or frightened. He sat up as his door opened.

The wafting air carried Heather's scent. Light from the hall silhouetted her motionless figure in the doorway.

"Heather. Come in."

After a second, she ventured in, closed the door, and crossed to his bed as he sat up.

The curtains were open, and the faint moonlight silvered her face and shadowed the curves beneath his white shirt.

Her husky voice was a whisper. "Can I...sleep...with you?"

"But of course." He held the covers up so she could slide in, then pulled her close. Her head lay on his shoulder, and he helped her rest her injured arm on top of his chest.

Snuggling closer, she sighed contentedly.

He kissed the top of her head. How had he forgotten she was a wolf? Of all the shifters, they needed others the most. Wolves often spoke of the happiness found as cublings in a puppy pile.

Why hadn't she called her pack to rally around her?

Stroking her hair, he frowned. Female wolves occasionally lived alone, but rarely so far from the others. Could the pack here be as dysfunctional as everything else in this territory?

With a slow breath, he let the worry go. This was not the time to try to solve another problem.

"Sleep, *ma chère*. You're safe here," he murmured. He rubbed his chin on the top of her head. She felt good in his arms. Not fragile, but soft and warm.

Holding her felt...right.

In his earlier years, he'd bring home a female to see how she'd fit with his life and his brothers. None ever won favor with Niall or Madoc. No surprise there since the occasional female who caught Niall's attention never pleased André. And Madoc had never been interested in a female outside of a Gathering.

Eventually, André had accepted that he and his brothers formed their own circle. He'd come to be content.

But now...

Niall's feelings appeared clear. Madoc's interest, though, might not be the forever kind. Until the trail forward was clear, he'd have to move very carefully so neither the bear nor Heather would get hurt.

CHAPTER TWENTY-SEVEN

The next morning, everyone came together for breakfast. With a smile, Niall watched the younglings next to him. After a taste of Madoc's cooking, the cubs had dug into the sausage-egg biscuits and hash browns with enthusiasm. They were already on their second helpings.

Heather, too, was eating heartily.

He smiled, pleased to have her in their home. And even more pleased he'd heard her voice in his brother's bedroom last night.

When he'd teased André, his littermate stated nothing happened, and she'd simply needed comfort.

Niall had smothered his smile. Because holding someone during the night could be even more intimate than mating.

Aye, André *liked* Heather, and a wayward hope rose in Niall's heart. Could they, maybe, someday have a family holding more than the three of them?

"Hey, guys." When everyone at the table looked up, Heather laughed. "I'm so outnumbered."

Madoc grinned. "Question or request?"

"A question. How can Canadians buy land here without a lot of paperwork?"

"Because we have citizenship here too. Under almost the same names." Niall cradled his coffee mug between his palms. "Our wandering parents found it useful to have separate identities as US citizens. When we were born in Canada, they registered us there, then crossed the border in the mountains with us, and did the same in the US. We're using our US papers here; a friend mailed them down."

"If we didn't have those"—Madoc waved toward Niall—"he'd create new ones."

Heather's eyes widened. "Seriously?"

Should he mention how much he loved creating fake IDs? "Some. Passports, no. And the new-fangled chipped drivers' licenses...not yet, although I can create all the documentation needed to get them."

"Calum will want to talk with you. He wants ways to keep long-lived shifters off the government radar."

Niall grinned. "As it happens, I'm open to work." With his office finally set up, he could start taking on remote jobs. "Speaking of work"—he looked at André—"are we starting the cub-hunt today?"

"*Oui.* While Ina and I work on opening the communal house, you and Madoc will search for the homeless younglings." André turned his attention to the cubs. "Talam, Sky, are you willing to talk with your friends? Tell them we have a place for them to stay?"

They shrank in their chairs.

Why would they be afraid of other cubs? Niall's eyes narrowed. "Are the other younglings mean to you?"

Talam shook his head. "They're okay, especially Mateo and Alvaro."

Perhaps it wasn't the boys they feared, but the unnamed boss who sounded like the Fagin character in a Dickens novel. They were probably right to worry.

"Hey, cubs. No matter where you go today, I'll be close by and so will Madoc." Niall ruffled Sky's hair. "We're your bodyguards, eh?"

The blond lad looked uncertainly at his brother. Talam was definitely the alpha of the two, much like André with Niall and Madoc.

After a moment's thought, Talam turned to André. "Yes, Cosantir. Uh—" He looked at Niall in an unspoken plea for the right words.

Niall winked, bowed his head, and whispered, "Your will, Cosantir."

Both boys bowed their heads and repeated the words.

Without a hint of a smile, André inclined his head in the formal response.

As the cubs sat up, straight and proud, Niall felt a delighted pride at the fine shifters they were becoming.

An hour later, Talam sat at the dining room table and pretended to read his book. The males were loading equipment into Niall's new pickup while Sky napped.

Heather was in the kitchen, making tea, and it was Talam's turn to watch over her in case she needed anything.

He hated it. Not because he didn't want to help, but because she had scratches on her face the healer hadn't fixed. And she was barefoot because all her shoes were gone. And she didn't have the little cabin in the forest.

Because of what he and Sky had done.

Only they wouldn't've burned her cabin if they'd known it was Heather's place. Mr. Wendell *lied* to them, and they'd believed him because he was—had been—the Cosantir. What kind of Cosantir would lie? Or burn a female's house? It was...wrong.

Frowning, Talam stared out the window, then heard Heather

say, "Cat-scat," real quiet. He stood up and saw her trying to open a honey jar one-handed by pinning it to the wall with her hip.

He hurried over. "I can get it."

Her eyes were red like she was going to cry. But she didn't yell or anything. "That'd be great, Talam. The lid is awfully tight. I guess these males are way too strong."

It was tight, but he got it open and felt almost useful.

"Thank you, sweetie." She poured the honey in her tea and then just stared at it.

"I...uh...don't you drink coffee?"

"I had some with breakfast. I'm having tea now so I can pretend it's calming." Her smile was crooked. Sky looked like that when he tried not to cry.

I did this to her. He was the reason she broke her arm and couldn't open a jar and had to drink tea. "I'm sorry."

"Oh, youngling." Putting an arm around him, she pulled him close. "I don't blame you for doing what a grown-up male told you to do. Especially if you thought he was the Cosantir."

He could feel her taking a big breath.

"I'm going to be sad and angry about what happened, probably for a while to come. But I'll never be mad at you or Sky. It's not your fault, Talam."

"Why—" His voice cracked, and he had to start again. "How come André is the Cosantir and not Mr. Wendell? I thought Cosantirs stayed till they died or something."

"Oh, I guess I'm to blame." She gave him a squeeze and let him go, then picked up her cup of tea. "Tell you what—sit with me, and I'll tell you the story."

When they were sitting back at the table—and somehow, he had a couple of cookies and a glass of milk in front of him—she started, "You see, Pete—Mr. Wendell—was Cosantir for a long time, but he stopped doing the job. He wasn't protecting the women and children or enforcing the Laws. So, when I saw a fight where a male broke the other male's bones, I..."

As Talam listened, his stomach got tighter and tighter until he pushed the cookies away. He'd heard about the scary, dangerous Call to the Gods in stories and stuff. Heather was really brave. He swallowed hard. "Did Mr. Wendell know you asked Herne for a different Cosantir?"

Heather nodded. "Yes, I told everyone during a work day at the Gathering House—and Pete was there."

Scatty poop. Talam wrapped his arms around himself. What should he do? Surely she knew Mr. Wendell hated her. Did she need to know more?

If he told her Mr. Wendell was who lied to him and Sky and had them burn her house, then he'd come after him and Sky. Hurt them.

Only what if Mr. Wendell tried something else? What if he went after her—or *killed her*—because she didn't know how crazy mad he was? Talam shivered.

"Talam?" She put her hand over his. "Honey, you're shaking. What's the matter?"

"He hates you," Talam whispered. "He—Mr. Wendell—he was the one who took us out to your house to burn it. And...and he said he'll turn into a bear and rip us to pieces if we tell. But you have to be careful, Heather. He hates you."

"Oh baby." Drawing him close, she held him as he cried.

And for the first time in a very long time, he felt...safe. So very safe.

That afternoon in Ailill Ridge, Madoc moseyed along, pretending to be window-shopping, but tracking the cubs' reflection in the glass. On the other side of the square, Niall was doing the same thing. They'd be close if their charges found trouble.

Would the mangy-tailed, coyote-livered weasel of an ex-Cosantir really go after them?

Madoc still had trouble believing any Daonain would threaten cubs—let alone a shifter who'd been a Cosantir.

No wonder Herne ripped Wendell's powers out.

Unfortunately, the God had left the weasel alive and free to seek revenge on Heather and the cubs. And probably André, if the opportunity arose. Because Herne didn't haul off and simply execute shifters.

Sometimes Madoc thought that was a shame.

Well, when found, Wendell would face Cosantir's Judgment. Not only for instigating the burning of the cabin but for embezzling from the clan and worse—using *cubs* to steal for him.

Madoc growled under his breath. The way he felt, Wendell would be lucky to survive to stand before André.

They just had to find him. He wasn't at his house. Roger, the pack alpha, had moved out and didn't know where his littermate was. Every evening, André did his Cosantir scanning thing, seeing what shifters were in his territory. Wendell wasn't. He might have taken off for a whole new state...or simply be hiding just outside of the territory in a human town. There was nothing to prevent him from returning. Unless André was actively scanning at the time, he wouldn't know if Wendell was here.

Which meant, until they found the weasel, they needed to guard his victims.

Madoc moved in closer to the cubs.

Circling the square, Talam and Sky slowed at each opening between buildings and whistled an odd tune. After making the circuit once, they started over.

A whistle came from one dark opening. The cubs stopped... staying within Madoc's sight.

Four slightly older lads stood in the shadows, all equally ragged and thin.

The sight about broke Madoc's heart.

And it made him wonder... A Cosantir could draw strength from his land and his clan. Did the bond go both ways? Did a

Cosantir's spirit affect his clan? Had Wendell's laziness and indifference infected his people?

Madoc chuckled, because if the link went both ways, the clan was in for a shock. André was neither lazy nor indifferent, and the shifters here might well feel as if they'd gotten a sharp nip to their furry asses.

As Talam and Sky talked, hope lit the other cubs' faces.

After a few minutes, Talam headed for the Shamrock, and the other cubs followed him like ducklings after their mother. Grinning, Sky brought up the rear.

Alert for threats, Madoc crossed the square after them. He didn't scent Wendell anywhere.

But the human Chief of Police watched the procession with narrowed eyes and a pissed-off expression.

Putting a foot up on a bench, Madoc pretended to tie his shoe and eyed the cop as questions arose. Why hadn't the police done anything about the wayward boys? Didn't humans take responsibility for orphans? The chief couldn't have known these were shifter children.

Or could he?

As the boys entered the Shamrock, the cop walked away.

Niall stopped in the doorway and glanced back at Madoc.

Since the boys were safe inside, Madoc pointed toward where Wendell's house was located. He'd wander over there and have another sniff to see if the weasel had returned.

He wasn't a cahir like his brother, but he never minded lending a paw in the name of justice.

And his paws were damned big.

Leaning against the long counter in the Shamrock, André winced as the sound of a circular saw assaulted his ears. Near one wall, the Moreno's all-Daonain construction crew were working on the salad bar Madoc had wanted at the last minute.

On the opposite side of the room, Heather and Ina were talking with the selected communal house residents.

André smiled as he watched them. Heather had refused to stay home and rest. Instead, she insisted on helping choose the shifter who would manage the communal house. Apparently, one of her friends had been bullied when living there last winter.

Since there would be parentless cubs in the house, André wanted someone who lived there to be in charge.

Talam had told Heather if she wanted to manage the house, he and Sky would help her. Before André could tell the lad no, she'd gently explained that she could afford to rent a house and shouldn't take a room someone else really needed.

At the door, Talam came in, followed by four boys, perhaps thirteen and fourteen years old, then Sky.

Thanks to the Mother. André pulled in a relieved breath. He'd been worried Wendell might have taken the other boys off to steal.

As they drew closer, he caught the wild scent, indicating the new cubs had already experienced First Shift. One worry gone since a cub required a mentor for First Shift—someone they completely trusted.

Talam and Sky's First Shift was still a concern. At this time, the only adults they even vaguely trusted were Heather, him, and his brothers. For now, the cubs needed to stay right where they were.

He walked over to a table in the center of the room and took a seat. No need to loom over the wary younglings.

Standing in front of him, Talam made the tiny bow he'd learned from Niall. "Cosantir."

"Talam." André smiled at them. "Thank you for coming."

The four new cubs stared at him. Thin, ragged, dirty. And trembling with hope.

He tilted his head. "I'm André, the new Cosantir—and I hope to take better care of you."

The blue-eyed one, trying so hard to be brave, stood straight. "Yeah, what do we have to do for it?"

His littermate elbowed him, hissing, "He's the Cosantir, scat-for-brains. Be polite."

Ah well, a cub learned by watching. André smiled gently and pointed at the chairs around the round table. "Sit, please."

Despite nervous glances toward the open door to ensure their escape was possible, they obeyed. Talam and Sky sat to his right.

"I know Talam and Sky." André smiled at the brown-eyed cub next to Talam. "Can I have everyone's names?"

The short, brown-eyed cub next to Talam spoke up first. "I'm Mateo Galves." He touched the lad next to him. "And my brother, Alvaro."

"It's good to meet you. I'm guessing thirteen years old?" André's estimate received a quick smile and nod from Mateo.

He turned to the other pair of littermates and waited.

"I'm Kathan." The sturdy blond cub turned and nodded at his equally stocky, brown-haired, blue-eyed brother. "And he's Hamlin...uh...Pfeiffer. We're fourteen."

"A good summing up." At André's approval, the fourteen-year-olds also smiled.

"Cosantir." Heather came out of the kitchen with a basket filled with donuts and small cartons of milk. She set it on the table. "For your meeting."

The female was wily as a fox. What youngling would walk away from donuts? "Thank you, Heather. Join us, please."

"Your will, Cosantir." She took the empty chair on his left, adjusting her sling as she sat.

The boys—even Sky and Talam—stared at the food, not believing it was for them.

"*You* are my meeting, lads." He motioned to the food. "Eat."

They still hesitated, as if thinking he'd change his mind. But when Talam took a milk carton and a donut, the rest did the same. Warily. Watching him closely.

Pity vied with anger in his soul. No cub should ever go hungry—or be so afraid. But it was quite satisfying to watch them eat and begin to relax.

Leaning closer to Heather, André whispered, "You are a wonder."

A charming pink filled her cheeks. "Just doing what needed to be done."

In his opinion, she always went several kilometers beyond.

Eventually, the younglings slowed and started giving him nervous glances.

André smiled. "You asked what you had to do..."

Hamlin, the cub with the quick mouth, bit his lip and nodded.

"I'm sure Talam and Sky said you'll live at the communal house."

They all nodded.

André folded his hands on the table. "You'll have a temporary foster parent for each set of littermates. Obey them and the house manager. Be polite and work together with everyone else there." He gave them a stern look. "You'll also obey the laws of the country and the Daonain."

"That means no more stealing." Everyone heard Talam's whisper.

The newcomers flushed and looked at the table.

"Aye," André agreed. "No stealing. If Pete Wendell tries to talk with you, tell your foster parent or the manager or me."

Off to one side, Niall raised his hand. "Or me."

André grinned. "Or the cahir."

As the cubs eyed Niall, André could see their tension ease. Like Talam and Sky, they were terrified of Wendell coming after them.

"Will there be food there?" Mateo asked carefully.

"Plenty of food. Clothes. Beds. Showers." André raised an eyebrow at Heather in case she wanted to add something.

"You'll be in school, of course, and along with fun times, you'll help keep up the house in return for an allowance."

The news of an allowance received delighted smiles.

She continued, "And...the Cosantir hadn't planned to open the communal house until it was fixed up, but after hearing about you, he's opening it today." Heather smiled at them. "Which means you'll get to help paint the walls. If the carpenters need help, go for it. You might learn a new skill."

"I like carpentry." Kathan straightened in his chair.

"He's good at it too," Hamlin chimed in.

"Perfect. You'll get a chance to help." André motioned to Ina's group waiting off to one side. "Heather will introduce you to your foster parents and the others who will be living at the house. I'll be here if you have questions or concerns afterward."

A second later, he was sitting with just Talam and Sky.

"We...we could go to the communal house too." Sky stared at his hands.

What with an upcoming First Shift and then Wendell's threat, he'd prefer they stay right where they were. But if the other boys were their friends, would they be happier at the communal house? "Would you prefer to go there?"

Both lads shook their heads vehemently.

"Then, until we've dealt with Wendell, you'll stay with us. Yes?" André smiled at the gusty sighs of relief.

A female's voice rose. "Why, I know—knew—your mama! I didn't realize she had returned to the Mother. Heather, let me foster these two."

André checked the corner. Kathan and Hamlin were being hugged by a middle-aged female. Smiles made him think things were going well. And Niall was lurking nearby. He'd have a report later.

"You!"

André looked up to see the Chief of Police crossing the room...from the kitchen. How long had the human been there?

The chief had an angry expression on his face. "I hear you're the new bigshot, come to take over the town."

André stiffened. How much did the man know about the Daonain? In a territory, there were usually a few humans who'd been told about shifters. Very few, though, because betrayal meant the death of the human *and* the shifter.

It was the Law.

"Chief Farley." André rose. "I'm André Crichton. What brings you here today?"

The chief looked André up and down, then his lip curled. "You don't seem particularly threatening."

"That's good to hear. Again, what brings you here today?"

"I know what you are." Farley moved closer, his voice dropping. "What you turn into."

Around the room, shifters tensed. Farley obviously didn't realize that shifter hearing was more than adequate to catch what he said.

"I see." André leaned a hip against the table. "And you are here because...?"

"Pete and me, we had a deal."

This wasn't looking good. "I hadn't heard about it." André opened his hands, palms up. "If you would, please explain."

"I told him how to put the brats to use, even taught him the tricks. I get a ten percent cut of everything they pull in." Farley dropped his hand to his firearm. "You took over Pete's job and the little shits. I expect my cut from what they steal."

"I see." André eyed the chief. *No, don't jump the idiot.* Risking females and cubs was unacceptable.

From the corner of his eye, André saw Niall silently moving in from the side. Behind the chief, Madoc appeared in the kitchen doorway.

Excellent. "I regret to tell you the children will no longer participate in illegal activities."

Anger darkened Farley's face. "Then you had best look to giving me my cut anyway. A thousand a month should cover it."

"And if I do not?"

Farley's mouth edged with a cruel smile. "Then I tell the media about people who turn into bears."

This was going downhill quickly. "A bear?"

"Fuck, don't play innocent with me. Pete showed me what you people are. Jesus, I about lost my fucking lunch." He sneered at André. "Since you took over, I guess you're a bigger bear than Wendell?"

"I'm a bigger threat," André said mildly. He glanced at Niall who'd come up right behind Farley. "Secure him, please."

A second later, the cahir had Farley restrained in a full nelson, arms beneath the chief's armpits and hands locked behind his neck. When the man kept struggling, Niall tightened his hold, coming close to breaking the lawman's neck.

No one in the room would object. The human's doom had been sealed the moment he threatened to reveal the Daonain.

Unfortunately, a dead police officer would draw attention.

There was another way to deal with the human. Not one André liked. His stomach twisted in sudden nausea. Yet he had no sympathy for a law enforcement officer who'd use children to feather his nest. "I fear, Chief, neither of us is going to enjoy this."

Niall held Farley as André laid his hand on the chief's face. When he opened the channel to Herne's power, the surging fire ripped a path across his soul as if he was riding a lightning bolt.

Bowing his head, closing his eyes, he pushed into the human's mind, ignoring his high scream of agony. With the flames of the God, he burned away the memories of weeks... months. All Farley's interactions with Wendell and the children —gone.

Go further. The God's command reverberated through André.

Continuing, he wiped the memories back to the man's first hint of what the Daonain might be.

Years...gone.

As the thunder of the God faded from his spirit, André dropped his hand.

The room was silent except for the rasp of the unconscious chief's breathing. The shifters stared at André in an uncomfortable mix of horror and respect.

He pulled in a breath. The clean certainty of a Judgment faded. Sickness at what he'd just done remained.

Stepping back, he met Niall's understanding gaze. His brother murmured, "Sometimes the job sucks."

A cahir would know.

"Thank you, brawd." André's words came out an ugly rasp. "We need to decide what to do with him. He'll be incapacitated for a while—and he's lost years of his past."

"Drop him off at a human hospital?" Madoc joined André and bumped his shoulder in support.

"No." Heather joined André. "Hospitals have security cameras outside. Your vehicle and face would show up."

Niall nodded. "She's right. Could we simply dump him somewhere?"

"*Oui.*" André rubbed the back of his neck. Abandoning a confused person, even if a criminal, was distasteful. "Afterward, I'll call emergency services to report an injured man on the roadside."

"No, the phone would—" Niall and Heather spoke together, then Niall continued, "They'd be able to track your phone."

"Use a disposable phone, an' hang up real quick." Sky and the other cubs had moved closer. When everyone looked at him, he flushed and muttered. "Mom and me liked to read thrillers."

"It's a good idea." Niall wrapped his arm around Sky's head and ruffled his hair. "I like clever cubs."

The sick feeling inside André diminished at the proud tilt to the cub's chin. And at remembering how the chief and Wendell had used the younglings. The balance was fair.

He looked at the small group around him. "It appears we have a plan."

An hour later, Heather couldn't quite get past what she'd just seen. Admittedly, she'd heard about how other Cosantirs banished and even killed shifters.

But this? André had wiped out years of a person's memories. *Years.*

"Here, Heather." Murtagh handed her a cheap phone from his stock.

She tucked it into her sling.

Then Sky, Talam, Mateo, and Alvaro climbed into the back two rows of André's Toyota Sequoia. Realizing the chief had been the one to set them up to be exploited, the younglings wanted to see him out of their lives.

Opening the back hatch, Madoc put the unconscious chief in, donned gloves, and jumped into Farley's police car. He'd follow them to the dumping site.

"Here goes nothing," Heather muttered and settled into the passenger seat.

Niall laughed and started the car. "We'll be fine, pretty wolf."

The drive toward Ellensburg seemed far too long, probably because Heather kept imagining how everything might go wrong—like getting discovered with the chief in the back.

Finally, Niall turned down a deserted road and slowed. "There's a likely boulder." Getting out, he left the car running. "Stay put, everyone."

With Madoc's help, he lugged the chief out of the SUV, knocked his head against the boulder, and let him fall.

As Madoc wiped any fingerprints from the door latch,

Heather eyed the blacktop shoulder, pleased to see the pavement showed no footprints or tire tracks.

Niall jumped back in, followed by Madoc. The police car would remain there, parked on the shoulder.

After buckling into a seat beside Sky, Madoc stripped off his gloves.

"Why'd you hit his head on the rock?" Talam asked as Niall did a U-turn and drove away.

"I wanted the boulder to be marked with his blood. It'll look as if he fell and thumped his head there. It explains why he's unconscious and will be confused."

Heather closed her eyes for a moment. Confused was an understatement, Heather thought. The chief wouldn't be able to remember the last years of his life. A prison sentence might be easier.

"I guess it's my turn." She punched 911 into the phone.

"911. What is your emergency?"

She made her voice high and frantic. "I...I saw a man. Lying beside the road. I think he's unconscious or dead or something. It's um, outside Ellensburg, barely south of the Manastash and Mellergaard intersections. There's like, nothing out here. Please send someone to check on him."

"Is he breathing? Or bleeding."

"I'm sorry; I didn't stop." *Oh cat-scat.* Why would a person not stop? "I—uh, I have a car full of children." True enough, right?

"Ma'am, I need your name—"

Catching Madoc's nod, Talam screamed in a high voice, "You pisser, you give that back!"

"No! It's my game," Sky yelled. "Ow! Mo-om, he *hit* me."

"No, no, it's mine." Mateo jumped right in. When he slapped his hands together like he'd hit someone, his littermate gave a yell of fury.

"You kids stop. Dammit!" Heather ended the call a second before she burst out laughing.

She turned to the grinning cubs in the back seat. "You were amazing." Hand in the air, she high-fived Talam and Sky in the closest seats, then gave a thumbs-up to the other two. "Brilliant idea."

"Yeah, when we were littler, we used to drive Mom crazy." Talam's expression held a mix of humor and grief.

"Us too," Mateo agreed.

Madoc was laughing. "The dispatcher—or any parent—will know exactly why you didn't stop to help a victim—or talk on the phone."

Within a mile, the four cubs in the back were quiet, playing an I-Spy game. A few miles later, Niall took the phone from her and threw it out the window into a deep ravine.

Heather sighed in relief. "Mission accomplished."

"Except for Wendell." Niall's jaw was tight. The grimness of his voice brought home to her who exactly would have to deal with Pete. Because Niall was a cahir.

Heather pulled in a breath.

Pete had told a human about the Daonain. He'd broken the Law. The Cosantir had no choice but to order the cahir—Niall—to kill Pete. To return him to the Mother.

"I'm sorry." Heather lay her hand on his hard thigh.

"Thanks." He moved his shoulders in a shrug. "That's the job, though."

Being a cahir took a very special kind of male.

After a minute of silence, she frowned. "Speaking of jobs..."

"What?"

"What are we going to do for a police chief?"

CHAPTER TWENTY-EIGHT

Stretched out on his favorite couch the next night, Niall listened half-heartedly to the conversation on the other side of their great room.

Heather and André had been discussing the lack of a police chief. Then Ina and Murtagh had shown up and joined in.

Maybe it was time to retreat to his work den? Yet... Niall didn't move. He'd built a nice crackling fire in the big fireplace, and the soft warmth radiated outward.

In the flames, a salamander was dancing with mesmerizingly sinuous movements. It was smaller and a lighter red than a lot of the fire elementals he'd seen. Must be a young one.

A prickle on his neck made him realize he was being watched. The conversation across the room had stopped. When he turned his head, Ina and Murtagh were staring at him. Heather was frowning.

André rubbed his neck and explained. "Brawd, they want to know if you would be the police chief."

Fuck me sideways. He bit back his first answer that would probably put the Elders in shock. "Absolutely not."

"But cahirs can be law enforcement," Ina protested. "Alec up in Cold Creek is the county sheriff."

Niall had met the big tawny cahir from the North Cascades. Good male. "Alec likes to be around people. I don't."

Ina blinked.

"There's a reason I work with computers. No people needed."

Ina looked startled. "But...you're a *cahir*."

Niall gave the Elders a slightly mean smile. "As such, I don't do diplomacy. I just break necks."

Murtagh snorted a laugh, then held up a hand. "Forgive us. We sometimes forget the Gods-called have their own personalities."

Niall nodded and went back to his job of dozing. Fair division of labor, right?

In the fireplace, the salamander was still playing. After a showy pirouette, the fire elemental rose up the chimney. A second later, it reappeared in a spiraling dive—but hit the side of a log and landed in the coals. Sparks exploded up the chimney.

Obviously humiliated, the little salamander disappeared behind the burning wood.

Niall let out a laugh.

Coal-black eyes glared at him from under a log.

Oh fuck. Next time he tried to start a fire, the damn elemental would undoubtedly snuff it right out—several times. Salamanders held grudges.

Across the room, the discussion about the police chief continued. It was a shame André didn't have a clone.

But they did have someone much like him. "Brawd, you might ask Bron if she'd like a change."

"Bron?" André's brows drew up, then he grinned. "She *was* complaining about being bored."

"We could use another cahir anyway." Niall's gut tightened. "The States have more hellhound activity than Canada."

André's mouth flattened. Because one cahir taking on a hellhound was essentially a death sentence. "I'll call her."

"Who is Bron?" Ina asked.

"Ah, our aunt—one of the few female cahirs—and also in the RCMP." André smiled. "She's the one who talked me into being a Mountie."

Niall added, "She's tough, but a good cop. Has even worked here in the States before. And she likes people."

"Nice fire, cahir." Heather joined Niall, standing beside the couch.

Seeing it had an audience, the salamander began to dance again, showing off its twirls and dives.

"C'mere, female." Wrapping an arm around Heather's hips, Niall pulled her down to sit on his belly. A wonderful weight, nice and toasty. "Thanks. I was cold."

Her resonant laugh burst out as she eyed his bare feet and T-shirt. "Might I recommend more clothing and a blanket?"

"Where's the fun in that?" He laced his fingers with her good hand. "You know, my room is the one next to André's. You're welcome to join me anytime. For snuggles and sleep, or for exercise then sleep."

She tilted her head to one side, considering him. Such beautiful eyes, filled with intelligence. "I thought you didn't like people."

"You're not people, pretty wolf. You're turning into family."

Her eyes gleamed with tears for a moment before she said softly, "What a lovely compliment. Thank you."

It wasn't a compliment, merely a fact, and one he was trying to come to terms with. She was becoming...important.

When she wasn't around, the world felt a little less alive.

CHAPTER TWENTY-NINE

Standing behind the counter of his restaurant, Madoc opened his senses and smiled at the scent of pizza and the buzz of happy customers. From behind him came the cheerful voices of the kitchen staff.

The evening was drawing to a close—and it'd been a great opening day for his restaurant. And for him.

Sure, he hadn't achieved everything he wanted, but this was a fine start. Even better, the atmosphere had the homey feeling he'd aimed for.

He figured this was one way he could help André. A healthy territory would have several places where clan members could mingle. Gathering Houses, of course. Pack houses for the wolves. Occasionally a bar, like in the North Cascades. Often a diner or a restaurant.

This would be a family-friendly restaurant where people could linger. There were tables for parents around a small, designated play area. One corner had board game tables where customers could play and eat—and talk.

Yeah, it was a family restaurant—and his family had helped tonight. Despite her arm still being in a sling, Heather had supervised the waitstaff for the first few hours. Talam and Sky helped bus tables during the rush. Niall and André pitched in to take orders or clear tables when needed—and shocked the traditionalist Daonain.

But since Madoc had worked in or managed restaurants for over three decades, his littermates knew exactly how and when to assist.

Now, Heather and his brothers were sitting at a table near the fireplace. Talam and Sky had happily accepted a pizza to share with Mateo and Alvaro.

"Amazing pizza, Madoc." Zorion Moreno, followed by Ramón and Moya, swung by the counter. The construction crew boss glared at his brother. "I'd planned to take some home for breakfast, but greedy gut there finished it off."

Ramón laughed and patted his flat belly. "It was too good; what can I say? You can get another one tomorrow, brawd."

"Actually, you can't." Smirking, Moya poked Zorion in the shoulder.

"What—why not?"

"Tomorrow's not a pizza day."

Both of the brothers turned to stare at Madoc.

He shrugged. "She has it right. There's a different menu each day we're open. Saturdays are pizza. Sunday will be barbecue."

"By the Gods. Meat, all the meat." Ramón moaned. "I gotta have me some of that."

Zorion laughed, told Madoc, "Guess we'll see you tomorrow," and led his littermates out of the restaurant.

Madoc leaned on the counter with a smile. Yeah, this was going to be great.

CHAPTER THIRTY

"I think I ate too much breakfast." In the great room, Heather yawned, not nearly ready to start the day.

"You look like you need a nap, pretty wolf." Smiling, André set a cup and a book on the coffee table.

"I woke up barely an hour ago. I swear, all I've done for days is sleep." Although she hadn't slept last night worth a darn. After all the excitement of Madoc's restaurant opening, she'd ended up with nightmares about her cabin burning. "No more naps."

"I haven't seen you sleeping much at all. You've been at Madoc's restaurant, doing bookkeeping, working with the cubs—and shopping. So, yes, you need a nap." With a wicked smile, he plucked her right out of the chair.

He sat on the couch, swung his legs up, and leaned back against the armrest. She ended up sitting on his lap. "*André.*"

"Yes, this should work." With firm hands, he positioned her to snuggle against him with her head against his shoulder, then flipped the throw blanket over her. "Sleep, Heather. I'll guard you."

There was no way she'd get to sleep, but...this really was

comfortable. He was so *warm*. With every breath, his chest slowly rose and fell. His heart rate was equally slow.

Padding over, Greystoke surveyed the situation, then jumped up and curled into a ball against her stomach.

"Now you have to stay put." André chuckled, stroking his hand down Heather's arm. "Everyone knows disturbing a sleeping cat is a sacrilege."

Greystoke was purring. She was warm and comfy and getting petted. This just wasn't...

Sometime later, she woke to the sound of voices.

"I'd get up, but I'm rather handicapped at the moment, you understand," André was saying. The smoky-smooth, deep voice made her think of long nights of making love.

She blinked and remembered she'd been lying on the male. His arm was a heavy weight over her waist.

"Now...how does it happen our sister is sleeping on you, Cosantir?" Her brother Daniel sounded quite irritated.

"Perhaps because she was tired?" The amusement in André's words was far too obvious.

Her brothers could be overly protective...and why were they here? She opened her eyes and reluctantly sat up.

With an annoyed chuff, Greystoke jumped to the floor and stalked away, ignoring Tanner's, "Hey, kitty," greeting. Greystoke had never approved of people who smelled like dogs—and the ranch had a couple.

Sitting up, she pushed her hair back, fighting the lethargy of a good sleep. And...oops, she was still sitting on André.

She looked down into dark, dark eyes filled with laughter and frowned at him. "You seem so serious, but you're as much of a troublemaker as your brothers."

"But no, I'm sure you must be mistaken," he murmured.

She thumped his chest in response and rose to give her brothers hugs. "Hey, dudes, what are you doing here?" She'd called them days ago to tell them about her cabin and reassure them she was all right.

Daniel gave her a hard squeeze. "We needed to see you, make sure you weren't feeding us a line of bullshit."

"I wouldn't." At his grin, she shrugged. "Okay, so we all make light of problems, but in this case, I really am all right. My sling is even off."

Tanner scowled. "You could've died." He took her shoulders gently, because he'd learned when young that his strength could hurt. "Gods, Heather." He closed his eyes for a moment, then managed a smile. "Hey, we brought you some shit."

"Your language." She shook her head, then recalled her own manners. "Cosantir, do you remember my brothers, Daniel and Tanner?"

André had already risen to his feet. "I do. Welcome—and can I get you a coffee or tea?"

Daniel tried to glower at him and totally failed. "No, we're good, thanks."

She almost laughed. The Cosantir's charm had scored again.

"We're all going for a furry run in an hour, if you'd care to join us. Madoc would love to have a couple of bears to wrestle with." With a nod, André headed back to his office.

"We've got some boxes for you in the pickup, sis." Tanner motioned toward the front door. "Hold on while we fetch them."

As she waited for them, her cell rang. The display showed GRETCHEN. Oh spit. She pulled in a breath. "Gretchen, what can I do for you?"

"I received an invitation to the housewarming for the Cosantir. Of course, I knew right away any party should be held here in the bed and breakfast. This is the—"

"No, Gretchen. It's a housewarming, which means it's held at the person's house." Tilting her head back, Heather looked at the ceiling. Because rolling her eyes would be childish.

After a moment, the female sighed. "Fine, then I need to be

helping prepare the party. You don't know anything about what—"

"No, Gretchen. Everything has already been planned. Oh, I need to go; my brothers are here."

Heather ended the call and pocketed her phone with a sigh. Murtagh must have caved to pressure and revealed that Heather had been part of the planning group. The Elders had come up with the idea, but Heather helped map out where everything would go and what would be needed for the day-long party.

She smiled. It was time the clan showed their appreciation for André and welcomed all three brothers properly. This would be good for everyone.

"Lead on, sis." Daniel carried in a big box, followed by Tanner.

Upstairs in her guest room, her brothers prowled around the room while she opened a box. It was filled with the spare clothing she'd kept at the ranch.

"We figured it'd take a while for you to replace everything. Once you have, you can bring the spares back." Daniel stood at the window, looking out at the forest.

"This is perfect. I bought some things yesterday, but...yes, it's going to take a while." She pulled out a couple of flannel shirts and hugged the age-softened material.

Before she could pull more clothes out, Greystoke jumped into the box. He circled once, curled in a ball, and gave her a look: *Mine*.

Being a wise female, she simply grinned. "Right. I'll finish emptying it later."

Tanner snickered. "No wonder the Crichtons like you. You already knew how to get on with cats."

The next box had...

Her eyes filled with tears as she pulled out a cashmere-soft blanket—one her mother had knitted. They'd all received a couple of the throws, but hers had burned in the fire. "Thank you."

Next was a photo album. Frowning, she opened it. "This is yours, Tanner." Mama had made one for each of them, although the pictures were all the same.

"Since we made it this far together, I figure Daniel and I can share his." Tanner's voice was gruff. "You should have one of your own."

The bottom of the box had a couple of framed photographs. Ones of them all together. Her voice came out wobbly. "You knew the things I'd miss the most."

Daniel shrugged.

Her brothers, so very male and hating emotional displays. Yet sensitive enough to bring her memories of their mother.

Wiping her eyes, she smiled at them. "So do you two want to come and run with the Crichton crew?"

"Play with another bear?" Daniel grinned. "You bet."

In cougar form, Niall leaped into a tree right outside the house portal and stretched out on a thick branch.

Madoc had already gone down the trail with the younglings. André had taken a phone call and was still in the house. Inside the portal, Heather was talking to her brothers, their voices drifting out the open tunnel door.

"Why didn't you come back to the ranch after you got hurt, sis?" The voice was the one named Daniel.

Niall's tail flicked at the annoying question. Heather was right where she was supposed to be.

"A couple reasons," Heather replied. "They had Lord Greystoke here. And my arm was in a sling. You would have insisted on staying home and taking care of me."

"Damn straight," the deeper, rougher-voiced Tanner said. Niall liked him for the instant agreement that caring for their sister was their duty.

"You don't have time for tending to me this month, bro—and, really, the cubs needed to do something. They still feel guilty, but I think it helped."

"Poor younglings." Daniel came out of the tunnel, followed by Tanner. "Being lied to is bad enough, but hurting someone you liked? Major suckage."

"So where is that bastard Pete, anyway?" Tanner asked.

"No one knows." Heather joined her brothers. "You know, he was a lazy, egotistical Cosantir, but how come he grew so much worse in the last few years?"

"When you lose your way, things can go downhill fast," Daniel said slowly. "He and Roger lost their female. Roger took it hard, but Pete... He was never the same afterward."

"I think you're right, Daniel." André came out of the portal behind them. "The connection to the God is much like a river—and negative emotions can close it off."

"So he cut off Herne, then everything started spiraling out of control?" Tanner shook his head. "I bet he blames everyone except himself."

Daniel scowled. "We're not in town often, but we'll help hunt him when we are, Cosantir."

André inclined his head in acceptance.

"We talked to Murtagh at the grocery store before coming here." Tanner scratched his back against a tree trunk. "I guess Chief Farley was in a bad accident—hit his head, and he's messed up."

Score. Niall licked his forepaw.

"No great loss there," Daniel muttered.

Heather nodded. "Ina said he called the town council to resign since he's moving back east to be closer to family who can help him. The town council will hire someone and put Farley's stuff into storage for him until he sends for it."

Tanner glanced at André. "Can we make sure the next chief is a shifter?"

"Since the Daonain Elders on the council outnumber the humans, I think it's assured."

Niall gave a chuffing cat laugh. It was assured because André had told the Elders to make sure it happened. If their aunt responded, Bron would undoubtedly get the job.

In another year, they'd see if they could coax Heather into running for mayor. She'd win hands-down—and she'd be amazing at the job. Then she could run the town, and André could run the clan.

"Enough serious stuff. Let's go play." Heather shifted to her wolf.

"Let's start with squish-a-wolf." Daniel grinned at his brother, and they both trawsfurred into bears.

Niall blinked. The two were as big as Madoc. They grappled with each other for a minute, then turned and trapped their sister in a corner of bushes.

Typical brothers.

Friendly play, however, there would be no picking on Heather here. *Not on my watch. Nope.* With a chuff, Niall alerted André.

When the first bear lumbered close enough, Niall leaped off his branch right onto Daniel's furry back and knocked him over.

Heh, this is fun.

Daniel let out a shocked huff.

Shifting to cougar, André swatted Tanner's ass from behind. As the bear spun, André sprang into the nearest tree.

The diversion worked like a treat.

With a taunting *ooo-ooo-ooo*, Heather scampered down the trail, leaving her brothers in the dust.

Niall heard André's pleased chuff before he dropped out of the tree. They rubbed heads, mutually happy.

Because the pretty wolf was theirs to defend.

CHAPTER THIRTY-ONE

Talam tapped the last key, finishing his test, and let out a whoop.

"Shhh." Mr. Quintrell tried to sound pissed, but his lips tipped up in a little smile. The short, gray-haired wolf shifter was really chill.

Also finished, Sky held out his hand, and they fist-bumped.

"Since you're both done, you can head over to the restaurant, if Madoc agrees. Hold on a sec." Their teacher pulled out his cell phone.

Their homeschool—but it wasn't at home—opened yesterday in the warehouse behind the Shamrock. Mateo and Alvaro were there, along with three other bunches of littermates.

Since Ailill Ridge was small and close to Cle Elum, the middle and high school students were bused to the bigger town. But when the Cosantir found out, he said being bused to a human town was unacceptable for cubs within a year of First Shift or who hadn't proven they could control their trawsfurs.

So he'd found Mr. Quintrell, who taught middle school before he retired and was happy to teach them cuz he'd gotten bored.

This morning, Niall came in and set up a bunch of computers.

He told Talam shifters should have paws in the world of today as well as the world of legend.

Sometimes, Niall could sound a lot like a bard.

Madoc never did. But boy, could he cook. One of warehouse doors was right behind the restaurant kitchen. And the smell of fried chicken was making Talam drool worse than a gnome.

"Talam, Sky, Madoc is expecting you. Off you go," Mr. Quintrell motioned toward the door and added, "Don't forget you have homework tonight."

"Yessir." Talam slung his backpack over one shoulder. Followed by Sky, he headed for the restaurant.

Madoc wasn't in the kitchen, but there were a couple of waitstaff talking to the Cosantir.

Talam skidded to a stop in the doorway.

André was always awfully nice, but Talam couldn't forget what he'd done to the chief of police last week. Later, when he and Sky had talked, Sky said André looked sick afterward, like he didn't like doing the judgment stuff.

Watching André, hearing his quiet voice, Talam remembered how Heather stated he hadn't wanted to be Cosantir at all. Herne dumped the job on him cuz she'd asked the God to get rid of Pete.

Would Mr. Wendell still be Cosantir if André hadn't taken it? That would be...bad. *Hey, uh, Herne. Thanks for making André the Cosantir.*

Even if André was really scary.

After getting a plate of food from one of the staff, André spotted them in the doorway and smiled. "Cubs."

Talam bowed his head. "Cosantir."

Sky did the same.

André glanced at the clock above the door. "So school's out. Are you here to keep Madoc on his paws?"

"Yessir." Sky grinned and looked at André's plate. "Maybe he'll have extra food too."

"I have no doubt he'll feed you. If he doesn't have work for you, you can come over to the gift shop and help me paint."

Talam brightened. "Sure." Painting was almost as good as helping build.

They didn't run out the door because Madoc told them waitstaff never ever ran, and it was good they didn't since customers were already sitting down at the tables.

The big bear was behind the counter. Talam grinned, remembering how, on Saturday, Madoc had tossed pizza dough into the air to stretch it to pan size. So cool.

When he'd let them try, Talam ended up with a hole in the center—and part of it in his hair. Madoc laughed and tossed him a new one to try again.

Because the Crichton brothers were all about the thing called *perseverance*.

Like at the communal house when Talam wanted to quit after bending a bunch of nails.

Niall had handed over another nail with a grin. " 'Never give up. Never surrender.' "

Recognizing the words from the *Galaxy Quest* movie they'd watched together, Talam had laughed, settled back on his knees, and tried again. And two more nails later, the nail went in. In fact, he was getting pretty good at pounding in nails.

And he'd get better at tossing pizzas.

He *would*.

"Yo, younglings. Wash your hands, please. Then Talam, take three glasses of ice water to table eight. Sky, a glass of Diet Coke to the same table." Madoc grinned at them. "Then you can head into the kitchen and grab what you need to keep you going for a while."

Talam grinned at Sky, and they chorused, "Yessir."

A little while later, they took a corner table with their plates full of chicken and mashed potatoes and gravy.

"This is great." Sky talked around a mouthful of food.

"Yeah." Talam started on his food and moaned at the taste. Just think, they'd be right next door all winter for school. "I'm glad André wouldn't let us go to Cle Elum."

"Yeah, me too." Shoulders hunching, Sky lowered his voice. "I mean...what if something happened, and we had first shift, like, on the bus."

Surrounded by humans, out of control. Talam shivered. But Sky was already scared, so he didn't say all the bad shit that could happen. "What do you think we'll be?"

"Dunno." Sky frowned. "Mom was a bear, but we're Gather-bred, so who knows what our sires were. You might be a wolf and me a cat or something."

"No way—you're too clumsy to be a cat."

Sky's hard foot hit Talam's ankle.

"Ow! You mangy-tailed ninnyhammer."

When Sky smirked, Talam grinned back...because his brother wasn't worrying about First Shift anymore.

Talam had his own worries. Like what would happen when Mr. Wendell was found.

Because...what would happen to him and Sky when they didn't need to be guarded anymore?

Where the fuck are you hiding, Pete Wendell?

Sniffing here and there for Wendell, Niall patrolled Ailill Ridge. Unofficially. The town council was still arguing about who to hire for the chief of police. The police station had two human officers, but the young men had been so beaten down by Farley, neither was up to taking over the chief's position. Duffy, the only shifter officer, refused point-blank.

André was adamant the chief needed to be Daonain. Even with firearms, a human cop might not win against a belligerent shifter, especially a werecat. And a Daonain police chief could cover up inadvertent shifter exposures.

The difficulty was in finding a Daonain with law enforcement experience. André had left a message on their aunt's voicemail, but Bron was on holiday and undoubtedly deep in the wilderness somewhere.

So Niall was keeping an eye on the town.

"Morning, Niall," Murtagh called from the grocery store doorway. "Fine weather we're having."

"It is." Niall lifted a hand, not wanting to stop. The male could talk a shifter off his paws.

At the end of the square, he saw Madoc's restaurant was filling rapidly. The bear would be quite chuffed.

Next to it, the door stood open to the forthcoming gift shop. A few people stood outside, probably waiting to talk with André, either about crafts for the store or clan concerns.

Poor André. Then again, the cat liked people.

In the car park, he noticed lights turning off in the warehouse. The school day should be over. Talam and Sky were probably helping in the restaurant or doing homework until André could take them home.

Good cubs. He could swear they'd grown an inch and put on several pounds now they were being fed regularly.

Talam was all action and hands-on. Sky was more sensitive, loved stories—and had a voice. If he had an interest in the future, they'd see if a bard would take him as an apprentice.

A new bard would be a fine thing.

Niall thought of singing in front of an audience as their mother had, and his nose wrinkled.

I'm so glad I'm a cahir.

Minutes later, when the stink of rotting oranges and carrion hit his nose, he ate those words. Because the scent was that of a hellhound.

Herne help him.

The hellhound must have been here after Sunday's rain, or its scent would have been washed away. In human form, no one would have realized what it was.

Ice crawled up Niall's spine. The demon-spawn couldn't have missed the wild fragrance of shifters...or of children.

Niall followed its trail farther into the parking lot. An abrupt disappearance indicated it had a car.

Standing in the middle of parked cars, he stared blindly back at the peaceful town square, remembering the few hellhound attacks he'd witnessed. The savagery, the blood. The deaths. Over the years, several of his cahir friends had died trying to save their people.

He scrubbed his hands over his face. *Guess it's my turn.*

A few minutes later, he stopped in the gift shop doorway and looked over everyone's head at his brother. The Cosantir.

André was talking to three people, but whatever was in Niall's face had him rising. "I'm very sorry, people, but it appears I'm needed."

Scowling, one male turned, saw Niall, and swallowed hard. "Cahir."

"People, let's get some supper and finish discussing what the Cosantir proposed." One of the females gave André a respectful nod and guided her group through the side door into the restaurant.

Niall drew his shoulders back. "Cosantir."

André walked over and set a hand on his arm. "Let's walk, brawd, so we won't be interrupted."

They crossed the square to the creekside park and veered away from people until there was only the tranquil sound of flowing water. A pixie chittered in a happy greeting to the Gods-called rather than a territorial warning. The wind rustled the trees and carried the fragrance of glaciers on the high peaks.

André bumped their shoulders together. "Now, tell me what raised your hackles."

"A hellhound." Merely saying the word made Niall's jaw

clench. "The scent was in the square's parking lot. From a day or two ago."

"That's...not good."

Niall met his brother's concerned gaze and felt it radiate like a warmth along their littermate's bond.

He was loved.

And he was a cahir who had his duty to the clan. He straightened and spoke—not to his brother, but to the guardian of their territory. "Cosantir, I'll do my best, but...I don't know of anytime a single cahir has prevailed against a hellhound." His death was guaranteed. Worse, there was far too high a chance he couldn't kill the demon-spawn before dying.

"If you don't face it?" André asked quietly.

Since demon-spawn could only shift to hellhound form on the dark of the moon, shifters could hide behind iron bars and sturdy doors until the sun rose.

But the hiding strategy wouldn't work here. "There are too many homes without adequate protection." *May the previous Cosantir's testicles shrivel into walnuts.*

And left unchecked, the hellhound would go on a killing rampage through the town, feeding on shifters' terror as well as their flesh. An exorbitant number of brave males often died trying to protect their females and cubs.

Putting his foot up on a boulder, André rested his forearms across his thigh. He studied the sunlit stream as if it would provide answers.

Niall sure hadn't come up with any. They had no time to do everything that needed to be done.

"What buildings in town are safe?"

"Downtown—the Shamrock, grocery, and bank. Couple of others." Niall considered. "Elsewhere, maybe a third of the residences are unprepared." Their own home had iron window guards and sturdy doors. The communal house still needed new doors.

"All right." André rubbed his face. "If the hellhound was near downtown, it'll follow the Daonain scents into the square first. Then, if denied prey there, it'll range outward."

The thought made Niall's gut twist. "To the unprotected houses."

"*Oui.* However, we can limit the losses by ensuring anyone without reinforced housing spends the night in a protected house."

"André, the hellhound will simply keep looking. We won't be able to notify everyone before tomorrow night."

"And so we have a step two."

Turning, André called, "Bear, we can use your help."

Madoc was still a distance away, and Niall hadn't heard anything. Just how sensitive were a Cosantir's senses anyway?

The bear joined them. "I saw you walk past the restaurant, and you..."

Probably looked like an open grave, Niall thought.

Madoc leaned against the table. "What's wrong?"

"We have a problem..."

After hearing Niall's explanation, Madoc took a minute to think, then he straightened. "I'll get the restaurant prepared for people to bring sleeping bags and hole up for the night. What's step two?"

"I'll ask Calum to send an extra cahir or two if the North Cascades isn't at risk. He has five cahirs there." André frowned. "We shouldn't rely on help from there. They've been hit frequently this year."

Niall's momentary hope died. "Was that step two?"

"No, brawd. Asking for help is simply common sense." André rubbed his shoulder against Niall's. "On to step two. Do you remember meeting Shay and Zeb last summer?"

"Briefly, aye." Niall turned to Madoc. "They're two of the North Cascades cahirs. Wolves. Lifemated."

"I talked with them—about how they fell for a beguiling female from Seattle." André's smile didn't reach his eyes. "After they taught Breanne to shoot, she returned to the city to save her human friends from a hellhound."

"Herne's horns and hooves, *no*." Madoc looked like he was already bracing for disaster.

Niall had to agree. A hellhound's scales were bullet-proof. Only the belly and the tiny, recessed eyes were vulnerable. Even knowing the female was alive and well, he felt his gut clench.

"She's a canny lass." André's smile didn't reach his eyes. "She planned to bait it into a narrow passage where she'd have a chance at hitting its eyes."

"Not completely suicidal, then." Niall caught the scent of his brother's thoughts. "You want to funnel a hellhound and do target shooting? I'm not the finest of shots."

With merely a slight turn of its head, bullets would ricochet off the hellhound's head rather than entering its eye.

"Actually, it was the idea of directing a hellhound's movements that caught my attention." André glanced at Madoc. "Remember when Uncle Gabin taught us about traps used on animals?"

"By the Gods, he had us terrified of going into the forest." Madoc grinned. "For a good day or so at least."

Niall snorted, then straightened in shock. "You want to *trap* a fucking hellhound?"

"I want to *kill* it, brawd. Remember Uncle's drawing of the medieval *trou de loup*?"

"The wolf hole?" A hole in the ground... "You mean the angled pit with a stake hammered into the bottom—sharp end up."

"Exactly. It's a nasty—but popular—design. It was used in the days of Julius Caesar, was called a tiger pit in the East, the Vietnamese used it in the American-Vietnam War."

Madoc snorted. "You and your history books."

Niall bumped the bear's shoulder in sympathy. When they were ten, André researched and built a trebuchet...then used it to catapult potatoes to pound holes in Madoc's snow fort.

But what about this wolf trap? Niall narrowed his eyes. "You want the hellhound to fall in and be impaled on the stakes. Because it has no armor on its belly."

"Exactly so."

"Even if it doesn't die right away or doesn't go in belly-first," Madoc said slowly, "if it can't escape the trap, it'll change to human at sunrise and can be killed then."

Unlike the Daonain, the demon-spawn could be in the hellhound form only on the night of the new moon.

Niall watched the water flow for a minute. "It's worth a try." Even if the trap didn't keep it contained for long, he'd have a much better chance to kill it before he died.

André slapped his arm. "Then let's get to work. There's only this evening and tomorrow until sundown to get this put together."

Turning to his brother, Niall saw the determination in his gaze and took heart. Maybe...maybe this would work.

Curled on the couch with Greystoke in her lap, Heather watched salamanders dance in the fire. The young one had found himself a friend, as salamanders were wont to do, and the two were making twining spirals in the flames.

By the hearth, André, in cougar form, had been sprawled on the thick shag rug and pile of blankets. Now, with a fang-exposing yawn, the cat rose, gave a polite nod of his furry head to her and Niall, and padded upstairs.

To her amusement, Lord Greystoke jumped off her lap and trotted after the werecat. The little rascal adored hanging out with the cougars. Niall and André didn't mind and simply laughed when they found the gray furball snuggled up to them.

André had the right idea. It was growing late. The cubs had been sent off to bed long ago. Madoc followed shortly after. She smiled slightly. When she'd run upstairs to check on them—

because it was obvious they were remembering their mother who'd been killed by a hellhound—she'd heard Madoc's deep voice coming from the third floor. He was telling funny stories to the younglings.

The big deadly bear had a wonderful heart.

In a nearby chair, Niall was working on his laptop, something he could do for hours.

She really should go to bed. Her body was tired enough. For hours, she'd cut sod to conceal the two hellhound traps. Thank the Gods her sling had come off Monday. And that she hadn't needed to dig.

Because they'd had a ton of volunteers.

The memory sent a small glow of satisfaction through her. Using what was becoming an excellent phone-tree, the Cosantir had sent word out to the clan. Shifters were warned about the hellhound and instructed to find a protected home before tomorrow's sunset.

At last full moon, he'd already instituted a sunset-to-sunrise curfew on all dark of the moon nights. But...there would always be those who ignored good sense.

However, when he'd asked for volunteers to help prepare homes, to create the pit traps, and even to fight the demon-dog, a downpour of shifters flooded the park.

By dark, the pits were nearly dug and the concealing sod ready to use. Tomorrow, they'd prepare the stakes and put the cover on.

Her book couldn't keep her interest, and she yawned. Unfortunately, despite her tiredness, her mind wouldn't stop. Because there would be a hellhound in their town tomorrow night. *Gods*.

Leaning forward, Niall set his laptop on the coffee table, and the fabric of his black T-shirt sleeves strained against his thick biceps. So many muscles but such a price to pay for them.

The God gifted extra size, strength, and speed to his warriors because they were a clan's protection against humans, ferals...and hellhounds. Niall would be out there with a hellhound tomorrow.

I don't want you to die. She put her book down because she was shaking too hard to read the words.

A big hand covered hers, and the cushions compressed as Niall sat beside her on the couch. "Little female, I didn't think anything scared you."

"I'm frightened fairly often, actually." She laid her palm gently against his cheek. "But tonight, I'm more scared for you."

"Ah." He moved his shoulder in a faint shrug. "It is what it is. Who knows, maybe the trap will work."

Firelight sent shadows across his square jaw, his sharp cheekbones, shadowing the laugh lines next to his eyes and mouth. The warrior liked to laugh. Loved his family...and his computers.

"I don't want to lose you, Niall. I've lost too much this year." Her eyes filled. "Gods, I sound selfish, don't I?"

"No, you sound as if you have a heart that knows how to love." Niall rose and picked her up, then laid her on the blankets in front of the fire.

The soft heap sank beneath her weight. She lay on her back, slightly propped up, and frowned at him. "What in the world?"

"You're cold and didn't even know it." Dropping down, he stretched out on his side next to her.

"Oh. I guess I was." As the warmth from the flames on one side and Niall on the other spread through her, she sighed as the tenseness in her muscles released.

"Better." He ran a finger over her cheek. "Now, tell me about your year. Who did you lose?"

She tilted her head. She'd told André the night she got drunk, and it seemed he'd kept her confidences private, even from his littermates. That was...lovely.

Niall waited, his gaze on her. His white-blond hair fell over his broad shoulders. His slightly darker eyebrows and lashes were pale against his tanned skin. And his eyes were so green, the pixies probably thought he was one of them.

"You're awfully gorgeous, you know."

He snorted. "Female, compliments won't let you escape my question."

Gorgeous...and annoyingly persistent. When had he become such a good friend? Maybe when her cabin burned and he'd come to help her?

"Heather?"

Her eyes dampened again, so she spilled everything in a rush, "First my mother died, and then I lost my unborn cubs."

"A miscarriage?" At her nod, he pulled her close. "*A thaisce,* I'm sorry."

"So"—she fought the sob rising inside—"y-you have to stay alive. It's an order."

"Bossy female." His firm lips curved, showing the captivating dimple in his right cheek. "I'll do my best."

"Okay. Okay then." Blinking hard, she turned to stare at the cheerfully crackling fire. The salamanders had curled under the biggest log like contented cats. "Your turn, then. What happened to bring you into the States, all shot up like you were."

He rubbed his chin on her upper arm in a cougar's affectionate caress. "It was ugly, Heather. Are you sure?"

Moving closer until the side of her body pressed against his front, she studied his grim expression. "Yes."

"All right." He propped his head on his hand and looked down at her. "My cybersecurity company asked me to mentor two new hires on their first job. Someone was stealing information from a Calgary client. Trevor and Sydney were just out of college, barely drinking age. After working all week, on Friday night, I told them to stop, take the weekend off, and I headed back to my small town. Instead, they copied the files, went back to their flat, and kept working. They discovered the thefts were terrorist related and sent the information to the Canadian Security Intelligence Service before calling me." His voice roughened. "Fuck me, they found *terrorists*."

At the pain in his face, she wrapped an arm around him. "Go on." Even more than she needed to know, he needed to share.

"I ordered them to go to a hotel immediately, but...they were too slow. By the time I arrived at their apartment building, they were dead, and the place was on fire. I scented the three murderers outside."

"Were they the ones who shot you so many times?" Only three men?

"No. When I caught them, they told me how to find the ones who'd given the orders. This was the same group who'd blown up a daycare the previous week. I drove the killers' car to the warehouse and found the terrorists loading a truck with illegal munitions." His face was hard as the rocky crags. "I killed them, Heather. All of them."

Dear Mother of All.

His chuckle was midnight dark. "I still have nightmares. Sometimes of the humans I slaughtered. Usually of the younglings who died in fear. Who I failed."

Touching her shoulder, he stared at his hand as if he saw only blood there.

"Oh Niall." She took his hand and kissed it, then laid his palm against her cheek. "If you never failed, Herne would expect you to take his place."

Startled, he chuckled. "What an appalling thought."

Laughing, she leaned in, tipping him onto his back with her half on top. Her heart set up a staccato patter at the intimacy of it...but this was where she wanted him. Because she loved him, this male whose intelligence was only surpassed by his protectiveness.

The unhappy tension faded from his expression to be replaced by a dark amusement. "You have me at your mercy, little wolf. Be kind."

"No." Straddling him, feeling the hard shaft under her ass, she sat up and pulled off her shirt. "I don't think kind is what either of us wants right now."

Niall's mouth went dry at the sight of Heather's breasts. She wasn't wearing a bra—she often didn't—and the light of the flames cast a burnished glow over her pale skin.

He slid a hand behind her back, leaning her forward so he could fondle her breasts. Her skin was so fucking soft against his palm. Under his touch, her nipples hardened into peaks.

He paused for a moment to listen to the quiet house. Yes, everyone had gone to bed. Good enough.

His cock was already hard and throbbing. Sliding his hand behind her head, he drew her down so he could capture her lips. Her kiss was deep and urgent enough that he rolled and pinned her beneath him. After stripping off his shirt, he kissed her again.

She ran her hands over his chest, then pulled his hair when he moved down far enough to lick and suckle her breasts. Her low moan of desire and heady demand, "More," sent heat raging through his blood.

"I'll give you more." It took only seconds to have her stripped so he could breathe in her feminine musk before burying his face between her legs. With fingers and tongue, he drove her up. He wasn't one to tease like André, and Heather was also obviously in a straightforward mood. She was so hot and slick on his fingers, he ached with the need to take her.

To his surprise, she stopped him. "No—I want you inside me when I come. Now."

When her grip on his hair turned painful, he laughed. "As you will, pretty wolf." Taking a moment to shed his jeans, he lay down beside her and put her on top. "Ride me."

Her eyes were heavy-lidded with desire and her smile bright as she rubbed her wetness over him, making him groan.

He yanked her forward to kiss her hard, before smiling against her lips. "Now, get to work."

Her husky laugh sent tingles up his spine, and she lifted slightly, positioning him at her entrance, and slowly lowered onto him.

She was fucking hot and wet and tight. A shudder ran through him, one he could feel in her as he closed his hands over her breasts.

She rose off him, then slid back down. Up and down, continuing way too slowly for what he wanted. But for long, wonderful minutes, he let her drive them both to the place where only need existed.

Then he groaned in frustration, and her lips tipped up in a teasing smile. Ah, the wolf wanted to play. "You have a wicked sense of humor. Really, you should be a cat."

He pinched her nipples and smirked as her cunt clenched around him. "Play-time's up, *cariad*."

Closing his hands on her hips, getting a good hold, he lifted her most of the way off his dick then slammed her down. Hard.

She gasped, her back arching. "*More*."

Oh yeah, they were running the same trail. Grinning, he rolled them both over, staying firmly planted deep inside her. And then it was *on*.

He loved how she met him, thrust for thrust, no matter how fast and hard he went. A female who could match him; he was in awe.

When she neared her peak and her cunt tightened around him, he tipped sideways far enough to get a hand between them. So he could stroke over her clit.

That was all it took.

"*Aaaah*." The sound of her pleasure was incredibly satisfying as were the pinpricks of her fingernails digging into his shoulders.

When the waves of climax broke over her, she tightened

around him so hard his balls pulsed. Heat boiled up into his engorged cock and out in a white-hot eruption of pure pleasure.

By Herne's titanic tallywhacker. His heart was slamming within his ribcage, and Heather was gasping for breath. A laugh escaped him. "We'll kill each other before the hellhound gets a chance."

She laughed.

Capturing her ass, he stayed inside as he rolled onto his back, and she settled down, a limp weight on top of him. Soft breasts on his chest, her hair loose on his shoulders, her perfect ass in his grip. He sighed his pleasure. "I'd die happy."

"No, cat. If you let a hellhound hurt you, I'll slap you into next week." She sat up and fixed him with a stern blue-green gaze, then smiled slowly. "More."

By the Gods, he loved her.

At the realization, he stared at her, stunned. How had he reached a place where he had so many ties to his heart? More than just his brothers, but cublings and now this female.

Putting his hand behind her head to kiss her, he felt words rising to his lips. The love words he'd never given to any female before. And wouldn't tonight, either.

Because she'd grieved enough. He wouldn't risk her heart.

But damned if he wouldn't do everything in his power to stay alive to return to her.

CHAPTER THIRTY-TWO

A thick layer of clouds blockaded the afternoon sun, and the wind off the mountains held a biting chill. André glanced up at the sky. Rain was coming, but it might hold off until tomorrow.

"Hi, hi!"

André turned. A three-year-old lass had targeted him like a flower fairy spotting a tasty rose. The cub's mother was chasing after her.

Bouncing off Andre's legs, the girl raised her arms to be picked up.

Who could resist? When he obeyed the mini-alpha, he got a strangling hug around his neck.

"Little rascal." André rubbed his cheek against hers, and the tiny giggles made him laugh. With a smile, he handed her over to her mother.

"Sorry, Cosantir." The mother smiled ruefully. "When my mates insisted that you're a youngling magnet, I didn't believe them. Now, I do. My girl is normally afraid of strangers."

"She's a fine cub."

Beaming at his compliment, the mother headed off.

Joining Madoc at the end of the square, André walked past the sawhorses blocking off the greenway. Signs were posted here and there: THE PARK IS CLOSED FOR WORK ON THE SEWAGE LINES. More sawhorses formed a path from the pedestrian bridge to the square, and a couple of shifters were on guard duty.

They couldn't risk having a human seeing either of the hellhound traps.

Down the leaf-strewn path, through a stand of trees was the north trap.

With his arm around Heather, Niall watched the digging being done.

André smiled...because she was leaning against the big cahir.

After a momentary frown, Madoc barked a laugh. "It's probably good for him to chase a female instead of being the prey."

"It is, isn't it?" André brushed his shoulder against his brother's. They'd need to discuss Heather soon, but first, they had to focus on tonight and keeping everyone alive.

"Any problems getting into the chief's house?" Madoc asked.

"No. Being on the council, Murtagh had the keys."

Duffy, the shifter police officer, had mentioned Chief Farley had kept a personal arsenal at home. Firearms were of limited use with a hellhound but better than nothing, and André's handgun was in Canada.

"Did you find his firearms?"

"*Oui*. I must admit my law-abiding conscience had fits." André watched as the volunteers hauled dirt out of the pit. "There was a nice S&W M41 he probably used for competition shooting. It fires twenty-twos."

"Just the ticket for aiming at a hellhound's eyes."

"Exactly." Even so, if the demon-dog was moving, the chances of hitting the sunken eyes were slim. "I also stole his Desert Eagle."

Madoc frowned. "Cool name. What is it?"

Like many Canadians who weren't hunters, military, or law enforcement, Madoc wasn't particularly interested in firearms. "It's a .50 caliber semi-automatic pistol."

"Brawd." The way Madoc kneaded his forehead suggested he thought André's wits had gone missing. "A massive bullet won't go through the eye socket, and nothing except teeth penetrates a hellhound's armored plate."

"True. However, remember when I survived getting shot because I wore body armor?"

"Oh yeah." Madoc's jaw tightened. "Not something I'd forget."

"Getting shot felt like getting bashed with a baseball bat." André rubbed his chest at the memory. "It half-stunned me—and might do the same for a hellhound, you understand."

"Could come in handy, then."

André nodded. "And a heavier bullet might embed in the armor rather than ricocheting." Ricochets were a major drawback to shooting at hellhounds.

"Cosantir," Jens, a wolf shifter, called from the bottom of the pit. "Is this deep enough?"

André checked. It could be deeper, but there were stakes to plant and the covering to put on. "Aye, it is. A fine job, shifters."

As the last buckets of dirt were hauled out and tossed into a pickup, the males climbed the ladder. The large number of Daonain who'd helped was gratifying. They were coming together as a unified clan far sooner than he'd expected.

"I'll let the Morenos know it's their turn." Madoc headed toward another group. The construction crew would hammer in the metal stakes, then weld sharp points to each one.

To be sure the hellhound couldn't escape, the bottom of each pit would be filled with the iron-tipped stakes.

"See you later." Heather went up on tiptoes to kiss Niall, raised a hand at André, and headed back to the town square.

Silently, Niall joined André.

Seeing the unease in his brother's eyes, André held off teasing.

If—no, *when*—they survived, there would be time for banter. "Let's go see how the south pit is coming."

"Sure." Niall looked around with a frown. "Where'd the cubs go?" His piercing whistle hurt André's ears.

Talam and Sky came running, followed by two other orphans, Mateo and Alvaro.

"Hey, Niall, they're putting in the stakes." Sky pointed to the pit.

André smiled. Madoc had joined the Moreno crew to help pound in the metal poles.

Talam frowned. "Why would the hellhound even come this way?"

"That's what bait is for, youngling." Niall's face was expressionless.

Razors shredded André's heart. Niall insisted he'd be the one to goad the hellhound into chasing him across the pit.

André couldn't gainsay him. Niall was correct; this was a cahir's duty.

Closing his eyes for a moment, André sought for some semblance of calm. At least the pits evened the odds.

In the creekside park, the traps were located north and south of the square in locations where copses of brush and trees would channel the hellhound. The *bait* would do the rest.

André set his hand on Talam's shoulder. "Predators seeing their prey fleeing will instinctively give chase. Niall will lead the hellhound to a trap."

"But...it'll see the trap and go around or something." Sky looked back at the open pit.

Smart cubs, bright as dew on a summer's day. "You're right, which is why we're camouflaging the trap with a grass and leaf-covered board so that the cover will look just like the path."

At the puzzled expressions, Niall added, "The board will be held up in the middle by a pole—and will swing down when the hellhound steps on it. Like a seesaw." He held his hand horizontally, showing how the top would pivot and drop the demon-spawn onto the stakes.

Talam scowled. "Won't you fall in too?"

"We'll pin yellow leaves to the pivot pole to show the one spot where it's safe to land," André said. "It'll take a big leap to get there and another leap to reach the path on the other side."

"What if the hellhound lands there?" Sky asked, his brow furrowed with worry.

"A hellhound is a lot heavier than I am. It'll break the pole." Niall gave André a wry smile, because André had insisted on several tests to ensure they had the right thickness of pole to hold the cahir's weight.

This was the best strategy to defeat the hellhound with the least chance of losing shifters. If it didn't work—or if they couldn't get the hellhound to go after the bait, then it'd be on to plan B where volunteers would attempt to keep the demon-spawn distracted so Niall could roll beneath it and slice open its unarmored belly. It was a technique developed by some North Cascades cahirs. Unfortunately, it required close to a cahir's strength to penetrate the thick hellhound skin.

The alternative was a stiletto or bullet to the eye. André had told the volunteers to carry .22s and long, slender daggers. Niall would be carrying the same weaponry. They'd be prepared if any opportunity presented.

He rubbed the back of his neck, frustrated anger simmering in his gut. A month hadn't been enough time to get the territory ready for a gods-cursed hellhound.

Please, Mother of All, let this work.

Welcome to the dark of the moon. As a cub, Niall had loved the moonless nights when the stars could reign in the black sky.

As a cahir? It'd taken only one sight of the savaged remains left by a hellhound for horror to set up residence in his soul.

At the front window of Madoc's restaurant, he looked out at the night. The sun had set an hour ago. The vintage, wrought-iron streetlights around the square created yellow pools of illumination. Nothing moved out there.

Niall pulled in a slow breath, hoping against hope the hellhound would attack somewhere else. With time—and André's charisma—they'd get a couple more cahirs to move here.

If there were other cahirs, he'd be out patrolling the night. But there was only him, and for the trap to work, the chase had to start here. The square was where the demon-spawn had located its prey—shifters—so this was where the hellhound would come first.

After tying his hair back, he cracked his neck, left, then right. He'd be ready.

"Is it out there?" Voice shaking slightly, Sky came up on Niall's right.

Talam took the left.

"No, nothing yet." Niall set a hand on Sky's shoulder, then Talam's as well. Both lads were trembling slightly.

Fuck. How could he have forgotten a hellhound killed their mother. Sliding his hands down, he pulled them into a rough hug. "Don't worry, lads. You'll be safe in here."

"But you won't," Sky whispered. Tears shimmered in wide blue eyes. "Can't you stay inside too?"

He wished.

Instead, he shook his head. "It'll hunt until it finds a home without window guards. Not everyone will be in a protected place."

Earlier, the Moreno construction crew reported the communal house's window frames needed to be replaced, or a hellhound could simply bust through. So those shifters and cubs were here.

Roger, the alpha, had quite a few of his wolves in their pack house. So that helped.

Not enough, though.

At full moon, André had told people to get their homes secured, and many had complied, thank the God. But there were always procrastinators as well as those who wouldn't take refuge with someone else. Or those who had nowhere else to go.

André had been outraged at the number and asked Heather to get their names and addresses. By next month, those shifters would be far better prepared, or he would know the reason why.

Niall smiled. It was amusing to see people meet the immovable rock that was his brother.

"People, time to move the tables and set out your sleeping areas," Madoc called.

Niall glanced over his shoulder. The warehouse and gift shop were closed off due to the construction mess, so the restaurant itself was packed with shifters, from cubs to seniors and all the ages between.

In one corner, Heather arranged sleeping bags and blankets while chatting with nearby Daonain. Her practical advice with a side-helping of humor implied nothing was as bad as it seemed. Other blanket piles formed around her as her calm competence attracted the anxious shifters like a magnet.

He knew how they felt. Gods, he wanted to be over there with her, too, hearing her throaty laugh, seeing the serenity in her eyes.

"Hey, sis, got room for mine?" Heather's brother, Daniel, shoved his shaggy brown hair out of his eyes. His brother, Tanner, had stayed home to protect their Daonain ranch hands, but Daniel had volunteered to be one of the fighters here. He'd shown up with a twelve-gauge shotgun.

Good male.

"Cubs." Niall gave the lads a nudge. "Go help Heather while I stay on watch. Then you can hang together with your buddies."

"Yessir," Sky whispered and gave Niall a hard hug before following his brother toward Heather.

Niall watched before shaking his head. Why hadn't anyone warned him how cubs could steal a heart faster than a hungry feline?

Movement outside caught his attention. Tensing, he leaned forward, expecting to see a grizzly-sized monster with a sharklike head.

No, it was a female, carrying a baby of maybe six months old. Another cub was in a backpack carrier.

What. The. Fuck.

At the closed grocery store next to the gift shop, she tried the handle. Sitting the infant at her feet, she pounded on the door. "Murtagh, I need food for the kids. Let me in!"

This wasn't good, but...if she was human, the hellhound wouldn't bother her—not with the scent of Daonain in its nose. Niall glanced around. André was already crossing the room at a fast clip with Madoc following.

Heather joined Niall. "What's going on?"

"Who's the female?" He pointed.

She looked out and stiffened. "Portia. One of our shifters and her two cubs."

A shifter. If a hellhound was around, her yelling would target her like a spotlight. He squeezed Heather's shoulder, wishing for more, so much more—and then dashed for the door.

A scream broke the quiet night. Cowering on her knees, Portia didn't even try to run from the huge hellhound stalking across the square.

The sight of it would terrify anyone. Grizzly-sized with ankylosaurus-like armor plating. Eyes the color of old blood. Claws the size of his fingers.

And just like that, their wolf pit plan was fucked. The demonspawn was too close to Portia for Niall to lure it away. It already had the scent of fear. Of babies.

"Run, female!" He dove at the beast, hitting it with his shoulder. It felt like he'd slammed into a concrete wall.

The hellhound staggered sideways, spun, and savaged Niall.

Pain seared through his leg as its jaws tore into his flesh. Kicking its head, he rolled away. To his horror, the female hadn't moved.

Roaring a challenge, Madoc in bear form slammed into the hellhound at an angle and dashed away.

Niall regained his feet and ran. The hellhound lunged after him.

Madoc charged again.

The booming crack of gunfire announced André had arrived.

Hands pressed to her mouth, Heather stood inside the door, dread shaking her. The males—*her* males—would die.

Behind her, she could hear Daniel shouting orders at the volunteers who'd come to fight.

Another shot rang out. André's bullets didn't kill the hellhound, but it stopped and shook its head.

Why didn't the brothers move back, regroup, *something*? In front of the grocery next door, they stood in a semi-circle far too close to—

Mother's breasts, they're protecting Portia and the babies. Hunched down on her knees, the female didn't move. Too scared. One baby sat at her feet, arms up. Crying.

The males couldn't do anything with Portia there.

I have to help. Heather's heart pounded as if to beat out of her chest. Her mouth was dry with pure terror.

Don't panic. Move!

She raced out the door, straight to Portia. Bending, she snatched the red-faced baby up, tucking him into one arm. Reassured by the high little wail, she turned to put her body between him and the hellhound. Grabbing the front of

Portia's shirt, Heather yanked the female to her feet. "Move your tail!"

Dragging Portia like downed prey, Heather ran back to the restaurant.

Rifle in hand, Daniel trotted past Heather. "Good rescue, sis." A wolf and a cougar followed him, then two more males.

Even as Heather went through the door into the restaurant, his rifle cracked.

The hellhound snarled.

Someone yelled, "The Cosantir's down!"

Pain ripped through André's shoulder as the hellhound shook him like a trapped rat.

With the deep, cracking sound of a heavy shotgun, the demon-spawn let out a shriek—and released André.

Madoc hit it from the side, buying André enough time to scramble away. *Thank the Mother.* Sweeping up his pistol, he regained his feet, staggering, hot blood streaming down his side.

Turning, he saw Heather had reached the restaurant with the female and babies. *Bless you.*

"Shooters, aim for the head," Niall yelled, pulling his knife. "Animals, charge its rear."

Taking aim with his left hand, André opened fire. Daniel and two other shifters did the same.

As the shifters in animal form attacked from behind, the hellhound was stymied for a moment.

Taking advantage, Niall dove under it and stabbed upward— even as the hellhound charged forward.

Its unholy shriek rang out. Blood splattered on the ground.

Niall had wounded it. But not enough. Whirling, it grabbed Niall's leg and flung the cahir across the street.

Then it attacked Daniel, who was frantically reloading.

André's pistol clicked on empty.

Madoc tore forward on three legs, his speed not nearly fast enough.

A female yelled. "Flashbang. Three-two-"

Merde. André dove to the ground, covering his eyes and ears.

As everything flashed white, a sound like the crack of doom almost ruptured his ear drums.

Was that lightning? Ears ringing, Talam shook his head as the splotchy after-images made his eyes water. But he could see good enough. Nose pressed against the glass, he told Sky, "The Cosantir's bleeding bad."

Sky's hand gripped his. "Niall can't run. His leg's all tore up. He can't be bait."

Talam's heart sank. Most of the shifters out there were down or hurt. "Nobody out there will be quick enough to stay in front of the hellhound."

"I run fast." Mateo bumped his shoulder. Alvaro stood beside him. "We both do."

Talam's breathing was too fast, and there was a buzzing sound in his head. Cuz he was scared—like when Mom had left them in the root cellar. And made the hellhound chase her.

She'd saved them. Because she loved them.

He made his hands into fists cuz his stomach was twisting like he'd puke. "I run fast too."

Beside him, Sky's face was pinched, but he nodded. "We should scream an' yell. Like prey."

"Yeah." Talam looked at Mateo. "We'll take the left trap; you go right."

They darted to the door, dodging people who grabbed for them.

And then they all ran for the park, screaming like they were scared.

Only he really was scared. He *was*.

. . .

Madoc flung himself at the hellhound standing stunned over Daniel. Above the ringing in his ears, he heard high shrieks. So high.

The hellhound's head turned with a jerk—and it charged after four younglings.

That was Sky's blond head. Talam was with him.

By the Gods, no!

Sprinting incredibly fast, the cubs reached the park and split, two going south, the other pair going north. Being bait.

Already in motion, Madoc chased after them with all his strength, ignoring the jolting agony in his hip where the hellhound had savaged him.

At the park, the demon-spawn paused, nose in the air. Obviously following the upwind scent, it turned left.

After Talam and Sky.

Faster, bear!

Madoc had almost caught up, and the hellhound was nearly to the younglings when they reached the trap. Hand-in-hand, the cubs sprang for the leaf-marked center. They came down right on the pivot pole and leaped again.

Sky's jump fell short, his belly hitting the edge.

"No!" Talam grabbed him before he fell in...but the trap cover tipped down.

At the seesaw motion of the camouflaged top, the hellhound skidded to a stop.

"Fuck that." Madoc rammed the hellhound from behind with all the fury in his heart.

It was like hitting a boulder.

Thrown forward, the hellhound crashed down into the trap as Madoc landed on the edge of the pit.

Gut-wrenching shrieks filled the air.

. . .

Half-running, half-staggering, André chased after the hellhound and Madoc—and cubs, by the Gods. His right shoulder was ripped to shreds, his arm hanging limp, and each hard footfall sent pain blazing through him.

Niall had tried to follow and collapsed. Thank the Mother, Heather had already been there, yelling, "*I've got this, André. Go.*"

Even as André reached the park, he could hear her barking orders to get Niall, Daniel, and the other wounded inside.

"Do you have more bullets?" A female ran beside him in the dark night. An inch or so above his six feet, muscular, short black hair and—

"Bron?"

"Aye, nephew. Sorry, I'm late."

Her arrival explained the flashbang. She did love the bloody things.

Footsteps sounded from behind as others tried to catch up.

When screams of pain broke the night, André's heart almost stopped. But no—it wasn't the cubs.

It was the hellhound.

At the trap, Madoc had shifted to human and tossed the top of the trap away. Now, his arms were wrapped around the cubs.

André looked down. The hellhound was badly wounded, but its thrashing had dislodged most of the stakes. One iron point dangled from its belly as it clawed the sides of the pit, trying to climb.

"Gods, it might be able to get out," Bron breathed.

"Aye." André pulled the other pistol he'd carried. The S&W .22. "I can't hit anything with my left hand."

He offered it to Bron who shook her head. "I'm not accurate enough for eyes."

"I am." The gravelly voice came from behind them.

André glanced over his shoulder to see two huge cahirs. One was darkly dangerous, scarred...and holding a handgun.

The fair-haired other had the appearance of an Irish prize-fighter.

"Shay, isn't it?" André asked the dark one. They'd met at the festival last summer.

"Zeb and Shay, aye. Sorry we missed the fight. We ran a patrol in Cold Creek before getting on the road." The prize-fighter smiled. "It's good to see you again, André."

He started to hold out his hand, then his eyebrows rose. Elbowing his partner, he bowed his head slightly. "Cosantir."

"Gnome-brain, that's André," Zeb growled, then he blinked and also bowed his head. "Cosantir."

"Enough," André growled. "Please finish this, cahir." *Before I pass out.* He motioned to the side of the pit.

Joining him, Zeb took aim and fired. It took several shots before a bullet finally hit one of the tiny, recessed eyes.

The hellhound dropped. It was done.

Seconds later, he was getting hugged by two—then four—over-excited cubs.

As the world darkened around him, he heard someone say, "Tell Calum we need Donal. Bad."

Gods, would the night ever end? Carrying a tray with a pitcher of water and glasses, Heather glanced around the Shamrock Restaurant.

At the tables near the walls, the people still awake were talking. Most of the cubs were curled in blanket piles, watched over by their loved ones.

All the wounded lay in one corner. On each side of André, Madoc and Niall sat on the floor, backs against the wall.

Setting down the tray, Heather knelt beside the Cosantir. Blood still streaked his shirtless, muscular chest. Biting her lip, she checked the pressure dressing on his shoulder. The bleeding had slowed but not stopped. He hadn't woken since they carried him in.

His brothers watched, worry in their expressions. "Shay says the healer is on the way," she told them.

Please hurry, Donal.

But André would live. He must. Her hands shook as she brushed the dark hair off his forehead.

His eyes opened, so dark a brown, so very alive.

"André," she whispered.

"Heather." His lips quirked, then capturing her hand, he kissed her fingers. "Thank you, *ma chérie*, for leaving safety to save the female. Your courage warms my heart."

Tears prickled her eyes at the words. At the respect in his gaze.

Leaning down, she brushed her lips against his. "Says the male who stood against a hellhound with only a pistol."

"Who's the female, anyway?" Niall frowned toward Portia, who sat across the room. Two females with her were caring for her two babies.

Typical lazy Portia behavior. She'd been freeloading in the communal house until Pete closed it. "She works at the RV camp downriver. She knew about the curfew but..." Heather lifted her voice to mimic Portia's higher one. "*I forgot to shop earlier, and the grocery should have been open.*"

André's eyebrows drew together, and his eyes darkened.

Madoc snorted. "Oh, she's in for it now."

After a second, André shook his head, and his eyes returned to their normal dark brown. "No. The hellhound was enough of a lesson."

"Probably so." Heather huffed a laugh. "She was so scared, she peed her pants."

"There you go then." Trying to sit up, André made a muffled sound of pain.

"Stop it." Was he crazy? "Stay *put*. You lost—"

Chuckling, his also-injured brothers helped him so he could lean against the wall like them.

Heather's head threatened to explode. "You are the most sprite-brained, crow-cursed feline I've ever met."

All three burst out laughing.

She eyed the tray of water. *Pour it on their stupid heads?*

With a sigh, she filled the glasses. "Maybe it's blood loss making you idiots. Drink up."

As they did, she checked Niall's leg and Madoc's hip. Daniel had also been ripped up, but his bleeding had stopped.

"André's awake!" The squeak of delight came from the blanket pile next to Niall. In a flurry of motion, their two cubs crawled over to join Heather.

Talam bit his lip, his gaze on the blood-soaked bandage on André's shoulder and how his arm was bound in place. "You got hurt so bad."

"It was worth it to keep our people safe," André murmured. "Don't you think...young warrior?"

After a moment, Talam nodded.

With his good hand, André touched the cub's face, then smiled at Sky. "You almost scared my fur off, but I'm very proud of you both."

Heather was too. And maybe, when she stopped choking on the memory, she'd tell them so. By the Gods, she'd never known such fear as when the hellhound had gone after them.

Or when Madoc had chased after them on only three legs. He hadn't even hesitated. She'd been so terrified for him—and for André who'd been half-staggering.

If Niall had gone after them, she would have smacked him flat, but he'd managed only one step before falling.

Stubborn, stubborn males.

A noise at the front door made her look up.

Donal, Margery, and Tynan had *finally* arrived.

Heather shot to her feet and waved them over.

Followed by his lifemates, Donal joined them, his gaze going from Daniel, who hadn't woken, to Madoc and André.

When his eyes fell on Niall, he scowled. "Cahir, you flea-ridden, fart of a feline, did you fuck up the same leg I just fixed a few weeks ago?"

As the cubs' eyes widened, Heather burst out laughing.

Her males were going to live.

CHAPTER THIRTY-THREE

André woke to the mouth-watering scent of bacon and felt his tail lash. They'd better leave him some.

When in fur, he usually preferred his food raw. But...*bacon*, he'd eat no matter what form he wore.

Lifting his head from Niall's furry flank, he yawned. Food sounded good.

Last night, after Donal healed him and his brothers, they'd shifted to animal form. After Heather trawsfurred, Niall—being a generous brother—tucked her between him and André.

Unable to shift yet, the cubs had curled into little human balls between André and Madoc.

Before André had fallen asleep, Heather's brother, Daniel walked over, Mateo and Alvaro trailing behind him. "Got a couple more cubs who're feeling shaky. Can we join you?"

André had shifted to human long enough to praise the younglings for their courage in baiting the hellhound to the park. They'd all been very lucky. Normally, the hellhound would have gone after cubs who'd already gone through First Shift in preference to Talam and Sky. But they'd been downwind, and the demon-spawn had turned to follow the scent on the wind.

These two had been incredibly brave.

After adding more blankets to the pile, Daniel had trawsfurred. Then Mateo and Alvaro shifted to small wolves, and they all piled in. A cuddle pile was just what cubs needed to feel safe.

Everyone was asleep within minutes.

André had shifted back, curled a paw over Heather's back, and followed suit.

But now, there was daylight slanting through the front window blinds, and the fur pile had diminished to him, Niall, and two strange wolves. He lifted his nose and sniffed.

Ah, Margery and Shay. Shay and Zeb had generously patrolled the town for the remainder of the night. And Margery, the healer's lifemate, had not only bandaged up the lesser wounds, but also provided extra energy to Donal so he could heal the major damages.

There had been a lot of injuries.

André pulled in slow breaths as he thought over the events of the night. But...final result—the hellhound had died. His clan had lived.

Now, it was time to get his tail moving.

The restaurant itself was emptied of all but a few. Several people sat at a long table. Two of Madoc's waitstaff were picking up the clutter and mopping the floor.

Pushing to his paws, André chuffed as his bruises and scrapes set up a painful clamor. A glance ascertained no humans were around, so he trawsfurred to human and dressed in the clothing piled next to the blankets. Heather's light scent lingered on the fabric, indicating she'd been the person who'd found him something to wear.

However, she was a sneaky wolf to have slid out from under his paw without waking him.

Finger-combing his hair, he followed the aroma of food across the room. He could hear Heather, Talam, and Sky in the kitchen with Madoc.

Maybe he should go there first. He needed coffee very badly.

But then, he noticed the people around the table. Aunt Bron and Zeb were talking with Donal and his littermate, Tynan, who was a deputy sheriff.

"Good morning, everyone." André bent and hugged his aunt. "Nice use of a flashbang last night. You saved Daniel's life—although my ears may never be the same."

She laughed.

"Did you get any sleep?"

She nodded. "I joined Zeb and Shay in patrolling until near dawn then grabbed some sleep at the bed and breakfast." Bron wasn't the type to join in a fur pile.

"Thank you for watching out for the town," André said to her and Zeb. "Were there any problems?"

"All quiet, Cosantir." A corner of Zeb's mouth tipped up. "Gotta admit, it felt odd to be back here patrolling."

Bron's eyebrows rose. "You used to live here?"

"Aye, we both did." Buttoning his shirt, Shay joined them. "When Pete—the Cosantir here at the time—decided he didn't need us, the North Cascades Cosantir requested our service."

At a low growl from the male who was mopping the floor, André turned to look at him.

The other male collecting the trash ducked his head in a bow. "Sorry, Cosantir. It's"—he faced Shay, then looked at Zeb—"Cahirs, I...the clan here would like to apologize. When Pete insisted you were worthless, we believed him. We had no idea..."

"No idea a Cosantir would lie," the one mopping put in. "Since then, other cahirs told us Pete's an idiot, and you two are the best ever known at killing hellhounds, and we'd regret not doing everything we could to keep you here."

The first worker nodded. "Aye. That's what I wanted to say."

The second bowed slightly. "Thank you for coming to help, despite how you were treated."

Zeb's expression didn't change, although the dark eyes held shock.

Shay shook his head, then smiled at the two males. "You're welcome. It's nice to hear we're welcome here."

"Always, cahirs." With smiles, the two went back to their cleaning.

"Can't complain." Zeb's voice was a gravelly growl despite a slight smile. "By leaving, we met our Bree."

"And found a home." Shay sat down at his partner's side. "Still, in some ways, Rainier is nicer."

"It's a beautiful territory, true." André took a seat by Bron.

"Here, Cosantir." Heather set a plate of food and coffee in front of him. "Eat while you talk. Healing needs calories."

He smiled. Her sweetly bossy words veiled a caring heart, one he was growing to cherish. To need. "Thank you, *ma chère*."

He caught her hand, kissed her fingers, and rubbed them against his cheek as he held her gaze. Such luminous blue-green eyes. He'd seen how courage sparked in them, how they went liquid with tears, how they went molten with desire...

A breath brought him her sunshine and roses scent with a very tempting hint of interest, and his lips curved.

She narrowed her eyes and pulled her hand away, saying so only he could hear, "*Bad* Cosantir."

As she stalked back to the kitchen, he chuckled, regretting he couldn't follow. Instead, he returned his attention to the conversation about the beauty of Rainier Territory.

"I agree the town is charming." Niall took a chair beside him. "Unfortunately, a hellhound carcass is a tawdry kind of tourist attraction."

Sky's high giggle sounded as the cub set breakfast in front of Niall.

Niall smiled. "Thanks, cub."

Talam gave Bron her food with a curious look. He'd probably never met a female cahir.

Their aunt grinned. "Thank you, youngling."

Talam smiled back and lingered, listening. A typical curious cub.

André swallowed a bite of toast. "Disposing of the hellhound's body will be the next chore, brawd." At least the corpse was in human form and easier to handle.

"Ew," Talam muttered, even while looking fascinated. *Cubs and blood.*

"Zeb and I would be happy to assist if we can check out your trap," Shay said. "How'd the cubs get across it, but the hellhound didn't?"

"Aye, I want to see it too." Tynan lifted his cup in a toast. "Brilliant construction."

Zeb nodded. "Could save lives."

"It worked better than expected. We didn't invent the design, although we modified it for the demon-spawn." Multiple stakes had been a good idea, André knew. "Now it's been tested, we can improve it."

"Deeper would be wise." Bron curved her fingers into claws. "Eventually, it might've managed to scrabble its way up and out."

Shay turned to André. "Zeb and I train cahirs in how to kill hellhounds. We'd like to teach them how to use a...does it have a name?"

"A *trou de loup* or a tiger pit." André glanced at Niall. "To avoid digging the holes again, we should cover the pits with something."

"The Wainwright brothers should be able to contrive a secure lid." Niall turned to Shay. "I'd like to attend your hellhound class if possible."

"Give me a call, and we'll fit you in."

"Count me in, too, please." Bron grinned at Niall. "Since we'll be working together."

Pleasure swept through André. "You'll stay, Aunt?"

"My favorite nephews are here." She tilted her head. "You mentioned a possible law enforcement job for me?"

"Aye." André shook his head. "The American law enforcement jobs appear to be rather a hodge-podge. For our province—no, our *county*—the sheriff and deputies are human. We'd prefer not to use them."

Tynan laughed. "We're lucky since our Azure County is tiny, and we own it. The sheriff's office is all shifters."

"We don't have that option. Instead, this town was incorporated so it could manage its own law enforcement. Thus, we have a Chief of Police and police officers." André smiled at his aunt. "Way back when, you worked in the States as a police officer. I plan to get you elected Chief of Police."

"The chief?" She snorted. "Is this revenge for recruiting you into the RCMP?"

"Totally." Madoc's big laugh rang in the room. Settling down at the table with a plate of food, he told Bron, "As a new Mountie, he'd return from some cop disaster and swear he would pin your hide to the wall next time he saw you."

André smiled...because he'd loved the job. But being Cosantir might be even more fulfilling. The territory had taken hold of him, as had the clan. The land and the shifters had become *his*.

With a plate and coffee in her hands, Heather came out of the kitchen and paused.

Before André could move, Niall slid his plate to the right, then rose and held his chair out for her to sit.

After a surprised look, she took the seat between them.

André shot his brother a smile.

Eyes narrowing at them, Bron then glanced at Madoc who had an unreadable expression. When Bron turned back to Heather, she was frowning. Their aunt had never approved of the females who chased after Niall.

She'd learn soon enough it was Niall chasing after Heather.

Finished with breakfast, André put an arm around Heather

and gave her a gentle squeeze. "Thank you for your care last night," he murmured.

"Thank you for not dying after tackling a hellhound with a *gun*." After a righteous glower, her anger disappeared like fog in the morning sun, and she kissed his cheek.

"If no one else will yell at you, I will," Bron snapped at André. "A Cosantir doesn't belong anywhere near the fighting."

Before he could respond, Heather huffed a laugh. "You could scold him for days, and the next time his brothers engage in a no-win battle, he'll jump right in beside them. Again. Why waste time yelling if it won't effect a change in behavior?"

Bron frowned. "You have a...very good point."

André coughed to hide his laugh.

"As it happens, I enjoy dispensing a good scolding." Donal scowled at the Crichton brothers. "I'll allow you to walk to the trap and talk for a bit, but then the three of you *will* sleep for the rest of the day. Don't test me on this. Am I clear?"

André smiled. The healer was incredibly skilled—and more irritable than a pixie during the first frost. "Clear, healer. We'll follow your advice."

"That's more order than advice if you hadn't noticed." Heather's under-her-breath comment made Niall snort.

"We're grateful for your help and the banfasa's—and for the long trip you and yours made to get here." André bowed his head to them, then smiled at Shay and Zeb. "Our gratitude goes to you two, as well."

Shay held up a hand. "Hey, you had everything handled without us."

"Without *you*." Zeb's lips tipped up in an almost invisible smirk. "At least, I was useful."

"You were. As it was, our success was poised on the edge, and if we'd failed, the hellhound would have slaughtered far too many." The thought made André's gut tighten. "Thank you both for coming."

"Actually, I have a tangible thank you." Madoc disappeared into the kitchen, and a minute later, returned with two boxes wafting a tantalizing butter and sugar scent.

Donuts, André would guess.

Carrying their own sacks, Talam and Sky emerged long enough to wave, then disappeared back into the kitchen. Off to the warehouse school for the day.

"I hear they live with you." Bron glanced at André. "How about I get them after school and keep them busy so you can sleep."

"Aye. Thank you. Your help would be most welcome."

"Thanks, Aunt." Niall smiled at her. "I'll admit—I'm fucking exhausted."

"Same here." Madoc set a donut box in front of Shay and Zeb. "Food for your trip back, with our thanks." He gave the other box to Donal and Tynan. "For you and the banfasa."

Donal lifted the lid, and his eyes lit. "Want help next month?"

Showered and wearing loose cotton pants, Niall leaned on the inner balcony outside his bedroom, too unsettled to sleep. The dismal view out the front picture windows mirrored his mood—black clouds, pouring rain. Heavy thunder reverberated through his bones.

Bracing his forearms on the top rail, he hung his head. Fuck, he ached. Although Donal had healed the hellhound's bites and slashes, he was left with a myriad of bruises and pulled muscles.

The damage would mend in time. And he had time...because he wasn't dead after all.

Looking down at the empty great room, he thought about how Heather had felt in his arms. Remembered her laughing with his brothers and teasing the cubs.

He was damned grateful to be alive today. So why was his mood this dark?

Stepping out of his room, Madoc silently joined him. Wearing only sweatpants, the bear still had wet hair from his shower. Healed claw marks and bites from the hellhound showed pink against his darker skin.

A minute later, André came out, and then the three of them were together, shoulder-to-shoulder-to-shoulder. Strengthened by blood and experiences and love, their bond was a solid shining rope tying them together.

A moment later, André straightened. "My room feels too empty. How about we make up the bed in the mate's room and sack out there. Together."

Niall let out a breath of relief. Yes, their company was what he needed.

He thumped his fist on the railing in agreement even as Madoc did the same.

Heather had taken a very, very long bath. A lightly scented oil in the tub had dispelled the last whiff of blood, pain, and hellhound. When her skin turned pruney, she'd finally climbed out—and then lotioned up as if fixing dry skin would calm her lingering anxieties.

After the night spent helping with the injured, she was exhausted. Yet her jittery mind couldn't move past the shrieks of the hellhound. The blood pouring down André's side. Seeing Niall fall. The cubs screaming. Madoc on three legs, charging after the demon-spawn.

A shudder ran through her.

Sleep wasn't going to happen anytime soon. Picking up Greystoke, she took a cuddle. He purred happily as she rubbed her chin on his head.

He was fine. No worries here.

But how about the others in the house? Were the brothers all right?

Maybe if they were sleeping peacefully, she'd manage to nap. Okay, she'd go check them. But nothing more. Absolutely nothing more.

Besides, she should make sure their phones were turned off so they could sleep for a few hours uninterrupted.

She set Greystoke down with a couple of kitty treats to forestall his complaints. Yanking on fleecy joggers and an ancient flannel shirt, she left her bedroom.

To her surprise, the males' bedrooms were empty. So was the downstairs. No one was on the porch or patio. There was no clothing in the portal room, so they hadn't gone for a run.

Frowning, she went back up to the second floor then noticed the door across the way stood open.

Huh, she'd never been in that room. Was it a den?

She headed around the U-shaped balcony. Maybe she wasn't a cat, but curiosity? She had it in spades.

The males' scent came from inside. She pushed the door farther open.

Oh, how lovely. It was an old-fashioned Daonain suite for a mated female. What would it be like to be so beloved?

A cozy sitting area opened to a huge bedroom. She peeked inside. The heart of the room was a custom bed twice the size of a king.

The three brothers were in it, tangled together, sound asleep.

Her chest felt too tight to breathe. They'd risked themselves for the clan. Had been covered in blood, bites, slashes. Had nearly died.

It wasn't good, not at all, how merely the possibility of losing them could upset her this badly. *Don't even go there, girl.*

She started to withdraw, then spotted the phones piled on a nightstand. Right, she'd wanted to turn them off.

Tiptoeing over, she glanced at the males again. All three were shirtless, sleeping on top of the bed with not even a throw blanket.

Mmm.

The carved features of André's face were softened in sleep, and his ripped musculature was a work of art. Such a stunning male, but what really caught her was his personality. The way he wanted the best for all their people, from the cubs to the seniors.

Niall's long blond hair lay tangled on his huge chest. She smiled, remembering the disconcerting feel of his steely muscles under the taut, velvety skin.

Niall was fair-skinned, Madoc, shades darker. The bear lay on his back, one arm over his head. Brown chest hair couldn't conceal the wonderfully heavy slabs of pectoral muscle. His short, neatly trimmed beard hugged the rough angles of his hard face.

But his lips...his lips could be so soft.

As her body heated, even she could smell the interest in her scent. *Focus, wolf. Turn off the phones.* With silent laugh, she picked up the first cell, set it to silent, and moved to the next.

"The Gods sent us a present, eh?" Niall's sleep-roughened voice startled her. His powerful arm curled around her waist and pulled her onto the bed. He rolled her over his chest, then over Madoc, and dropped her on her back between André and Madoc.

André blinked at her sleepily and obviously caught her aroused scent. A corner of his mouth tilted up. "Heather."

The sound of her name in his deep, accented voice sent a thrill through her.

Rising on an elbow, he tangled his fingers in her hair to hold her for his kiss.

Oh, he could kiss. The bed seemed to rock as she sank into a lake of desire.

"What's going..." Madoc's rumbling voice came from behind her. "Little wolf. Did you want to celebrate being alive?" He slid a callused hand under her shirt and cupped her breast.

She gasped at the jolting pleasure...and realized Madoc was right. She totally wanted to glory in their survival. Common sense tried to surface. "You're supposed to sleep."

"Later." Niall chuckled. "After seeing you in danger? Every instinct makes us want to verify that you're alive...in the best way possible."

"You can always call a halt, *ma chérie*." André studied her for a long moment, undoubtedly seeing her longing. Smiling, he kissed her again.

When he rolled off the bed, Niall moved into his place. His big hand cupped her cheek, and he took her mouth.

The bed dipped next to her feet. Standing at the end of the mattress, André stripped off her joggers.

"He's right. You're overdressed." Madoc's hazel eyes glinted with laughter as he unbuttoned her flannel shirt. There was a wash of cooler air before his mouth closed on her nipple. His lips were velvety, his tongue all wet heat, as he teased and sucked. The brush of his soft beard was incredibly tantalizing.

She closed her left hand in his heavy, thick hair and her right in Niall's lighter, silkier locks.

All she could do was hold on.

Three males. Her thoughts fragmented under the onslaught of sensations. Niall's drugging kisses. Her breasts swelled and tingled under Madoc's attention.

André spread her legs and settled between her thighs. As his warm breath bathed her groin, her muscles tensed in anticipation.

"Mmm, she smells like roses again." He ran his hands over her stomach, down her hips, up her thighs. With a purring sound, he parted her labia, and his tongue ran over her.

Her startled inhalation made all three males chuckle.

Gods, she wasn't sure she was ready for this. She couldn't even move with Niall's hand in her hair, Madoc's heavy arm across her waist, and André pinning down her legs.

The sensations grew overwhelming.

She could feel the tight points of her nipples. Madoc's tiny nips alternating with licks and sucking made her engorged breasts sensitive to the lightest flick.

André was teasing her with lips and tongue, sucking on her clit, rubbing with his tongue, and then he slid a finger inside her.

"*Ooooh.*" The volume of sensation ratcheted right into the red danger zone. Her muscles tightened as pressure built inside her, drowning out...everything.

"Come for us, pretty wolf." Thrusting fast and hard, André pulled her clit into his mouth and sucked.

"*Ahhh!*" Blinding pleasure crashed over her in stunning waves of release, leaving her shuddering and limp.

André lifted his head, feeling the aftershocks of Heather's orgasm around his fingers. By the Gods, he loved driving her high enough her practical mind shut right off. Watching her surrender and climax was a glorious satisfaction.

Just look at her. Her eyes were closed, her fingers still tangled in Madoc's—and Niall's—hair. Her chest rose and fell with her panting.

Waiting for his instructions, Niall and Madoc were stroking her lightly. It was tempting to bring her to climax a few more times before moving on, but she'd had a long night. What came next would test her endurance.

There were three of them, after all.

"Strip, bear." André made a roll-over motion with his index finger. "On your back, legs off the side."

"Aye, brawd." Madoc shed his sweatpants and rolled, angling so his legs dangled off the bed.

Niall sat up and gripped Heather's waist. "Here you go, little wolf. A treat for you." He set Heather on top of Madoc.

With a knee on each side of Madoc's hips, her pussy was well positioned.

André waited for her to understand where she was.

She blinked for a second before flattening her hands on Madoc's big chest. "Well." Her voice was beautifully throaty. "I think I know what comes next."

Reaching down, she played with Madoc's shaft, teasing the head against her pussy, then rubbing her thumb on the wetness.

As André knew, she was a generous lover. He smiled as his brother's face darkened with need—and surprise. During full moons, females in heat wanted only fast and hard. Madoc had never experienced the joy of slow and sensual.

Today would be good for him.

Eventually, Heather sank down onto Madoc's erection in one smooth move. Her pleased inhalation was as much a delight as the bear's deep groan.

Slowly, she rose up and down.

Exchanging smiles, André and Niall stripped down.

"Heather." André stroked his hand down the smooth skin of her back. "Can you multi-task and use your mouth too?" He motioned for Niall to kneel beside Madoc, and a second later, she was giving the cahir a blowjob.

André watched for a minute. His brothers were as lost in pleasure as Heather was. As her need grew, she'd lost her coordination, and Madoc had taken over lifting her hips up and down.

André opened the drawer on the nightstand. When they'd moved in, he'd put supplies in both his room and up here. It was the only time they'd lived in a home with a mate-sized bed, and he'd hoped to put it to use.

That the first time was with Heather made him happier than he could say. Because...she fit. Her personality was a match for all three of them.

So. Time to see if she could *take* them all as easily.

With a small bottle of lube and condoms, he stood between Madoc's parted knees.

Meeting his gaze, Madoc moved his hands to Heather's buttocks and spread her apart to reveal her puckered asshole.

André's cock hardened further as he put a finger in one condom, lubed it up, and circled the rim.

She let out an adorable squeak of surprise and sat up slightly, looking over her shoulder at him.

"I will go slowly, *mon trésor*." When she didn't object, he held her gaze, watching for any sign of distress, and slowly inserted a finger.

Her tight muscles closed around him as Madoc squeezed and massaged her ass cheeks.

"Continue?" he asked. There were females who didn't like being penetrated by two males. He had a feeling Heather wasn't one of them, but the decision was hers.

She breathed out as he worked the muscle to make room for himself. And then she nodded and returned to pleasuring Niall.

His brother grinned. "If she bites me, I'm blaming you, brawd."

Madoc laughed and resumed lifting her hips up and down on his cock.

André moved to two fingers, then three. Slowly, carefully. It was obvious she wasn't unfamiliar with the act but hadn't been taken this way in a while.

Pulling the condom off his hand, he rolled a new one onto his cock and liberally lubed it and her. He chuckled when she shivered at the cool gel.

"Brace, pretty wolf." He pressed his cock against the rim of muscles and went in a few centimeters. "So tight."

Her shoulders tensed, but she didn't protest.

Steadily, he continued. When the head of his cock popped in, her muscular ring closed around the narrower part of his shaft, giving him a burst of pleasure. "Mmmm."

"Gods." Her low sigh held both pain and arousal.

André smiled at Niall. "Sorry, cahir, your time is over."

"There's a shame." Niall pulled out of Heather's mouth, then bent to kiss the top of her head. "You're awesome, *mo leannán.*"

André blinked at the term, one a shifter might use to a lover.

Well. André met Niall's gaze, each of them recognizing the same wish.

"Come here, Heather." One arm under her adorable breasts, André drew her almost upright. Reaching around between her and Madoc, he slid his fingers over her slick clit.

Madoc gave a grunt of surprise as her muscles clenched around him.

Looking up at her—and André—between half-lidded eyes, Madoc smiled slowly. "Nice position." He reached up to play with her breasts, and each pinch of his fingers made her cunt and asshole clench.

Smiling, André bent his head to nibble on her neck, feeling little shivers course through her.

By the Gods, she was tight, having taken both him and Madoc. And when she tightened around him? His cock demanded for him to move.

Patience. He couldn't think of anything more enjoyable than having Heather orgasm with them inside her.

Half in, he held steady while using a single finger to trace circles around her clit.

Her soft body stiffened, her hips wiggling delightfully. And she softened slightly around his shaft as her body adapted.

Now. Slowly, he penetrated deeper. The tight anal ring moved down his shaft as velvety warmth surrounded the rest of his cock.

He pulled back, feeling the wash of cool air. *In and out.* With each thrust, his cock was engulfed in heat.

His brothers waited, giving her time to grow comfortable.

"Heather."

She didn't react, lost in the sensations.

André nipped her shoulder. "Heather." He waited until she

looked over her shoulder. "Are you ready for something more vigorous?"

Her face was flushed an appealing red, her eyes slightly unfocused. So beautiful like this. After a moment, she nodded.

André nodded at Niall, then met Madoc's gaze, and they began.

Madoc took over playing with her clit. Kneeling beside him, Niall was already enjoying teasing her breasts.

Still standing, André gripped her hips, lifting her off Madoc's erection, even as he thrust in. Pulling out, he pushed her down onto Madoc.

Her whole body tightened, her back arching.

André didn't halt. One shaft in, one out, making for a coordinated dance of mating. He could feel the friction of his brother's cock passing his with only a thin membrane between them.

Together, they shared Heather in the most intimate of ways.

The rhythm was glorious, but slow. Before he could pick up the pace, Heather moaned and tried to do it herself.

His grip on her hips tightened, holding her immobile. "No, *ma chérie*, you will take only what I give you." He bit the curve between her neck and shoulder, holding the muscle between his teeth until he felt her tremble—and soften.

Ah, he had forgotten. She was a wolf.

André *bit* her. Rather than tensing, Heather's muscles went limp as her inner wolf surrendered completely to his quiet order. To *him*.

As she instinctively bowed her head, her desire soared to new heights. Every single cell in her body grew even more sensitive.

He licked where he'd bit, then kissed up the side of her neck, making her moan.

"*Ma louloutte*," he whispered in her ear, "now, we will give you what you want."

Lifting her almost off Madoc, André drove into her ass. Then he slammed her down onto Madoc's cock as he withdrew. Up and down. Faster and faster.

Gods, she'd never felt so full, so out of control. Sensations bombarded her. Niall's demanding hands on her breasts, Madoc's fingers sliding over her clit. And being impaled on one cock, then the other. Every single nerve in her whole lower body had roused, leaving her teetering on the precipice of coming.

Then everything inside her detonated in a soul-shattering burst of pleasure. She came and came, writhing on the two relentless shafts.

Dropping forward, she braced her hands on Madoc's huge chest, sucking air as if it had disappeared from the room. Everything inside her was shimmering with pleasure. "Gods."

"Fuck, you feel good when you come." Growling, Madoc gripped her hips, his hands beside André's and pounded into her from below in hard, hammering thrusts. With a subterranean growl, he came inside her.

Under her palms, she could feel the hard thudding of his heart.

His hazel eyes met hers, and he smiled slowly. "Thank you." He cupped her cheek, bringing her down so he could kiss her, slowly and beautifully.

"Ready, brawd?" he asked André.

"Aye." André closed his arms around her, holding her against him tightly, still deep inside her. He lifted her off Madoc and lay down with her on top.

Her head spun. After a moment, she realized she lay supine, her back against André's chest with him beneath her.

He was still deep inside her. Even deeper, if that was possible.

They were at one corner of the bed with André's feet braced on the edge of the mattress. Hers dangled off the bed.

Niall moved between André's knees and lifted her left leg up in the air.

"What..."

"My turn, pretty wolf." Niall grinned down at her, positioned himself, and slid deep into her pussy.

She sucked in air at the glorious, overly full sensation.

Grasping her other leg, he raised it, too, and braced her knees in the crooks of his elbows.

André was still deep inside her ass, one hand on her clit, the other around her waist, pinning her in place.

Standing beside the bed, Madoc was playing with her breasts, gently at first, then his teasingly sharp pinches to her nipples sent electricity shooting to her clit.

Using his hold under her knees, Niall lifted her hips up. As André's cock withdrew, Niall slammed into her, then dropped her back down on André. The in and out was much like Madoc and André had done, only this time, she had even less control of... anything. Not the speed, the position, the penetration.

The helpless feeling melted her insides, waking her arousal again. "More."

With a darkly masculine laugh, André rubbed his cheek against hers. "More you will have. Niall...go."

Within seconds, they were dual-pistoning into her, filling her so deeply, so intensely, her need rose, hard and fast.

Every nerve inside her tightened at the exquisite simultaneous torment of André rubbing her clit, Madoc fondling her breasts, and the two cocks inside her. *Gods.*

Her breathing stopped as the devastating sensations drowned out everything, taking her to the edge. And then... In a cataclysmic release, waves of pure pleasure swept through her body, totally obliterating her.

There was a roaring in her ears; the world disappeared. And the merciless pounding continued. Another climax surged across her nerves, rolling her in pleasure.

Niall came with a shout, then André with a deep, pleased purr. And as satisfaction dissolved her body, she went limp.

. . .

A short time later, they were all sprawled out on the bed, and Niall felt more content than he ever had before.

He lay on his back with Heather draped over him, all soft and female. Her face was pressed against his neck, and he could feel the small puffs of her breath on his damp skin. Her hand gripped his hair. His arms were around her shoulders, holding her to him.

His brothers were on either side of him, André stroking Heather's back, Madoc with his hand on her ass. All connected.

And that was good too. He'd needed this badly.

After seeing her risk death to rescue the female and babies, his cat had needed to be with her in this way, to affirm in the most basic of ways that she was all right.

Because, admit it, down deep, he thought of her as his mate.

He rubbed his cheek against her hair to mark her with his scent, despite having done so rather thoroughly already. He breathed in and grinned. The room held all their scents...along with the heady fragrance of sex.

He'd needed this time with his brothers too. Fuck, but when the hellhound attacked André... Niall took a slow breath. Then there had been the sound of Madoc's bellow of pain.

They'd come so close to dying; the knowledge still shook him right to his bones.

Sharing the female he adored with his littermates was a brilliant celebration of life. And more special than he could have ever realized.

Smiling, he tightened his grip and fell into sleep, surrounded by the ones he loved.

CHAPTER THIRTY-FOUR

Why did he feel so weird? Sitting at the school desk, Talam looked over his shoulder at the windows. At the door. Again.

He was so *tired* but all twitchy at the same time. Whenever he started reading, he could feel a hellhound right behind him again. Or smell it—the puke-stink of garbage cans with fish heads in 'em in summer.

But when he turned to look or sniffed the air? There was nothing.

All day, the kids had asked questions—all the questions—about the hellhound, being bait, the trap, the hellhound screaming, the blood...

Talam shivered, wishing he couldn't remember how André had been bleeding so bad. And how Madoc's fur had been all matted with blood, and Niall's leg looked like ripped-up meat.

Earlier, after about the zillionth time he'd turned around, Mr. Quintrell called him over about a homework problem. Only instead, the teacher had talked about a fight with a feral bear and being anxious for days afterward. He said lots of people had trouble settling after being in danger...and it would get better.

Talam sighed. Maybe he wasn't totally a gutless coyote, after all. Mr. Quintrell told him to talk with Niall about it.

And to get extra hugs from Heather. Talam liked the idea. Heather gave great hugs.

He worked a while longer on adding stupid fractions together and then the door to the parking lot opened.

Bron, the Crichton brothers' aunt, walked in and went over to talk to their teacher.

Talam eyed the sword-shaped cahir mark on the female's face. He hadn't known females were cahirs. It was pretty cool. She was really tall and had some major muscles. Okay, not as big as Niall or the two massive cahirs who came to help last night. But *big*.

Beside him, Sky grinned.

"What?"

"She looks like the woman in the Matrix movie we watched with Niall. You know—Trinity."

Talam tipped his head. Short black hair, eyes kinda gray, a pointy thin nose and chin too. "Yeah, she kinda does. Bet she kicks ass like Trinity too."

"That would be major."

Their teacher motioned to them to come forward. "Talam, Sky, did you meet Bron?"

"Uh, kinda?" Did seeing someone introduced to someone else count?

"I'm Sky. Good to meet you, ma'am."

When Sky kicked his ankle, Talam remembered the manners Mom'd taught. "Pleased to meet you, ma'am. I'm Talam."

Bron had a cool laugh, not quiet at all, but more like Madoc's. "It's good to meet you both. I'm looking after you until supper, since André and his brothers need to sleep after being healed."

"Oh yeah, gotcha." Sky grinned. "I was all sleepy, too, after the healer fixed me."

Her eyebrows went up. "So young and already acquainted with the healers."

They both backed up a step. Telling her about burning down Heather's house? *Uh-uh.*

She looked at them hard, then shrugged. "The carpenters are making covers for the traps. I know André will want a report, so shall we check it out?"

They nodded, although Talam wasn't happy. Sure, it'd be cool to see how they'd keep people—especially humans—from falling into the pits, but he didn't really want to remember all those screams.

At least this Bron cahir seemed to be nice.

Heather woke some time later and simply enjoyed. She was sprawled over Niall, inhaling his masculine, woodsy scent with every breath. Her breasts were flattened on his hard chest, and he had a hand on her shoulder and his other hand behind her head.

André lay to her right, his arm across her middle back, Madoc to her left had a heavier arm over her low back.

She was thoroughly pinned in place...and had never felt so cherished. How had she never realized she wanted to be cuddled after mating?

But maybe it was only true for *these* males? Somehow, they'd set up residence in her heart like no one had before.

No, foolish wolf, don't think that way.

Silently, she lifted her head, pleased no one woke.

Niall's eyes were closed. Faint pink claw marks showed on his cheek and jaw from the crow-cursed hellhound. She smiled, seeing his lips were slightly swollen—from kissing her. She'd left a bite mark on his shoulder, and the territorial mark pleased her wolf immeasurably.

Beside her, André was sound asleep. His color had improved, back to the light olive tone. Her fingers twitched, wanting to trace the firm line of his mouth. His stern jaw held the shadow of a beard. His face was all forbidding razor edges. Only the humor always lurking in his dark eyes kept the male from being downright terrifying.

Turning her head, she saw Madoc was also deeply asleep.

His brown hair was tangled over his shoulders, his beard a shade darker. The hard planes of his face were like granite, but laugh lines creased the edges of his eyes. And a corner of his mouth was tilted up as if he was dreaming of something happy. Unable to resist, she kissed the top of his head.

He was so easygoing and sociable...except around her whenever he remembered she was female.

She huffed a silent laugh. He'd sure realized she was female today. As at the Gathering, he'd taken her with an open enthusiasm that still made her tingle.

The memories of this afternoon, she'd have forever. André's dark-velvet voice giving instructions, his far-too-knowledgeable hands on her body. Niall moving her as if she weighed less than a doll. Madoc's hearty laugh. The way they'd shared her, the way they'd been so pleased when she climaxed. The way they'd taken her for their own pleasure.

Feeling the tingling in her girl bits, Heather rolled her eyes. If these over-sized males took her again, she'd be walking bow-legged for a week.

And if one of them smiled at her, she'd roll over and say *go*.

Time to get out of here.

After cleaning up—and boy, she'd needed it—Heather went downstairs to see what she could pull together for supper. A fancy cook she was not, but she could manage the basics.

If Bron was cub-watching, she might well stay for the meal. Madoc had mentioned his aunt had booked a room at the B&B.

Heather shook her head. Would Gretchen give Bron as much trouble as she did most females? The cahir didn't look the type to put up with Gretchen's nastiness.

Checking the fridge, Heather found packs of ground beef. And look, the cupboard held taco shells and burrito wraps. *Perfect.* Since Madoc had three crockpots—crazy chef—she could prepare everything and let the guys sleep as late as they wanted. Whenever they came downstairs, there'd be food ready.

A while later, as Heather lowered the heat on the crockpots containing taco meat, refried beans, and rice, a vehicle came up the long drive.

A couple of minutes later, Talam and Sky bounded into the kitchen.

"Smells good. I'm *soooo* hungry." Talam went over to Greystoke to give him a quick stroking.

"Me too." Sky's big eyes were hopeful.

Laughing, Heather gave them quick hugs. "Have you ever not been hungry? You two eat more than gnomes."

They grinned, no longer worried about being teased.

"Here." She set out carrots and dip. "Start on this. If the brothers don't come down soon, we'll eat without them."

"See, Bron. Heather won't make us wait for them," Talam called to the cahir who walked in the back door. With a suitcase.

Oh. Heather blinked. Why hadn't she realized the aunt wouldn't continue paying for a B&B when she could stay with her nephews? Especially since there were empty rooms here.

Bron's dark eyebrows came together. "You stay in the Cosantir's home, eat his food, and won't wait for him?"

Ouch. The way she phrased the question did sound bad. Bron must be a traditionalist.

Heather thought to ignore the comment, but Talam and Sky had hunched down in their chairs. There would be no making cubs feel bad about being hungry—not on Heather's watch.

She gave Bron a level look. "If you know André at all, you know he wouldn't want younglings having to wait for their meal."

Ignoring the comment, Bron tapped her suitcase with her boot. "What room has been prepared for me?"

"As far as I know, none." The males wouldn't have had time; they'd simply fallen into bed. And then...they'd been doing other things. Hoping she hadn't flushed, Heather started setting out the taco fixings on the kitchen island.

The cahir grunted. "Fine, make me up a bed in the room beside theirs."

Talam shook his head. "Heather's in the room next to André."

"Isn't that nice." Bron's tone was flat. "Why am I not surprised? Females are always trying to move in with Niall—and now there's a Cosantir to go with the cahir."

Did she imply I'm a—how did Vicki put it?—a Gods-called groupie? Exerting control over her temper, Heather gave Bron a thin smile. "There's an empty room next to mine. I can help you if you feel you need assistance in making a bed."

The cahir looked as startled as if Heather had hissed in her face.

Gods, I'm acting like a cat. The aunt was simply guarding her nephews from what she thought was a pushy female. Cahirs were overprotective by nature. Heather smiled more naturally. "I'd be happy to help."

"No need." The female picked up her suitcase. "Which room?"

"I'll show you," Sky set down his carrot stick and jumped to his feet.

"Thank you, cub." Bron motioned toward the stairs.

"Sky." Heather ignored the cahir. "The brothers are still napping, so please be very quiet. The healer insisted they needed their sleep."

As Bron and Sky went up the stairs—quietly, Heather was pleased to see—Talam frowned. "Bron was nice to us, but she wasn't nice to you. Did you step on her tail or something?"

Trying not to feel unwelcome, Heather smiled and ruffled his hair. "Or something, I guess."

No, she didn't want to cause problems between the cubs and the brothers' aunt, even if the aunt was acting like a bee-stung badger. "Maybe she's cranky because she didn't get any sleep last night. It was wonderful of her to come to help with the hellhound."

Feeling the bed rock, Niall started the path upward to wakefulness. By the Gods, he'd slept hard. As he rolled onto his side, dull aches made themselves known here and there. But sleep had made everything better.

So had the mating.

Inhaling, he breathed in the scents of his brothers and the lingering fragrance of female arousal and sex.

Of Heather.

He sat up in the massive bed. André was already getting dressed. Madoc was still asleep, so he nudged him. "Time to rise and shine, bear."

Yawning, Madoc scratched his chest. "Is it morning?"

Smiling, André fastened his pants. "No, brawd, it's almost eight in the evening. We need to clean up—again—and head downstairs."

The cubs would be back. And Bron, as well.

Niall eyed the bathroom. It had a huge shower and a big tub, both designed to be shared. Wouldn't Heather look lovely with her auburn hair curling in the steam, face rosy. Breasts...

Feeling himself stir, he turned his thoughts away from mating and instead thought about what more he wanted. From her. With her. "Heather. I want to keep her."

Sitting up, Madoc frowned. "She's not a pet."

"No, I mean..." Niall scrubbed his hands over his face.

"By 'keep her,' do you mean for a week or two...or *longer*?" André asked quietly.

"Longer. Much, much longer." Niall turned. "Madoc?"

Climbing out of bed, Madoc grabbed his pants. Expression unreadable, he shook his head after a moment.

Niall sat still, trying to deal with the painful rejection. Brothers had to agree on a mate. But...it hurt. He couldn't even think of what to say.

Silently, the bear pulled on his sweatpants, then hesitated, looking between André and Niall. "I don't know. I wasn't thinking of being serious about her. Gods, I've never thought of serious when it comes to any female."

"We know." André studied Madoc. "I have noticed you look at Heather differently than you do other females."

"Perhaps. Maybe." Madoc turned to Niall. "Let me ponder for a while."

Niall managed to keep his mouth shut and just nodded. A *maybe* was far better than a *no*.

And the bear couldn't be rushed. He'd think and think, until a brother wanted to knock him into a lake from frustration. But when Madoc finally came to a decision, it was invariably a wise one—and then he'd flatten any obstacles in his path.

As Madoc left, Niall looked at André. "You?"

His brother smiled slightly. "Oh, much, *much* longer sounds about right to me."

Niall grinned.

As usual, Madoc was the last to get downstairs. Maybe it was because his brothers were cats, but they always managed to get moving faster than he did after waking.

Stomach rumbling with hunger, he followed a spicy aroma to the kitchen. His littermates were already at the dining room table with loaded plates. Hopefully, someone had cooked enough for him to have a helping.

André and Niall smiled at him without slowing down at all. Not surprising. The aftermath of being healed included a savage appetite.

In the great room, Heather was sitting on the couch. On the floor, Sky and Talam sat on each side of her legs, using the coffee table for their homework.

Spotting Madoc, Heather gave him a warm smile, which lightened his heart.

And made him want her again.

By the Gods, he was confused.

For *much, much longer*, Niall had said. The thought of her living here, of her being their mate was unsettling, yet... Why couldn't he imagine a time when he didn't want her nearby? When her scent in the air didn't make him happy?

"Madoc. *Madoc*." Bron was trying to get his attention from the kitchen.

"Aye, Aunt?"

"What can I get you to drink?" She glanced toward the great room with a frown.

"Water is fine for me, thank you." He ran his gaze over the food on the island and smiled. More than plenty remained. He loaded his plate with tacos, burritos, refried beans, and rice, then joined André and Niall.

Bron brought him a glass of water. Returning to the kitchen, she stopped to make nice with Lord Greystoke who—after a suitable period of aloofness—allowed her to give him scritches.

Felines. No matter the size, they all had outsized egos.

After filling a plate for herself, Bron took a seat at the table.

Madoc hardly noticed, being busy vanquishing the hollow place in his belly. These tacos weren't gourmet food, but were solidly satisfying, and the biting spices vanquished the last lingering taste of hellhound. "This was exactly what I needed. Thank you, Bron."

Her mouth twisted. "Your... Heather cooked."

Startled at the unpleasant tone, Madoc stared at her, then turned toward the great room. "Thanks for the food, Heather. I was starving."

Her smile lit the room. "I've been healed before. I know how it feels."

Sky patted his stomach. "Like a wolf is gnawing on you from the inside."

"A *wolf*, huh?" Heather poked Sky's shoulder.

"Yeah," Madoc grinned at her indignant expression. "Gotta watch out for wolves."

"Honestly." Heather sniffed in mock annoyance. "*I* think extreme hunger feels more like a mangy *bear*."

"Mmm, better watch out for those bears," Niall agreed. "They have an appetite, especially if it's been a while." His glance at Madoc was wicked.

It was true enough. And when the little wolf turned red, Madoc chuckled right along with his brothers.

As he worked his way through a couple of burritos, he listened to the cubs asking Heather questions. "Math homework," he observed with a grimace. "Better her than me."

She heard him and called. "Personally, I think it's easier than cooking."

Talam nodded vigorously, and Sky shook his head.

André smiled and lowered his voice, "Complete opposites, those two."

There were some litters where the siblings had almost identical personalities. In some, as with Madoc and his brothers, each was different. That was why he'd been certain they'd never find a female to share. Of course, there was the fact he didn't want a mate at all.

"So." Bron pushed her plate back. "Sky told me Heather's

cabin was burned down. I must commend you all on your care for your clan by taking her in. He also mentioned you repaired the communal house, which is wise. You can't open your home to all the strays."

Bron's tone was interesting. Very even, but with an underlying edge. Was this animosity he was hearing? Madoc glanced at André.

His brother's eyes narrowed slightly.

"Heather, since I haven't started my duties as police chief yet, I'll assist in moving you to the communal house tomorrow." Bron's smile was thin as she looked at Heather.

Niall scowled. "Aunt—"

"You can't leave, Heather," Sky protested. "You belong *here*."

"Yeah." The worry in Talam's young face was distressing.

Feeling much like the cubs, Madoc wanted to snap his teeth in his aunt's face, despite knowing why she was being as aggressive as a wolverine.

Still... The thought of Heather leaving was...wrong. He wasn't ready. Not yet.

"Actually, Bron is right." Leaning forward, Heather put an arm around each cub. Her voice dropped, but Madoc could still hear her. "You were wonderful in helping me, my cubs, but my arm is all healed up. It's time I found my own place to live."

The younglings had tears in their eyes.

Heather turned toward the table. "No need for help, Cahir Bron." Her warm contralto had chilled. "Everything I own fits in one bag."

"No." Niall's face darkened. "You can't—"

"Heather." André's soft voice interrupted Niall and stilled Madoc's protest, as well. "As with the cubs, you're the focus of Wendell's animosity. You *will* remain here. When he's out of the picture, we can revisit the subject of your living arrangements."

Her mouth opened, but she didn't respond. André's voice held an unyielding note, and they all could hear it.

Her frown disappeared when the cubs buried her in hugs.

And Sky whispered, "What's ani-smosity."

Madoc frowned. Wendell had already displayed a vindictiveness rare in shifters. André was correct. The little wolf needed to stay here where they could protect her.

The thought of her getting hurt was...unacceptable.

An hour later, Heather tidied up the great room. The brothers had all gone upstairs to put Talam and Sky to bed, which had made her throat get tight. The three were still shaken at how close the cubs had come to dying.

Bron was in the kitchen, putting away leftovers and filling the dishwasher.

Hating the prickly territorial feeling, Heather told herself it was nice to have help. But still... Bron had been up all night and all day. Why hadn't she gone off to bed?

The house normally felt like a serene refuge, but the female's attitude had destroyed any peace—at least for Heather.

Gathering the dishes from the younglings' bedtime snack, Heather carried them into the kitchen. With a forced smile for Bron, Heather loaded the cups and plates into the dishwasher.

"The plates should face forward rather than back," Bron stated.

Still bent over the dishwasher, Heather growled under her breath. Aside from the short nap with the brothers, she'd been up all night and day as well. Her tolerance for assholeness, as Vicki would say, had worn thin. It was time to set some boundaries.

Removing the plates and cups from the dishwasher, she set them on the counter. "There you go. From now on, the cubs and I will leave our dishes here, so you can load the dishwasher to your exacting specifications."

Bron's jaw went tight. "You'd make someone else deal with your dishes?"

"When someone criticizes whatever I do simply because she has a hair up her ass for whatever reason? Absolutely." Heather started to walk out and bounced off Niall.

Beside him, André squeezed her shoulder and stepped around her. "A word, Aunt."

Oh, I really don't want to hear this. Grabbing her coat from the hanger by the back door, Heather walked out.

Once outside, she stopped and pulled in long breaths of the clean cold, rancor-free air. Unfortunately, she could still hear Bron. "I knew she was a lazy, rude—"

"Herne's pole and pebbles, what is wrong with you, Aunt?" Niall snapped. "You've been—"

Heather broke into a jog to get out of hearing distance. Yet the way André and Niall had jumped to defend her set up a warm glow inside.

The glow faded quickly.

She should have politely put up with the pig-headed aunt. Bron *had* come to help the town and her nephews. Really, from Bron's view, Heather did look like a charity case.

She wasn't, though. She had plenty of money. Had friends too. But, after falling for Madoc's *"we have your cat,"* ploy, she'd simply not wanted to leave. Especially since the cubs were there. And so were the clan's accounting books and files.

And, if she was confessing, so were the brothers.

Bron was wrong; Heather hadn't chased the males for being Gods-called, but face it, she *was* falling for them.

Talk about foolish.

When the trail split, Heather frowned. To the right, it appeared as if the forest path led downward into a narrow valley—a direction she'd explored before.

Glancing back at the distant house, she could see in the lit kitchen, Bron waving her hands in the air.

Yep, keep walking.

As she veered to the right, the fir needle-covered trail was soft under her sneakers. And she had some thinking to do.

Tomorrow, she'd ignore André's dictate and find a place to live. A Cosantir had a hard enough job to do without dissension in his home. Really, none of the males should have to tolerate such unhappiness.

When it came right down to it, leaving was the right choice for her too. She didn't want entanglements, and from what she'd observed, neither did the brothers.

So she'd leave before her heart got involved. *Right, okay,* before her heart got any *more* involved.

This afternoon sure hadn't helped her to stay unattached. She shook her head. There were no words for how wonderful it had been.

She realized she was smiling at the memory, but who wouldn't? The males had incredible stamina and control. And more... They'd been so tender with her, and André so dominating in a way that made her wolf shiver and submit. And sweet... How could such tough males be so sweet? They'd totally reduced her to a sated, happy mess.

And, oh, she wanted to go back and do it again.

No, absolutely not.

At the bottom of the slope was a grassy clearing where the scent of calm water and damp grasses filled the air. In the center, the dark water of a tiny lake reflected the night sky.

Beautiful.

Near the lake, she spotted a carved log bench. The wood was cool under her touch, and she took a seat, then tipped her head back. In a moonless sky, the stars shone all the more brilliantly.

Peace settled like a soft mist on her shoulders.

A few minutes later, she heard the soft scuff of footsteps on the trail. Her eyes narrowed. Who had come after her?

If it was Bron... Not good. Hitting a cahir was simply asking to get flattened. And Heather had never liked physical combat—not like Vicki.

But it was Madoc who appeared. Who studied her for a long minute before sitting down a small distance from her on the bench. He didn't speak, probably allowing her to decide if she wanted him to leave.

He could stay.

As sociable as the bear was, he wasn't a chatterer. Instead, he carried a stillness within him. In the quiet night, he fit in well.

She didn't break the silence with words.

And he didn't leave.

When a light breeze on the water rippled the reflection of the stars, she could feel his pleasure. A deer on the opposite shore came to drink, setting the undines beneath the surface to swirls of translucent beauty.

Eventually, when she felt as if she'd bathed in serenity, she turned and laid her hand on his muscular forearm. "I'm sorry about causing a fight." Well, she hadn't caused it, but—

"You didn't cause it." He chuckled. "Bron poked at what she thought was a bunny and found a grown wolf instead. If her finger has fang-marks, it seems only fair."

His straightforward defense felt far too good. "She did have a—"

"Hardly. She was rude without any cause. I'm sorry for it."

Nonetheless. "No, Madoc, she did have a point. It's time for me to find my own place."

He made a gruff sound in the back of his throat. "Little wolf, didn't André say you were to stay? Because Wendell might come after you?"

It was a good reason. And Gods, how she wanted to stay. Yet she knew better. She'd already learned what would happen with her and males.

It would hurt to leave. She felt her lip tremble and pressed her lips together hard. *Grow up, fool. Pixie dreams are for cubs, not adults.*

If she was going to keep her heart intact, she needed to get away from temptation. Should get out of the area entirely.

Otherwise, the next full moon... She knew all too well what would happen.

"Actually, I'm thinking about moving to Cold Creek."

The shock of her words turned Madoc's entire body to stone. By the Gods, what was the female *thinking*? "You'd leave the whole *territory*?"

Her laugh contained no real humor. Didn't sound like her at all. Pulling her legs up, she wrapped her arms around her shins and rested her chin on her knees. "It's not far away. I have friends I can stay with until I find a place to live."

"But...we...you have friends here." Bears weren't known for smooth-talking, but he didn't usually stumble over his paws like this. "We...I don't want you to disappear."

"I can still do your business accounts. We already set them up to be mostly online, anyway." Her gaze met his. "I received the impression you don't care for females. You might be happier with a male accountant."

For the second time in one day, his past rose up to gnaw on his tail.

And although she was obviously trying to keep her voice level, he had ears. His avoidance of her had left wounds.

He'd hurt her. The realization created an ache deep in his chest.

How could he fix this? What kind of a pitiful worm was he to be unable to face his past?

"All right, let's talk."

"What—no, we don't need—"

He took hold of her ankles, firmly pulled her closer, and set her legs over his so she was facing him. *Better*.

"First..." He rested his arm along the back of the bench and partly over her shoulders. Because he wanted to touch her. Needed to. "I have scars from when I was younger. It's not you."

"Really, it's all right. You don't need to explain."

She didn't believe him. Gods, he was making a muck of this. He ran his hand through his hair in frustration. "I was fostered in a Daonain village up in the Yukon Territory. There were other shifters around my age, but bears can be slow to grow. And I'm a black bear."

"What does black have to... Oh." She nodded. "You have grizzlies up north, don't you?"

Aggressive, huge grizzlies, yep. "Mmmhmm. I was small compared to the fast-growing wolves and cats—and the grizzlies. And I hadn't grown up there."

"Oh ow. Teens and outsiders. Did you get picked on?"

"To put it mildly." Knocked off trails, flattened under cougars, left out of games. "It's probably why I hate bullies. When I finally grew tough enough to hold my own...there was this female."

"Uh-oh." The worried expression on Heather's face was heartwarming. The sweet female was all concerned for the cub he'd been years in the past.

"Gods, I was gone over her. Totally in love. We were high school seniors, and I'd just attended my first full moon. Since you females don't start your heats until around twenty, she wasn't old enough to mate, but I didn't mind that I'd have to wait for her." Needing more contact, he laid his hand on Heather's thigh, feeling the solid muscle under the denim. She wasn't frail or weak, in body or spirit.

"And her?" She asked softly.

"I thought she loved me. She asked me to wait for her, said she'd be my mate."

Heather sighed. "You were way too young, Madoc. What happened?"

He almost smiled at the cynical tone in her voice. "Some of us were playing on the rocks beside a flooding river...not far above a waterfall. Teens never think they can die, do they?"

She set her hand on his, squeezing hard. "An accident?"

"A werecat slipped on a mossy rock and landed in the river. He couldn't swim worth a damn. I shifted to human and dove off my rock. Pulled him close to the bank and grabbed a low tree branch. But he panicked. Climbed me, leaped off my shoulder, and knocked me loose and into the current." Gods, he'd been powerless against the rushing water. "I went over the falls."

"Mother of all." Her grip on his hand was painful. "Madoc."

"Rocks banged me up good. A shifter couple was fishing and dragged me out, mostly drowned. Trouble was I'd cracked my head on the rocks. Everything else healed, but my brain... It left me clumsy and barely able to talk."

She closed her eyes for a moment as if in pain. "I'm guessing your girlfriend couldn't deal with it?"

"Tossed me away faster than a dwarf finding coal in his pile of gold." He gave her a pained smile. "She was with someone else two days later. Joined the others in making fun of me."

Heather's dark growl made Madoc blink. "Point her out to me. And the others. I'll—"

"You're a vicious little wolf." His laugh was unexpected, especially with the thickness in his throat. "It was years ago, aye? As it happens, André and Niall took care of them."

Niall told him later that in protecting Madoc, he'd learned he wanted—*needed*—to be a cahir.

"Didn't this happen during your fostering years? Your brothers shouldn't have been there."

For teens after First Shift, most littermates were separated and sent to distant relatives to give each cub a chance to grow in independence.

"Apparently, my pain—and misery—came through our littermate bond. André ran away from our uncle, detoured to BC to fetch Niall, and they covered over a thousand kilometers to get to me. Their guardians were more than pissed-off."

"I bet. Good for André and Niall." She was blinking hard, and he saw wetness on her cheeks. "You must have been hurting so bad for them to feel it."

"Mmmhmm." Was she crying? Over *him*?

She turned away and wiped her cheeks. "So...are you still longing after your girlfriend?"

"Not even." He smiled slightly. "She's still in the Yukon, and according to my uncle, latches onto a new male every year."

"Oh. Well." Heather released his hand, leaving dents behind. "But you got better. I mean, you're certainly not clumsy or inarticulate."

"It just took a long time to heal. If I'd been older, I might have been out of luck."

"Cubs are resilient, thank the Gods." She was silent for a while. "But, Madoc, avoiding all females simply because of a bad one seems..."

She bit her lip and looked away. "Sorry. I was being judgmental."

But truthful. It was one of the things he liked—her blunt honesty. "Well, she did break my tender, young heart."

His words came out lightly, but he was also being truthful. The pain of her betrayal had been far worse than the blinding headaches he'd suffered from. "When Herne made Niall a cahir, I saw how females chased him for his genes or status. So many times, a female would lead him on; he'd fall hard for her, then get chucked like two-day-old garbage when she moved on to the next status symbol. He'd be fucking miserable for months."

Heather winced. "Poor Niall."

"So yeah, I stay away from females outside of Gatherings. I only wish I could completely avoid the ones chasing after Niall... and now André."

"Wait, what?" Heather snorted. "Dude, seriously? The only females you talk with are the ones chasing the Gods-called?"

He shrugged. "Yeah."

"Madoc, you do realize not all females are like those? That's like deciding all birds are predators after watching only the hawks."

Could she be right? By Herne's hairy hocks. "I, ah, might not have realized I was judging females based on a sub-group."

Her expression...

"Yeah, go ahead, call me a gnome-brain."

Her lips twitched. "Didn't you meet nice females at the restaurants where you worked?"

He shrugged. "The places were human-run." To avoid shifter females.

"Oh honestly." She shook her head, then laughed. "I'm afraid your time of avoiding my gender is over, what with owning a restaurant and having to help the Cosantir."

"So it seems." The thought wasn't particularly appealing. Especially if one shifter female wasn't going to be around.

Gods, he didn't want her to leave.

Time to try again. He took her hand again. "Maybe I was wary of you at first, but that hasn't been the case for a while."

She blinked and pulled her hand away.

You can't stop me from making my point, little wolf. "How many hours have we spent together, working on the restaurant? Or this afternoon in bed?" Keeping his arm around her shoulders so she couldn't move away, he stroked the sweetly curved legs lying across his thighs.

He really did like touching her.

"Madoc."

"Heather. I don't want you to leave. You can mark it off as a reason."

She huffed at him like a bear might. Fucking lovable. "Your

aunt wants me gone, and I'm not going to cause a fight within your family."

Because she was a peacemaker—and how rare was that?

"Bron doesn't know you yet, Heather." He sighed. "Between the females chasing after Niall and the ones harassing her cahir friends, she has as warped an opinion as mine. As mine *was*."

Heather narrowed her eyes. "Even without her beliefs, I doubt we'd get along."

"She won't stay in our house long. In the past, any visit lasting over three days made us as irritable as if we'd rolled in grit. Her, too. She prefers to live alone."

"Oh. Well..."

He gave her another verbal nudge. "André told you to stay. Do you really want to upset a brand-new Cosantir?"

"Now you're playing dirty."

Laughing, he pulled her closer, then fully into his lap. "You want to play dirty, little wolf?" Tangling his fingers in her hair, he pulled her head down so he could kiss her.

And wasn't it an amazing feeling when, after the smallest of hesitations, she wrapped her arms around his neck and kissed him back.

When his hand closed on her breast, he could feel the full-body shiver she gave.

And then he had the joy of mating with her under the stars. Of taking all the time he wanted, of hearing her throaty cries of satisfaction.

It was a long, long time before they returned to the house.

Talam felt something grab his arm; the hellhound charged out of the mist, and somehow, it was already biting him. He screamed and hit and hit.

"Ow!" The voice was Sky's.

Did the monster have *Sky*?

"Wake up, ninnyhammer."

Ninnyhammer. That was what Mama called them when they were stupid. Why did—

The hellhound shook Talam like he was a rat.

"Wake *up*."

Jerking awake, Talam sat up real fast. Everything was dark, only no, there was a light down low. An owl was flying in front of the moon. Why was the moon by the ground?

It was the nightlight. He was in bed. At the Cosantir's house.

Next to him, Sky dug his fingernails into Talam's shoulder.

"Ow." Talam scowled. "Did you shake me?"

"Uh—maybe?"

There was a tap on the door. "Cubs, are you all right? May I come in?" It was Heather.

"Yeah." Talam's voice was hoarse, and he swallowed hard. He really, really wanted her to come and be with them. He swung his legs out of the bed.

Sky had already jumped up and let her in. "Hey."

Walking in, almost as quiet as André and Niall, she patted Sky's arm. Then she looked at Talam, and her smile went away. "Oh baby, did you have a nightmare?"

Talam bit his lip. "Did I wake you up?" He kinda thought he might have screamed out loud, like a scaredy-mouse.

"No, I read for a while after my walk and was getting ready for bed when I heard you."

Scat, had *everybody* heard him? "Did I wake up anyone else?"

She shook her head. "I think your bed is above my guest room. I doubt the brothers heard you." Still in jeans and shirt, she sat on the bed and put an arm around him, pulling him close. Kinda like Mom used to do.

Sky took her other side, and she hugged him too. "You know, nightmares happen after scary things. Shifters recover better than humans and usually the dreams and jittery feelings go away. But if not, we have soulweavers and shepherds to help us. Our big, bad cahirs use them too."

"I bet cahirs get really bad nightmares." Sky shook his head. "I mean, they *look* for hellhounds. Not me, nope, never."

"I guess." And... Talam frowned. If he and Sky hadn't made the hellhound chase them, then people would've died. Niall and André almost did and so did Madoc and Heather's brother. They'd been safe, because of what he 'n' Sky had done.

He'd protected the clan almost like a cahir.

He snuggled closer to Heather and wondered if grown-up cahirs got hugs too.

CHAPTER THIRTY-FIVE

The next morning, in the warehouse behind the Shamrock restaurant, André finished talking to the carpenters about sectioning off the back for a half-court for basketball.

As he crossed the huge building, sunlight from the big windows brightened the freshly painted walls and gleamed on the refinished hardwood floor. Freestanding room dividers created smaller spaces.

Progress. The building was now functional, although rather bland. This winter, he'd have the clan's artists paint murals on the walls.

But, despite the construction noise, shifters were already using some of the sectioned-off spaces. In one, a couple of Daonain were using the computers Niall had bought.

A craft corner with comfortable chairs held three females and two males knitting as they talked.

It was a start.

A *good* start.

On the other side of the building, Niall entered, followed by Madoc with a carryout tote in his hand.

"Brawd, come and eat breakfast with us," Madoc called.

A meal with his brothers. He could think of nothing he'd like better.

Or maybe there was one possible "better." As he bumped shoulders in greeting, he asked, "Is Heather joining us?"

Madoc's jaw tightened as he shook his head. "Should we walk down to the park?"

Noting the interested gazes from the shifters in the building, André nodded. The park was much more private.

As they crossed the square, the brisk wind held a decidedly autumnal chill. In the creek, undines were riding the crests of the small whitecaps.

"Here's a good spot." André took a seat on a picnic table behind a windbreak of bushes.

His brothers joined him, and Madoc started unpacking the tote.

Stomach rumbling, André devoured the first sausage biscuit. "Thanks for this. I didn't realize how hungry I was."

"You must have left at dawn this morning." Madoc's heavy brows pulled together with his disapproval.

"Aye. I slept too much yesterday and last night."

"You're an unnatural cat." Niall smirked. "*I* can always sleep late. Or nap."

"Only because you're lazy." André helped himself to a coffee thermos. "Was there something we need to discuss, or did you just miss me?"

Madoc grinned and made kissy noises until Niall thumped him.

At Madoc's grunt, Niall made a satisfied chuff, then turned to André. "We always miss you, brawd, but we wanted to catch you up when the cubs were absent."

André stiffened. "What's wrong with the cubs?"

Madoc set a hand on his arm. "Merely a concern, nothing major."

Niall nodded. "After Madoc took the cubs to school, Heather

said Talam had a screaming nightmare last night. Sky's unsettled too."

André relaxed. But...the poor younglings. "I'm not surprised."

"I didn't hear any screaming." Madoc frowned.

"Healing sleep is deeper than normal," Niall muttered. The cahir would know.

Madoc frowned. "It's a shame there are no soulweavers or shepherds in Rainier Territory."

"There are none in the North Cascades, either." It was why last summer at the festival here in Washington, they'd encouraged a shifter suffering from PTSD to move to Canada where he could get help. Tilting his head back, André inhaled the cold, moist air. There was so much to do yet. "We'll have to work on attracting one to this area."

Madoc huffed agreement. "The clan's had rough times. A soulweaver would have plenty of work."

"I'm not sure hearing about work is an enticement." Niall's voice was dry. "Here, shepherd, let me share my worst nightmares with you."

Sipping the hot coffee, André considered his brother.

Niall had suffered ugly nightmares in his early years as a cahir, especially after the first time he sent a feral back to the Mother. All too often, a shifter who lost all bonds to others would disappear into their animal, savagely attacking and killing other shifters. There was no cure but death, ordered by the Cosantir, carried out by a cahir. The feral could be someone the cahir knew, even loved.

Cahirs might be the supreme predators, but their spirits could still be damaged. André bumped Niall's shoulder. "You've picked up some coping techniques over the years. Can you take Talam and Sky on a few hikes and do some sharing?"

"I don't have..." Niall stopped, then half-smiled. "I guess I do have ways to bounce back. Mostly ones I learned from old Bram up in the Kwadacha Territory Elder Village. He'd draft me for his carpentry projects and entertain me with advice hidden inside his stories."

Back when Niall had only been a cahir for a couple of years, they'd met the retired cahir when visiting a great-uncle who was nearing the total of his days.

"All right." Niall scrubbed his hands over his face. "I'll talk with the younglings. Put them to work maybe."

"Got a project you can use." Leaning back against the top of the picnic table, Madoc stretched out his legs. "Down the lake trail, there's a beautiful old log bench crying out for refinishing."

"Sounds like a perfect cub-sized job," Niall agreed and told André, "I got this."

"Thank you, brawd." André turned his regard to the bear who had followed Heather out last night. "You found a lake, a bench, and...perhaps a beautiful female?"

"Maybe." Madoc scowled. "So what?"

Niall groaned. "Bear, you're killing me."

It appeared Madoc and Heather had talked, at least. Last night, seeing him go after her, André had hoped the two would connect. His brother had a tender heart for wounded souls.

André had hoped for more than talk, but there was time.

"You two." Madoc shook his head, his expression hard as mountain rock...and then burst out laughing.

"What the..." Niall stared.

Thumping his palm on the picnic table, Madoc grinned. "So I love that female. When are we going to lifemate her?"

André choked on his coffee.

Niall's biscuit dropped onto the table. "Say again?"

"What? You're telling me you don't want her for our own?" Madoc smirked.

"I...fuck, yes, I want her for ours." Niall shook his head like a half-drowned cat. "I never thought you'd take a female seriously."

"Yeah, well"—Madoc pushed his hair back—"it's time to move past old shit."

André managed to clear his throat. "From back when you were hurt?"

"Aye. It warped my feelings about females." He bumped Niall with his shoulder. "And the incredibly pushy females after you—how they didn't want you for yourself."

Niall's eyes narrowed. "And you were thinking all females were like them?"

"I've met a few good females. None who were single. So...yeah."

Niall sighed. "Sorry, brawd."

"Dirt under our paws." Madoc held up his hand, and Niall slapped it.

They turned to look at André.

"You in?" Madoc asked.

"I've simply been waiting for my slug-witted littermates to catch up." André raised an eyebrow. "They're, perhaps, a few leaves short of a bush."

"Flea-ridden feline." Niall smacked the back of André's head.

André grinned...because all three of them loved Heather.

The future seemed to be filled with light.

"So how do we handle this?" Niall asked.

"Slowly, I would think." André pinched the bridge of his nose as he considered. "She fears being hurt again. We might simply live together for a time until she learns to trust the way we feel about her."

"Sounds like a good plan except for one problem." Madoc picked up his coffee. "Last night, she was planning to move to Cold Creek."

"Because of Bron?" When Madoc nodded, Niall scowled. "By the Gods, she was way out of line."

"Our aunt also has...issues." André didn't know how much his cahir aunt had shared with his brothers. "And she's still very protective of us, especially Niall."

Niall set his size fourteen foot on the bench and braced a forearm on his huge thigh. "It's because I have delicate feelings," he told them earnestly.

With a snort, Madoc back-armed Niall and his delicate feelings off the bench.

Trying not to laugh, André cleared his throat. "We will move slowly, but be prepared."

"Prepared?" Madoc asked.

"Aye. Did you know there's a blademage in Cold Creek?"

Grins met his hint. Then three fists thumped the table in unanimous agreement.

At a desk in the dusty bar office, Heather rubbed her burning eyes. Nikolaou's writing was so pinched as to be nearly unreadable, and the lighting in the room was abysmal. Next time, she'd bring in her own desk light.

Still, she welcomed the work. To create order out of chaos, to make numbers jump up and do her bidding—this was her crack. At least, here, she was in control.

Unfortunately, when it came to her emotions about Madoc, Niall, and André? Talk about a chaotic mess.

"How's it going, Heather?" the booming voice of Nikolaou, the owner of Bullwhacker, made her jump.

She smiled at the stocky human with his extravagant graywhite mustache. "Your bookkeeper kept good records." Nik had used the same accountant as the clan. Old Harold had been very competent. "Once I have everything gathered, we'll look for ways to cut costs and find more deductions."

"Exactly what I'm hoping for." His gravelly laugh reminded

her of Madoc. With a sweeping gesture, he set a glass of soda beside her.

"Thanks, Nik." The gruff bar owner was a sweetheart.

She worked another hour before calling it quits. After putting everything away in her laptop bag, she stepped out of the office.

Still cool, the barroom held the lingering scent of stale beer. The Bullwhacker wouldn't open for another hour or two.

In the back, Nik was talking to a couple of delivery men. "Yeah, someone tried to bash the poor guy's head in last night."

Are they talking about Ailill Ridge? Heather paused, eavesdropping like some snoopy feline.

One of the delivery men asked something, and Nik answered, "Local banker. Good guy. I don't know who'd want to try to kill him."

A banker. "Friedrich?" she called, crossing the room. "You mean Friedrich Schumacher?"

"Yeah, him." Nik held up his hand. "No, he's all right, missy. Ended up with a headache, but he dodged quick enough the shovel didn't crack his skull open."

"A shovel?" one of the humans repeated.

"He'd been planting daffodils and hadn't put it away." Nik tugged on his mustache. "We don't usually have trouble around here. But last month, some bastard burned your cabin, Heather. Then after the police chief's position goes empty, we hear a horrendous fight in the square. And last night, Murtagh's grocery gets the window busted out, and Friedrich is attacked. Don't know what the town is coming to."

Heather frowned. The horrendous fight would be the hellhound attack. But the rest... Pete was behind her cabin fire. Was he also attacking the Elders—Murtagh and Friedrich?

She shivered at the thought of any shifter losing his way so badly as to try to kill other Daonain.

I need to call Ina and warn her. And André too. "I guess we better get a new police chief hired quickly." No matter how annoying, it was good Bron was here.

"The sooner the better," Nik agreed.

"Well, I should get going." Reaching the door, Heather turned. "See you Monday, Nik."

His loud voice, "See you then," followed her out onto the street.

Frowning, she hitched her bag onto her shoulder. It would feel good to keep the Bullwhacker going. Maybe she should talk with Calum and get some small town bar ideas.

"*Heather.*" Talam's high voice cracked to a lower one. Someone was reaching puberty.

He and Sky jogged toward her, leaving—Gods help her— Bron in the middle of the square. The cahir must have picked up the kids after school.

Smiling, Heather opened her arms and gave each cubling a good hug. Once the hellhound attack was further in the past, they'd undoubtedly return to being independent young teens. But for now, if they needed hugs, she had plenty to give.

"Look at that female. Always got the males around her." The easy-going voice with a southern drawl came from a big tanned cahir with disheveled golden-brown hair and sharp green eyes.

Delighted, she laughed. "Alec!"

He caught her up in a hard hug before giving her a long assessing stare. "I heard about your cabin. Are you all right?"

"I'm okay, yes. Merely considering my options."

"Of course you are." The big cahir chuckled. Growing up, he'd teased her and his brother, Calum, about their insistence on being organized.

"What are you doing out of the North Cascades?"

"I came to see y'all's trap. Ben and Ryder came with me in case you need help with construction and hellhound-proofing your buildings."

"Ben and Ryder?"

The two strolled over, grinning at her. Ben was a massive grizzly cahir. His littermate, Ryder, was a shade darker and a couple inches shorter with shoulder-length black hair.

"Whoa." She beamed up at the two and teased, "Are we stealing all the Cold Creek cahirs?"

"Gretchen was right." Bron's tone was as harsh as last night. "You'll make a play for any of the Gods-called. Why don't you get a damn job rather than sponging off my nephews?"

Heather let out an exasperated breath and turned.

Anger steamed off the female cahir. If Bron had been in fur, Heather might well have her throat torn out. Bron glanced at the Bullwhacker Bar, and her lip curled up. "Isn't it a little early to be drinking? You're a fine example to the cubs here. Or was there a cahir in there you were sniffing at too?"

Crossing her arms over her chest, Heather considered ripping the female a new asshole. Then her gaze landed on Talam and Sky.

The cublings had gone pale. They sure didn't need more violence to add to their stress. And they'd have to live with Bron until the female moved out.

Besides, having a spat in the middle of town was just plain stupid, as was using terms like *cubs* and *cahir*. What was the female thinking, anyway?

"Bron." Heather's carefully moderated tone wouldn't carry to non-Daonain ears, "I hope you're quite finished. Please do recall this is a mixed *human* and shifter town."

Bron glanced at Alec, then Heather. "Let's hope you keep your mating off the street, then."

I have had enough. Heather's simmering temper boiled over, and it was an effort to keep her voice low. "Cahir, you're insulting not only me but your fellow Gods-called. You're indiscreet *and* a disgrace to your calling."

Bron's color rose to dangerous levels. "You—"

"*Pffft.*" Heather turned away as dismay...and grief...filled her.

Because her words had eliminated any chance of a friendly relationship with her loves' aunt.

She paused only to squeeze the younglings' shoulders and then walked away.

Now what was she going to do?

"No, Heather." Talam started to run after her, but Bron grabbed his arm, then got Sky too.

Spinning, Talam kicked her leg hard, making her curse. Sky bit her at the same time. But she didn't let them go—and by then Heather had disappeared.

Gone. Talam realized he had tears on his cheek—and he kicked the stupid female cahir even harder.

"Whoa, cub." The big male Heather had hugged—the one called Alec—pulled Talam away from Bron. "I think the cahir received your message that you didn't like what she said." His voice went cold. "I didn't either."

Talam blinked.

A rumbling growl sounded kinda like Madoc's, only it was from the really, really huge cahir. He'd taken Sky away from Bron.

All three of the males were pissed-off, not at Talam and Sky, but at Bron. Well, *good*.

"Heather was right. This isn't the place for a discussion." Alec's green eyes seemed sharp enough to cut. "Walk with us, cahir."

Bron's jaw was hard, like she was going to keep spitting out nasty shit, but then she nodded. "Name's Bron."

"Alec." The cahir motioned to the bigger male, then the shorter darker one. "Ben. Ryder. From the North Cascades. How about you, cub?"

Talam looked up.

Alec still had a hand on his shoulder. When he grinned, he

kinda looked like he'd be a cool male to know. "Would you happen to have a name to share with me?"

Name? *Oh*. "I'm Talam—and he's my brother, Sky."

"Solid names." The darker male who wasn't a cahir gave them an approving nod. "Good to meet you."

Alec's hand stayed warm on Talam's shoulder as they walked to the park. In a spot where there wasn't anyone close, they all stopped.

"Now can you explain to me what just happened?" Alec frowned at Bron. "I do believe my mate might call it a royal goatfuck."

Sky made a choked sound at the swear, and if he hadn't still been so mad, Talam might've laughed.

Bron crossed her arms over her chest. "I came to help my nephews and discovered they have that...female...living in their house. Sponging off them. She's another of the leeches who suck the life out of the Gods-called."

"Rather harsh." Ryder ran his hand over his jaw where he already had a beard shadow. Talam might have one like his someday.

"Just the facts," Bron snapped.

"No, I'm afraid your facts are all messed up." Alec had a different sorta voice. Soft and slow, but it reminded Talam of petting André when he was a werecat—all soft fur, but his muscles were like steel underneath.

Alec cocked his head. "You accused her of sniffing around cahirs—because she hugged me?"

Bron nodded.

Alec snorted. "Growing up, Calum and I ran around with her and her littermates. Now she's best friends with our mate and *caomhnor* to our daughter." He held up his arm, showing the life-mating bracelet.

Sky had inched away from the giant cahir—Ben—until he was

beside Talam. He leaned over and whispered, "Isn't Calum the Cosantir in the other territory?"

A flicker of Bron's eyes showed she heard. *Oops*.

"Besties with our mate too." Ben showed his wrist.

Bron's mouth got all pinched like Sky's did when he was gonna be a butthead. "She's still sponging off my nephews."

"Now, cahir, I'm doubting there's any sponging going on." Alec scratched his cheek. "Heather isn't hurting for money."

Ryder chuckled. "Hardly. She's the one who taught me how to manage our investments. Since she recently sold her company for a whack ton of money, she could live the rest of her life without working at all."

Bron stared. "She's...rich?"

"Not billionaire rich, but yeah." Ryder shook his head. "She's one of the few shifters who had the control and big enough balls to get a college degree. She's a CPA."

"She's doing the"—Talam searched for the word—"the books for the clan. An' for Madoc's restaurant."

"The bar owner hired her to help him figure out how to save money," Sky added. "She says she's missed helping little businesses pros—prosper."

"Small businesses," Talam corrected.

"Yeah, that."

"If she's so well off, why is she staying with my nephews?"

"Ah, I heard why." Ben's laugh was almost a booming sound. "Margery, the banfasa, told our Emma the story. When Heather's house burned and she was hurt, all her friends in Cold Creek were fighting to get her to stay with them, but one of your nephews won the battle. He told her, '*We have your cat.*' "

"Gotta appreciate a sneak attack like that," Alec said.

"She had to stay with us." Talam scowled at Bron. "Her arm was busted and in a sling, and she needed us to help her. It was *our* job."

"Cuz we burned her house," Sky whispered, looking at the grass.

"And you're picking on her, and she doesn't even have a house go to. Because of *us*." When a sob sneaked out, Talam turned around, trying to rub the tears from his eyes.

"By the Gods." Alec put an arm around him.

Talam shoved his wet face against the male. Would Heather really leave? The thought was an aching hole under his ribs.

"Cat-scat and wolf-piss." Bron turned and stood staring at the creek.

Why didn't anybody say anything?

After a minute, Talam straightened, trying to wipe his eyes. The Alec male let him move back a bit but kept an arm around Talam's shoulders. It was almost like André was there.

When Bron turned back around, she looked like someone had kicked her in her belly.

Talam knew how that felt.

She went down on a knee in front of him and Sky. "Cubs, I'm sorry. It appears I was misled. Gretchen told me—"

Sky scowled. "Gretchen hates other females. Everybody knows she lies."

"Gods-dammit." Bron said under her breath. "I was wrong—way wrong. Your Heather didn't deserve my words or the way I've been behaving."

Talam turned his face away.

But his brother was nicer—he'd always been nicer. "Why? Why were you so mean?"

When Bron didn't answer, Talam turned to look at her.

Hands on her knee, she stared at the ground and seemed almost old. And sad. "Most of my friends are cahirs. Even though the younger ones enjoy all the attention from the females, the older they get, the less they like it. Or they've been burned…"

"Burned?" Sky asked.

"Hurt," Bron explained. "It's what happens when a shifter falls in love, then learns his female only wanted his status and easy meals."

"Heather's not like that." Sky didn't yell the words the way Talam would've.

"No, it seems she's not." Bron rubbed the back of her neck like how André did when he was unhappy. "One of my sons is a cahir. He and his brother fell in love, whiskers over paws, for a female. And she dumped them when a new cahir came to town. She boasted she owned the heart of every cahir in the territory. My sons were so hurt..."

Sky reached over and took her hand.

She had tears on her cheeks. "My cahir son nearly died during a fight with a feral. Because he didn't care if he lived or not."

Talam stared in horror, and suddenly, he understood. If Niall had almost died cuz of a female, Talam would hate her forever. "Is he okay? Your son?"

"He is. Finally." She swiped at her face, rough, like Talam did when he didn't want anyone to see he'd been bawling. "It took a few years. He and his brother mated a healer last year."

"They chose a Gods-called," Ryder said.

"Yes." Bron shook her head. "They'd grown too bitter to trust their love to a female who wasn't."

Talam scowled. "Heather isn't Gods-called, but she's just as good as one."

"Yeah." Sky put his hands on his hips. "She is."

"I'll apologize to her." Bron looked Sky then Talam right in the eyes. "And, if she'll let me, see if we can be friends. It sounds as if she'd be a very good friend."

"I guess. Okay." Sky nudged Talam with his shoulder.

Talam was still thinking. It was good Bron realized Heather was amazing, but he and Sky had hopes for more. Would Bron be a problem? He crossed his arms over his chest. "The Cosantir and Niall and Madoc—they really like Heather. A lot."

At a sound, he looked over his shoulder. Alec had his hand over his mouth and made a coughing sound.

Bron's smile was kinda twisted, but it was still a smile. "Go on, lad. Does Heather like them back?"

"Uh-huh. A lot. But I don't think she's..." He ran out of words and glanced at Sky.

His brother bit his lip, then offered, "She's maybe like your sons who got hurt."

"Ah." Bron frowned. "She needs time to learn to trust them with her love?"

Talam nodded, unable to talk through the clog in his throat. He and Sky wanted to live with Heather and the brothers. But they weren't family, not real family, and soon enough, he and Sky would get dumped in the communal house.

But at least, Heather would be happy. The males would take good care of her, and she'd love them.

Cuz she was good at love.

At her guest room desk, Heather started writing a note to the males. The first few words had taken forever to write. Because her eyes kept blurring. She sniffled, thinking of Niall's note to her, left on her table so many weeks ago, back when he thought he was leaving. The one she'd tucked away in her purse.

Was a piece of paper all she'd have of him in the future?

No, don't be crazy. She was simply going to spend the weekend in Cold Creek...after she cleared her stuff out of their house.

With a sigh, she pulled out her cell phone and called Ina, only to find the Elders and the Cosantir had already been informed of Friedrich's attack.

Good. This is good. No need to call André, then. Or hear his dark smoky voice—or have him pick up on how upset she was. Because he would.

As she shoved her phone in her pocket, it rang. Now what?

The display showed: GRETCHEN.

Gods, I do not need this. The female was undoubtedly calling to nag some more about taking over the housewarming party. Heather's jaw tightened.

The female had lied to Bron about Heather and made everything worse. *You mangy cur.* Growling, Heather threw the phone toward her tote bag and...anger messed with her throw. The cell hit the bed's iron headboard with a loud crack.

Oh cat-spit. Picking it up, she saw the shattered black screen. It wouldn't power-up. *Broken.*

Like her.

No, not like me. Absolutely not. Snarling under her breath, she dumped her phone in the wastebasket and finished writing her note.

Then headed out with suitcase and tote bag.

Greystoke was already in his special oversized travel condo, which took up most of the back seat. Since she always kept it in the Jeep, it hadn't burned with her cabin. She tossed her suitcase in the cargo area. "Ready to leave, baby?"

When he let out a plaintive meow, she felt her breathing hitch. He didn't like traveling.

She didn't much either. "Me too," she whispered. "Me too."

An hour passed, then two.

She'd planned to use the long drive to think over her options. But making plans didn't happen at all. Every time she thought about what had happened, her eyes would get teary.

They felt so far away.

And why did it seem as if the moment she let herself hope, everything had been derailed.

Coming up behind a car with stick figures of a mother, father, and three short children on the back windshield, Heather winced. *The cubs.*

Really, she should have spoken to Talam and Sky, so they'd

know she'd see them on Monday and was thinking of them. They didn't have phones, but she could text André with a message for them.

She reached for her phone and... *By the Mother's breasts.* Her phone was broken and in a wastebasket.

Because she'd thrown her phone. *Seriously, girl?* She'd acted like a toddler having a temper tantrum. *Maybe I should buy myself a blankie and a stuffed teddy bear.*

Or if she decided to truly leave the area and take one of those job offers, she'd add a condition to the acceptance letter. *Sirs, I'm pleased to accept the position of chief financial officer; however, a condition of my employment would be the provision of a binkie and a rattle for personal comfort and wellbeing.*

Sure, that would go over well.

The drive to the North Cascades was interminable. With every added mile between her and André, Niall, and Madoc, her heart ached more, almost like there was a bond fraying apart.

So she snarled at the traffic—and Greystoke added his yowling complaints.

They were a sad, sad pair.

By the time she reached Cold Creek in the early evening, all she wanted was to be in fur. So, rather than heading for Breanne and the Wildwood cabins, she drove to the Wild Hunt tavern.

After giving Greystoke some crunchies and petting, she cracked the windows of the Jeep and locked up.

In the tavern, the familiar scents of malty beer and roasted peanuts were so comforting, her eyes burned with tears.

Behind the bar, Calum started to smile and frowned instead. "You smell like anger and sadness. What has happened?"

"Nothing. Just a rough day." It was good Alec hadn't known she was coming here, or he'd have called Calum with a report. She put a hand on the bar. "May I use the portal? I need to run."

"Of course. Always."

As she headed for the back hallway, she felt his gaze on her back.

In the cave system beneath the tavern, she breathed in moist cool air with a rocky, metallic tang. Stripping, she pushed her clothing into a carved-out rock cubby.

And then she trawsfurred. As the loving caress of the Mother swept up from the earth, her heart filled with gratitude. Here was a constant love.

Out of the cave, she broke into the comfortable trot she could maintain for hours. As her wolf took over, her worries and regrets, her hopes and needs fell away under the needs of the moment.

As a soft breeze ruffled her fur, her ears pricked forward to catch the slightest rustles in the brush. The air held the fragrance of evergreens, of small prey in the undergrowth, of deer and coyotes.

A scratching noise came from next to the trail. She pounced and caught the unwary shrew between her teeth. It made a fine warm snack.

Miles fell beneath her paws.

The sun was down, and the night air cold by the time she started back. Her mind had emptied, filling with peace in the quiet of the mountains.

Back at the Wild Hunt, when she shifted to human, the pain of being so far from André, Niall, and Madoc swept over her again.

Once dressed, she climbed the stairs. Time to have a beer and think about her next steps. But first, she should get a cabin at—

"Heather."

She blinked, realizing she stood at the bar, and Calum was saying her name.

His lips twitched. "The run did you good. Now sit by the fire and finish the cure."

"Ah, good idea." Taking the beer he handed her, she obediently headed toward the fireside seating.

And stopped.

The chairs and couches were occupied.

"Heather!" Bree and Vicki called.

"You had a long run." Darcy rose from a chair.

"It's about time you returned." Emma set her drink down.

Smiling, Margery stood.

And they engulfed Heather in hugs and pats. The unconditional support tightened her throat.

When they separated, Bree and Emma sat on one couch, Darcy had a chair as did Margery. Vicki drew Heather down to sit beside her on the other couch.

"What are you all doing here?" Heather picked up her beer. "Am I interrupting a meeting?"

There was a snort from Darcy. Known as a tinker who could fix anything from toasters to cars, the female had wavy black hair and big brown eyes.

Heather loved how blunt she was. Normally. "What?"

With a sweet, summery nature and hair all the shades of sunlight, Bree smiled. "Silly, we're here for you. Calum called Vicki to say he was worried about you."

Heather turned toward the bar and narrowed her eyes at her childhood friend. He hadn't changed any from those days.

Catching Heather's look, he inclined his head. Totally unrepentant.

"Meddling cat Cosantir," Heather muttered.

"Perfect description." Vicki grinned, then frowned. "He said you'd been crying. What's wrong?"

Heather sighed. The retired Marine could give Darcy lessons in bluntness.

"Does it have anything to do with those three brothers you talked about last time?" Bree gave her a mischievous smile. "Zeb told me that when you slept in a puppy pile, the Cosantir wrapped a paw around you. And you used the cahir for a pillow."

The memory was a glow in her heart; she'd never felt so safe and happy. But still... "A puppy pile? They're not wolves, for Herne's sake."

"Oooh, we should find a better term. A cougar cuddle?" Emma guessed. "Or maybe a happy huddle?"

"Sounds like over-friendly football players," Vicki muttered.

Emma continued, "A fur heap, a cuddle huddle?"

"A cuddle huddle? Gods." Margery snickered. "No more alcohol for you, bard."

But Emma was on a roll. "A clan cluster? Shifter stack?"

Everyone cracked up.

Vicki held up her hand for a halt. "We need details." She turned to Heather, "So you got up close and furry with the brothers in a clan cuddle. Tell us more."

"There's nothing to tell. Really. It was after the hellhound fight." Heather took a hasty sip of her beer. "Totally innocent. There were cubs in the pile."

"Oh, I love piles with cubs." Emma laughed and talked about being woken up by her adorable Minette. The five-year-old was always bringing home her friends.

Smiling, Heather listened and tried to think of what she was going to do. And how she really should have spoken to one of the guys before leaving.

But explaining why she needed time away? Too difficult. The last thing she wanted was to cause problems between them and their aunt.

Which meant...she really should stay here in Cold Creek, at least for a while.

A burst of laughter caught her attention, and she looked up.

Her friends noticed.

"You've been lost in thought." Vicki frowned. "Honestly, is anything wrong? Something we can help with?"

"No." She was used to keeping her problems to herself.

However...these were her friends, almost like sisters. She'd helped them with their troubles. Given advice. "Maybe."

The Gods knew she could use some help. "Yes."

Darcy hmphed. "There's a definitive answer."

Heather looked around at the smiling faces. Gods, she loved each and every one of them—and could think of nothing better than to share her troubles.

She pulled in a breath. "I need some advice."

"Our turn to give back? Yes!" Bree pumped her arm in the air.

"Problems with those three males, maybe?" Emma guessed. "It was rather obvious you were falling for them."

"I am." No, be honest. "I did."

"How about them? Have they shared how they feel?" Bree asked softly.

"I think they care for me." Heather bumped her arm against Vicki's. "Here's a Daonain problem the humans don't have. Since shifter brothers share a mate, they all have to fall in love with her. If one doesn't, they keep looking."

"Holy fuckdoodle. There's a clusterfuck I managed to avoid." Vicki picked up her beer and drained it.

"Right?" Darcy shook her head. "Add in how males avoid talking about emotions, and it probably takes forever for litter-mates to hash things out."

"Especially with three brothers." Margery looked appalled. "*Three*."

"Three." Vicki snorted. "Girlfriend, you are cray-cray."

"Tell me about it," Heather muttered. "I've thought males liked me before, and they changed their minds. Backed away. Including the last ones who fled at the thought of raising cubs."

Vicki slung an arm around her shoulders. "Give us the names of the last set. We'll go fuck them up."

"Gods." Emma burst out laughing. "I keep forgetting how violent she is."

Darcy curved her fingers into claws. "I'll help with the shredding, Vic."

"I can shoot." Bree raised a hand. "Testicles make nice, fat targets."

Heather was torn between laughing and crying. By the Mother, she had fine friends. "Thank you...but those males left the territory. Their balls are safe."

"Okay, so you care, and it sounds like maybe they care. Only you're here. And have been crying." Emma frowned. "In all the songs, that means something is keeping you apart. Either the males are blind, deaf, and dumb, or there's something else." The bard was one of the most perceptive people Heather knew.

Everyone turned to look at Heather again.

Darcy frowned. "It must be something else."

"Sounds like they're taking too long to make up their fucking slow-as-slug minds," Vicki said decisively. "You're living in their house, right?"

"Well...I was."

A lesser female would be cowed by all the scowls. And Vicki snapped, "Explain this *'was'* bullshit."

"It's a story," Heather started—and saw Emma lean forward. *Bards*. "Their aunt—a cahir—came to help with the hellhound as well as take over the Chief of Police position, and she's decided..." Heather laid it all out for them. A relative who hated and vilified her, about Talam and Sky, about thinking she'd start a business in Ailill Ridge, only...maybe not.

"Oh wow. There's a tangle." Margery shook her head. "So what are you thinking?"

"I'm thinking it'd be best to move here to Cold Creek for a while." Merely saying the words made Heather's heart sink. But... "It gets me out of their home—and the territory, so I wouldn't be causing fights between them and their aunt. And my absence would give Bron a chance to calm down and settle in."

"I don't like her at all." Darcy pressed her lips together. "Are you sure she should be in law enforcement?"

"I think I'm getting a one-sided view of her," Heather

decided. "The brothers love her, and André thinks she'll be an excellent chief. She must have good qualities."

Emma frowned. "But as chief, she might cause you problems."

"Maybe." Heather shook her head. "But if I'm in town and Bron keeps bad-mouthing me, people will start taking sides. After everything André and his brothers are doing to pull the clan together, I can't stay there and create a huge divide. A war, no. I'll simply remove myself from the battlefield." *Even if it breaks my heart.*

"The plan makes sense, but I'm not liking it." Margery brightened. "Although it means we'll see more of you. In fact, you should come and stay with me."

"Wait, no. She stays with me." Bree turned to Heather. "In the lodge or in a cabin, whatever your heart desires."

They were sincere.

Emma bounced on the couch. "We have a guest room; it's wonderfully cozy."

"I can understand the logic in moving to Cold Creek, at least for a while." Vicki cut off Darcy who had her hand in the air.

"Or forever," Bree said. "You could stay here."

Heather started to shake her head.

"Girlfriend." Vicki leaned forward, resting her elbows on her knees. "Is it wise to plan your life around your enemies?"

"What?" Heather frowned.

"So Bron may or may not continue to be a problem. Giving her time makes sense. But...you've conceded the battlefield without checking in with your allies. Did you even talk to those males before you left?"

Heather sagged back against the couch. She hadn't. "I left them a note."

Vicki let out a laugh. "Fucking-A, that sounds familiar."

Gods, it was exactly what Vic had done when she ran from Calum and Alec. Heather started to grin. "You did—because you were a cowardly little furball...and so am I."

A note. Honestly, how insecure could she be? Was she too afraid to talk with them about how she felt? About what they wanted? Was she trying to make sure they didn't have to decide between her and their aunt?

Maybe a little. Maybe a lot, yes.

She sighed. She loved them. With all her heart. And being here in Cold Creek actually...hurt.

Having them not return her love would hurt even more, but to run before finding out? Sure, she could tell herself that Cold Creek wasn't too far away...but it really was. She was being a coward.

She needed to tell them she cared. Wanted more. How many times had she told them she wanted no entanglements? They probably didn't even realize she'd changed her mind.

Yet the thought of putting herself out there, leaving herself vulnerable, made her shake inside.

The last time she did, the males left the territory.

She huffed. Kind of like she just had. Gods, she was a fool. "Okay, I need to go back and talk to them. Let them know how I feel. Ask them what they want."

Emma nodded. "You know your heart. Give them a chance to show you theirs."

The day had been a long one, and Niall was dragging as he pulled his new pickup into the garage. "I'm so glad to be home," he told André and received a tired smile in answer.

First, he and Madoc had visited Cold Creek's blademage. Then once back in Ailill Ridge, Madoc headed for his restaurant, while Niall joined André in finishing up the communal house repairs. At the urging of the residents, they'd stayed there for supper.

All evening, Niall had felt increasingly irritable, almost like when he hadn't been in fur for too long. But this time, he was missing Heather. He'd texted her to invite her to join him and André at the communal house, but she hadn't answered.

Once out of his pickup, he saw it was late enough that Madoc was home from the restaurant. His CRV was there.

Heather's Jeep was missing though. Had she planned to hang out with Moya? Maybe for one of the book club meetings?

Following André inside, he saw Madoc flipping through a recipe book at the kitchen island. Leaving off his muttering about the lack of Saskatoon berries, he looked up as they entered. "Do either of you know when Heather's returning? I have an invoice I wanted to check over with her."

"Don't know." Niall automatically glanced at the back door where they hung their coats. Heather's hook was empty of both her coats. Odd. Even stranger, her rainboots were missing, too.

There'd been no rain today. He started upstairs.

Her room was bare, the bed stripped.

"Fuck, fuck, fuck." Niall spotted the note on the desk. André and Madoc stood on either side, reading over his shoulder.

André, Niall, Madoc,

I realize leaving a note is taking the coward's way out.

Madoc, you really did talk me out of leaving last night. But after further thought, I know staying in your home will continue to create strife, and while you work to sort out the town, your home should be where you can find peace.

Niall's hand closed hard on the paper. What peace could there be with her gone?

I'm going to stay in Cold Creek while I do some thinking.

· · ·

Madoc made a sound as if he'd been kicked in the stomach.

If you've called me, I'm sorry. I broke my phone.

Please tell Talam and Sky I'm sorry not to have waited to see them before I left.

And thank you so very much. For coming to find me at the cabin, for caring for me afterward, and for sharing your home.
 Heather

Palms down on the desktop, André bowed his head as if he'd been gutted.

Niall understood the feeling. He couldn't seem to move, unable to feel anything except the tearing sensation in his chest. "No. Not when we finally found our mate. *No.*"

"Brawd." André set a hand on his shoulder.

Niall wrenched out of his grip. "Don't tell me to be reasonable." Turning, he met Madoc's gaze. The hurt in his brown eyes almost buckled Niall's knees.

"She'd agreed to stay." Madoc pushed his hair out of his eyes. "Something happened today to change her mind."

"Bron," Niall gritted out. Over the years, their aunt had seen females wreak havoc on her fellow cahirs, breaking hearts and egos. When her cub nearly died because of a heartless female, Bron's tolerance had turned to hatred. Last night, when they'd tried to talk to her about Heather, she'd walked away.

They should have tried harder.

"Bron," André agreed. "Let's see what happened."

The clatter of the cubs sounded from downstairs.

Niall's gut tensed. "Let's send the younglings outside in case this gets ugly." The cubs didn't need to hear shouting.

Out of the room, Niall stopped on the interior balcony and looked out the front picture window. Car lights were heading down the drive.

Frowning, he called down to the younglings in the great room. "Cubs, why is Bron leaving?"

"She's gonna stay at the B&B." Sky looked up at Niall. "Till she makes up with Heather."

Oh. Fuck.

Once her decision to talk to the brothers had been made, Heather was able to relax. She'd spend the night and head back in the morning. And then confess all.

Meantime, she'd enjoy being with her friends.

Or not.

They were laughing about Gods-called powers, the extra strength of the cahirs, and then teasing Vicki about bedding down with a Cosantir. Trying to find out if God-like powers made for more interesting matings.

When Vicki dodged the questions, the eyes turned to her.

Emma, of course. "Sooo, a new Cosantir might not be completely in control of his powers. During the full moon, did you—"

Heather chugged the rest of her beer. "Oh, look, I need another drink. Be right back."

Laughter followed her cowardly retreat. Maybe someday she'd want to share, but...those times with the males had been so very special.

When she reached the bar, Calum was delivering a couple of beers to the "Reserved" table he kept for dwarves. Although the

HEART OF THE WOLF

OtherFolk usually avoided businesses where there were humans, the beer in the Wild Hunt was too good for them to resist.

She could wait. By the time she returned with a beer, the topic should have changed to something else.

"Heather, good to see you." Donal joined her at the bar.

His littermate came up behind him. Tynan wasn't in uniform and had a drink in his hand, so the deputy was off duty. "Evening, Heather. Did I lose track of the days, and it's the full moon?"

She rarely showed up in Cold Creek except for full moons—or if summoned for something by her friends. "Just a visit."

"How are all the injured in Rainier?" Donal asked. "Did your three obey my orders and sleep the next day?"

"They did." Aside from indulging in enough exercise to turn her into a boneless, satisfied female. But afterward, they'd slept harder than hibernating pixies.

"Well, and isn't that an interesting smirk." Tynan had a light Irish accent—and a pleased smile.

How had she forgotten how observant the cop was?

Donal grinned.

"I swear, you two act like you never reached the age of First Shift." Heather sniffed and turned her back on them.

"Now, my sweet." Donal slung an arm around her. "We worry about you, down there with all those..."

When his voice trailed off, she glanced up him.

His face was unreadable, his silvery-gray eyes distant, the way he looked when he healed. "Hmm. This is unexpected."

She tried to pull away, and his arm tightened. "No, be still."

Mother of all, what was up with him? She had no injuries to heal.

"Is there a problem, healer?" Calum's deep voice was easy to recognize, the faint English accent remaining from his years in England. He set a beer for her on the counter.

"No, Cosantir, not a problem." Donal released her, and a smile tilted his lips. "Blessings of the Mother upon you, Heather. You're with child."

She stared at him. "I'm..." Her hands automatically flattened over her abdomen.

Calum's eyes darkened; his voice deepened. "The clan increases."

"But I"—her eyes filled—"I can't carry. I lost..."

"The miscarriage you had was meant to be, I fear. I could tell there was a problem with the chromosomes, but... It wasn't something I could heal." Donal shook his head, his eyes sad. "There *was* a chance."

A chance was why he hadn't warned her.

"Will I lose these too?" Her hands pressed tighter.

"Everything looks perfect." Donal's grin flashed. "Well attached, very strong embryos. The sires must be interesting."

Sires. The only males she'd mated with at full moon, the time of fertility, were André, Niall, and Madoc.

"You'll have a little while before your scent changes enough to notice." Then the healer smirked. "Before *everyone* knows."

"Behave, brawd." Tynan smacked his brother's head, then smiled at her. "Congratulations, Heather."

Pregnant. I'm...pregnant. Turning, she fumbled for the beer only to have Calum move it out of reach and hand her a glass of sparkling water.

When she glared at him, he just grinned.

She remembered how annoyed Vicki had been during her pregnancy about giving up her favorite drinks.

Ah well. She gave her belly a gentle pat and picked up the drink. "Thank you. Do you have any refills I should take back with me?"

His gaze went past her to check the sitting area, then he poured a glass of wine. "For Darcy."

"Got it. On my tab, please." Drinks in hand, she smiled at Donal and whispered, "Thank you."

"Babies are the best part of being a healer." He touched her cheek. "Call if you need me, sweetness."

Her eyes prickled at the offer. "Thank you."

Back with the others, she sat on the couch beside Vicki and handed the wine to Darcy. "Calum sent this for you."

"Thank you." Darcy frowned. "Your eyes are red. Were Donal and Tynan mean to you?" The tinker looked ready to jump up and kick some furry asses.

"You do look upset." Hands fisting, Vicki leaned forward. "What'd they say?"

Her protective friends could give cahirs a run. Needing time to process the news—*she was going to have cubs*—she shook her head. "Nothing bad. It's been an emotional month."

"I can't even imagine." Emma smiled gently at Heather, then told the others, "I was in a forest fire once, back when I was living as a bear. I tell you, it was..." And like magic, the empathetic bard swept the attention off Heather, giving her time to get her emotions back under control.

Nearer the fire, Margery gazed toward the bar, and Heather realized she'd probably seen her mate Donal go into healer mode. She glanced at Heather's drink—water rather than beer. With a soft smile, she met Heather's eyes...and remained silent.

Heather gave her a nod of gratitude. The tender-hearted banfasa, the Daonain equivalent of a nurse practitioner, was the soul of discretion.

Heather took a sip of her drink and wrinkled her nose. Sure wasn't beer.

But it was all right. She was *pregnant* with little lives growing inside her. Her heart melted at the thought of a mini-André.

Or might she be raising Madoc's cub—a little bear? Or a tiny kitten with almost white hair and Niall's green eyes?

Cubs. She was going to have cubs.

But she already had cubs. In a way, at least. Talam and Sky

were such a wonderful mix of sweet and tough. So proud to help her and the males. So courageous to bait the hellhound.

She'd love to have them for her own. If things didn't work out with her males—the thought was like a claw to her heart—she could bring them here to live with her. If it was what the cubs wanted.

If they needed a home. Once Pete was dealt with, would the Crichton crew send the younglings to the communal house? They wouldn't, would they?

But the males were all so busy. How could they care for the boys?

Lifting her glass, she watched the bubbles rise to the surface.

When she talked with the males tomorrow, she'd make sure they knew the cubs would always have a home with her.

Talk with the males tomorrow... Oh Gods. She was carrying their babes.

André had overseen the Gathering. He'd know full well she hadn't mated with anyone except him and his brothers.

"Heather, if you keep glaring at your glass, it's going to melt into a puddle." Bree laughed.

"Ah, right." Heather set the glass down.

"Are you all right?" Darcy asked. "Did you change your mind about going back in the morning?"

"No, not exactly. No." Heather shook her head. "Things just became a bit more complicated."

Now she had their full attention. Was this how Emma felt when she sang for a crowd?

Heather snorted. "You see, Donal told me I'm with child."

Eyes went wide. Vicki's, "Oo-rah," rang over the happy squeals from the others. Heather received hugs and more hugs. Their enthusiasm was so unstinting her eyes went damp.

"So do we know the sires or are they gather-bred?" Emma asked. When Vicki and Breanne looked appalled at the question, the bard rolled her eyes. "I keep forgetting you two were raised by humans."

"It wasn't a rude question." Margery held out her hands. "Being gather-bred is a fact of life and not something immoral. After all, unless a female is lifemated and exempt from attending Gatherings, her babies will likely be fathered at one."

"Because all the females ovulate at the full moon." Vicki rolled her eyes. "Another Daonain quirk."

"I'm gather-bred." Heather put her hands over her stomach. "As are these." She hesitated, then shared. "But as it happens, I was only with the three Canadian brothers."

"Oooh, interesting," Bree said. "The last Gathering I attended, no one except Shay and Zeb appealed to me. Because I was in love."

Love. There was no denying it, not with the joy filling her heart. She smiled at her friends. "Same here."

CHAPTER THIRTY-SIX

The next morning, André woke in an unsettled mood that didn't improve. The previous night, unable to rest until he knew Heather was safe, he'd called the North Cascades Cosantir. To everyone's relief, Heather had been in Calum's tavern with her friends.

Niall and Madoc were all for heading up there immediately, but Calum, overhearing, had pointed out they wouldn't arrive before the wee hours of the morning.

After a moment, Madoc added a cautionary thought. If Heather was in a tavern, she'd be drinking. Waking up an already irritable female who would either be intoxicated or—worse—suffering a hangover seemed...unwise.

Today, they'd head for Cold Creek.

Once downstairs, André found Madoc and Niall arguing about which vehicle to take. Talam and Sky weighed in with their own opinions.

André snorted. "We'll take mine."

"Yours?" Madoc frowned. "I thought you couldn't leave the territory."

"Cosantirs can leave for short periods. It's simply not prudent when a Cosantir is new to the land."

"You're still new, brawd," Niall pointed out.

Pouring himself a travel mug of coffee, André growled, "If the God wants this fucking job back, then so be it. I'm going after our mate."

"Okay, cat." Laughing, Niall held up his hands in surrender. "If Herne burns your whiskers off, don't yowl at me."

Madoc grabbed a jacket. "Your car it is."

Before André could get a sip of his coffee, the doorbell rang, making everyone jump.

Niall hissed. "Remind me to turn the sound down on the cursed thing."

"I'll get it," Talam called, running for the front door with Sky behind him.

When they opened it, shifters poured in. "Happy Housewarming!" Carrying a covered basket, Ina led the way followed by Murtagh and Maeve.

André looked out through the picture windows. Cars were lining the drive. People were walking up the steep hill. "Ina, what is this?"

"The clan wanted to welcome our new Cosantir and his family properly. We have food coming." She set her basket on the table. "Volunteer cooks with portable grills. Even music."

More people streamed in, smiling at him with open happiness, bowing heads and murmuring, "Cosantir."

Wrapped presents began to cover the dining room table.

By the Gods. His burning need to find Heather warred with an inescapable fact. He was trapped. So were his littermates. He turned.

His brothers' expressions held the same frustration.

"We can't let them down." André barely kept from growling. "We'll go after her tonight."

"I can't believe I forgot about the housewarming," Heather told Greystoke. "It sure looks like a lot of people showed up."

Talk about bad timing on her part. *Oh well.*

Cars lined the long drive, and she was lucky enough to catch someone pulling out, so she parked in a shady spot under a wide-canopied oak tree.

Ina, Murtagh, and Friedrich had planned for the event to last the entire day in order to give everyone a chance to come for a few hours and not overcrowd the house.

Heather half-smiled. André and Madoc would enjoy a long party, but poor Niall would probably end up hiding in his office.

Maybe he'd let her join him...if he wasn't too annoyed with her.

Courage, wolf. She cracked the back door windows to let in the cool air, then checked the cat condo. "I need to leave you for bit, sweetie."

Snuggled in his favorite blankie, Greystoke opened his eyes once before returning to sleep. She checked the litter box at the end of his long carrier. All clean. The dish had water. She sprinkled a few crunchies for him to nibble if he grew peckish.

Closing the car door, she looked up the hill at the house. Had they found her note? Had Talam and Sky told them what happened with Bron. Were they angry?

Had they missed her?

She'd missed *them*. Gods, she really had.

For the entire drive, she'd tried to think of what she wanted to say. How she wanted to act. It wasn't as if she could walk up and say to André, "I love you. How do you feel about me?" Maybe being so direct might work for monogamous humans, but not when she'd have to turn and ask the same question of Niall, then Madoc.

"Why wasn't I born human?" she muttered.

"Human, seriously? *Girl*." Moya turned from where she was opening her car trunk and patted her heart dramatically. "Give up on shifting to wolf? *Never*."

Annoyed by the histrionics, a pixie in an overhanging bush grabbed Moya's hair and pulled.

"Ouchers. Bad sprite." Moya huffed, then pulled a grape from a shopping bag in the trunk and held it up.

The sprite took the offering and disappeared back into the bush with a victorious chitter.

"Then again, humans don't have pixies. I'm starting to see the appeal." After smoothing her hair, Moya grabbed the shopping bag and closed the trunk.

"No, girl. Pixies are everywhere. Humans just can't *see* what's pulling their hair or tossing twigs and pinecones at them."

"Huh." Moya wrinkled her nose. "In that case, never mind."

"I must admit, there are more pixies around here than there were even a week ago. The Crichton crew seems to attract them." Heather grinned up at the tiny sprite who was sampling the grape. "So what's in your bag?"

"My amazing fruit salad."

Right. This is a potluck. And *oops*, she had nothing to contribute.

As they walked past a dark sedan, she frowned. "Is this Roger's car?"

"It is. Maybe he's decided to make nice with the Cosantir." Moya wrinkled her nose. "I thought he might follow Pete—wherever he went. But Roger's not the type to give up being alpha."

"I don't like Roger, but if he quits? As beta, Brett would probably take his place in the pack."

"Oh." Moya looked horrified—and worried. "Roger's a bully, but Brett's even worse."

"Exactly. Let's hope Roger stays until someone nice comes along to replace him."

"In your dreams. Alphas are never nice."

Heather glanced at her friend and stayed silent. Maybe someday, Moya would share the origins of her troubles with authoritative males.

"Hey, Heather. Moya." Out of uniform, Duffy was stationed at the front door, undoubtedly to ensure no humans entered the Cosantir's home.

"Have you noticed the pack alpha and betas are never chosen for guard or enforcer duties?" Moya muttered as they entered.

"None of the Crichton crew nor the Elders are fairy-witted," Heather whispered back, getting a laugh.

Walking slower through the crowded great room, Heather looked for Talam and Sky. Would the younglings hate her? How could she talk with them or the brothers in this mess? "Do you see André, Niall, or Madoc anywhere?"

Moya stood on her tiptoes and scowled. *Lovely,* all she could see were chests and stomachs. Then again, there *were* some excellent abs to appreciate. "Girl, I can't see anything. This being short—it sucks dirty gnome-toes."

From her added height of an extra five inches, Heather looked down and grinned. "Let's go this way." She veered to the right.

"Sure, I—*oomph*." Turning to follow, Moya ran right into an extremely solid male and bounced.

"Whoa, there." Hard hands gripped her upper arms, holding her up until she regained her balance.

She looked up into black eyes so deadly that a shiver ran up her spine. "I... Sorry." Feeling the dominance pouring off the black-haired male, she backpedaled quickly...and bounced off another granite wall of male.

A humiliating squeak escaped her. *Gods, just claw out my throat.*

She spun halfway—not wanting to turn her back to the dark-eyed one—and met blue eyes as pale and cold as ice. This male put a hand under her arm to steady her, then stepped around her and walked away. The other male followed.

"Now, what are they doing here?" Joining her, Heather watched the two males.

"You know them?" Moya wrapped her arms around herself, still feeling the terrifying shock of an alpha's power swamping her. "Who are they?"

Please, let them be visiting, not staying.

"Remember the Daonain who were imprisoned by the Scythe in Seattle? Those two were the leaders of the shifter-soldiers."

"Oh." A momentary feeling of pity for them was drowned out at the memory of what the males had done for the Scythe. They'd been used as assassins. No wonder they scared her.

"They're probably between jobs and wandering through the territories."

"More over-testosteroned males. Let's hope they don't start any fights here." Feeling her fear subside, Moya sighed. "I'd better get my salad out to the food tables on the patio."

"Go on out. I need a diet Coke first."

"Those are so bad for you." Holding up a hand in farewell, Moya walked out onto the patio. And the two strangers were there.

They didn't even see her—naturally not. No one noticed cute, round females, and even if the mating stuff was still scary, it burned a bit to be ignored.

To her disgust, they were watching Miss Perfection strutting across the patio. Gretchen was trailed by four males who obviously couldn't see past their dicks.

As the obnoxious blonde walked past the two strangers and disappeared into the house, the black-haired one murmured to his icy-eyed buddy, "Now, *there's* a beauty."

If Moya'd been a cat, she'd have hacked up a hairball.

On the way to the kitchen, Heather checked the rooms. No Crichton crew, no Talam or Sky, although she spoke to their cubling friends, Kathan and Hamlin, in the great room. They'd come with the people from the communal house. Mateo and Alvaro hadn't shown, though. Apparently their new foster mother didn't enjoy socializing.

Heather shook her head as she entered the kitchen. Her nerves were jangling, and her stomach all twisted. She opened the fridge to grab a diet Coke, both for her stomach and to give her hands something to do.

"Gods, I might have known you had no manners." The shrill voice was all too familiar.

Straightening, Heather closed the fridge door, diet Coke in hand.

At the island, Gretchen pointed accusingly at Heather. "How could you steal from the Cosantir in his own house? You're a thief."

Face unreadable, Bron stood behind the blonde B&B manager. Everyone in the wide-open ground floor turned to watch.

A noisy face-off. How very Gretchen.

With a sigh, Heather opened the can and lifted it in a silent toast to Murphy. Of *course*, she'd run into Ms. Perfection rather than the males she wanted to see so badly. "Gretchen, I bought the sodas last week. If you think André, Niall, or Madoc would ever touch a diet Coke, you don't know them at all."

Several shifters snorted.

Bron chuckled. "She's right. A very serious youngling instructed me how the pop is Heather's and must not be touched."

As the shifters in the room grinned and returned to their conversations, Gretchen gave Bron a betrayed scowl and stomped off.

The cahir had called Gretchen on her accusation? How unexpected.

Bron turned to Heather and studied her for a long moment.

Bracing to endure more insults, Heather gave Bron a level

look. "I'm not here to move back in—or even stay. I simply plan to talk to the Crichton brothers and my cubs and then leave."

At Bron's flinch, Heather realized she shouldn't have called Talam and Sky her cubs. Oops.

"I'm sorry."

Heather blinked. "What?"

"I was wrong about you, and even if I wasn't, it isn't my place to tell my nephews who they can be with. Or live with. Or love. My past blinded me—and I acted like a troll. I'm sorry."

By the Hunter and the Mother, what had happened here? Heather realized her mouth was open. She closed it. Cleared her throat. "Right. Of course." No, do better. "You were rude because you care about them. There's nothing to forgive."

"You're very kind. Thank you." Bron actually looked relieved. Then, with a flickering smile, the female glanced at the patio door. "They're all outside."

Whoa, doggies. The cahir was being helpful? And here she'd been dreading running into Bron here. What a waste of all her worrying.

"Thank you, cahir." Only now...now she'd have to face André, Niall, and Madoc. Oh Gods. Trying to find her courage, Heather took a hefty swig of her drink.

And amusement lit Bron's eyes. "Good luck." She strolled out through the double doors. People on the patio greeted her, and the cahir smiled and chatted...just like a normal person.

Heather could see why the brothers loved her.

Well. Okay. Time to deal. With a sigh, Heather checked her diet Coke and mentally added the caffeine content to her daily total. Two hundred milligrams max which was basically, only one coffee and one caffeinated soda.

Pregnancy sucked.

And wasn't it going to be...fun...to tell the males she was with child. *Not.*

And not today. Today, she'd simply say she cared for them.

Maybe give them a moment or two where they could, if they wanted, say something in return. Let her know how they felt. But even if they didn't, she'd tell them she hoped to see them. Or... somehow convey, *I'm here and open to having a relationship.*

Pulling her courage around her, she walked out onto the wide stone patio. A built-in grill sat near the edge with smaller charcoal kettle grills set up near it. The mouthwatering aroma of hamburgers and hot dogs hit her with a wave of nostalgia. Her grandparents had loved hosting big barbecues overflowing with guests.

She smiled at greetings, accepted hugs, and didn't let herself get bogged down in conversations. Instead, she moved to the less crowded edge of the patio and continued her search.

High shouts came from the lawn stretching between the patio and thick forest. A myriad of younglings kicked soccer balls for several small wolves and two bears to chase. Farther away, some young cougars were playing king of the mountain on a wide, chest-high tree stump. But none of her males were out with the younglings.

She turned to check the crowded part of the patio—and caught sight of a huge, white-blond cahir. Niall. Everything inside her froze as her heart spun in circles like a happy puppy.

He was politely talking to several shifters on the other side of the patio, although his lack of expression seemed like he wasn't fully engaged.

And there was Madoc.

She pressed her hands against her sternum. *Crazy heart, stop pounding.* Closer to the food tables, Madoc was speaking with a group of business people. He, too, seemed as if he wasn't completely involved in the conversation.

Her feet took her a few steps that way.

No, wolf. The males were occupied—and this party was for them. *Really, what were you thinking?* She should have waited. Come when they weren't busy.

Why in the world had she come today?

She huffed under her breath. *Be honest, girl.* It had nothing to do with logic, and everything to do with wanting to see them so badly she hurt.

Continuing around the edge of the patio, she searched for a glimpse of André.

Where was he?

André chatted with the five shifters around him, trying for more than simple politeness. They'd gone to a lot of trouble to welcome him and his littermates, and it truly did warm his heart. Two of the females had come over to talk about the gift shop. Unfortunately, the three younger females reminded him of the ones who fawned over cahirs.

Gods, as if he wanted any females. Just one. His heart had throbbed painfully all night as if to remind him Heather wasn't within his reach. He needed her here, in his arms, in their bed. Needed to know she was safe and happy.

But today was for his clan, and he'd give them his best. They were honorable people, he'd discovered, but under Wendell's neglect, they'd grown lazy. Like muscles, character needed exercise to stay strong. With time, the clan would remember who they really were.

As the two craft-loving females headed off to eat, Murtagh came forward with a male beside him. "Cosantir, have you met Roger Wendell, alpha of the wolf pack?"

The burly male gave a perfunctory bow of his head. "Cosantir."

"It's good to meet you," André said. Roger appeared to be a more muscular version of his brother Pete. Equally arrogant, it appeared.

After exchanging a couple of inanities, André frowned. "You

aren't looking particularly well. Have you been ill?" Shifters were sturdy, but illness did happen.

The alpha hesitated, then pressed a hand to his chest. "I think it's my brother. The bond between us is...wrong."

"Have you seen him recently?" Murtagh asked.

"We fought the last time I saw him." Roger's shoulders sagged. "Brett says Pete went into the forest a few days ago."

Was the littermate bond between Pete and Roger thinning? Losing bonds could be dangerous.

Before André could ask, Murtagh did. "You have another littermate, a female over in...Idaho?"

"Wyoming, aye." Roger rubbed his chest. "Our bond is still there. Strong."

André relaxed slightly, then frowned as one of the females moved closer to him.

Now what should she do? At the edge of the patio, Heather stood by a portable charcoal grill close enough the heat from the glowing coals almost scorched her side. Stainless-steel tools lay on the side table beside a plate of hot dogs ready to cook.

Considering how hard the cubs were playing, they'd be hungry soon. But her? She had no appetite at all.

She should probably leave and return once the party was over.

Before she could take a step, the tilt of a dark head caught her attention.

Across the patio, André was surrounded by shifters with a couple of the inevitable groupies.

A wave of joy welled inside her at the sight of him. His head was tilted slightly as he gave all his attention to the male who was speaking. Having been on the receiving end of André's concentrated focus, she knew how compelling it was.

Unable to help herself, she let her gaze linger on the sharp planes of his tanned face, on the way his wavy hair curled over his shirt collar, on how his shirt sleeves were rolled up the way he liked.

When a female moved closer and ran a hand over André's bare arm to capture his attention, possessive jealousy dug fangs deep into Heather's self-control.

As if he felt her watching, his gaze went past the female straight to Heather. As his eyes met hers, everything inside her shook with longing.

I love you.

She hadn't spoken aloud, but the flare of warmth in his dark gaze suggested he'd heard her anyway.

With the tact he had in abundance, he excused himself from the group and headed for her. His shrill whistle caught his brothers' attention. Following his gaze, they spotted her.

Oh Gods, what have I done?

Niall shoved his drink into someone's hands, Madoc shouted in glee, and they abandoned their groups. Moving toward her, they were slowed by the press of people covering the patio.

Then two more voices made a whooping sound.

"Heather!" came Sky's high voice.

Talam's shout cracked on the second syllable. "Hea-ther!"

Gods. She braced for the onslaught, and her heart rejoiced. They hadn't given up on her.

The cubs reached her first and slammed into her like small freight trains.

Trying not to cry, she hugged them both. "I missed you two. Even for just a night, I missed you."

Talam looked up, eyes reddened, and—

"Fucking brats!" a male shouted, and the cubs squeaked in fear.

That voice. It was Pete.

She turned in a circle, trying to locate him.

Behind André, the alpha, Roger, pressed his hands to his chest and moaned.

The next bellow of rage was almost deafening. "Traitorous cunt!" It came from the forest. Where...?

With a sob of fear, Talam pulled out of Heather's arms and stepped in front of her.

There. Mud-spattered and naked, Pete ran across the lawn. His eyes were crazed, his expression enraged.

Halfway across, he trawsfurred into an enormous black bear. Fangs exposed, he roared until froth and spittle flew from his muzzle. He charged straight for her and the younglings.

As terror battered her senses, Heather froze.

The bear knocked two males out of his way without slowing, and terror-filled screams filled the air. His small, maddened eyes fixed on Heather and the boys.

"Out of my way!" Niall shouted from back in the crowd somewhere. Like a knife, his frantic voice cut through Heather's paralysis.

The bear was too close.

No one would reach them in time.

Gripping Talam's and Sky's collars, she yanked them behind her. Snatching up a long barbecue fork, she used it to hook the red-hot grill from over the coals. With all her strength, she flung the grill in the bear's face.

The overheated metal hit the big nose with a sizzle, and Pete shrieked in pain. He stumbled, shaking its head.

"*Run.*" Still gripping the fork, Heather tried to push the boys away. Instead, Talam picked up the BBQ spatula as if it would delay the monster for even a second.

"Cahirs, the bear is feral," André called, voice deep with the God's power. "Protect our people."

Screaming came from the crowd. Ferals were mindless, driven to savagely kill other shifters.

"Your will, Cosantir," Bron called, acknowledging the order. She trawsfurred to a large, dark gold cougar.

Arms extended in front of the cubs, Heather took step after

step, backing them all away from the bear. Her fingers were still clamped around the eighteen-inch steel fork.

Foam dripped from the bear's gaping jaw as Pete fixed his gaze on them. He rose to his hind legs, at least seven feet tall.

Her heart stuttered.

Bellowing, he swung at them with huge, clawed paws.

She jumped, shoving the cubs back. Claws ripped her shirt, and she slashed his muzzle with the steel fork.

Roaring, he—

A huge furry body slammed into Pete from the side, knocking him away from them. It was Madoc—even bigger than Pete.

Heather's breathing froze in fear for him.

Both bears rolled to their paws, jaws wide, fangs exposed.

A cougar—Bron—landed on top of Pete, biting and clawing, then springing away. Two wolves attacked the bear from behind, snapping at its hind legs.

Retreating with the cubs, Heather glanced over her shoulder.

Behind her, André had trawsfurred to cougar and guarded a group of younglings. More shifted adults lined up in front of the cubs and older shifters.

After snapping at the wolves, Pete rose onto his hind legs again, focusing on Heather and the younglings.

Madoc plowed into him once more, knocking him back on all fours.

With a loud snarl, a huge gold cougar—Niall—leaped onto Pete's back. As the two wolves and Bron trapped the bear, Niall's powerful jaws closed on the bear's neck to bite through the spinal cord.

The bear dropped. A moment later, with a shimmer of magic, the body turned into Pete's human form.

Heather sucked in a breath and just stood, shaking. So close. Too close. For her, for the cubs. For the cahirs, too. If the God hadn't made cahirs so big, the bear would have won.

Stomach twisting, she swallowed hard, not wanting to look

but afraid not to. Half expecting the body to turn back to a bear and attack again.

But two cubs were clinging to her, shaking as hard as she was. Putting her arms around them, she turned so they wouldn't see Pete's body. "It's over, my babies, it's over," she whispered.

Face hard, Bron stepped in front of her, dressed once again, although her T-shirt was torn. "Heather. Excellent defense with the grill. You think on your feet and have an abundance of courage." Bron's quick smile reminded her of Madoc's. "I approve."

Heather stared. *Huh*.

The two wolves who'd harried Pete were shifting—and Heather recognized Patrin and Fell.

Bron nodded to them. "Nice job, shifters. Thank you."

The two grinned.

Turning, Bron snapped at a couple of younger males. "You two. Get a tarp and carry the feral down to my car."

"Yes, cahir," one of them stammered.

"She'll make a most effective police chief, won't she?" Heather said under her breath. Still hugging the cubs, she started to head for the house. They needed a calm place.

In the center of the patio, André had pulled on his jeans and turned to face the defending line of shifters. "You put yourselves in harm's way to protect the defenseless." His eyes darkened, his voice holding a reverberation like thunder. "You are a credit to our clan. You should be proud."

And suddenly she could feel it—his pride and approval of them all.

She pulled her shoulders back and saw everyone else doing the same, holding themselves straighter.

In her arms, the two cubs stood tall.

Smiling, she kissed the top of Talam's head, then Sky's. "You two were very brave."

"Yes, you were." Wearing only a pair of jeans, Niall joined her, stealing the younglings for his own hug. "You did good. I'm grateful you were there to defend Heather."

Despite being pale, the cubs both grinned, looking more like themselves.

Niall ruffled their hair. "Can you two give us a few minutes with Heather? I—we—want to talk with our missing female."

Talam grinned, Sky snickered, and they sped off quickly.

"Missing?" Heather sniffed. "I knew where I was the entire time."

And then she flung herself into his arms.

"Gods, yes, this is what I needed." His arms closed around her so tightly her bones creaked—and she wouldn't complain for the world.

Here was comfort.

"I fought hard." Madoc stood behind her. "Do I get a reward too?"

Her laugh was shaky as Niall handed her to his brother.

Like Niall, Madoc wore only jeans, and as she hugged him, she pressed her face against his wonderfully furry chest, breathing in his light citrus scent with a hint of chocolate. Someone had been in the kitchen.

"I missed you." His deep voice was a rumble against her ear.

"I missed you back."

"I didn't fight." André spoke in a worried voice although his lips curved up. "Does that mean I won't get a hug?"

"Nope, no hugs for you, brawd," Madoc said sternly, even as he handed her over.

"*Mon amour*, we've been worried." His arms were like steel, but as he buried his face in her hair, she could feel the tension ease. "Your note was most inadequate."

"Sorry?"

He chuckled, stepped back, and cupped her face with his hands. His eyes were penetrating...and tender. "Heather. As it happens, we love you. Seeing you in danger or going missing is...unsettling."

Her lungs forgot how to work. "You...love me? Really?"

"Aye. And we would...we want..."

When Madoc rumbled in annoyance, Niall could only agree. Their brother, never at a loss for words, had choked.

He bumped André's shoulder to take his place. Gripping Heather's hand, Niall felt the warmth of their connection like the sun had come out. "Ah, what he wanted to ask was..."

When her luminous turquoise gaze met his, his mind went blank. What if she refused them?

She wouldn't, she couldn't. She loved them; he knew it.

"It's not rocket science, oh geek." With a bear's huff, Madoc took her other hand. "He's trying to say we love you and want to know if you love us back."

"Oh." Heather's lips curved. "Yes. I do."

As happiness bubbled up inside Niall, he heard André chuckle.

"This is why the Gods give us two or three males to one female. It takes that many to make it even." Still laughing, André tugged her forward and kissed her.

Taking his turn, Niall bent and fell into the kiss. Her lips were soft, and she smelled like sunshine and roses.

Then Madoc made a grumbly sound and Niall had to laugh. After years of avoiding females, the bear was all on board.

Because it was Heather, their own personal miracle.

Off to one side, he heard the B&B manager whining. "Honestly, doesn't she know better? Displays like this are for full moons, not at a party. It's not like they're mated or..."

"Can't get a better lead-in," Niall murmured to André.

His brother's eyes lit. "Agreed." André turned. "Madoc. The time is now."

With a last lingering kiss, Madoc glanced over, and his eyes caught fire. "Aye."

They stepped back, the three, shoulder-to-shoulder-to-shoulder as was right and knelt together.

Body heated from the kisses, heart spilling over with love, it took Heather a moment to realize...

André, Madoc, and Niall were kneeling in front of her.

And three palms held out lifemating bracelets.

"Heather Sutharlan," André said softly, "we love you. We want you as our lifemate, to carry in our hearts and souls through this life and into the next."

The traditional words, sometimes used, sometimes not. Of course the Cosantir would use them.

She pressed her hands over her mouth, trying to keep shocked —happy—sobs inside.

Dimple on full display, Niall smiled up at her. "We need you, pretty wolf. My brothers and I made a perfect circle, but our circle lacked a center. A balance. You're everything we need. Come and be the heart of us."

Madoc's voice was a low rumble. "In turn, we'll give you everything we are—our time, our laughter, our joy, our cubs.

André's smile flashed. "Holding you when you cry or need comfort...or a mandatory nap."

"Feeding you, singing with you, making love with you, watching night skies together." Madoc's warm hazel eyes were focused on her face.

"Protecting you from any and all dangers, from hellhounds, Scythe mercenaries," Niall added with a huff of laughter, "and your annoying brothers."

A strangled laugh escaped her and opened her throat so the words could escape. "Yes, oh yes."

They rose, and André kissed her fingers and slipped a bracelet on her wrist before pulling her into his arms. "By the Gods, I love you." He looked deep into her eyes before kissing her thoroughly. She could feel his power simmer around her.

He handed her to Niall, who cupped the back of her head, looking into her eyes as if to see if she'd really agreed. Then his smile appeared, and he slid his bracelet onto her wrist. "I love you, Heather Sutharlan." His kiss was long and wonderful.

When he turned her to Madoc, she went into the bear's big embrace. Here was happiness and comfort. For a long moment, she clung there, like a pixie safe in the hollow of her tree. Then he took her shoulders, moving her back enough so he could smile down at her. "I love you, little wolf." Carefully, fingers fumbling, he put the bracelet on her, and his kiss held all the love in the world.

Oh, how she loved them all.

As she stepped back, she heard Sky's whisper. "Don't the males get those lifemating things too?"

Laughing, Heather lifted her eyebrows. "As my friend Vicki would say, don't I get to tag you too?"

"Seems only fair," Niall agreed. Each male dug in a pocket and held out the heavier version of lifemating bracelets.

"I love you, Madoc." Sliding the bracelet on his heavy-boned wrist, she took his hard, callused hand in hers. "You're my shelter in the storm—and I'll be yours. Whether you're strong and healthy or injured or old, I'll be at your side."

"I know you will." His soft words of trust melted her heart.

She braceleted Niall. "For the rest of my days, I'll take on the job of protecting you from evil cahir-hunting groupies." When his sunlit green eyes filled with laughter, she grinned back. "I love you so much."

"I love you, André." She held his hand as she put the bracelet on his strong, corded wrist. "When the weight of the God gets heavy, I'll be there to listen, to help...and to share my lunch."

Smiling, he lifted her hand and kissed her fingers.

Then she gave him the traditional words in return, looking at the others to include them. "For as long as life shall last and long beyond, I'll be your lifemate."

As the people busted out into cheers, Talam quickly swiped the wet off his face. This was good. Really it was. Heather needed the big males to watch over her.

And the brothers, they weren't happy without her. It'd sucked when she disappeared.

"Major cool." Sky perched beside him on top of the picnic table and grinned really wide. "Maybe we should look for a lifemate?"

Appalled, Talam stared at him. "We're, like, *twelve*. What's *wrong* with you?"

His brother snickered. "Gotcha."

"Ninnyhammer." Talam shoved him. He glanced over and saw Heather and the brothers were surrounded by people doing congratulation stuff.

Yeah, he was happy for them. Only...now what? What would happen with him and Sky?

"Yo, bro." Sky frowned. "What's wrong? It's all good, right? Mr. Wendell can't hurt us, and Heather came back and everything."

"Uh." Talam hesitated, then sighed. He should warn Sky so his brother wouldn't be surprised. "Since Mr. Wendell is gone, why would the Cosantir keep us here?"

Sky's mouth dropped open, and his whole body kinda drooped, like when they forgot to water the plant Heather'd put in their room. "They'll send us to the communal house."

"Yeah, I figure." Talam tried to smile. "It'll be okay." Only it probably wouldn't. Mateo and Alvaro weren't there anymore. They'd gone to live with some female who wanted a family and took a shine to them. The communal house would only have a bunch of adults they didn't know.

Sky nodded. "Sure."

"Now, just one little minute here." Heather pushed her way out of the group of people. Standing at the end of the picnic table, she frowned at Talam and Sky. "You are going *nowhere*."

Shocked she'd heard them, Talam couldn't figure out what to say. But...she was wrong. The brothers wouldn't—

"I'm confused." Madoc put his arm around her waist. "Who's going where?"

"They think they're going to the communal house." Heather put her hands on her hips.

On her other side, Niall slung an arm over her shoulders. He cocked his head at Talam. "You don't like us anymore?"

Talam's eyes filled. How could he tell them he wanted to stay so, so bad?

Standing beside Niall, André put his foot up on the bench and braced his forearms on his thigh. "It seems we need to discuss this."

As Talam turned away, blinking hard, he could feel the way the Cosantir studied him.

"My brothers. Heather." André's voice was soft. "I realize I simply assumed the cubs would stay with us."

Talam turned back to stare at him. The Cosantir would let them stay?

André smiled at the others. "What do you think? Do you feel the lads will be better with us or at the communal house, eventually to get foster parents?"

"Us. Absolutely." Niall cracked his neck like he was ready to fight somebody. "They stay."

Beside Talam, Sky made a choked sound.

"Us," Madoc said. "Stay."

Talam realized his fingernails were digging into the wood on the table. Would Heather...?

"Well, as it happens"—her voice went soft—"I'm going to need a lot of help in the future, and I suppose this is the time to warn everyone."

Worry made Talam's voice come out all weird. "Are...are you sick?"

The brothers turned to her, looking just as worried.

"No, but it's like this"—her smile was so warm Talam could feel it in his chest—"when the next litter shows up, I will need you to be big brothers to them. Can you do that?"

"I can be a big brother?" Sky was such a gnome-brain.

Only Talam was thinking it too. They'd be...like a family.

"If you're up for it," Heather said.

Talam nodded and felt Sky bounce on the table. "Yes!"

Heather tilted her head. "To me, you feel as if you're already our cubs." She glanced at André. "Stay."

"Agreed." André thumped the table with his fist.

Two more thuds sounded from Niall and Madoc, and a second later, Heather's fist joined in.

And then Talam and Sky got hugged and hugged and hugged.

Hours later, leaving the quiet house, André stood on the patio and regarded the forest. The scents were not quite the same as in Canada. Each territory had its own unique fragrance.

But... He looked up at the dark sky. The stars were the same here as in the provinces.

As were the Gods.

He touched the lifemating bracelet on his wrist. A simple brush of his fingers over the beads brought the feeling of the Mother, an intriguing counterpoint to the often-overwhelming sensation of Herne within him. The open warmth of the Goddess was the same feeling he received from Heather. No barriers, no holding back, simply a streaming forth of all the love in her generous heart.

They were lifemated.

Footsteps sounded, then Niall joined him. "Hell of a day, eh, brawd?"

"Very." André cocked his head. "It's suspiciously quiet in there."

"Not to worry." Niall chuckled. "You missed out on some news. Ina called to tell Bron the town council gave her the job—and the position comes with a house. Chief Farley didn't own his house."

"Really." André remembered the foray he'd taken into the house for weaponry. "It was a good solid building."

"Yeah, Bron was pleased. It's been emptied and cleaned. She left to pick up the keys."

André blinked. "What's the hurry?"

"Weeeell." Niall pushed his hands in his pockets and looked up at the sky. "She took a notion that new lifemates should have a night alone. She packed up a bunch of sleeping gear and took the cubs with her."

A night with Heather and his brothers. Hope flickered to life inside him. "But...are the cubs all right with spending the night?"

"Get to explore a new place? Oh yeah." Niall grinned. "She'll take them to the café for breakfast and bring them home sometime tomorrow morning."

André smiled. "If this is Bron's way of making amends, she's doing a fine job."

"I know, right?" Niall nodded toward the door. "Heather's down from her shower. I made a fire, and Madoc decided to make hot chocolate. You ready to come inside?"

His brothers had always been tolerant of his need for space... which had increased since Herne had called him. "Hot chocolate, a fire, and Heather." And his brothers. "I can't think of anything finer."

Inside, Madoc was in the kitchen.

Wearing a calf-length fuzzy robe, Heather was lounging in the blanket pile in front of the hearth. And frowning. Now, why would she be looking so serious, even worried, on their first night together?

"Come, *mon amour*, let me hold you for a while." André sat down where he could lean his shoulders on a pile of cushions, then pulled her between his legs so her back was against his chest.

After a second, she relaxed, leaning her head back against his shoulder. "You are a very bossy cat."

"No, how could you say such things?" He kissed her temple.

Laughing, Niall sprawled on his side in the blankets, running his hand up and down her legs. "Pretty wolf."

Coming out of the kitchen, Madoc handed out mugs of hot chocolate. Sitting beside André, he took and held her free hand. "*Our* wolf."

Heather drew in a slow breath. This was what she'd needed, a quiet evening with her males. *My lifemates.* She looked at the three bracelets on her arm and again, her heart simply melted at the sight.

Resting against André, she could feel the slow rise and fall of his chest. Like a big cat, Niall was curled in the blankets, running his hand up and down her bare leg. Madoc was kissing her fingers and watching the fire. He'd made her hot chocolate.

She frowned. "You know, I'm going to get awfully spoiled if you keep this up."

"I think it falls under the duties of a lifemate."

When she looked at Madoc, he was completely serious.

"Okay." She squeezed his fingers and had to admit she was looking forward to feeling those big hands on her body later. "As long as you realize it goes both ways."

When he opened his mouth to object, she narrowed her eyes at him.

"Aye, fair enough."

She watched the fire where their resident salamanders had started to dance. "I think the little one's grown a couple of inches."

"I noticed." When the fire elemental did a showy spin and dive, André grinned. "It appears quite chuffed about getting bigger."

"Young things," Niall said.

Young things, indeed. She needed to tell them. But how? She bit her lip, stalling by taking another sip, then realized all three males were watching her.

"Heather. Can you tell us what's bothering you?" André ran his fingers through her hair, the gesture infinitely comforting.

"Well." Maybe she could come at this sideways? "We never talked about taking the cubs on. Are you really all okay with that?" As she'd found with her previous lovers, males weren't always eager to raise babies, no matter how much they enjoyed making them.

Madoc gave his deep laugh. "Aside from Wendell, have you ever known a Cosantir who didn't think younglings were blessings from the Gods?"

She turned her head.

André's dark eyes were filled with tenderness. "Talam and Sky are gifts."

"More fun than a basket of pixies," Niall agreed. "I can't wait to take them on mountain runs after their First Shift."

She turned to Madoc.

He shook his head. "I can't imagine life without them, can you?"

"No, I can't." Okay, this wasn't working. She was going to have to—

Madoc lifted their clasped hands, and she winced, realizing

she was squeezing his fingers. He made a sound deep in his throat. "Whatever's bothering her we haven't reached the bottom of it."

Like the cat he was, André rubbed his cheek against hers. "Tell us, Heather."

She wanted to bury her face against his shoulder. What if they were unhappy to hear about more cubs? The males from last summer had simply left her. Their abandonment had hurt, but if Niall and Madoc and André left? It would break her.

No, her lifemates wouldn't leave her. She knew it. *Stop being a coward.*

"Can't be that bad, little female." Niall's mouth tipped up at a corner. "What horrible thing have you done?"

She reached up to set her cup on the end table so she could press a hand against her belly. Over the new life there. "It's more what we've all done."

They straightened like they were going into battle.

"You said you like cubs." She pulled in a breath. "Are you...are you ready for more cubs in another eight or so months?"

Madoc squeezed her fingers. "More? Are there more homeless youngl—" He stopped, staring at her other hand that lay on her belly. "Babies?"

Beneath her, André went rigid. "You're with child?"

She tried to pull her hand out of Madoc's grip, wanting to wrap her arms around herself. Madoc didn't release her—and then André's arms wrapped closer around her, instead.

"We're going to have babies?" Niall looked...not angry, but like he'd seen the sun rise. Sitting up, he laid his hand over hers on her belly.

Madoc's eyes filled with joy. "We'll have a house *filled* with cublings." He reached forward to lay his hand on her stomach.

"The clan increases," André murmured, and his hand covered his brothers and hers...over the cubs they'd bring into the world.

EPILOGUE

Two weeks later

Niall wasn't in cougar form, yet he could swear he was purring in pure contentment anyway. Hands in his pockets, he moseyed down the trail after Sky and Heather.

It'd been an amazing two weeks since lifemating the most beautiful, amazing female in all the worlds.

They'd moved her into the mate room that very night—and had thoroughly enjoyed the massive bed.

He hadn't been sure how life with a female would work, but somehow, she made time for each of them. All of them ended up in her bed more often than not, even if just to sleep. He'd never realized, but he slept better with his brothers close. Maybe his subconscious knew nothing could get past Madoc and André.

It'd been rewarding to see Heather drop the last of her defenses and come to believe they truly did love her.

It had been almost as amazing to see Madoc's contentment.

The OtherFolk must have felt their happiness. Last week, a

family of brownies had moved in. As owner of the kitchen, Madoc had made a special trip to town for cream, then baked a cake. No one would miss not having to clean the kitchen.

And it left more time for being in the forest.

Up in front of him on the trail, Sky was bouncing around like he'd had a gallon of coffee for breakfast rather than milk.

Teenaged cubs. Niall grinned. He'd heard parents use a certain *I-survived-I'm-not-sure-how* tone when speaking of their younglings' adolescences.

After last week, he was beginning to understand why. Cooped up for several days of heavy rain and blustery winds, the cubs had grown as fidgety as nervous coyotes with a flea infestation.

Thank fuck the sun had finally come out today.

Even better, André had declared this a *"check the trails"* day—mostly to get the cubs out of the house.

But the irritable cublings had gotten into a brawl the first few minutes of the hike. So they'd split into two parties at a fork in the trail. André and Madoc had taken Talam.

Niall and Heather had Sky.

"Don't get too far ahead," Heather called as the cub disappeared around a corner.

Yeah, they needed to keep him in sight. Niall's mouth tightened. A couple of days ago, Talam and Sky said they'd started to see the door to the wild in their minds.

They were getting close to First Shift.

As a youngling, he'd been a cocky little git, not believing the rumors telling of cubs who didn't survive First Shift.

Unfortunately, the rumors were true. Cubs did die. Overwhelmed at finding himself in fur, a youngling might run himself to death or tumble off a cliff, or worse, not be able to find the doorway back to human.

On the trail ahead, Sky reappeared, running back to Heather to show her a rock he'd found. Having a home, being safe and loved, Sky was flourishing. He was much like Heather—and Niall too—happy to bury himself in books and computers. The way he took to numbers delighted Heather, and she'd been teaching him to play the stock market with virtual money.

But... Niall's gut tightened. Being so sensitive and possessing a vivid imagination weren't good traits for surviving First Shift. Sky was the type of cub who might well lose himself in the wild—and not be able to come back.

By Herne, they needed more time with the younglings. Needed to establish the kind of trust where the mentor's mere presence could make a cub feel safe. Could ensure they'd listen.

As the worries kept poking at his nerves, Niall growled under his breath until Heather looked over her shoulder in worry.

"Sorry. I'm having foxtail thoughts."

"Barbed seeds—a demon must have invented that kind of grass. I had to see a healer once when one burrowed into my paw." She wrinkled her nose. "So what painful thoughts are embedded in your brain?"

"Tell you later." And wasn't it a comfort he had her and his brothers to share worries with?

Up ahead, Sky had gone to work, trying to drag a small fallen tree off the trail.

"Good lad," Niall called and grabbed Heather for a quick kiss. Mmmhmm, she felt so good in his arms, he lost track of everything except her lips, her scent, her arms around his neck, her breasts pressed against...

Uh-oh. "I love you, pretty wolf," he grumbled and released her, "but you should come with a warning label."

As he strode up the trail to help the cub, she laughed.

"You're so gone over her." Sky shot him an impudent grin. "You're gonna be even worse with babies."

"True enough." His heart would probably crack right into pieces. "And you won't?"

Sky hesitated, then gave a teen shrug. "Yeah." A tiny smile appeared. "We're looking forward to being big brothers."

"They'll be lucky cubs to have you." Niall ruffled the soft hair, then started pulling the tree farther off the trail. "Can you get the branches?"

"On it." Sky filled his arms head-high with broken boughs. Trotting after Niall, he stumbled over an exposed root—and fell. "Ack!"

Suddenly, there was a small bear half-buried in fir branches and fighting its clothing. It let out a terrified bawl.

Oh fuck.

"Hold on there, Sky." Heart racing in panic, Niall bent and tried to disentangle the cub from his shirt. *Stay calm.* But what if the lad remembered how Wendell went feral—as a bear. What if he—

"Whoa, you're a bear, Sky." Heather's husky voice was quiet and...delighted. She took a knee beside the furry cub to free his legs from the pants. "How *fun*. Madoc will be so happy to have another bear to play with."

The cub shivered as he picked up a fat paw and gave it an appalled stare.

Get a grip, cahir. Niall knelt beside Heather. "Good paws there, youngling. You'll have to get Madoc to show you how he fishes." Gently, he rubbed his hand over the upright ears and studied the nose and spine. Looked like Sky was a black bear, not a grizzly.

Sky's panting slowed, and the cub started to look around.

"You'll notice everything's louder, and there are more smells, and it's just plain weird to be lower to the ground." Heather stroked a hand down the black fur. "Okay, Sky. Your first job is to find the door in your head. Open it and walk through."

The little head lowered. And nothing happened. *Nothing.*

Niall's hand clenched as he tried to keep the worry from his face. "Mine usually glows around the edges. Can you see it?"

A second later, with a shimmer of magic, the bear turned into a skinny naked boy.

As she might with a baby's first steps, Heather cheered. "Perfect job, Sky. Congratulations on your first shift!"

The cub's big blue eyes looked to Niall for confirmation.

And Niall's heart was simply gone. He cleared the thickness from his throat. "You're a shifter now, Sky, congratulations."

"I'm a bear." Grinning huge, Sky picked up his pants to dress.

Head buzzing with relief, Niall laughed. "Nah, we'll all shift and go find the others to celebrate." And in cougar form, he might stop shaking.

By the Gods, why had no one mentioned how terrifying being a parent was?

"Stupid rain. Look what it did." Talam scowled at the cliff where a slide had dumped a ton of rocks and boulders all over the trail. Cat-scat, they'd be clearing it *forever*, and he was already hungry.

"It appears we have our task set out for us." André started tossing rocks into the underbrush. He probably heard Talam's stomach rumble cuz he laughed. "We'll work for a while and then break out the food."

"Here, lad." Madoc tossed Talam a granola bar, then braced his feet and started rocking a huge boulder. When it started to roll, he pushed it right off the trail.

Halfway through the bar, Talam stared in pure envy. "I wish I was as big as you are."

"You have some growing to do, then." Madoc clapped Talam's shoulder and bent to the next boulder.

"You might well get to be his size." André chuckled. "At twelve, Madoc was Sky's size."

"Really?"

"Sure was." Madoc shoved the second boulder after the first. "The faster-growing wolves and cats picked on me, and then I wound up a foot taller than some of them."

Talam swallowed the last of the bar and grinned. *I could be as big as Madoc. Yes.*

With more enthusiasm, he started flinging the smaller rocks into the underbrush, then moved to bigger ones. Gotta grow some muscles, right?

Straining to carry one, he took a step, and his boot skidded off the loose stones. Trying to catch his balance, he dropped the rock. On his *foot*.

"Ow!" At the blast of pain, his world spun around and around. Falling, he landed on his hands and knees. Only...

He blinked at the fat, furry paws under his nose. And something kept blocking his vision when he looked down. *What...?* It was a really long, black nose.

He tried to scramble away from it, and something grabbed his legs, and he fell again. His yell came out high and squally, like a little kid.

Panicking, he let out another squeal.

A hand gripped his chin. "Talam, look at me." That was the Cosantir's voice. *André.* He'd make everything okay.

Panting, Talam looked up.

The dark eyes were calm. Yeah, André wasn't scared.

Okay. Okay.

"Look at you, youngling." Madoc knelt on the ground. Slowly, he reached out and stroked Talam's head. "You're a bear like me."

A bear? I'm a bear?

André was smiling.

Talam looked down again. Those were *his* paws? *Oh wow.* He tried to pick one up and almost fell again.

"Let me help you there, little buddy," Madoc pulled the T-shirt off one paw, then what must've been jeans from his legs. Back legs. Cat-scat, he had, like, four legs. How did they all work?

Talam studied his paws. Furry and black. And he could smell everything. He lifted his for-real long nose and sniffed.

Madoc let out a bellow of laughter. "Yo, the smells are great, aren't they? But first, get your ass back through the door in your head."

No way. This was too—

"Talam." André used the voice no one ignored, "the door, please."

Fine. With a huge huff of annoyance, Talam looked for the door in the back of his mind. Yeah, there, glowing around the edges. So cool. Opening it, he stepped through and felt total disappointment at having fingers and hands and arms.

"I was having fun," he grumbled.

"And you will again," André said. "Congratulations on your First Shift, Talam."

Talam looked up quick, but the Cosantir wasn't mad at his grumbling. His dark eyes were laughing.

"Good job, cub." Madoc held his hand up for a high-five. "Congratulations."

When André set his hand on Talam's shoulder, the last trembles disappeared. "How about we stow our clothes off the trail? We'll all shift and go find the others for your First Shift run."

"Yes!" Talam jumped to his feet.

Wouldn't Sky be surprised?

Heather led the way down the trail, her paws happy, her tail waving. *What a wonderful day.*

Behind her, Niall padded beside Sky, who was doing fine if he didn't think about having four legs.

She could still remember those days after her first shift when her paws would tangle, and she'd land snout first in the dirt. So embarrassing.

Daniel and Tanner had been even clumsier—and she'd taken total advantage. Bears were so nicely trippable.

Reaching the fork in the trail where they'd split into two work groups, Heather lifted her nose and sniffed at the scents coming down on the breeze. Cougar and bear and...bear?

She looked over her shoulder, wondering if she'd caught a whiff of Sky.

The sounds from upslope preceded the sight of a massive bear, a cougar, and...a juvenile bear.

Talam was also a bear?

Shifting without thought, she put her hands on her hips. "*Nooo*, I refuse to accept a family with three bears and two cougars. I'm so outnumbered!"

Sky raced past her, and then there were two bear cubs rolling and bumbling about.

Was anything more adorable?

André shifted and joined her. Putting a warm arm around her waist, he kissed her, long and slow before smiling down at her. "We appear to be infested with bears."

Madoc settled down next to the cubs, so obviously delighted she had to laugh. "It'll get worse. My brothers will descend on us for bear outings."

"At least we all know how to deal with having bears in the family." Niall bent for a quick kiss. "We also know how to annoy them."

Tossing his blond hair back over his shoulders, the cahir sauntered up the hill. "Hey, what do you call a bear with no teeth?"

All three bears looked up at his approach.

Trying to keep her face straight, Heather took up the cause. "I don't know. What *do* you call a bear with no teeth?"

Niall grinned. "A *gummy* bear." Seconds later, he was buried beneath a giant bear and two little ones.

Laughing her head off, Heather leaned back against André.

Arms around her, he laid his palms over her belly. As they watched the rest of their family playing, her heart simply overflowed with love.

Sometimes dreams really did come true.

DAONAIN GLOSSARY

The Daonain use a conglomeration of handed-down languages from the British Isles. Some of the older villages still speak the Gaelic (Scots) or Irish Gaelic. Many of the more common (and mangled) shifter terms have descended from Welsh.

Errors and simplification of spelling and pronunciation can be attributed to being passed down through generations...or the author messing up. Below are a few of the more common words and terms used by the shifters. And, just for fun, I added pronunciations (good luck with those).

- *a leannán*: sweetheart, darling [a le-anan]
- *banfasa*: wise woman/nurse (Irish Gaelic from bean feasa) [ban-FAH-sa]
- *brawd*: brother [br-ow-d. Don't need to roll the "r"]
- *cahir*: warrior (Irish/Gaelic from Cathaoir) [ka-HEER]
- *caomhnor*: protector/guardian of children (from Caomhnóir) [kuheeoo-NOR]
- *cariad*: lover, darling, sweetheart (Welsh) [core-ee-awt]
- *cosantir*: guardian or protector (Irish Gaelic from An Cosantóir) [KOSS-un-tore]
- Daonain: the shifter race [DAY-ah-nan]
- *mo leannán*: my darling / my lover [mo le-anan]
- *mo thaisce*: my treasure [muh HASH-keh]
- *prìosan*: prison [pree-soon]
- *trawsfur*: transform or shift (Welsh from trawsffurfio) [traws (rhyme with laws)-fur]

ALSO BY CHERISE SINCLAIR

Masters of the Shadowlands Series
Club Shadowlands
Dark Citadel
Breaking Free
Lean on Me
Make Me, Sir
To Command and Collar
This Is Who I Am
If Only
Show Me, Baby
Servicing the Target
Protecting His Own
Mischief and the Masters
Beneath the Scars
Defiance
The Effing List
It'll Be An Adventure

Mountain Masters & Dark Haven Series
Master of the Mountain
Simon Says: Mine
Master of the Abyss
Master of the Dark Side
My Liege of Dark Haven
Edge of the Enforcer

Master of Freedom

Master of Solitude

I Will Not Beg

Master of the Wilderness

The Wild Hunt Legacy

Hour of the Lion

Winter of the Wolf

Eventide of the Bear

Leap of the Lion

Healing of the Wolf

Heart of the Wolf

Bonds of the Wolf

Sons of the Survivalist Series

Not a Hero

Lethal Balance

What You See

Soar High

Standalone Books

The Dom's Dungeon

The Starlight Rite

ABOUT THE AUTHOR

Cherise Sinclair is a *New York Times* and *USA Today* bestselling author of emotional, suspenseful romance. She loves to match up devastatingly powerful males with heroines who can hold their own against the subtle—and not-so-subtle—alpha male pressure.

Fledglings having flown the nest, Cherise, her beloved husband, an eighty-pound lap-puppy, and one fussy feline live in the Pacific Northwest where nothing is cozier than a rainy day spent writing.

Made in the USA
Las Vegas, NV
31 October 2025